THE PALADINS

THE
PALADINS

TIMOTHY J. STONER

Third
Story
Window

The Paladins
by Timothy J. Stoner

Cover Design: Rick Devon
Cover Illustration: Jeff Walker

ISBN 1-58169-002-9
For Worldwide Distribution
Printed in the U.S.A.

THIRD STORY WINDOW
An Imprint of Genesis Communications, Inc.
P.O. Box 91011 • Mobile, AL 36691
(888) 670-7463
Email: GenesisCom@aol.com

DEDICATION

To Patty:
Who loves Him,
With sweet, childlike devotion.
Who runs the race,
With her eyes on the prize;
Whose crown no one will take.

Chapter One

The foggy darkness coiled in slathered layers on the damp ground. The watcher in the overgrown bushes along the circular drive peered through a telephoto lens at the imposing manor obscured by the mist.

Soon, he thought, *it should come at any moment.* He almost looked down at his watch, but the sound of the door hinges stopped him. "Come on," he whispered to himself, "let's see your ugly face."

His lens was fixed on the hazy outlines of a large, bearded man striding hurriedly out of the three-story Victorian mansion. In his arms was a bundle of metallic cylinders. The toe of his boot scraped on the drive and caught a pebble, sending it spinning into the bushes. It grazed the watcher's black sneakers and struck the camera bag laying open by his feet. The dull thud made the cameraman jerk. He sucked in a hissing oath, took a quick breath to steady his nerves and refocused on his subject.

Click.

The shutter blinked, freezing his quarry's glance at the turreted structure looming behind him. The cameraman smiled to himself as he captured the look of dread twisting around the man's pale blue eyes. As the watcher flexed his fingers, which had grown stiff around the cold lens, he had to agree there was a vague aura of evil about the building that was unsettling—even for him.

He adjusted the dark baseball cap over his close-cropped hair and shoved his chin into the folds of the wool scarf wrapped around his neck. Lifting the camera back up he stared at his subject 20 yards away. "You look cold, Red," he muttered grimly, "but I'm gonna make sure it gets lots colder for you before this is over. I promise you that." He wiped his nose with the back of his hand. The cold was getting to him too.

The lens magnified Rick "Red" Jaglowski's bearded face and the twitch at the corner of his right eye. Fingers of steam were being expelled

1

from his thin, cruel lips; and with each hurried step, a greasy ponytail flopped against the hood of his parka.

Gazing furtively around, Red waded through the white mist toward his van. He opened the back doors, exposing state-of-the-art movie equipment to the voracious gaze of the watcher's camera lens. Grunting, Red slid the metal tubes into padded shelves underneath floodlight tripods. He slammed the doors and turned angrily toward the brooding mansion.

An unnervingly high, falsetto drawl assaulted the watcher's inner ear through his earphones. "Shore takin' yore precious time in dere," the earphone snarled. "I can jest i-ma-gin' what yore up to."

Although the microphone was glued onto the luggage rack, it sounded as though Red's lips were inches away. The listener hurriedly turned down the volume. When he looked back up, Red was leaning against the van's front grill, stamping his cold, damp feet while continuing to stare intently at the large front door.

The watcher pulled back the sleeve of his jacket to take a quick look. *Three more minutes.*

Red coughed, then spat on the ground. The drapes at the front window parted.

"Geez—finally," Red's high voice grated, as he flung his hand up in the prearranged signal.

"*Seig heil,*" muttered the watcher.

The drapes closed. Again, the imposing oak door creaked open. A glint of candlelight leaked through the crack, revealing the dim contours of a man's body. A flash of light blazed near the man's face as he flicked on a cigarette lighter, revealing narrow lips surrounded by a fastidious goatee and a black silk cravat. A broad-brimmed hat dominated his head, covering longish hair, prematurely gray.

The camera shutter blinked repeatedly, recording the shadowed figure and what looked like an angry, red eye winking malevolently below the brim of his dark hat. He stood on the porch, motionless, poised like a panther smelling the air.

The watcher's wristwatch began vibrating. *Now!*

Grabbing his side as if he'd just been stung, the sinister figure on the porch yanked out a pager the size of a deck of cards. He held it up to his face. Swearing loudly, he ripped the half-smoked cigarette from his lips and threw it onto the slatted floor. A brief tail of fire cut the fog like a falling star.

"Let's get out of here!" he shouted to Red. "They'll be here in less than ten minutes." The dark figure raced toward the van with the smooth grace of a commando. The tension fairly crackled from him.

"Yes suh, Mr. Pieters." Red hurriedly flung open the van's sliding door and ran around to the driver's door. "Smart of yah to post a lookout." Red huffed as he jumped into the front seat shoving aside a video magazine with a bloody dagger on the cover.

"Red, there's one thing I've never been accused of, and that's being stupid."

"Riiight," murmured the man in the bushes, "wait till you see your ugly mug plastered all over the six o'clock news!"

Pieters' voice continued, "You're certain you picked up everything inside the house?" The listener in the bushes nodded appreciatively, making sure that his tape recorder was registering properly. The microphone hidden inside the van was now catching every word.

"We don't want—"

The engine turned over smoothly. "Nuthin' to worry about, boss. I think—"

Pieters cut him off, "I've told you before, I'm paid to think—and worry."

"Yeah, and you'd better, you filthy swine," the observer gloated, taking a final shot from his hide-out.

Inside the van, Pieters had pulled out the car phone and was punching in seven numbers. Covering the mouthpiece, he barked, "Let's go."

Steam poured out of the quivering tail pipe, shining yellow-red as it reflected the van's brake lights. Pebbles shot across the drive as the van jerked away from the mansion.

"It's all set. Filming of the conclusion will begin next Friday night," Pieters was muttering into the cellular phone. "—yes sir, it is the 13th. —I thought it was rather fitting too. —No—no problems, they all cooperated quite readily. —Yes, it's hot stuff. You'll like it. I'm sure of it."

The watcher smiled. Every word was stored on brown magnetic tape. The little electronic gizmo inside the van was working just fine.

* * * * * * * * *

Inside the darkened mansion, five teenagers huddled in blankets sat in a cluster roughly the shape of a pentagram. A bleached skull in the center

3

with a candle on top was weeping red streams of wax. The dying flames in the fireplace cast eerie shadows, which gyrated fitfully on the mildewed walls. A haze the color of burnt mustard had crept into the room from an incense bowl on the hearth. The pungent smell of sulfur and decayed flowers filled the room.

Four of the young people held a card, black on both sides; the fifth, Trent McCauley, had thrown his on the floor. It was face up in front of him. A white death mask leered at him from its bottom right corner.

"The sinister base," he murmured tonelessly, his red-rimmed eyes frozen in blank horror.

The observer crept out of his hide-out as the van's tail lights disappeared into the gloom and stepped carefully up the porch steps toward the boarded-up bay window. He peered through the crack in the warped boards. Pressing the camera lens up to the crack, he snapped a picture of the living room.

"Pathetic kids," he murmured, shaking his head sadly. Stowing the camera inside his bag, he flung it over his shoulder and headed for the front door.

Trent's face was ashen; his expression haunted, like that of a trapped animal. He stood up and walked unsteadily over to a portable stereo. With trembling fingers he turned on the volume and, instantly, "Death Maiden's" maniacal howls flooded the murky silence. He rejoined the group on the floor and began rocking hypnotically to the relentless, throbbing incantations.

The knob on the front door turned.

The squeal of the hinges was completely drowned out by the electric wailing of the damned.

Chapter Two

Across town, almost at the very moment the van's engine began pouring its plume of smoke into the fog-shrouded night, Jotham Lewis sat up in bed, eyes wide with fear, gasping for air. He found himself on top of his mangled blankets, chest heaving, cold prickles of sweat running down his spine. He knew he'd been sobbing, but no sound had come. There was a raw burning in his throat as if he'd actually been screaming. He recognized these symptoms all too well.

Sitting up, he reached out to retrieve his pillow, which had fallen off his bed. Doubling it over, he placed it under his head and laid back trying to sort the jumbled pictures careening through his mind: his old friend, Ernest Glampoole, white hair flying, swinging a poker at Jotham's drunken father, and bright red blood flowing from a wound on his dad's head. These were mixed with confused images of his old pals Bart and Carisa dancing wildly around his younger brother, Abe, who was holding the shaft of an ax to his lips like a flute. And of course, inevitably, the huge, foreboding oak tree dominated the background. As the other fragments faded, that sinister image came into sharper relief.

Quietly, like a swarm of vipers, the familiar whispers resumed their harsh chant: *You're going to turn out just like your father. You can't escape your fate. You're never going to amount to anything. You're a loser . . . a nobody—just like your dad.*

Jotham struggled to ward off their relentless assault, but the clamoring only grew louder: *You're losing your mind. Give up; you're crazy. You're pathetic . . . give it up.* The insidious whispers were now a shrieking chorus: *You nothing. You—are—a—loser.* Then, inevitably, the stinging bite to the heart: *It was your fault he left . . . He thought you were worthless, and soon everyone else will know it too.*

Sweat dropped off Jotham's clenched jaw as he strained to shut out the raging accusations. Remembering what his father had done to his family caused a boiling cauldron of hatred to pour over and extinguish the voices. The internal hissing was now that of a blanket of rage squelching the fire of fear and revulsion.

Anger was his most effective counter to the relentless attacks of self-loathing; consequently, he walked around with it simmering just below the surface. Most of his friends would describe him as fairly easygoing except when on the football field. Jotham hid his fury well.

Unable to return to sleep, Jotham threw his legs over the side of his bed and groaned. During practice "Jumbo" Nagurski, the team's largest player, had fallen on top of him. He pulled up the leg of his cutoff pajama bottoms. His thigh was a dark blue. Grimacing, he hobbled into the bathroom where he turned on the cold water faucet full blast. Before he had time to talk himself out of it, he thrust his head under the chilling stream. The shock of the frigid water on his warm skin took his breath away, but he remained under the current until his face went numb. It was a little ritual he endured each morning. It served both to wake him up and test his mettle.

Drying his reddened cheeks and thick brown hair, he rubbed the bristles which were beginning to appear on his square jaw. "You look terrible, man!" he told his reflection in the mirror, staring at the dark circles underneath the hazel eyes looking back at him. "Looks like you had another rough night."

Though it seemed that he'd been plagued with the haunting nightmare forever, it had actually begun only two years earlier—the day his father had slammed the kitchen door and walked out of his life. Gingerly, he walked back to his bed and sat down, trying to work out the soreness in his leg. He needed to be in top condition for tonight's game—his last as a high school athlete.

He started in surprise as the alarm clock radio broke into his reverie with the loud conversation of two local DJs. Forgetting his leg, he lunged to change stations before their first hearty guffaw. He despised their corny theatrics, but it was a highly effective means of getting himself out of bed in the mornings. He punched the preset button to the soft rock station as the red glowing numerals blinked 6:00 A.M., alerting him that he was 12 hours away from his final football game. The pain in his leg diminished as the familiar tightness in his stomach and chest took over.

Walking over to his pet owl's perch, Jotham stroked its downy head,

"Good morning, little buddy. You've been a good 'watchbird.' No one would escape alive if they ever broke into my room, would they?"

Plato had been abandoned by its mother after falling out of the large maple tree behind their house. Jotham had found him huddled at the base of the trunk and built a nest for him in a shoebox lined with soft rags. The forsaken owl slowly recovered but had lost the use of one eye. He had also remained quite small. His favorite perch was the corner of the bookshelf on Jotham's desk. From there, he could keep his good eye trained on his master who slept and studied beneath him.

Jotham decided that a hot shower might do his leg some good. When he was done, he put on a pair of old jeans—back pocket frayed and knees torn—and his favorite sweatshirt. It was black, with a Picasso-like silhouette of Segovia in gold, playing his guitar. His mother had given it to him several months earlier on his 18th birthday, in hopes of encouraging him to persevere with his acoustic guitar lessons.

Jotham snapped on the desk lamp, sat down and picked up his Bible. He felt a twinge of guilt as he opened it. At a youth rally he'd accepted the challenge to read through it in a year. Although erratic, he'd managed to stay relatively close to schedule. Right now, he was only a book and a half behind. One good week and he would be back on track. As he was pulling out the tattered envelope-bookmark, his brother's alarm buzzed loudly from the next room. With a low groan, he laid the leather-bound book down on his nightstand. I'll finish the book of Romans tomorrow, he promised himself, clicking off the light.

On his way downstairs he entered his brother's room and hit the alarm's snooze button. He paused. Peering at the bed, Jotham could distinguish a large lump emitting soft, steady snores. As his eyes adjusted, he made out Abe's curly black head poking out from underneath the comforter. Abe, two years younger, clearly favored his father's eastern European roots; whereas in Jotham, his mother's Celtic features predominated.

Listening to Abe clinging to the last sweet seconds of sleep, Jotham couldn't restrain himself. He reached for the rolled-up sock by his foot and bounced it off the rumpled mass. Abe groaned and turned over on his stomach. Needing a missile with more substance, Jotham threw a slipper, this time hitting his brother squarely on the head.

"W-hat?—Ohh . . . cut it out," Abe grumbled.

"If you don't get up, it'll be the Chinese water torture next," threatened

7

Jotham, ignoring the edge in Abe's voice. Abe responded by bunching his bedspread around his head and turning to face the wall. Picking up the leather soccer ball from underneath the bed, Jotham yanked back the covers and dropped it on his brother's exposed back.

Abe bolted upright, his eyes blazing, and grabbed the ball off the floor. He drew back his arm, aiming at his brother's teeth, but Jotham had hastily ducked out of sight and was heading downstairs. Jotham could hear the furious tremor in his brother's voice following after him: "You never know when to stop, do you! You've always gotta be—" Abe snapped off the remainder of his tirade and heaved the ball into his closet.

Standing inside the doorway of the kitchen Jotham saw that his mother was preparing pancakes for breakfast. She had her long reddish-gold hair tied in a simple ponytail. A well-worn, red and white checkered apron protected her green cable knit sweater and blue jeans. Tiptoeing quietly behind her, he gripped her shoulders and whispered loudly in her ear: "Morning, Mom!"

She gasped, dropped a plate on the floor, and in the same instant swung around with a spatula. It left a smear of batter on his cheek and white droplets across his carefully combed hair. Though small in stature, she packed a real wallop. In happier days, he'd frequently heard his father refer to Katherine as his "tough little Irish lassie."

"Jotham, you most certainly deserve that," she scolded when she had regained her breath. "How many times have I told you not to do that? It's no wonder I'm getting gray hairs," she continued, bending over to pick up the plate which, fortunately, was still intact. "You'll be sorry when I keel over with a heart attack after one of your scares."

"Mom, look what you did to my hair," he moaned looking at his reflection in the microwave door. "Now I'm gonna have to go up and wash it all over again . . . and I'm going to be late for Biology too." He started for the stairs. "If I get a detention, it will be your fault!"

Katie Lewis glanced over her shoulder, puckering her lips in an exaggerated pout of sympathy.

When Jotham returned, Abe was sitting at the kitchen table finishing his first stack of pancakes. He ignored his older brother.

"Mom, keep that weapon away from me," Jotham warned her, sitting down.

Piling three blueberry pancakes on his plate, she waved the utensil at him threateningly. He rolled his eyes at her, and after pausing for a perfunctory silent prayer, dove in with his fork.

When Jotham began to slow down, she asked, "Ready for your last game?"

"Yeah," he mumbled, his mouth full, "although my leg's a little sore." He took a drink of milk. "But I won't even feel it tonight. You can bet Marywood won't beat us again, not on our field."

Mrs. Lewis put her hand on his shoulder. "You sure you're all right, Jotham?"

He nodded his head, though not before she had seen the brief twinge of pain in his eyes. Football season aroused painful memories which Jotham preferred to leave buried. Although he loved the excitement of the games, he hated the hole left by his father's departure and the empty space next to his mother on the bleachers. No matter where she sat in the stands, the void seemed to follow her. He despised his father for leaving—for inflicting so much pain on the family—but the truth was, he felt responsible for it, and so he was unsure how to answer his mother's probing question.

Sensing his discomfort, Katharine laid her hand on her boy's broad shoulders and remained by him for several seconds before she walked back toward the sink and began cleaning the counter.

Jotham felt the rage beginning to build. Fighting off these pangs of guilt and anger could sometimes drive him into a white-hot fury. According to Coach Malloy, it was the secret of Jotham's success on the field; he called it Jotham's "fire." To Jotham it felt more like a raging volcano.

"You'd better hurry," she said, looking at the kitchen clock. Gulping down the rest of their food, the boys gave their mother a hurried good-bye. They threw on their coats and, clutching their packs, jumped into Jotham's red, '75 Mustang.

On the way to Rockville High, Jotham was lost in thought. Abe was accustomed to it. Fridays—game-days—always brought on this pensive mood. Normally, Abe would sit quietly, humming off-key along with the radio station, but today was different. He was still seething from their early morning skirmish. If school weren't so far away he would have stormed off on his own while Jotham was still stuffing himself.

As they drove past Plainfield Park, a few stray snowflakes filtered down on the windshield, harbingers of a hard winter to come. As the wipers flicked them off, Jotham glanced out the window at a large, deeply rutted hill. Turning to Abe he asked, "Remember when we used to go tobogganing over there?"

Abe did not respond.

Oblivious to the tension, Jotham repeated the question.

Abe cleared his throat. "Yeah," he muttered.

In a voice tight with tension, Jotham released the question that had been plaguing him. "Do . . . do you think he'll come tonight?"

The question hung in the air for several moments. Abe's anger subsided at the taut wistfulness in Jotham's voice.

Abe turned toward his brother. "I hope so." He tried to reflect confidence but his eyes betrayed him. He quickly looked out at the flakes drifting down onto the windshield. Although he had not made peace with his father's departure either, he understood that during football season, it was particularly difficult for Jotham who had gone out for the sport primarily to please their dad, a football fanatic.

"You're gonna do great!" he continued with more conviction. "Marywood won't know what hit 'em."

They made a left turn. The Mustang slid a little on the transparent film of ice that was beginning to coat the road. They continued along the last three blocks, down the quiet street lined with trees, brilliant in their russet hues like a row of British red coats at attention. As the light dusting of snow settled on the leaves outside, a melancholy heaviness settled down on the two inside the car.

Driving past the football field, Jotham's eyes ran fondly over the familiar white goal posts looming over the gray brick stadium walls. His chest tightened at the sight of a long icicle hanging from the crossbars. Immediately, the terrible image of the slashing knife, the ghastly, writhing, moonlit oak, and that awful groaning gripped him.

Jotham felt himself unraveling. *Oh God! Oh God. I can't take it . . . I'm gonna go crazy.*

He squeezed the wheel to keep his hands from shaking. The last thing he wanted was for his little brother to see him lose it. He had to be strong for all of them. If Abe ever suspected this weakness in Jotham, his status would be shattered.

He couldn't fail his family—he just couldn't.

The pressure in his chest increased. Jotham desperately began filling the stadium in his mind with hundreds of shouting fans, projecting himself running exuberantly onto the field, then intercepting a pass and running it in for a touchdown. He imagined the raucous celebration following the home team's victory and the sweetness of that final triumph. By the time they pulled into the parking lot of the sprawling red-brick complex, the vise around Jotham's chest had loosened. But the awful dread still clung to him like a warm leech.

Please God . . . please get rid of that awful dream.

He looked up hoping for some sign, but all he saw were ghostly fingers of steam rising from the ice on the blacktop . . . and they were writhing.

Chapter Three

"I knew it," moaned Abe at the sight of the unbroken rows of cars in the school parking lot. "We're gonna have to park in the Gulag!" he said, referring to the section furthest from the school where the snowplows left their mountainous deposits in the winter.

The sound of the car doors slamming was muffled by the hum of the generators at the side of the brick building as the boys jumped out and sprinted for the main entrance. Slipping on patches of ice they navigated their way up the broad steps in front of the modern structure. Abe ran in first and flashed his identification card at William Robinson, the gray-haired security guard.

Bill smiled. "Hey man, looks to me like he done beat you again," he said, slapping Jotham good-naturedly on the back as he tried to push past his younger brother.

"Yeah, well, he had a head start."

"If you ax' me, Jo, he beat you fair and square." Bill winked broadly at Abe. "I think you jus' forgot your Wheaties."

"It'd take more than a bowl of cereal for him to beat me, Bill," Abe bragged.

"Youze be nice to your big brother, son," warned Robinson, suddenly protective. "He's got a big game tonight. Don't be putting him down now." He was about to shake a large forefinger at Abe when his eye caught the clock. "Unless I'm mistakin', you boys bes' be running along."

Alarmed, the boys began racing for their lockers.

"Make us proud, Jo!" Bill yelled, waving his weathered hand at them. "Eat up their quarterback. He thinks he's Mr. Big-stuff."

Jotham's response was drowned out by the bell's ear-splitting ring.

Thanks to an almost photographic memory, school generally posed little challenge for Jotham, but on game-days it was difficult concentrating even in

12

Calculus, his favorite class. However, today, it was impossible. His thoughts bounced unpredictably, like a fumbled punt, from the math lecture to memories of his first game, then to his defensive assignments, and then deflected to blond-haired Trisha McCauley.

The "ball" came to rest there as he began refining the script of the dialogue which would result in Trisha's delighted agreement to go with him to the Prom. For the past several weeks he'd been hearing rumors in the locker room about her breakup with Don Ratthmun, the Bronco's field goal kicker. However, Jotham was nervous about asking her out so soon after an apparently painful split.

Dave Benoit, the senior class president, and its self-appointed counselor—as he termed it—"in delicate matters of the heart," had strongly advised him to take advantage of the opportunity.

"On the rebound or not, I wouldn't let it stop me," he said, tossing back his long black bangs for emphasis. "Shoot, man, she is hot! I'd ask her myself if I weren't already taking Samantha. Take my word for it—" Here he had shrugged his shoulders dramatically and held up both hands, the picture of utter sincerity. "—and, Jo, I do know about these things; there is no better time than this. As my uncle, may he rest in peace, advised me after his fourth marriage, 'Davey, Davey, you've got to strike while ze iron it eez hot.' I hated it when he called me that, but he did have experience with women."

"Mr. Lewis," his math teacher's reedy voice intruded itself into his wandering thoughts. "I know you have more meaningful endeavors in which to participate this evening, but I would greatly appreciate you at least opening up your textbook."

"Ichabod Crane," a nickname Jotham had bestowed on their teacher, Mr. Green, was as sharp-tongued as he was single-minded in his devotion to his science. His long, spare frame and nasal voice had prompted the name. A confirmed bachelor, he had no room in his life for "romantic entanglements." Jotham smiled, imagining what "Ichabod's" potential heartthrob might look like.

"Mr. Lewis, perhaps you could share your thoughts with us." Jotham was startled to realize he had apparently again been staring at the chalkboard. "They apparently are much more interesting and amusing than mine."

Jotham began lamely, "Well, Mr. Cra—" he caught himself as titters spread around him, "—Mr. Green, I mean . . . I—I was thinking . . ." then sudden inspiration struck, "—about how much I enjoy this class and how much I'll miss it next semester." He smiled innocently at his teacher.

Mr. Green's eyes bored holes through Jotham. "Thank you for your contribution, though I find it strangely unconvincing." Ripples of laughter swept over the room as Mr. Green turned back to complete an indecipherable formula.

Jotham congratulated himself at his quick thinking, noticing that Trisha had turned around to look at him, laughter playing at the corner of her lips. His eyes locked momentarily on hers. He was shocked. Her beautiful green eyes were bloodshot, as if she'd been crying. She broke free of his gaze and abruptly turned her head.

At lunch most of the football team ate together; however, today Jotham selected a small table by the east bank of windows, his back to the rest of the room. Perhaps it was the dream, his father's absence, Trisha, his last game, or a combination of them all that had made him feel both angry and depressed. Whatever it was had drained his appetite.

All he wanted was to be left alone.

Jotham stared out at the golden leaves cavorting in the breeze. His attention was drawn to a bronze leaf with reddish streaks, trembling alone in the top branches of an old maple. As he watched, it twitched, broke loose, and began its free fall to the ground. The leaf rocked in slow, descending arcs. The finality of the undulating flight sent a shiver of sadness through him. The tree's naked branches shook in the breeze, as if also mourning its final death throes.

The futility of the leaf's lonely battle touched something inside him: a strange, angry empathy ached in Jotham's heart. There had been a terrible poignancy about the leaf's inevitable surrender. It had held out heroically, but had finally, fully and utterly succumbed. He had a sudden, crazy vision of himself shaking the tree and shouting, "Live! . . . Live!" But the reality of his impotence mocked him.

The heat startled him when it came.

A stubborn resistance was welling up like lava inside him. His fists were clenched, his body rigid. *I won't give in, I won't. I don't care what my father did. My life is going to count for something.* He gritted his teeth, then let out a deep breath. *I'm going to make a difference!* he swore to himself.

A scornful whisper, dripping with sarcasm, chilled him. *Yeah . . . right! Forget it, Jo-boy. You're a loser, remember? After what you did to your old man? You're not gonna' amount to anything! Life stinks and then ya die, buddy.*

The warmth began to recede; then, so distinctly that it almost knocked him backwards, he heard another voice, very firm, yet gentle, declare: *Jotham, your life will make a difference! That is your calling! Trust in me.* The sweetness and certitude of the words instantly blasted the despair, leaving behind an empty husk like the brittle shell of a snake's skin.

When he regained his breath, he cautiously turned his head and looked out of the corner of his eyes to see who had spoken. No one was near him. Mystified, he glanced down at his tray shaking his head.

Did I imagine it?

He knew he hadn't.

He was tingling and shaking inside. He felt a sensation as if strong arms were embracing him. Pure, liquid peace flowed over him, and he became utterly still. Slowly, the awareness of being in the presence of Another faded away.

He looked out the cafeteria window again and saw the brilliant autumn splendor. Though the intrusion of the peaceful presence had been a surprise, the message itself had actually not been. As early as he could remember, despite frequent bouts of futility, there had throbbed the faint but stubborn pulse of an awareness of his unique destiny. He'd never dared share it with anyone; it had remained his own private, almost guilty, secret.

Now, certain he would be incapable of finishing his lunch, Jotham reached into his backpack and withdrew the letter he'd received almost two weeks ago. Looking at Bart's scrawling script gave him a comforting sensation of belonging. *It's only a stupid letter,* he reproved himself, a little ashamed. Nonetheless, as he began to open it, he again felt a surge of nervous anticipation.

Bartholomew "just-call-me-Bart" Crayford had been his childhood companion in mischief and adventure. Bart's father, Mark, had been the associate pastor at Rockville Community Church where Mrs. Lewis had begun attending when her marriage began to deteriorate. Returning to her childhood faith had caused her spiritual life to bloom. Whenever the doors were open she was there, two well-scrubbed children in tow, gratefully ushering her brood into the safety of that granite sanctuary. Ignoring their loud protests, she had even signed them up for children's choir, in spite of Abe's inability to carry a tune. The experience had scarred Abe for life, or so he claimed.

Since Bart Crayford was the only boy of Jotham's age in the choir, their shared misery had inseparably bonded them together. Their friendship helped make up for the hole in Jotham's heart left by a distant and frequently hostile father. Jotham grinned, recalling how Pastor Mark had threatened to claim him as a tax deduction because he slept over at their house so often. He'd last seen his friend five years ago when the Crayfords left for a pastorate in Tennessee.

Jotham took a sip of his Coke and began rereading the letter printed on Bart's LaserJet.

Hey Chill—

How's it going? I've got some great news! Dad and Mom decided to give me and Carisa part of our graduation presents early. They said we can come with them next week when they drive up to Rockville. Actually, believe it or not, Dad's going to be candidating (I've always thought it should be called auditioning) at Faith Christian Church. Yeah, ugh! Remember how we hated them as kids? They always beat us in softball. It feels kind of strange going there, like I'm committing treason or something.

Anyway, Dad's going to be doing his best juggling and tap-dancing routine, and Carisa and I have promised to be on our very best behavior so as not to blow his chances. Fortunately, he didn't ask us to sing. The days of the Crayford Family Quartet are definitely history. Maybe if he let us sing something with some electric guitars and drums, we'd reconsider. Fat chance—we have to worry about the "o" word. You know: "OFFENDING." We don't want to shock the church folks with the startling revelation that it really isn't 1955 any longer—sur-prise!

Whatever. Dad says I need to watch my attitude. I think I'm just being honest. But, as old Glump used to say, "I digress." (Is it okay to start a sentence with a "but"?—I digress again, sorry.) The point being, I'll be seeing you in a few days. Of course, it goes without saying, we're praying that some mighty delusion falls over the audience and they demand that Dad take the pastorate. A fat signing bonus would also be nice too. Right? Dream on!

Wouldn't it be great if we could return to Rockville though? What a blast that would be! After all this time, I still feel like a foreigner here in the South.

By the way, we're going to be bringing our bikes to hit the trails. Hopefully, your weather will cooperate. That would definitely be the one thing I'd miss: 80 degree weather in the winter. Very nice. Carisa bought a beauty last year. Mine got stolen (so much for southern hospitality) so I'm using "ole Bessy," my trusty ten-speed. Talk about an embarrassment! I'm saving up so I can get me a serious bike next year.

Well, that's about it. Say hi to Abe for me and tell him that Carisa sends him a big kiss.

Carry on mate . . .

Your friend,
(although just barely, based on your pathetic response ratio)
Bart

P.S. Carisa instructs me as follows, and I quote: "Make sure that Jotham knows that I am also sending him my fondest regards."
P.P.S. Hail Paladins!

Jotham was so engrossed in the letter, he failed to notice the attractive blond-haired girl standing behind him. Hearing a low chuckle, he turned quickly. It was Trisha McCauley. A fleeting look of embarrassment rose in her face as she came down off her tiptoes. He folded the letter and smiled at her, feeling a little foolish himself.

"I'm sorry, I—I didn't mean to interrupt you," she stammered. "I really wasn't reading over your shoulder." Then she grinned. "At least not very much," she added playfully. "May I sit down?"

"Sure."

She sat across from him and took a sip from her glass of ice water. "I have a huge favor to ask, but first, there's something I'm curious about."

He slipped the letter hastily into his back pack. "Go ahead. What is it?"

She hesitated. "How did you get the nickname 'Chill'?"

Feeling his cheeks begin to burn, he wished he'd never brought the letter to school, or better, had burned it. He looked down at his half-eaten plate of lasagna. "It's a stupid nickname the guys on the team gave me. I don't know why, maybe it's because they like my mom's chili."

Her exotic green eyes smiled innocently. "That's not what Don told me."

Jotham felt a stab at the casual mention of her ex-boyfriend.

"Seems like he said it had something to do with a helmet." Her eyes twinkled.

"He has a big mouth. . . . It's not like it sounds. I tripped over it during a scrimmage."

Actually, it had happened the day after his dad left home for good, three weeks to the day after his overdose on alcohol and antidepressants. Jotham had gone to the practice field enraged, like a bull elephant looking to prove a point. He'd found his opportunity in Dirk "the Brick" Mangione, a rival candidate for All-State defensive honors. Jotham's pretext was the Brick's unintentional blow to his head. He'd retaliated instantly by throwing a wild punch, ripping Dirk's helmet off and flinging it to the ground. When Jotham jumped on it with both feet, the facemask shattered. "Jumbo" had waded in and saved Dirk's handsome features. It was the only time in anyone's memory that a football helmet had been broken by a player.

That was the day Jotham's nickname was born. The double meaning was intentional—referring both to Jotham's need to chill out, and to his crazed look which, as he thrust his feet through the facemask, was downright chilling.

With a guarded expression, Jotham looked at Trisha over his soft drink.

"OK, Jo, whatever you say. I was just kidding anyway." She hesitated momentarily. "Do you mind answering one more thing?" Then, without waiting for his reply, she asked, "What are 'Paladins?' —I just happened to notice it at the bottom of the letter."

Jotham cringed; Trisha was beginning to make him feel like a little kid. Maybe the Prom was not such a hot idea after all.

He stuck a spoon in his chocolate pudding and began stirring it. "The Paladins were representatives of the King: knights who were chosen to perform special missions." He wished he could stop, but he suspected that he would be unable to deflect her inquisitiveness; she seemed to be just picking up steam. "It was also the name of a club a friend and I started when we were just . . . nine." His cheeks flamed.

"Was that friend named Bart?" Her eyes grew wide, "Hey, that letter wasn't from Bart Crayford, was it?"

An internal warning flag began to wave madly. "Yes, it was," he answered levelly. "He and Carisa were in the club along with my brother Abe. They're coming to visit us tomorrow," he went on, a slight edge to his voice. "And that was two questions, by the way . . . anything further, *counselor?*"

Trisha's face was now the one showing a bit of color. "I'm sorry," she said. "Don always said I should become an attorney . . . like my mother." She rolled her eyes, distaste etched on her face.

"I'd rather go into acting. Anyway, I really am sorry. I didn't mean to pry; it's just something I do when I'm really interested in getting to know someone." Jotham relaxed; the red flag went limp.

Trisha looked wistfully at the gray skies outside the window. "Bart's sister Carisa and I were pretty good friends. We just lost touch after they left, I guess." She stared past him forlornly. "Those were good times." No longer the coquettish cheerleader, she looked more like a trapped little girl. "Sorry for being so nosy, Jo; I don't mean to . . . Maybe I should just go . . ." her voice trailed away.

The sadness trembling in her green eyes melted Jotham. He longed to assure her that no one in their right mind could ever be mad at her, but the words stuck in his throat. Instead he remarked awkwardly, "It's all right, Trisha, don't go. I needed to get my mind off of the game anyway."

She leveled her gaze at him, pursing her lips thoughtfully as she weighed her next words. It was then that Jotham noticed the weariness in her face. "If you're sure you're not angry, then I need to ask if you would do something for me. It's terribly important."

"What is it?" He felt a twinge of apprehension at her somber expression.

"It's about my brother, Trent. He's in the tenth-grade and he's also on the Junior Varsity Team . . . or at least he was. Abe knows him."

"Yeah, I know him too. He's got really good hands. I haven't seen him practicing with the JV recently though; I thought maybe he got hurt."

She nodded her head. "Yeah, he did, although not in the way you mean. You're kind of his football hero." She reached out to grab his arm. "But please don't let on that I told you; he'd kill me if he knew." Her hands fell back onto the table. She began tracing nervous patterns in the condensation on her glass of Coke.

"Something's happening to him. He quit the team about a month ago. Since then, his grades have been terrible. He's been skipping school with a group of really scary kids, and I'm afraid he may be starting to do drugs." She stopped, her eyes filling with tears.

Wishing desperately that he knew what to tell her, Jotham looked at her bowed head and searched for an eloquence that eluded him. Nothing came to mind other than pathetic generalities; so he remained mute, his fingernails digging miserably into his palms.

Trisha gathered herself and said, "I realize it's an awful lot to ask, but I thought . . . I was hoping, that because he admires you so much, maybe you could write him or talk to him about staying with football. He feels like a total failure and my dad is no help. In fact, he's the main problem." Her hand squeezed the cold glass. "He's always on Trent's back about everything. After Trent dropped the football in the last game, Dad blamed him for the loss." Her white fingers released the glass and balled into a fist. "Can you believe it?"

Knowing he had no other recourse, Jotham gave her his best "everything's-cool-and-under-control" look and said, "Listen, Trisha. I'll be glad to give him a call and encourage him to keep going. He really does have talent, you know." He stretched out his hand reassuringly, but it came to a halt inches away from hers. "If he keeps working out, he's got a shot at making the varsity next year."

He thought for a moment, "I just had an idea. Maybe after the season is over he could join Abe and me for weight training."

Her hand reached out to rest on top of his. "Oh thanks, Jotham." Heat prickled up his arm. "Thanks so much. You have no idea what this means to me!" She stood up, eyes shining, and impulsively bent over, lightly kissing his cheek. Blushing, Jotham pushed his chair back as she began to leave. He bumped into Dave Benoit, who had chosen that moment to walk by.

Dave glanced at them with raised eyebrows and, smirking at Jotham, nodded his approval. "Hello, Trish. I see you've gotten over our good friend Don. I've always said that the Jo-man is one of the most irresistible dudes in our class—next to me of course."

"Shut up!" Jotham warned, grasping Dave's throat, threatening to choke his friend.

"Trisha," a high-pitched voice yelled out. Samantha was running toward them. "I've been looking for you everywhere. Your mom just called and said that you need to come home right away. It's something about your brother."

Trisha's face went white. She dropped her tray on the table, spilling her glass of Coke and ran out of the cafeteria. Through the windows, Jotham watched her athletic figure race down the hall and felt anxiety growing like a firestorm in his stomach.

20

Several hours later, during his last class, his uneasiness was forgotten. As the time for kickoff approached, anticipation mingled with an aching sadness had taken over. Once, he'd caught Jumbo's eye, and they nodded, communicating silently: *Tonight it's going to be over, buddy. Can you believe it? Our last game.* He looked away and blinked rapidly, staring studiously at his textbook.

Where did the time go? . . . Suddenly, like the sneering face of an unwelcome visitor, the painful question resurfaced: *Will Dad be there tonight?*

He smothered a faint surge of hope and instead pictured himself smashing through the line and driving Marywood's quarterback into the ground.

Chapter Four

The afternoon of the game broke brisk and clear. It was an idyllic, late fall day—Jotham's and his mother's favorite time of year. "Thick sweater and hot tea weather," she called it. It was that gracious midwestern interlude between the sweltering humidity of summer and winter's frigid, unrelenting assault.

Jotham smelled the air as he ran to the locker room. It had a crisp bite, like a tangy mouthful of cold cider. He jumped to give "Brutus," the white Bronco painted on the cinder block wall, its traditional pre-game smack.

It was a good day to be alive.

The team completed their emotion-laden, pre-game meeting and was now waiting on the stairs ready to take the field. There was only a hint of snow left in the air, and the breath of the clustered players seemed to billow like the smoke of so many dragons preparing for mortal combat.

Jotham loved that unique moment in which time seemed to quiver and stand absolutely still. It happened immediately prior to rushing out of the "tunnel" with the clamoring of hundreds of fans filling the small stadium. The exhilarating sense of power and pride was intoxicating.

He loved it. It served to help fill the hole inside, if only momentarily. The hairs on his arms tingled with anticipation awaiting the announcer's bellowing introduction. All the pain of practice was worth the rush of adrenaline as the team tore onto the field, racing over the manicured grass with the abandon of wild horses. After galloping crazily to the opposite sideline, he surveyed the stands and steeled himself against the inevitable stab of disappointment.

His father was nowhere to be seen.

He snorted angrily. Nothing was going to spoil his last high school game. Jotham let the pain combust into fire; it would be an unpleasant game for his opponents. He would make sure of that.

Early on in the first quarter, as both teams were still tentatively looking for the advantage, Jotham helped turn the momentum. Freddie Sanders, Marywood's ball carrier, who was short but surprisingly strong and elusive, had taken his team to within 12 yards of Rockville's end zone. On an earlier play he had faked so effectively that he'd left Jotham sprawled on his stomach, clutching handfuls of air.

A few plays later, assuming they had found a weak spot, Marywood ran it again. Freddie came barreling at Jotham, thighs high and cleats crunching on the hard turf. His eyes were wide and shifty. Jotham readied himself to lunge forward but held back and waited for Freddie to plant his right foot and slide by Jotham's grasp. Ignoring his clever footwork, Jotham threw himself forward, driving his helmet straight into Freddie's chest, swinging his arm down on the football. His fist landed hard. He felt Freddie's fingers give and the football come loose. Mangione, circling from the opposite side, fell on top of it and Rockville took control.

"Yeaah!" Jotham yelled, pounding the muddy turf with his hands. Freddie was on his back struggling to regain his breath. Getting up from his knees, Jotham rubbed his filthy hands on his thigh pads. A wistful thought suddenly intruded: *I wonder what Dad would have thought of that hit?* He clenched his jaw and reached down to yank his opponent up to his feet. Freddie ignored him and with eyes blazing ripped the ball from Mangione, throwing it at the ground.

Jotham scanned the sidelines as he ran exultantly off the field. For the first time he realized that Trisha was not with the other cheerleaders. A warning light flickered. It was immediately extinguished on the next play, when the Broncos' half-back broke through a tackle and nearly scored. Two plays later, Marywood intercepted a pass and Rockville's threat was turned aside.

During the second quarter Rockville mounted another long drive downfield, chewing up a lot of time and yardage. The temperature had begun to plummet as the game progressed, and as Jotham cheered from the sidelines, he felt his thigh stiffen and begin to throb. Toward the end of the period, it had become so cold his ears and fingers were beginning to ache. Several minutes later, the offense stalled again and the Broncos had to attempt a field-goal. Don's kick went wide by only a few inches, so at halftime the teams ran into their locker rooms with the game scoreless.

At the start of the second-half, Jotham could still feel that familiar tingling that usually indicated a solid game. He'd felt it when he awoke and it was proving accurate. He'd stopped Freddie for only a few short gains, had knocked down a pass, and had made several clean tackles. However, Marywood had taken the field with a vengeance and was moving methodically toward Rockville's goal line.

Tim Marinaro, Marywood's quarterback, was as cocky as he was good. He had apparently finally found his rhythm and was leading his team so impressively that a score seemed inevitable. Marinaro swaggered as he stepped up to the line, and the sound of his harsh, arrogant voice as he barked out the signals sent a surge of anger flaming through Jotham.

"Not today! Not on my field!" he growled loudly, fire in his eyes. He slapped both hands sharply on his thigh pads, the loud clap an unmistakable challenge. Marinaro's cool eyes momentarily held his.

Marinaro took the snap, pedaled backwards several yards, preparing for a pass. Jotham launched himself against Marywood's line, spun sideways, and with his blocker off balance, grabbed his shoulder pads and hurled him to the turf. Sensing his approach, Marinaro twisted and ducked trying to elude Jotham's rush. Leaping over the blocker's extended arm, Jotham lunged and grabbed the loose tail of Marinaro's retreating jersey. Holding on with one hand, he flung his body sideways and twisted Marinaro out of bounds. The quarterback's spinning body smashed into the Gatorade table, dousing the front of his white jersey with green liquid.

Jotham couldn't resist swaggering just a little as he ran back to the huddle, thrusting his fists into the air. Marinaro was unable to return for the next play and Marywood had to try a field goal. The kick was good and at the end of the third quarter the Broncos were behind, three to zero.

In the last quarter, Marywood's defense was unrelenting and kept forcing Rockville to give up the ball. The Broncos returned the favor by shutting down their opponents, refusing to allow them another score. Although Jotham broke through the line on several occasions, he'd been unable to catch their elusive quarterback again. Marywood's center got even for the earlier sack by shoving his fist through Jotham's facemask, bloodying his nose. On the next play, Jotham made sure to fall heavily on the center's stomach, knocking the wind out of him. As time was running out, Marywood again had possession near mid-field. On an earlier play Rockville's safety had twisted his knee, and Jotham was assigned coverage of Marywood's star receiver.

Marinaro faked a handoff, then dropped back for a quick pass. Jotham kept his eyes on his man, who was slanting directly toward him.

His chest tightened.

24

It was going to be a pass play over the middle. The receiver was fast, a lot faster than Jotham was, and worse still, they both knew it. Marywood had run the same play in the first half so Jotham had a hunch where the ball was going, and Marinaro threw the ball perfectly. The receiver launched himself high in the air to make a spectacular grab. Anticipating the location of the throw, Jotham timed his tackle expertly, hitting his opponent hard before his feet touched the ground. He heard the satisfying "ooomph!" and saw the ball squirt free in a lazy arc.

Time seemed frozen.

The noise of the crowd evaporated. The ball spun and glided down toward the wet grass. Jotham felt himself stretch out his body and reach out his arm. His fingers were taut and spread open wide. The cold leather smacked into his palm and lay still in his numb fingers.

He had 45 yards to go for a touchdown.

The stands exploded.

He angled across the field for 35 yards. It was just like he'd dreamed it a thousand times. The adrenaline rushed him through and past the arms of several tackles. Around the 15-yard line he sensed someone catching up to him. He glanced over his shoulder and saw Tim Marinaro racing toward him, his lips fixed in a snarl. Jotham gritted his teeth and tried to avoid his lunge, but Tim was too fast. His forearm hit Jotham's calf, tripping him three yards shy of the goal line.

As he fell, the ball spun out of his cold fingers. Sliding on the slick grass, he made a grab for the muddy ball and watched as it rolled out of bounds. His helmet struck a wooden bench, ending his skid and leaving him momentarily stunned. Jotham picked himself up quickly before Coach Mallory could run over to examine him. Staggering slightly, he walked off the field with Jumbo's arm for support.

Marywood's defense refused to buckle and drove Rockville back to the 12-yard line. It began to look as though the Broncos were going to have to settle for a field goal to tie the game. On third down, as time was about to expire, Coach Mallory called a risky pass play. Steve Benz, Rockville's sophomore sensation, faked a curling route over the middle, then dashed to the corner of the end zone where he made a diving fingertip catch.

Six points were on the board and Rockville's victory was sealed.

Moments later, after the extra point was made, the whistle blew. Rockville had won by four.

Running off the playing field with his screaming teammates, Jotham made a final survey of the stands. *Not there again!* He headed for the shower room, his eyes hard and glistening like translucent brown marbles.

Later, after celebrating at Mangione's Pizza King, Jotham drove home a little after midnight. He found his mother still up, finishing some paperwork from her job as office manager at Rest Haven Manor, a private nursing home. She jumped up, beaming proudly at her son. Wrapping her arms around his broad shoulders, she kissed his cheek. Then, staring up at his face, she shifted smoothly into her over-protective, motherly mode. "Jotham, are you sure your neck's all right? Did the trainer look it over? It looked like you hit that bench really hard!"

He nodded. "It's fine, Mom. I even did a headstand for five minutes while waiting for the pizza to come."

"Jotham Lewis!" she scolded, half seriously.

As he turned to drag his suddenly weary body upstairs, she reached out to grab his hand. "Oh, I almost forgot," she said, giving him an inquisitive glance. "A girl named Trisha called. She said to please call her tomorrow, and to tell you that it was urgent."

"Really? What time did she call?" The conversation in the cafeteria suddenly flashed back into his memory.

"It was around three hours ago. She said she knew you'd be home late, but that it was extremely important that she talk with you as soon as possible in the morning. She sounded terribly upset. I could tell that she'd been crying." His mother's face was now openly curious. "Who is she, Jotham? I don't think I've ever heard you talk about her before."

Heading up the stairs, he answered tonelessly, "She's a cheerleader, Mom. She and Don were going out. Her little brother needs help. I'll tell you about it tomorrow."

"Okay, but remember, the Crayfords are supposed to arrive in the early afternoon. So you can't sleep in very late."

"Yeah," he yawned as he began pulling his sweatshirt over his head. "I know. G'night, Mom."

As he fell into an exhausted sleep, he had a nagging premonition that the new day would hold something both unexpected and unpleasant. He pushed it out of his mind and hoped morning would never come. *One more step and I would have made it in!* he thought as he drifted into sleep. His last waking memory was the look of pure hatred on Marinaro's handsome face as he lunged to keep Jotham from scoring.

Chapter Five

Walking barefoot across the cold linoleum floor early Saturday morning, Katharine Lewis tightened the belt of her thick terry cloth robe around her. The house had yet to warm up. Since her husband, David, had walked out on them, she'd begun turning the heat down below 60 degrees at night in an attempt to pinch pennies. It made for chilly mornings. She searched around the kitchen and found her slippers in the entryway and made her way to the cupboard. She took out the hand-painted porcelain mug she loved—a Mother's Day gift from her boys—and poured a cup of coffee, holding it up to her face. The warm steam brought color to her cheeks. Katie turned up the thermostat and sat down at the kitchen table, drinking in the early morning stillness.

Looking out the kitchen window at the thick layer of discolored leaves on the lawn, she could once again see her little boys and David as they carried huge mounds of leaves in a sheet to toss into the empty lot next door. *Those were such good days! Where did they go?* The nostalgic memories were interrupted by the nagging question which had eaten at her since David left.

What did I do wrong?

A slow tear slid down her cheek, leaving behind a trail of confusion and regret. The sting of David's rejection was still raw. She suspected that the pain of his betrayal would probably never be fully relieved. She didn't know which she hated worse: her loneliness or David's occasional phone calls interrupting it. His call last month at Abe's birthday party had almost ruined the festivities. As always, his timing was terrible. The careless promise he'd made to be at Jotham's final game had rung hollow, but it had sparked a flicker of hope which, last night, he'd just as carelessly ground out.

A heavy thud from Jotham's room overhead deflected her thoughts toward the day's activities and helped push down the bitter swell which threatened to engulf her. The coffee in her cup had cooled, so she placed it in the microwave and pressed 30 seconds. A pile of clean laundry she had folded the night before lay next to it on the counter. Scooping it up she walked to the stairway. "Jotham, are you awake? I've got some clean T-shirts down here if you need them." There was no response. So she called again, "Jotham?" The microwave bell sounded, and with it came his response: "Just a minute Mom; I'm on the phone."

First thing in the morning! she mused, then smiled to herself. *I was right, Jotham can't hide anything from me. There is more to this Trisha than he let on.*

In his bedroom, phone in hand, Jotham was nodding his head nervous-ly. "Yeah, I've heard about that group —How long has Trent been hanging out with them? —Really? —Maybe he'll just get sick of those weirdos— Why not? —Black! —You're kidding! If I did that to my room my mom would shoot me!"

After a long pause, Jotham continued, "Yeah, your mom's right; the Crayfords are coming over this afternoon —So, she already talked with him? —Well, I guess I feel a little strange about it, but with Pastor Mark coming it makes a big difference. . . ." Hopeful of a last minute reprieve, he inquired, "You're sure Trent wants me to come?" He shook his head morosely at her reply. "Okay then, I guess I'll see you at 2:30 this afternoon."

He hung up and headed for the tub to soak his stiff muscles. When he got out, he threw on his old Harvard sweatshirt and jeans. As he was pulling on his sneakers, he noticed the Bible by his bed. Its open pages drew him. He loved the feel of its soft-leather cover and the crisp, gilt-edged leaves. The torn envelope, which served as his makeshift bookmark, had dropped onto the floor. He picked it up and turned it over in his hand.

It was obvious by the fine wrinkles over its surface that, at some point, it had been wadded into a ball. Over time it had been pressed flat, yet its surface remained marbled like a lizard's skin. Jotham glanced at the out-lines of three small, reddish-brown splotches. He turned it over; as always, the sight of the smeared red fingerprint on the flap arrested him. It was an aching memento left by his father which he wanted desperately to forget, although something inside him clung just as tenaciously to the ragged edges of that pain.

His hazel eyes grew hard and the corners of his mouth stiffened. He stuffed the envelope back into the book and slammed it closed, tossing it on his bed. He strode quickly out the door. Passing through the family room, Jotham saw Abe who was slouching on the sofa playing a video game. Abe hollered, "Great game last night! You showed that fat-headed quarterback. I loved it when you doused him on the sidelines—awesome tackle!"

"Yeah, thanks," he mumbled, choking back his rage. "I did get him pretty good. I just wished I'd made it into the end zone."

Abe grinned, "I warned you. If you'd taken more of those conditioning runs, rigor mortis wouldn't have set in at the ten-yard line."

Jotham stared at his younger brother's reclining form, a hot spark in his eyes. "You should talk . . . you're gonna be feeling more than rigor mortis yourself if you keep it up, you couch potato." Jotham kicked a mini soccer ball at him. It flew wide. Abe caught it deftly with one hand, inches from their mom's favorite lamp.

Sensing an opening, Abe pressed the advantage, "And don't try out for the soccer team either. You've got to be able to run and kick."

Jotham's cheeks flushed. "Right, squirt. But if you want to see how tough you are, come on out for football. That's a real man's game."

The words stung, but Abe pretended not to care.

When Jotham's face turned, Abe sent the ball sailing, smacking Jotham on the side of his head.

"Not in the house!" came the I-mean-business voice from around the corner.

Jotham sauntered over to the couch. "Okay, Mom; I'll tell Abe to stop," he yelled, stuffing a pillow forcefully into Abe's face.

Abe swung blindly, landing a glancing blow on Jotham's shoulder. "Stop, you big ox!"

"Jotham, come in and tell me about Trisha's brother," interrupted their mother.

Jotham menaced his brother with the coal shovel next to the fireplace, then walked out of the den. One glance at his mother and Jotham decided to divulge the information as quickly and painlessly as possible. Trisha's interrogating skills were nothing compared to his mother when she had a full head of steam.

Pouring himself a glass of orange juice, he began, "Trent dropped out of the junior varsity football team a few weeks ago. Since then, he's given up on everything, maybe even his life."

"What's he done?" Mrs. Lewis asked.

"Well, he's painted his bedroom black, is big-time into metal music, and has begun hanging around with a really strange gang: 'death-heads' Trisha called them. Apparently, they all forged excuses and skipped school yesterday. The police found them somehow. They called Trisha at school since her folks were both out of town on business." He filled his glass again.

Abe, who'd just sauntered in, looked at him quizzically, "Out of town? Again?"

"Yeah, that's what she said."

"They're gone all the time," Abe commented. "I remember Trent telling me that's why they hardly ever came to the JV games."

"Well, things haven't changed. Trisha mentioned it to me too."

"Maybe Trent's just trying to get their attention," Mrs. Lewis suggested.

Abe's eyes shone with a deep understanding as he spoke over a bite of banana. "Sounds to me like they're running away from serious problems. You know, kind of a passive-aggressive thing," he added, throwing out a term he heard on a talk show.

Jotham nodded his head in mock seriousness. "Riiight, Dr. Abraham *Freud!* Anyway, somehow the FBI's mixed up in it too. Trisha couldn't tell me how they got involved."

Abe stopped peeling a second banana. "That's weird. Why would the FBI be interested in Trent? Man, I didn't know the Feds went after you for playing hooky." He took a bite. "Talk about 'Big Brother!'"

Jotham sat down across from his mother and broke an apple bagel in half. "When Trisha's folks came home last night, Trent completely lost it. He started yelling something about dying. She told me that since slamming the door shut, he hasn't come out of his room."

Abe strolled over to the coffee maker and nonchalantly poured himself a cup. He studiously ignored his mother's it's-not-good-for-you glare. "I know the kids she's talking about," Abe said blowing the steam off his mug. "A couple of them are in my class. . . . You wouldn't believe these guys. Two of them have their heads shaved, except for long tails on the side. They remind me of Attila the Hun. On Halloween they all came to class wearing dark make-up around their eyes and black lipstick."

He grimaced. "Man, did they look sick!"

Jotham took the other half of the bagel. "There's a girl like that in my History class too. She's scary. I heard she was in a weird club that got together to do drugs and write poetry about death."

"What do your teachers do about these kids?" asked their mother.

Bouncing a soccer ball off his forehead, Abe responded, "What can they do?" He lunged to grab the ball before it hit the top of the stove.

"Abra-ham!"

Abe kicked the ball safely into the family room. "In Lit. class one of them read a poem he'd written. Ms. Stein-Friesen said that it was, 'veh-ry pertheptive and dah-rkly provocative.' I thought it was just plain sick. Whoever thinks death is 'a beautiful virgin dressed in violet' needs his head examined."

Their mother's face was becoming troubled. "But why did Trisha call *you*, Jotham?"

"Trisha said I was some kind of hero to her brother. She thinks I'm the only 'normal' guy he'll listen to."

Abe jumped in. "Sheesh . . . that kid must be seriously messed up!"

Jotham ignored him. "He hates his father and won't speak to him. . . ." He stared at his plate. "That, I can relate to." Seeing the lines along his mother's mouth tighten, Jotham hurried on. "In any event, after our talk yesterday Trisha told him I would be calling him. Then, Mrs. McCauley found out that the Crayfords were coming this week-end and asked Trent if Pastor Mark could come over. I guess Mark and Trent were really close before they left. For some reason, Trent told Trisha that it would be okay as long as I came along too."

She bit her lip, worry lines deepening. "Is he dangerous? Has he threatened anyone?"

"Not according to Trisha, but I really feel like I'm in over my head."

Abe nodded sagely.

"I promised her I would do what I could to try to help, but I was thinking of, you know, working out with him and stuff. I wasn't planning to give him psychological counseling."

"I think it's just an adolescent stage," Mrs. Lewis said hopefully. "It's nice that he looks up to you, though. He probably just needs a friend."

"I don't know, Mom. Something tells me it's more than just that. Anyway, it's too late now. I'm just glad Pastor Mark is going to be there— he'll know what to say."

After breakfast, when subtle hints proved ineffective, their mother handed them rakes and an ultimatum: "Rake the front yard before noon or forget TV for the next week."

The brothers dragged themselves outside, offering only token resistance.

Since their father left home, they had felt compelled to help lighten her load around the house. The boys had even agreed to set up a kitchen clean-up rotation after overhearing her crying in the bedroom. However, many were the evenings since then, as they stood staring at the greasy dishes, that they wondered what had ever possessed them to volunteer for such gruesome work.

The next few hours were spent in what Abe and Jotham called "hard labor." While carrying a bag of leaves to the curb Jotham, gave in to an irresistible impulse and dumped the contents on Abe, who was bent over filling up his own bag.

"What do you think you're doing?" yelled Abe, trying to dodge the deluge.

Picking up his rake, he charged Jotham who sidestepped the blow, stuck out his foot, and tripped him as he rushed by. Abe threw himself at Jotham's legs, twisting him to the ground. He jumped on Jotham, who was lying on his back laughing helplessly, and began shoving handfuls of leaves into his brother's face.

Tiring of the assault, Jotham took hold of Abe's sweatshirt and yanked him off. By this time Abe was also laughing in between coughing spells.

"Boys, cut that out!" their mother yelled from the kitchen window.

"No milk and cookies for you after we're done," muttered Abe, taking a swipe at Jotham with the rake.

As he dropped off another bag in the long row in front of their home, he stopped to look at the initials on the sidewalk: "JL loves SC." He had inscribed them on the wet cement when he was 12.

It was now just one more painful memory.

Jotham had used one of his father's pottery tools to carve out his first girlfriend's initials. He'd never seen his father so angry. Jotham's cheek was bruised for days from the slap he'd received. It was soon thereafter that his father had to close down his ceramic business and go to work at the foundry.

The childish letters were now cracked by a tree root which was breaking through the cement. He bent over to touch their outlines. He felt detached, as if they had been carved by someone else. The gnarled root prompted another memory—that of a writhing oak—and this one was much more painful than the last.

"Come on, get going," yelled his brother. "I'm not gonna do all the work. I remember last—"

"Yeah, yeah, I know all about it, you runt," Jotham interrupted, beginning to scrape the leaves into another pile. "Every year, it's the same sob story. The fact of the matter is, I can rake and bag before you decide what side of the rake you're supposed to use."

"Very funny. You ever thought about being a stand-up comedian? You'd have the audience rolling on the floor . . . in agony."

Jotham feinted at Abe's head then poked his brother in the stomach with the rake handle. Abe bent over, grimacing in pain. Jotham had hit him much harder than he realized.

Jotham turned away and tried to regain his rhythm, the nightmare oak now dominating his thoughts. In his dream it was always the same: he was alone and afraid in the middle of a foreboding forest. He was walking toward a monstrous oak tree with contorted branches reaching high into a moonlit sky. It stood grand and forlorn, glowing a silvery-blue. The night was windless and still. Suddenly, the tree would begin to sway in an unnatural and frightening manner.

It sent icy shivers through him.

The great trunk would twist and bend slowly, contorting as if in torment. The oak's awful pain was both terrible and compelling. It hypnotized him. He was drawn to it with shuffling steps; then, freezing the blood in his veins, a moan of haunting desolation came from its core.

What occurred next nauseated him.

He would see himself stop, draw out a long dagger and with careful, cold precision ruthlessly stab the trunk. In the dream, his eyes terrified him—they were pools of liquid hate. The tree's groaning now became a horrible and dreadful wail. His horror would erupt in wrenching sobs. This is what would inevitably awaken him.

Shaking off his nightmarish thoughts, Jotham raced Abe to finish the job. When they were done, the boys headed inside and grabbed some cans of pop from the refrigerator. Their mother was skimming around the kitchen like a tornado, while delicious smells beckoned the hungry teenagers. A frosty glance from her direction was sufficient to dispel any thought of sampling the aromatic delicacies.

"They'll arrive any minute," was all she needed to say.

To escape from the tempting smells, Jotham grabbed a basketball, yelling at Abe to join him. Unable to resist the challenge, Abe turned off the sports channel and followed Jotham out to the hoop at the side of the driveway.

Twenty minutes later when the Crayfords' mini-van drove up, Abe was leading the tiebreaker by one point. Jotham saw the van first and yelled,

"They're here!" When Abe turned his head, he stole the ball and sank the uncontested basket.

Jotham sprinted past his brother. "You lose," he gloated, tossing the ball back with a malicious grin.

Bart was the first to uncoil himself from the van's interior. He now easily surpassed six feet and was several inches taller than Jotham. As the familiar sandy blond head emerged, Jotham grabbed his old friend around the shoulders in a bearhug. Bart, in one fluid spinning motion, tossed Jotham over his hip.

"Judo," he stated matter of factly, smiling broadly at Jotham's dazed expression. Jotham dove at Bart's legs, pulling him to the ground; with a little effort, he pinned his lanky opponent.

Carisa jumped out with athletic grace, scornfully tossing her long tawny hair at the melee on the grass. Abe stood ten feet away transfixed. Her golden brown eyes still sparkled with an undercurrent of mischief, but the childhood resemblance stopped there.

She walked over to Abe; her smile dazzled him. He was standing awkwardly holding the basketball in his hands, completely stunned. "Hi ya, Abe," she said, giving him a warm hug. She ruffled his hair, her brown eyes gleaming. "Look at those curls; I always figured you'd turn out to be a heart-breaker."

Abe struggled to regain his equilibrium. He was usually pretty smooth with the crowd of girls who vied for his attention, but he was utterly unprepared for Carisa's transformation. Five years had done wonders. Though she still retained a childlike air of vivacity, there was no denying it—she had become an extremely attractive young lady; and for the moment, the metamorphosis had left him speechless.

He cleared his throat, and finally his tongue came unglued. "H-hi Carisa, you look . . . great! I'm really glad to see you again."

"We've been looking forward to coming. It feels like we're back home." She stopped, seeing Jotham talking to her father. "Come on and say 'hi' to Dad and Mom. They won't believe how much you've changed."

Pastor Crayford was giving Jotham a hard squeeze. Jotham hugged him in return. He always liked "Pastor Mark," as he preferred to be called, even though his sermons tended to run long. He had a dry sense of humor and a real passion for football. With his muscular build, Jotham always thought he would look more at home on the sidelines than behind a pulpit.

"Well, well, son, I guess I can't muss up your hair anymore. I was told you were a terror on the football field; now I can see why," Pastor Mark said approvingly.

Catching sight of Abe, he landed a playful punch on his shoulder. "And haven't you grown up? Looks like you've put some muscle on too." He turned toward his daughter and his tone grew serious. "Now Carisa, these are the kind of guys that—"

"Dad!" Carisa cut her father short. Abe glanced sheepishly at his brother.

"All I meant was: if you're going to be interested in someone . . ." Jotham's stomach began to knot up.

The front door slammed and everyone's attention was drawn toward Katie Lewis, who was running toward them. "Sharon! Mark! It's so wonderful to see you." She threw her arms around Sharon Crayford.

Sharon was unable to speak over the lump in her throat. Tears were running down both the women's cheeks. A lot of time and pain had been shared between them, forging a powerful bond.

"Katie, you haven't changed a bit," Mark eventually said, gallantly overlooking the faint lines which the last five years had become more deeply etched around her eyes and mouth.

Katharine was standing with one arm around Sharon and Carisa. "Thank you, Mark. But speaking of change, I can't believe your daughter. Carisa, you've become a beautiful young woman!"

Abe and Jotham silently and wholeheartedly assented.

Katharine smiled at the tall young lady next to her. "I don't know if I would have recognized you alone!"

Carisa leaned over and rested her cheek on Katharine's head.

"Thanks, Aunt Katie. You look great too . . . I've really missed you and Uncle Da—" she caught herself.

Katie patted her hand. "It's okay, honey . . . the boys and I miss him too."

Sharon grabbed Katie's hand, "Thanks so much for letting us stay with you; we could easily have stayed in the hotel. . . . We hate to put you out."

"I wouldn't think of it! Anyway, how else could you and I ever hope to catch up on all the news." She motioned the Crayfords toward the house. "Come on, let's get inside where it's more comfortable. The boys can bring in your bags."

Bart opened the rear door of the van and began taking out their suitcases. Grateful for something to do, Jotham went over to help his friend. His head was spinning. Carisa's remarkable transformation and the uncomfortable exchange with her father had robbed him of the capacity for intelligent conversation. Choosing to hide behind the mound of luggage seemed the best solution.

Carisa resolved his dilemma by going around to the back and confronting him with a reproving smile. "Hi, Jo. You weren't going to ignore me all day, were you?" She stretched out her hand. "It's usually considered good manners for gentlemen to greet guests when they arrive, at least it is down Sah—outh." She strung out the last word over several syllables as if she'd been born and bred in Dixie.

He blushed. "S-sorry," he cleared his throat miserably, "I was just getting your suitcases out." He reached out to shake her hand. She took it with a flourish of formality; then laughing, leaned over and gave him a quick peck on the cheek. His heart stopped; then lurched forward doing triple-time. He was having a difficult time swallowing. Every time she looked at him, he could feel an uncomfortable thickness in his throat.

Her golden eyes were warm but inscrutable. "Just ignore my dad; he hates Sonny, my boyfriend back home." The edge returned to her voice. "No one's good enough for his little girl, you know."

Jotham's heart sank.

She reached out to pick up her suitcase. "Here, let me take it," he offered.

She curtsied slightly. "Why tha-ank you, kind suh." She lifted her face at him and smiled. Her eyes were of the most unusual shape and color; they were hazel, flecked with green and gold. Their long lids had a slight droop at the edge that would have made a less spirited girl seem languid. But they captivated him.

He looked down at his feet, suddenly feeling foolish. It was impossible to tell if she was mocking him or just being funny. He was also becoming painfully conscious of the rip and the grass stains on his sweatshirt.

Why didn't I put on my varsity shirt? he groaned to himself, as he followed the rest of the group into the house. How could I have possibly guessed that Carisa would turn out like this?

36

Chapter Six

During lunch, Jotham explained Trisha's request to Pastor Mark. "I'd be delighted to go," he responded.

"We won't be gone very long," Mark promised, patting his wife's shoulder, "I may be the only pastor he trusts. We may have been brought here to do more than just candidate at the church."

"You're right, honey," Sharon agreed. "Tell Stephen and Connie hi for me. Katie and I have plenty to catch up on while you're away." She winked at him, "Stay as long as you want."

On the drive over to see Trent, Jotham was distracted by thoughts of Bart's astonishingly attractive twin sister. He struggled to brush those thoughts aside and concentrate on the upcoming meeting, which was becoming less appealing every minute. *Why did I ever let Trisha talk me into this? Pastor can handle this without me. What am I gonna tell that mixed up kid anyway?*

All too soon, Jotham pulled his Mustang into the driveway of the brick Tudor house. Through the windows in the garage doors, they could see that both of the McCauley's cars were gone.

Strangely, Jotham felt suddenly vulnerable and alone. "I wonder where Trisha's folks are; she told me they were expecting us this afternoon."

The curtains in the bedroom window upstairs fluttered as they approached the front door.

Jotham's eyes grew wide. An eerie picture seemed to be dancing before his eyes: a grinning skull with a red candle melting on top. He blinked to shake off the image, but it continued shimmering like a holographic picture just beyond his reach.

Chills ran up and down his back.

Mark knocked crisply on the front door and the skull disappeared. Jotham stood beside him, in cold misery, wishing he were far, far away.

Trisha met them with red-rimmed eyes. When she saw Pastor Mark, all she could manage was a choking sound as tears began to run down her cheeks. Gently Mark reached out and gave her a comforting hug.

"It's going to be all right, Tricia," he said kindly. Don't worry." He held her quietly for a few moments; then in an attempt to cheer her up, held her at arm's length and said in his best pastoral tone: "Well, well, young lady, you've certainly grown up. When we left Rockville, you were just a little thing playing 'hide and seek' with Carisa in the church basement."

A small smile broke out briefly. "It's been a long time."

Mark nodded. "Oh, that reminds me—Carisa said to say hello. She wants you to call her. She thought that maybe you could get together before we leave."

Her eyes brightened. "I'd love to see her again. . . . Thanks so much for coming over, Pastor Crayford."

"How's Trent doing?" Jotham asked.

She smiled gratefully at Jotham. "He's still refusing to leave his room. All he's been doing is listening to his stereo."

Jotham looked up in the direction of the heavy bass reverberations that were throbbing overhead. "Does he know we're here?"

"I just told him you were driving up." Trisha looked at Jotham intently. "I'm so glad you came; I know Trent will listen to you."

Jotham smiled weakly.

She motioned for them to follow her into the living room. "Please come in and take a seat."

"Where are your folks?" Mark asked, sitting down on the white leather sofa.

Trisha kicked at the leg of the mahogany coffee table. "They told me to apologize for missing you, Pastor. Mom got a call about an emergency meeting at the firm. They're in the middle of preparing for a big trial . . . and Dad had some kind of golf tournament he couldn't get out of."

Mark had a unique ability of making others feel totally at ease. He did so now, leaning forward, and clasping one of Trisha's hands in his. "Trisha, it's fine; these things happen. Let's talk together about Trent for a second. First of all, I've learned in my counseling experience that it's important to recognize your limitations." He spread out his hands and placed them on each of their shoulders.

"We have to realize that there are many psychological problems which are beyond the ability of lay people to address. Over the years I've seen several youngsters like Trent, who were so depressed they required professional therapy. It takes some time, but most can be helped. I remember Dr. Collins was the most effective therapist in town." He looked into their eyes. "It's wise to have realistic expectations; that way you keep from being disappointed."

Jotham felt relief flood over him. Strangely, the picture of the skull flashed back into his mind. He ignored it. He let Mark's reassuring words wrap a blanket of rationality around him, causing the cadaverous image to lengthen out into an indistinguishable red mass, then evaporate.

"Nothing is too hard for God, though," Mark continued, repeating counsel which sounded well-worn. "God can use our simple words to penetrate Trent's heart. We can pray that He will do that, even if it's only to let your brother know that we care. Otherwise, God may choose to use the help of a good counselor. My advice is that we just be loving and understanding, and trust God for the rest."

Grabbing a Kleenex from the lacquered box on the lamp table, Trisha wiped her wet eyes. "Pastor, can we pray before going upstairs?" Jotham was surprised at her request but turned a hopeful glance toward Mark.

Mark smiled warmly at her. "Of course we can." He removed his glasses and rubbed the bridge of his nose. Then, again placing his hands on their shoulders, he prayed briefly for God's blessing and wisdom.

When he was finished, Trisha clasped her hands tightly in front of her, her knuckles white and added, "God, please help my brother to be all right."

Jotham felt the familiar chill begin to freeze-dry his insides. He knew he should pray but couldn't muster up any coherent contribution. Disjointed thoughts skidded hollowly around his mind but remained out of reach. He felt weak and ashamed, like he'd felt as a freshman looking at the school's weight machine.

Heading up the stairs, panic was welling up inside him. Mark's back gave no hint of undue concern. Still, it failed to comfort him. Since entering Trisha's house, Jotham thought he'd detected a hesitancy in Mark's eyes—a flicker of weakness that scared him. A cold prickle of sweat broke out on his forehead and upper lip.

Suddenly, he wanted to run.

A dark, crushing terror began to coil itself around him. He clenched his teeth, pressing his lips into a tight, hard line. His eyes began to sting as a smell of decay settled over him. With each step, it grew more pungent and oppressive. The stench was so vile it nearly gagged him. The others, however, were oblivious to the odor. Jotham's heart began to race as he climbed into the foul thickness at the top of the stairs. His saliva turned acid with dread.

There was no way to escape.

Chapter Seven

They stood in front of the bedroom door. Harsh, driving music attacked them through the wood, like a gauntlet being thrown in their faces. Jotham thought, *Pastor Mark definitely looks uncomfortable.* His lips had begun to move soundlessly.

Trisha knocked loudly and called out her brother's name, repeating it several times. The wailing inside finally ceased, and a raspy voice barked, "Chill out." Jotham winced.

Trisha said, "Pastor Mark and Jotham are here to see you."

There was a long pause. "Great," the voice mumbled.

The bed creaked. Bare feet padded on the wood flooring and approached the door. Jotham steeled himself and out of the corner of his eye saw Mark attempt his most convincing smile.

Jotham felt as if an overwhelming weight had dropped onto his shoulders. He licked his lips; they were dry with a mounting panic.

Trent opened the door.

Trisha gasped. "Trent, what did you do to your hair . . . and your face?" His head was shaved high around the sides with the long patch in the middle dyed a startling vermilion orange, and dark mascara streamed from around his eyes. A contorted face dripping blood from its mouth glared from the front of his black sleeveless T-shirt.

He stroked the orange mane. "Gripping, isn't it? Do you think Dad'll like it?"

Something about the ghoulish design on Trent's shirt was oddly familiar, but Jotham couldn't bring it into focus. His tongue felt thick and his head strangely muddled.

"How're ya doin', Trent? May we come in?" Pastor Mark stuck out his hand, a smile fixed warmly in place.

Trent ignored the overture. "Yeah . . . whatever." He turned his back on his visitors and stalked back to the bed. The threesome stepped tentatively into the dim interior as Trent sat down on the edge of his bed.

Jotham decided to disregard the sullen hostility in the macabre death mask facing him. "Hey, Trent, what's up?" Trent's eyes failed to make contact, but he did manage to raise his hand in a brief salute.

A naked red bulb gleamed from the ceiling, shining a hellish hue on the room's glossy black interior. A smoky haze stung their eyes, burning the back of their throats. On the shelf over Trent's bed, a pair of small yellow eyes glowed unblinkingly at them. The hairs on Jotham's arm tingled.

As he drew closer, the pressure in his chest began to relax: they were only the burning tips of incense sticks. These were apparently the source of the pungent smoke which reeked of sulfur and some indistinguishable flower.

Jotham sat on the corner of the desk on the opposite wall. Mark pulled out the chair while Trisha dropped onto the beanbag on the floor.

Jotham floundered for words, realizing with a horrifying rush that, for some reason, it was up to "Trent's football hero" to break open the impasse. He swung at the first thing that came to mind. "The JV really missed you, Trent. They could have really used some good hands. I told—"

"Yeah, ri-ight. I'm sure they would have loved some more dropped balls in the end zone." Trent looked at them with a mixture of scorn and despair. "Look, Jotham, thanks for coming over and all that. But it's hopeless. Pastor, I know you mean well, but the cards have already been played." His words floated cryptically toward them through the smog.

Jotham could see Trent's eyes turn a feverish and hopeless glance above him. Jotham followed his gaze to a small card propped against the gargoyle incense holder. It was black with some kind of white design on the bottom right corner.

Pastor Mark waded in, leaning forward on his chair. "The cards are not what determine our destiny, Trent. We choose, and we reap the harvest from our choices. But God is merciful, and asks us to turn away from our wrong decisions and come to Him. No matter what you've done, He'll forgive you. He loves you, Trent."

"He's got a cute way of showing it," Trent snarled, eyes now as cunning and sharp as stilettos. He threw his head back on his pillow and stared at the murky ceiling.

Without hesitating, Mark continued, "He sent His Son to die for you to

42

prove it to you, Trent. I know you've heard this already. I remember when you and your parents were in the new members class and you all told me you believed in Christ. Later you and Trisha—"

"Yeah, my folks are great Christians—especially my dad! You have no idea what he's like. You wanna know what that wonderful Christian did? He hauled off and punched me!" His voice dripped with venom. "Great example, don't you think? I can tell you, I am *not* impressed."

Trisha pulled out a crumpled Kleenex. "Trent, you know Mom and Dad love you. Dad doesn't understand what's going on with you . . . and . . . he gets frustrated. . . ."

Trent snorted.

His voice grew flat and dull. "It's always my fault. I'm always the bad guy. And, you know, I've finally figured it out: he's right! So, the best I can do is remove myself and stop screwing up everybody's life."

Inspiration struck Jotham. "Trent, that's not true. I think God used Trisha to bring us here to show you that you're important to Him."

"Look Jotham, let's cut the crap." Trent sat up in bed with an unusual, hard brightness in his dark eyes. They bore a hole straight into Jotham's soul. "You barely knew I existed until my sister talked to you. The only reason you're here is to impress her, and it's Pastor's job to counsel crazoids like me—so don't give me any 'BS' about love and importance, blah, blah, blah." As he snarled his accusation, an angry tear smeared a dirty gray trail down his face.

Jotham's face was burning. Shame had drained all moisture from his mouth.

Pastor reached into his pocket and withdrew a thin leather Bible. "Trent, that's unfair. I believe Jotham is exactly right. God wants to preserve you and use your life for Him. Satan hates you and wants to destroy you." Trent's eyes narrowed; hot flames of evil began licking the pupils.

Mark was looking down and didn't notice. He reached into the inside pocket of his jacket and took out his reading glasses. "Here, let me read a verse from the Bible." As Mark leafed through the pages, the muscles in Trent's body went rigid. Trent leaned forward. He was coiling like a panther ready to pounce on an unwary prey, staring with burning hatred at the book in Mark's hands.

"Here it is. In James we are told that Satan is a—"

A low growl rumbled from Trent's throat.

43

It happened so suddenly, Jotham was paralyzed.

Trent's face had become a mask of incarnate evil. With ferocious power he leapt off the bed snarling, and hit Pastor Mark in the face, sending his glasses spinning. Four ugly welts split his cheek.

Trisha jumped up and started toward her brother, sobbing in fear. Jotham grabbed her and pulled her back toward the door. She struggled in his arms, wanting to run towards Trent. "Stop, Trent, stop! What are you doing?" she wailed.

Trent stood over Mark, who was now on hands and knees, growling at him in a guttural voice unlike anything Jotham had ever heard, "You weak, pathetic emissary. You don't have a clue what you're doing! I'm stronger than you. *I know you* and you can't defeat me." He spat out the words with utter, terrifying contempt. His eyes were dark pools of madness. Mark's strong frame seemed to wilt. He looked dazed and terribly afraid.

Trent again lunged at Mark, who managed to duck and throw both hands over his head. Instead of hitting him, Trent grabbed the Bible, which lay in an open heap on the rug, and clamped his teeth over its open spine. With one wild, exultant tear he shredded it in half and hurled it at Mark's bowed head.

"Get out of here!" he shrieked triumphantly, foam flecking his mouth. He flung himself back on the bed, his chest heaving, his shirt drenched with sweat. In a dangerous, controlled rasp, he whispered, "Leave, before I do some serious damage." He threw out a stiff arm menacingly.

"And take that damned book with you."

Mark picked his glasses and the loose pages off the floor. His hand shook as he motioned for Trisha and Jotham to go. Walking unsteadily, he guided them out of the bedroom.

As soon as they were out the door, the pounding music assailed them again. Down the stairs they were followed by Death Maiden's electronic shrieks.

Somehow, the music jarred Jotham's memory. He finally made the connection—the skull on Trent's T-shirt was identical to the holographic-like image he'd seen when he drove into the McCauleys' driveway. Jotham was too stunned to try to make any sense out of it. He just wanted to get out and away from the house as quickly as possible.

Waving off Trisha's apologies, Mark asked for the phone. He tried to smile but his face was drawn and white. The red welts stood out painfully.

She pointed to the den and handed him a wet cloth for his face.

Jotham and Trisha retreated into the kitchen where they quietly filled glasses of ice water. Jotham's throat felt parched. He had almost finished his second glass when Pastor Mark strode in looking more composed.

"Dr. Collins said that he didn't think there was any real danger at the moment." He dabbed the cloth against his cheek. "It sounded to him like a lot of suppressed anger and adolescent rebellion, mixed in with self-esteem issues. However, he recommended that you give him a call immediately if he makes any specific threats regarding suicide.

Mark took a deep drink from the glass Trisha offered him. "Thanks, Trish, I needed that . . . You can tell your folks later. It may not be the best timing right now. It might be just the excuse Trent wants to blow up at your dad. He definitely needs some time to cool down."

Mark and Jotham headed for the front door. Trisha looked ready to collapse. She tried to speak, but no words came.

"It's going to be all right." He smiled soothingly. "The Lord won't let you down. He'll work it out for good. Just try to prevent a confrontation between Trent and your father. It would be the worst thing right now."

As they walked past the credenza in the hallway, Jotham noticed a business card on the glossy surface. The FBI's seal was emblazoned in silver, with the name Agent Jack O'Tulley printed beneath it. A phone number was scrawled on the bottom. The card registered momentarily on his consciousness, but he ignored it. Nothing was going to keep him in that house an instant longer.

During the drive home, Mark and Jotham were silent. Once, their eyes had met and a queasy sensation unsettled Jotham's stomach. It was there again: a vague weakness in Pastor's eyes that jarred him. The skin on his neck prickled. He decided to keep his focus on the road.

Despite the silence inside the car, Trent's mocking challenge rang loudly in his ears. It reminded Jotham of a humiliating childhood encounter with a gang of bullies. He felt that same shameful exposure washing over him now.

When they arrived at Jotham's house, they downplayed the incident at the McCauleys'. Jotham, needing to forget the horrible encounter, had suggested they go biking to some of their favorite haunts. They would later recall that Carisa had been the one to propose visiting the Glampoole Estate.

Anxious to take advantage of the remaining sunlight and the clear weather, they changed quickly into their biking suits. They ran outside, took down the bicycles from the roof of the Crayfords' van and raced away, heading for the place where, years earlier, they had first encountered the supernatural.

Chapter Eight

Across town, in the area where Rockville's "old money" lived, the bike riders dismounted. They had taken the "scenic route" and wore the evidence of their wild dash splattered over their calves.

The four stood in front of a black wrought-iron gate. It was set into a ten-foot high brick wall which surrounded a three-acre compound. Its once pale stones had been darkened with years of grime. Climbing English ivy, its leaves turning deep russet and purple, twined up in disorderly profusion. Years of careless growth lent an air of neglect to the entire place. The gate was bent slightly backwards, as if doing an inverted bow. Its lock had rusted and broken off, and pieces of the corroded chain lay on the loose pebbles of the circular drive. Etched regally on the stone column supporting the gate, the Gothic script was still visible: "Glampoole Estate – 1823."

Jotham and Abe pushed on the tilting gate; it groaned open in protest, making reluctant room for them to squeeze through. Not wishing to intrude on the serenity of the compound, they chose to walk their bikes up the winding drive. On both sides tall firs stood like overgrown green sentinels ushering them to the three-story turreted building that had once served as the Paladins' "clubhouse."

Bart rested an arm on Jotham's shoulder to steady himself as he scraped mud off his shoe. "It almost feels like old times, doesn't it?"

Jotham was silenced by the weight of the memories flooding over him.

The Victorian mansion was much like he remembered; except it was now bowing under the burden of years of desertion. Its shutters were askew: some had fallen off entirely, giving it the appearance of an English gentleman gone to seed, in desperate need of a new suit and a shave. Several windows were boarded over, and the once-proud wraparound porch that dominated the front was beginning to sag.

Carisa maneuvered her bike around bits of broken glass and stopped next to Jotham. "I can't believe it," she said staring at the forsaken house. "It makes me feel so sad. Jotham, have you been here since 'Glumpuddle' died?"

Glumpuddle, or Glump, was their nickname for Ernest Glampoole—the last known heir of the Glampoole estate. It had been Bart's idea, and the others had readily adopted it.

"No, I haven't. I guess I figured it just wouldn't be the same without him. Abe and I talked about it after he died, but we never came back." He stopped, looking at the debris scattered around the ground and then at the house's decrepit condition. "Now . . . I guess, I'm kinda' glad we didn't."

Abe walked over to them wiping his face with his sleeve. Not surprisingly, during the race to the mansion, he'd managed to get more mud on him than the rest of them combined. Abe was always more than willing to sacrifice his body in order to win. "Wasn't there a newspaper article about the city waiting seven years or something in case an heir showed up?"

Jotham nodded his assent. "You're right; it also said that the estate's attorney had been unable to find a valid will. Glumpuddle had revoked the only one drafted before he died." He grinned, "It stuck in my mind 'cause the attorney's name was Warren B. Slick. I thought it was appropriate for a lawyer."

His eyes grew suddenly distant and a shadow fell over his face. "Man, I can still see the way Glumpuddle looked at us from the hospital bed . . . Remember, Abe?"

Abe was bent over, pulling a stone out of his shoe. "Sure do. And how about that nurse—the one who thought you were 'Ivan something or other'? She was really hot!"

Carisa looked over at Jotham. "Ivan who?"

"It was kind of strange," Jotham explained. "She said that Glump had been delirious and had been repeating something that sounded like 'Ivan Eklibrius.' She had thought he was talking about his equilibrium, but then decided he was calling for someone. We told her we never heard him mention anyone by that name. Anyway, when we walked in, Glump recognized us right away." He shook his head. "He couldn't smile but the corners of his mouth twitched. He gave us that big wink, like we were in on some huge secret. He died the next day. That was not long after you guys left Rockville."

Jotham became very quiet. Carisa came over and rested her hand on his arm. "I miss him a lot too, Jo. He was one of the neatest people I've ever met."

"Kind of like a really cool grandfather," he smiled, "though kinda odd at times."

Carisa's eyes danced as she laughed with him.

Bart interrupted, "How long ago was that, anyway?"

Carisa dropped her hand, turning toward her brother with a trace of exasperation. "Well, we were 13 when we left, and we just had our 18th birthday, so figure it out, Einstein."

They pushed their bikes closer to the old mansion. Despite its evident decay, the gabled building retained the aura of mystery which had always surrounded the Glampoole family. There were dark whispers that the males were required to swear a blood oath never to allow it to leave the family. Some of the Glampoole boys had died in unusual ways, and it was reported to have been caused by their desire to sell the family dwelling.

In each generation there was at least one child who could be described either as highly eccentric or slightly mad. Ernest Glampoole, the last of the clan, fit admirably into both categories. A reclusive bachelor in his late 70s, the quartet had made his acquaintance under humiliating circumstances.

Carisa had come up with a scheme to topple the old outhouse behind the mansion and pull it to their church. The plan was to set it up on the front lawn, next to the church's sign-board with the letters "Occupied" spelled out. It had seemed like a hilarious idea at the time. Late one evening they had climbed the gate, crept up next to it, and began trying to push the shabby building over. When it started to rock, Carisa had been the only one to exercise caution by jumping back.

It had fallen with alarming suddenness.

The boys were unable to keep their balance and were catapulted into three feet of fetid ooze. Their loud wails had roused Ernest Glampoole, who appeared on the back porch dressed in a striped night shirt and an incongruous tasseled fez. He held a candlestick in one hand and a thick yardstick in the other.

"Be gone, be gone!" he had shouted out wildly into the darkness, holding the candle in front of him. As he peered into the night, he resembled a tall stoop-shouldered stork. As the light played around his deep-set eyes, his appearance was alternatively horrible and ludicrous. Drawn by their despairing yells, he had marched across the backyard toward what now looked like a huge casket lying on the grass. Carisa was stretched out prone against its side, shaking in fright.

49

Mr. Glampoole had gazed down somberly at the three filthy children, their eyes wide in faces contorted with fear and disgust. None of them would ever forget what happened next. After staring at them for several moments in complete silence, he suddenly broke out in a high cackling laugh and launched into a maniacal jig around their pit. Over and over he kept repeating the strange phrase: *Deo gratias est dies irae . . . Deo gratias est dies irae.* Later they'd found out that it was a Glampoole family saying and was Latin for: "Thank God, it's judgment day!"

Concluding his bizarre dance, he pointed his yardstick at the boys and began to chortle: "Be sure, be sure, your sins will find you out." Then, stopping as suddenly as he'd begun, he peered quizzically down at them and asked glumly whether they had enjoyed their time in the Slough of Despond.

Only after the four had solemnly agreed to return the following day to right their wrong, had he offered to pull them out. This he accomplished with a great deal of huffing and oblique complaints about his weak back.

Having gained the old man's confidence by keeping their word, they'd been invited inside the imposing mansion. They were served tea and hot scones, which they soon grew to love. It was a good thing, since that is all he would ever offer them.

Whenever they inquired about his family, he would sorrowfully bemoan his lack of cleverness and his brother William's intellectual superiority. "I'm just simple, you see," he'd murmur with a profound humility, and then continue sadly, "I never could do much." In the middle of this mournful monologue, he would inevitably interrupt himself with the words: "But I don't want to talk any more about that. I ought not to speak so much about myself." He would turn away gloomily but then with comical sobriety turn around and begin recounting how he'd not been able to achieve anything significant in his life.

The library was by far their most favorite room. It had floor to ceiling oak bookshelves lined with thousands of books of every size and subject. The Glampooles had their evident failings, but ignoring good books was not one of them. Glumpuddle had proven to possess a gift for reading out loud, having an amazing ability to change characters and accents at will. They had read through several adventure classics while having tea together. These stories had stoked in the children a deep yearning for the heroic. Although rarely alluding to their "unholey" misadventure (as they referred to it) while reading *Pilgrim's Progress,* Jotham was certain he'd seen the sides of Glumpuddle's mouth twitch suspiciously during Pilgrim's difficulties in the Slough of Despond.

Now, over five years later, they were once again laying their bikes down on the long grass, but this time next to a red-bordered "No Trespassing" sign. It glared at them from the bedraggled flower garden next to the front steps. It had been placed there under the authority of Rockville's Historical Society. Bart took a pebble and struck the "No" a sharp, disrespectful blow.

"Looks like I haven't lost my touch," he commented smugly.

"Big deal," countered Carisa, "anybody could hit it from this close." She picked up a stone and as she threw it Bart nudged her shoulder, causing the missile to bounce off a window pane.

"You cheater!" she yelled, chasing him around the side of the dwelling. Laughing, he dodged around a pillar, then froze in his tracks. Carisa tried to stop, slid on the stones, and skidded into his back.

They turned and silently motioned for Jotham and Abe to come quickly. Following the curve of the drive, which wound toward the four-stall garage in back, the brothers saw it at the same moment: a purple-black van which gleamed with the obvious sheen of a new vehicle. Its tinted windows gave no clue as to its contents.

"Maybe we'd better go," Abe muttered.

"Yeah, it could be people from the city. If we got caught we'd have to pay a $100 fine," agreed his older brother.

Shaking her head, Carisa said, "If it were an official city van, it would have some kind of logo on the side." She stepped forward to examine it more closely. "And guys, come on! Does this look to you like the kind of vehicle the city would own? Plus . . ." she hesitated for dramatic effect, "I don't think Rockville would install Georgia plates, now do you?"

"Very clever, Sherlock," Bart said.

"Thank you, Watson, elementary really," she said, flicking at his nose.

"Why don't you walk over to the van and put your hand on the hood to tell us how long whoever it is has been here?" he suggested.

"Maybe I will do just that," she snorted, rolling her eyes at him, "and by the way, the owner is a he." She raised her eyebrows melodramatically, her shoe obscuring a large print left by a cowboy boot.

"Yeah, and he's right-handed with a scar on his left buttock," Bart mocked.

"Laugh all you want, you simpleton. You'll come crawling when you see the results of my excellent detective methods."

"All right," asserted Jotham, taking command, "let's find out who he is. But let's try the front door first."

With Jotham in the lead, they walked gingerly up the stairs over planks which were beginning to bow and split, avoiding the broken glass scattered on the weathered boards. Jotham was relieved to observe that the ponderous oak doors with the Gothic "G" engraved on leaded glass insets appeared intact. He'd always loved their rich craftmanship. Tentatively, Jotham raised the ball and claw door knocker, which still clung stubbornly to the frame.

He let the brass claw fall. The sharp clang echoed emptily inside.

Abe glanced around nervously. From the time they had approached the mansion, he'd felt eyes fixed on the four of them. Of course, being the youngest made it impossible for him to reveal his suspicion.

Carisa shuddered theatrically, gripping Bart's arm in mock terror at the gargoyles leering down from the top of the door jamb.

"I can't hear anyone moving around," Jotham said. He dropped the claw again, this time from a greater height.

No one answered.

The drapes in the adjacent library window quivered, parting slightly. None of them noticed.

"Maybe whoever is here is out checking the grounds," Jotham remarked.

"When all else fails, my good man, do the obvious," Bart suggested, motioning toward the door handle.

"Good idea, Columbo," Jotham responded. He cautiously twisted the knob and found it turning easily in his hand. The four looked nervously at each other. Carisa nodded her encouragement. Without a word they stepped into the quiet building.

Carisa was the first to note the missing pieces. The large grandfather clock, which had once dominated the hall, was gone as was the embossed suit of armor on the landing of the circular stairs.

"We should report this to the police," Abe whispered. "We don't want some lousy thieves making off with all Glumpuddle's stuff. It should be in a museum or something."

"Here, here!" agreed Bart, beginning to talk more loudly, as he headed toward the paneled living room. "Maybe *we* could turn this house into a museum and charge admission. We could make a bundle!" Stooping to peer into the dark recesses of the fireplace, he picked up a charred stick. "Hullo, what have we here!" he exclaimed in a high-pitched English accent. "Ahha, the plot thickens. Looks like there's been some visitors here within . . ." he rubbed the coal between thumb and forefinger, "approximately 39 and one-half hours, give or take 15 minutes."

Carisa walked over to examine his discovery. "What's that?" she asked, noticing a pile of papers in the far corner opposite the mammoth fireplace.

Abe was bent over concentrating on something in the middle of the floor. He went over to pick up the bundle and held it up to the light. "Hey, check out what I found!"

Bart ran over to look. Abe held in his hands a wad of photocopied pages torn from what appeared to be a video magazine. Underneath was a video cartridge. He held the plastic cartridge in the dim light, puzzled. "It's called *The Suicide Club*. Strange—I never heard of it."

"If you haven't, then it must have just come out over the weekend," commented his older brother wryly.

"Sounds like a real fun video to me. Let's take it home and watch it tonight," Abe joked. "There's probably a bunch of other gems in here too," he said holding up the papers.

"Let me see those," demanded Jotham, suddenly suspicious.

He took one of the pages and drew back the drapes. He glanced down at the pictures and felt his face flush.

Striding toward Abe, he barked, "Give the rest to me." Jotham grabbed them from his hands.

"Hey!" Abe protested, "What's the matter?"

"You don't want to know." Jotham muttered. He folded them, stuffing them quickly into his back pocket. Walking through the dining room, he looked down at the floor. He bent over. "Guys, check this out." He scraped it with his shoe. "It isn't . . . blood, is it?"

"I thought so too, but it's not." Abe said, scratching a bit off the oak parquet floor. He put it near Jotham's nose. "See? It's red wax."

There was something oddly familiar about the smell. "It's sorta like decaying flowers," Jotham said, wrinkling up his face.

Carisa joined the huddle. "Let me smell." She took a deep breath. "Yeah," she agreed, "It's violets."

53

Bart was uninterested. He'd been born without a sense of smell, so violets or honeysuckles, it made no difference to him. "I'm gonna go check out the library," he said.

The others turned to follow him. He walked up to the French doors, but before swinging them aside, he slapped the armored knight's dusty helmet which stood guard outside. "Good to see you again, Sir Gallahad. Looks like you've been neglecting your pike though. Have it sharpened forthwith. Carry on."

Bart winked at Jotham. "The troops have gotten a little sloppy in our absence, Captain." He put his hand on the crystal knob and hesitated. Slowly he opened the glass paneled doors of the room which held a mystical fascination for them. The interior was dim since the heavy drapes were drawn tightly over the large bay window that covered the span of the far wall. Bart walked over and carefully pulled them aside. Still, only limited light filtered in through the boards covering the broken panes.

Looking over the shelves, Bart exclaimed in a hushed voice, "They're still here!" He gazed reverently around at the rows of books that lined the walls.

Carisa stepped inside, holding her breath as if entering the sacred confines of a cathedral. Jotham and Abe followed her closely, sensing the familiar awe pressing down upon them. They stood quietly in the middle of the darkened room illuminated by three arrows of sunlight, reluctant to utter a sound.

The angle of the sun's afternoon rays slicing through the gloom drew Jotham's gaze. His breath caught in a lump. The bright shafts seemed possessed of their own life as they danced and sparkled before him, evoking a painful longing inside.

Jotham remembered reading somewhere that there are moments when beauty is so heavy that words are too weak to bear up under their weight. This seemed to be such a time.

Bart broke the spell by walking over to the shelves that ran the length of the near wall on both sides of a stone fireplace. He ran his fingers gently over the dusty bindings and pulled a book out. Embossed on the book's red leather spine was the title, *The Count of Monte Cristo*.

"What was it he used to say when he finished reading one of these books?" he paused momentarily, caressing the raised lettering. "He'd close the cover, sigh, and say—"

"Ars longa, vita brevis," Jotham and Carisa responded in unison. Their eyes met and they smiled at each other.

"That's right!" Bart exclaimed. "That was it: 'Art is long, though life is short.'" He stopped abruptly, then covered his mouth to restrain a sneeze.

"Dust!" he muttered in disgust, stopping two others in quick succession. Blinking watery eyes he continued, "Thanks to Glump, I got into Latin." He waggled his eyebrows at Jotham, "You can't imagine how it impresses the babes."

Carisa shook her head, "You are so-o shallow."

Walking over to the sofa along the side, she felt the tapestried upholstery. "Right here is where it happened," she murmured softly. "Do you remember, Jotham?"

Jotham walked over and sat down. "How could I possibly forget? It was the most incredible experience of my life."

"What do you guys think it meant?" Abe queried.

"I've wondered that too, many times," she admitted.

Jotham looked over at the flagstone fireplace, "I think it was sort of like a calling."

"What do you mean?" asked Bart.

"Well, think back over what happened."

They had each been engaged in chess matches against Glumpuddle. He had seemed unusually distracted, and as a result, the children were making impressive headway. Like a gangly frog, he had hopped back and forth between the four card tables, waving his arms excitedly and muttering to himself. He had stirred the fire a dozen times, and the youngsters were taking advantage by making aggressive gambits. They winked at each other when his back was turned, anticipating their first victories.

Suddenly, he spun around, the poker swinging wildly over their heads. *"Deo gratias! Deo gratias!"* he bellowed. "I remember."

They were then told to sit down together on the "sacred Glampoole sofa" dubbed in honor of his father's obsessive attachment to the overstuffed monstrosity, which dominated that side of the wall. They obeyed, and to their dismay, he shoved aside the card tables, scattering chess pieces across the floor.

"He told us about his dream or vision," Abe said, "then he prayed over us."

Bart sat down next to Jotham. "It was awesome, wasn't it?"

Glumpuddle had begun, "I had—well how should I put this? Modern children like you have no confidence in such things, but not to put too fine a point on it, I had a vision about you last night. I was reading *Ivanhoe* before retiring. I've told you it's one of my favorite books, haven't I?" Four heads nodded. He mentioned it almost weekly. "When I looked up, I saw you all standing by the door, dressed in suits of armor and holding great swords in your hands." He stared at them, looking as startled as if they had just materialized in the room at that moment.

"You were shining so brightly that my eyes were watering; then I heard a voice calling you Paladins. It said that you had been chosen by Almighty God and I was to serve you. I asked what I was to do, and the voice said: 'Knight them as I knighted my Son.' When I woke up it was almost too late for breakfast. All day, I knew I needed to tell you something and I finally remembered it. My memory isn't what it used to be, I'm afraid. Ever since—" he coughed in embarrassment, "Well, I'm sure you're not at all interested in that. My infirmities are not your concern, of course. My brother had the constitution of an ox; but I, on the other hand, took after my mother's side—may she rest in peace. Anyway, ahem, I digress. I apologize for going on about myself. It is not a particularly appealing trait, is it?"

Four heads again dutifully nodded.

"Yes, well, when I picked up this poker it finally came to me . . . I wish I had a sword, but this will have to do. Please kneel in front of the sofa."

They knelt with an awareness that despite the oddity of the situation, something important was occurring. Glumpuddle awkwardly approached each of them, touching the tip of the ash-covered poker to both shoulders, and intoned words that burned into their memories: "I knight you Paladins, set apart by Almighty God, in the name of the Father, the Son, and the Holy Ghost."

After knighting them, Glumpuddle turned away rubbing his chin. The children eyed each other, but before they could rise he spun back toward them and began praying over them in a remarkably powerful voice. Blessings had poured out of him like an overturned pitcher of rich oil. There was a passion in his words that had scared them a little. He gently laid his hand on each of their heads, and as he did so, electricity seemed to pulsate through them from the top of their heads to the bottom of their feet.

"When he finished praying over us, he shook our hands and told us that he felt privileged to know us," Jotham recalled, his voice soft.

"But I'll never forget what he said next," Carisa said, "as only he could." Imitating their enigmatic friend, she made a wide sweeping gesture and bowed. "I would be honored to be considered your *amicus usque ad aras—*"

Bart interpreted, "—our friend to the last extremity."

"The last thing he said was that prophecy about our future," she added. They all recalled how, with an odd gleam in his eye and a thickness in his voice, he had told them of their unique destiny.

Carisa softly repeated the words which had both thrilled and terrified the four children: "He told us, 'You are destined to be great heroes and enjoy mighty exploits.'"

As she spoke, the drapes in the far corner of the library began to part. A sinister metallic click jolted them out of their reverie.

Their heads jerked toward the noise. Carisa sucked in her breath. The hard muzzle of a gun was pointing directly at her from behind the embroidered fabric.

A harsh, mocking voice assailed them from the dark recesses of the room. "Hah! Some heroes. I think you punks' destiny jus' done run out!"

Chapter Nine

Behind the folds of heavy material they could make out the bulky out-lines of a man's body. The shafts of light had failed to illumine the corner of the room where he had been hiding. Before any of them could move, the drapes were angrily tossed aside and a large form materialized.

He was a little over six feet tall, just shorter than Bart, but a good 50 pounds heavier. His knee-length parka was open, revealing a broad chest and a surprisingly fit physique. A twisted smile creased his face underneath a large flattened nose. His long red hair hung in loose strands around a bushy beard. His eyes were pale blue. There was a deathly coldness in them.

"Red" Jaglowski threw an empty whisky bottle, smashing it against the fireplace in front of them. Shards of glass rained down onto the stone hearth. He stumbled sideways, then recovered his balance.

Red jerked the short barrel in Abe's direction and spat on the floor.

"You—sshquirt," he snarled in a grating, high-pitched voice. Its tone, despite a slight slurring due to the drink, brooked no opposition.

Abe stood frozen in a shaft of sunlight. He felt as though he were held captive by an alien force field. It was too late now to warn his companions of his earlier fears.

"I'm talkin' to you, yah little runt." The man loomed menacingly over Abe, weaving slightly. He shoved the barrel harshly into Abe's ribs.

Jotham could hear his blood pounding in his ears. He was ready to explode but didn't dare make a move.

"What'sha have in yore hands?"

Still unable to speak, Abe brought his hands into view, revealing the video cartridge.

"Yea-ahh! Theah it is!" With the speed of a striking cobra, the bearded man ripped the cassette out of Abe's hand. As he grabbed it, he shoved Abe backwards with the gun barrel. Abe stumbled back, tripped over the coffee table behind him, and fell heavily onto the floor, the corner of the table striking him sharply in the chest.

Jotham lunged toward his brother.

The loud bang of the hammer hitting the firing pin exploded in the dusty air.

Carisa screamed.

Jotham's heart stopped.

Red's high-pitched cackle pierced them like a bullet. "Ha, ha, ha. You can shtop, right dere, Mr. Hero, unlesh you wanna be Mr. Shwish Cheese." He wiped the back of his mouth with a freckled hand. "The next chamber is loaded." He cracked open the weapon, spinning the chamber in front of them for emphasis. "I leave one empty to make a point if I haff to . . . a little trick Uncle Sham taught me in 'Nam." He cocked the hammer impassively, his eyes going dead. "But the next squeeze ain't no trick."

Carisa choked back a sob.

His attention swiveled in her direction. His eyes began to blaze darkly. He walked over, leering at her. Holding the gun with his thumb and forefinger, he carefully laid the barrel on the palm of her hand.

"Do you like guns?" he smirked, his hot breath potent with alcohol.

Carisa pressed her teeth down on her lower lip to keep from crying out. The weight of the weapon on her open palm shocked her.

He stared at her striped biking suit. "Well, well, aren't you the cute little tiger in that thang yore wearin'." He stroked her hair with a large filthy hand. "May I say Mish, you Yankee girls shore are mi-ghty fine." Fiercely, she jerked her head away.

He yanked the gun back, grabbed a handful of auburn hair and ran the gun barrel menacingly along her cheek. "Ha! Could use some tamin', tho'. I like that in a woman . . . I most certainly do."

Jotham and Bart tensed, ready to pounce.

Red's and Carisa's eyes were locked.

Red's gaze broke first. With forced bravado, he barked a scornful laugh and pushed her to the floor.

He waved the gun menacingly at Bart, who had moved to help her up. Defiantly, Carisa pushed herself off the floor, her fists clenched in anger. Their attacker strafed the group with remorseless eyes. It was obvious that death had long ago lost any meaning for him. His legs were spread out in a stance which seemed altogether too purposeful. He held up the video, caressing his lips with its black edge.

"Here's my . . . problem," he whispered confidentially with a tight smile. "I got what I come for, but I alsho got me four things I didn't. Y'all done stuck yore noses into somethin' that jes' ain't none of yore blasted bizness." He stroked his tangled beard. "Now I gotta figure out how to clean up thish here mesh—if'n you know what I mean."

Bart stared back, a scowl contorting his face. He placed his arm around Carisa's trembling shoulders. He could feel her heart pounding.

The bearded man's cold blue eyes became harder looking than ever, as if a shroud had been pulled down behind his pupils. He smiled cruelly at them. "I'm thinkin' we're gonna go for a little drive. Why don't y'all file out like good little sholdiers." He jerked the gun at them and motioned in the direction of the kitchen.

Rubbing his side, Abe pulled himself up and joined the others. As they turned to head out the door, they heard the snap of the safety being released. Jotham, seething with fury, headed out of the room first. He tried not to leave too quickly—a plan had materialized that required total surprise. The instant he left the dark confines of the library he slid over to his right, slipping the blunt spear out of Sir Gallahad's chain-mailed hand. The three other Paladins followed more slowly behind.

"Shtick together or I'll blasht yore girlfriend here and now," the shrill voice threatened.

Jotham put a finger to his lips as Abe emerged. Taking his cue, Abe turned left toward the kitchen, scraping his feet loudly. Bart also grasped Jotham's intent immediately. To draw Red's attention, Bart tripped over the threshold as he and Carisa walked through the French doors.

"Get movin' . . ." their assailant growled, shoving the revolver at Bart's spine.

The moment Jotham could see the barrel, he swung the spear ferociously.

The sound of bone and wood cracking, combined with girlish shrieking, bounced hysterically off the walls. The gun clattered to the floor. Their attacker fell onto one knee, cradling his arm. Jotham swung again, landing another solid blow on his neck, and another on his shoulders. Moaning, Red fell face forward, landing on top of his weapon.

"Run!" Jotham screamed.

The four bolted through the kitchen and burst through the backdoor. Ignoring the stairs, they vaulted the low porch railing and flew across the yard. As they darted past the black van, they heard high pitched obscenities begin to reverberate inside the house.

"Forget the bikes, there's no way we can get to them before he gets out," yelled Bart, dashing ahead of the group. "We're going to have to go through the woods."

"Yeah, we'll lose him out back and climb over the wall behind the gardener's shed," Jotham shouted.

Abe was struggling to keep up, one arm holding his ribs.

"Come on," yelled Carisa. "We don't have much time!" She reached to grab his free hand.

They scattered into the dense grove that stood behind the Glampoole residence. When they were hidden from view, they made a sharp turn and headed toward the shed against the east wall.

The kitchen door slammed. The enraged man was hurtling his way out of the house after them. They heard him stop, then begin running toward the trees.

When they reached the shed, their hearts sank. The roof had caved in completely and would afford them no platform to scramble over the brick wall.

Standing motionless, Jotham motioned for the others to follow suit. He peered through the foliage. "Be quiet. Move very slowly along the wall. Maybe we can outflank him and get out through the gate.

Far to their left they could hear footsteps crashing through the brush. As if he had overheard their plans, Red's voice yelled out: "Forget the gate, punks, I've called for back-up and they're gonna be parked out front."

The footsteps ceased.

They could almost hear him daring them to give away their position.

They remained frozen, holding their breath. An eternity later, the crunch of feet began moving away from them.

Jotham motioned for them to gather around him. "He may be bluffing, but we can't risk it." Glancing up at the bricks, he whispered, "Let's look for a tree that we can use to climb over the wall."

Pointing at an ancient elm with a wide trunk and limbs stretching out at fingertip level, Abe began inching quietly toward it. The others followed cautiously in single file. Abe walked around the base of the elm and disappeared.

When Jotham craned his head around the other side, Abe was nowhere in sight. He looked up at the branches but they were bare.

"Abe," he hissed, "where are you?"

The crunching sounds heading away instantly stopped.

"I'm in here," Abe's words echoed hollowly from the tree. Jotham peered into a gaping hole in the base of the trunk. "Down here." His brother's sepulchral voice was coming from the ground beneath him.

He looked down and saw Abe's head sticking out of an opening in the ground. With one hand he was holding open a small trap door.

"Get in quick. There's a passageway down here. Hurry!"

The footsteps were now crashing wildly toward them.

Jotham grabbed the other two. "Quick," he urged as he squeezed Carisa into the opening. "Bart, drop that branch over the door when you close it!"

He watched as Carisa's head disappeared into the dark hole; then he pushed himself down through the gap. He found himself on a ladder clambering down wooden rungs into the pitch darkness. He could hear Abe and Carisa breathing heavily below him. Bart dropped swiftly into the shaft. Above him the trap door closed with a muffled thud.

They froze on the rungs, their breath aching in their heaving chests. Jotham's forehead broke out in a cold sweat from the close dankness of their narrow cave. He imagined that the walls were closing in on him like the coils of a giant boa constrictor. His heart was thudding wildly.

The cracking of twigs was followed by the chilling sound of a gun butt angrily striking the trunk above them. The reverberations through the wood sent chills through the four below.

Jotham's chest felt as if it were ready to explode. Prickles of sharp pain began spreading like a spider's web through his thighs as the muscles began to cramp.

The words, "Where are those damn . . ." could be distinguished with dreadful clarity above them.

Silence.

Their assailant was poised like a snake licking the air for scent. Finally, steps could be heard striding hurriedly away.

After another eternity, Jotham suggested that it was safe for Bart to open the door. The sounds of his grunting and straining soon filled their dank cubicle.

"What did you pull over the top—a rock?" hissed Jotham.

"No, it was just a hunk of that dried-out bush."

"Bart!" Carisa's quaking voice sounded close to panic. "What if he's holding it closed!"

Jotham reached down and laid a hand firmly on her head. "Carisa, come on! Don't lose it! If he knew we were down here, we'd know about it pronto. He's not the kind to play those kind of games."

"You're—right," she whispered, gulping down her fear. "S-sorry."

"Jotham, what's the deal with the door?" Abe asked from the depths below.

"I dunno. I think it might be jammed."

Bart continued struggling above them. Bits of dirt and dead grass rained down on the three below. "I can't . . . I can't budge it!" he groaned. "It feels like its locked or something."

Jotham fought down a wave of panic. "What's below, Abe?" he asked.

There was silence for a moment as Abe investigated. "There's a dirt floor down here. I can't feel the other wall . . . Hold on! Everyone, quiet! I think I hear voices!"

The three, their muscles already aching from their awkward posture on the ladder, were forced into another period of tense immobility. Fear flooded the dark hole like sewage. Jotham's ears throbbed with each lurch of his heart.

After a few minutes, Abe's tremulous whisper floated up to them. "I can't quite make it out, but it sounds like chanting or singing." Abe's feet began sliding along the dirt. He was feeling his way forward, taking hesitant steps toward the sounds with his arms outstretched. His fingertips made contact with something hard.

"Hey! There's a door here." He felt around for a handle, but there was none. Both hands began tracing its wooden contours. His right hand felt rough, corded fibers. "There's a rope hanging here, but no handle."

"Pull it carefully," instructed Jotham.

Carisa felt a vague premonition. "I don't . . ." She was unable to finish. Her words were drowned out by the terrifying peals of a huge bell. It seemed to be thundering all around them. They began swaying back and forth as if they were inside the iron carillon itself and the ladder were its clapper. Jotham heard Carisa's terror-stricken voice beneath, then above him. They were being flung about like playthings at the end of a string.

Suddenly, they began to spin. They whirled as if in a giant gyroscope, slowly at first, then with mounting speed. They twisted sideways at increasing angles, until they were spinning perpendicularly. They could never be quite certain what happened next. Whether from inside or outside themselves, they heard a roaring like that of an oncoming locomotive. The roar seemed to affect their skin, alternatively stretching and contracting it. Ripples of current flowed all over their bodies.

Then, without warning: stillness.

Everything stopped. They were enveloped in darkness and an almost painful quiet.

"Bart? . . . Jotham? . . . You guys, where are you?" Abe's high-pitched voice quavered.

"Here . . . right in front of you," Jotham responded, grabbing his brother's arm. Carisa and Bart moved toward his voice. "Everybody stay close together," Jotham urged.

"W-what happened?" Carisa stammered. Childhood nightmares of being trapped in a huge, pitch black cave assailed her.

"Who knows," her brother responded. "But it was kind of fun, like riding the Cyclone at the amusement park." His voice sounded different to Jotham, as if the excitement had raised it several octaves.

Jotham felt the frayed end of the rope that Abe still clutched in his hand. "Man, what in the world did you pull?"

"I—I don't know; it was really scary." His voice trembled. ". . . anyway, *you* told me to pull it!" Abe continued petulantly.

"All right, you boys, don't start," interrupted Carisa. "We've got more important things to do, like figuring out how we're going to get out of here."

Jotham, who had no stomach for carnival rides, was surprised to find that he didn't feel the slightest bit nauseous. He felt as if he'd been through a huge laundromat: paddled clean, then spun dry.

A small trickle of water could be heard plopping slowly into a pond off to their left. Its hollow reverberations echoed off a ceiling far above them. They were clearly in some kind of cavernous room.

Bart, closest to the water, began edging his foot sideways. Suddenly the ground fell away to nothing.

His foot was hanging over thin air!

He jumped backwards. The floor apparently fell away into a pit, less than a yard from where they were standing. They were on the edge of a precipice. Before he could alert the others, from the opposite side of the cavern, appeared the shadow of a hooded figure walking rapidly toward them with a flaming torch.

Chapter Ten

The Paladins were frozen in terror. The menacing figure was similar in height to their assailant, but the jerking shadows made it impossible to judge the remainder of his shape. The torch came to a stop.

"Halt!" The command was spoken brusquely in a reedy voice that was oddly familiar. The words echoed eerily from the cavernous heights above them. Jotham's tension eased slightly. The voice was clearly not that of their attacker.

The monkish figure thrust the flame toward them. It cast his cowled face into a deeper shadow. From where they were standing, he now appeared to be close to seven feet tall. From his side hung a formidable sword, glinting in the flashing light.

"As one of you has already discovered, you are in a precarious position. One false move and you will have a frigid, although perhaps much needed bath." He stopped, coughing to cover his enjoyment at his own cleverness. "But enough levity. Despite your attire, you are here on serious business for the Great General himself." Bringing the torch down to the level of their chests, he squinted through the flames at their biking clothes.

"Bahh," he grumbled, "Justar always chooses the unlikeliest sorts. But I never expected four harlequins." He turned scornfully on his heels.

As the flickering torch had advanced toward them, it seemed to Jotham that his friends were strangely altered.

Abe grabbed Jotham's sleeve, which was now hanging loosely from his arm. "What's going on? It's like we're in the Twilight Zone or something!"

Jotham shook his head, hopelessly confused.

"And, who's this General dude?" Bart hissed in a squeaky voice. He gestured toward their guide. "Man, Alfred Hitchcock would really love this guy!"

Carisa interjected, "Where are we? Jotham, do you know what's happening?"

As Jotham was trying to construct a reasonable response, the monkish figure turned his head grumbling to himself. "Baah! Children! What is happening, you ask? As I explained once already, and that rather clearly I might add—you are here on express orders of the Great General, Justar, himself." He covered his nose with his sleeve, only partially succeeding in stifling a sneeze. "Had you been paying closer attention, instead of gaping impertinently, you might have heard me the first time, and I wouldn't need to be standing here repeating myself, catching my death of cold."

He jerked back around and shuffled up stone steps which led to a narrow tunnel, muttering loudly, "My work is becoming harder and harder, but I shan't complain." His shoulders stiffened, and coming to an abrupt halt he barked into the darkness, "It is my duty but to do and . . ." He stopped, rubbing his chin. "How does that infernal saying end?"

"Die?" Carisa suggested helpfully.

The towering figure spun toward her. "What did you say?"

Carisa shrunk back, "I . . . I said, 'die' . . . sir. It is your duty but to do and . . . 'die.'"

"Well, of course, thank you." The monk's yellow teeth gleamed from the recesses of the cowl. "Regardless of how foolish you look, you appear to have a quick wit. Strange though that you would know that, I thought it was our creed, not yours." He continued walking toward the passageway. "Follow me," he instructed them, not looking back.

Bart looked over at Jotham and raised his eyebrows questioningly. He had a queer expression on his face as he stared at Jotham.

Jotham raised his shoulders in an expression of complete bewilderment.

Abe whispered, "Should we follow this crazy dude?"

"I don't think we have much choice," Carisa responded, looking at the darkness behind them.

They hurried to catch up to the receding torchlight. The ceiling was so far above them it was not illuminated by the light. To their left was a wall; and on their right, a precipice with water somewhere far below.

They entered the tunnel; it was cold and damp. The four kept close to each other. Soon Abe's and Carisa's teeth began to chatter. She reached out and squeezed Bart's hand tightly. It was less reassuring than she remembered. He grasped hers with equal intensity. Their feet slid on the scummy stone flooring as they hurried to keep up. The ceiling quickly became lower, forcing their guide to hunch over.

Carisa had been staring intently at the stoop-shouldered monk. Strands of white, unkempt hair glimmered against the dark material covering his head. He had a gangling frame and narrow wrists that seemed in danger of disconnection from his arms. His shoulders were rounded with age; but despite his advanced years, he moved with tremendous agility. However, it was his slightly hunched posture which settled the matter for her: the resemblance was unmistakable.

She smiled broadly in recognition, then burst out incredulously, "Glump . . . I mean Mr. Glampoole, is it really you?"

He jerked around, bumping his head on the ceiling; he tottered and almost extinguished the flame as it hit the wall to his right.

"Wha . . . Wha . . . Who? I mean, did you call me? I'm sorry, I'm a bit added. I've been rather busy getting ready for your arrival—at rather short notice I might mention. You could have given us some advance warning, you know. But I will not complain. I do my work. My duty it is."

He held himself erect. Holding his torch at attention, he declared: "It is my duty but to . . ." he interrupted himself, adding sheepishly, "Well you know already." As he turned to continue up the incline, he slapped his forehead and exclaimed: "I did it again. You'd think after all these years I'd remember . . ." He peered intently at them, "I sincerely apologize." He bowed his head abjectly then pulled back his cowl.

The four gaped at him. He was Glumpuddle's exact double, except for his eyes. Instead of light blue, his were dark brown, almost black—wine-black. Still, the resemblance was uncanny. His eyes projected an expression of latent doubt, their vagueness sheltered beneath beetling eyebrows that served as a protective overhang for his pointed nose and high cheekbones. Nevertheless, there were flashes of penetrating intelligence in his eyes. They held a bright, wild inquisitiveness which reminded Jotham of his owl, Plato. Above his brow, like a whimsical crown, his tousled white hair stuck out in all directions. Carisa fought an impulse to run up and hug him.

Glumpuddle's clone stuck out a long, bony hand. "I forgot to introduce myself. Bad form, I'm afraid. My name is Slimgilley." He shook their hands with remarkable solemnity. As each of them introduced themselves, he nodded somewhat distractedly—as if he knew them already. He placed his hand over his heart and bowed deeply. "By the by," he said in his nasal voice, "welcome to the land of Issatar." He waved the torch. "Don't worry yourselves, it will get lighter presently."

"Perhaps he really is related somehow to Glumpuddle," Jotham whispered to Bart, staring at their tall, stooped guide.

"Who knows," Bart responded, still looking oddly at Jotham. "In this weird place, I suppose anything is possible."

The ritual completed with the utmost gravity, they resumed their uphill trek. Despite their initial disappointment, the four were still somehow comforted. It felt as if they were once again in the company of their old friend. In a few minutes, they came to a stop in front of an arched doorway. It was set off by an expertly crafted stone archway. A tasseled rope hung next to it. The tall monk grasped it and the four jumped toward him, shouting, "No!"

But it was too late; he had already given it a sharp pull.

They stiffened, anticipating another chaotic whirl. Instead, a silvery jingle could be heard from behind the slatted wooden door. Without a sound, it immediately swung open on well-oiled hinges. Slimgilley stepped inside, looking back, shaking his head at them with a quizzical expression.

Standing beside the door was a dwarf, completely bald, but with a waist-length curly red beard. He had dark brown eyes that sparkled in a sunburned leathery face. His head shone in the light of several lanterns that lit a well-appointed, comfortable room with hand-sawn beams along the walls and ceiling. A cheery fire beckoned them from a rounded fireplace made from stones and crystals, which scattered bright prisms throughout the room. Through a window, they could see an armful of roses of various colors swaying gracefully from a trellis in the evening sunlight.

In the dining area, a rough oak table was prepared with six place settings. In the middle was a large bowl overflowing with small, crusty loaves. The room smelled of hearth-baked bread and roasted venison. Simple metal stemless goblets surrounded a large pitcher with foam quivering on the spout.

As he removed his hooded robe, Slimgilley cast a shrewd eye at the table then twisted his head to glare sternly at the dwarf. "Flaggon, you scoundrel. Testing out the quality of our ale again, were we? I wish I could say I was surprised. You simply couldn't wait to begin the celebration, could you?"

He tossed his robe on a rocking chair by the fire. "Well, I can see what your word is good for—apparently nothing." The blushing dwarf hung his head dejectedly. Out of the tops of his eyes he looked at the Paladins hoping for some sympathy from the visitors.

Slimgilley, now clothed in a simple white tunic with a gold crown embroidered on its right corner, turned his head away dismissively, muttering in disgust, "I certainly hope it met with your approval. Without doubt, you've certainly had enough experience to become the General's own personal taster."

The dwarf's face and beard were now of the same, dark red hue. He slowly drew himself up, snorted, growling under his breath, but loudly enough for all to hear, *"Abusus non tollit usum."*

Slimgilley retorted with the speed of a whipsaw, "While that may be true, my imbibing assistant, let us of course not forget its corollary, *"Ab ennt studia in mores."* He turned his wild gaze at his four visitors. "Is that not correct, young Paladins?"

How'd he know our club name? Jotham wondered. He looked at the others only to see ignorance written patently on their faces.

"Sir . . . we don't understand what you just said," Jotham admitted meekly.

"My goodness!" Their host's dark eyes grew large and incredulous. "What do they teach young people where you come from?" Without waiting for a reply, he translated, "My impetuous helper justified his misbehavior by claiming the well-worn aphorism that simply because something is abused—such as fermented drink—it is not sufficient argument against its proper use. I, of course, responded with the more telling maxim that practices which are zealously pursued (such as in imbibing spirits at every hour without restraint) inevitably pass into bad habits."

Slimgilley rubbed his hands together and glanced frigidly at his barrel-shaped assistant. "I must apologize for my undisciplined companion. My only hope is that he left enough for me after his own private festivities. You, on the other hand, have nothing to fear: Flaggon made his father's special recipe just for you." He gestured toward the table. "Please take your places; the food is ready. Thankfully, Flaggon didn't have the temerity to also break bread behind my back." He looked darkly at the oven. "I sincerely trust that he managed to restrain himself from consuming the meat."

Slinking toward them with his eyes downcast, as if wishing he had a tail to drag behind him, Flaggon spoke in a gravely voice: "Now now, sor, I wuldna thot of it. I only wonted to make sure that the drink was suitable for you, sor."

The four didn't know whether to laugh or cry. The fawning little baldheaded creature was comical enough, but when they looked at themselves they were stunned—they had each shrunk several inches! Apparently, in their spinning plunge into Issatar, they had actually been catapulted backwards and were now five years younger.

Jotham rolled up his sagging sleeves and leggings, folding them over three times, forming thick sausages around his wrists and ankles. They all gazed wide-eyed at each other, their mouths open. Though internally Jotham could discern no major change, physically he felt spindly and puny. He fumed—Carisa was again an inch taller than he.

Carisa ran her fingers through her hair, now considerably longer and finer. She gaped at her figure and then quickly at Bart who was attempting to stifle his laughter. She tossed her hair at him and flounced down onto a chair, emphatically ignoring him. The rest followed.

Slimgilley and Flaggon sat at each end, the children in the middle. Clearing his throat loudly, their tall host gestured with his thumb to the iron stove behind him. Flaggon stood up quickly and scurried to bring the meat.

The bearded dwarf grimaced apologetically as he placed the massive roast on a trencher next to the bread bowl and set beside it a tall pewter jug. "Sorry, sor. Almost forgot the main dish." Nodding his head briskly as if it were on a metal spring, he beamed at them with a sheepish smile. "Shoulder of venison, young sors and miss, with fresh cooked carrots and onions . . . our favorite." He glanced apologetically at the loaves. "The bread is simple country fare, but it is hearty and we much prefers it to wastel cakes. With more warning—"

He was interrupted by Slimgilley's abrupt cough and the sound of his chair being pushed back from the table. Their host stood erect, holding the jug and began to fill the Paladin's goblets with pink brew. "This is a specialty of the house: rhubarb, lime, and crabapple with crushed mint leaves."

When he finished filling their cups, Slimgilley took up the other pitcher. Flaggon's eyes began to glow, and the tip of his tongue moistened his lips as their host began pouring out the foamy, amber contents. However, when the dwarf saw that his tankard had only been half filled, his lower lip almost dropped to the table.

When Slimgilley was finished pouring the libations, he and Flaggon remained standing behind their chairs. Staring at the Paladins, Flaggon wiggled his bushy eyebrows pointedly. They looked back and forth at each other in confusion. Slimgilley again cleared his throat loudly and picked up his cup, holding it aloft. Flaggon's eyebrows were now fairly dancing. Carisa, the first to take the hint, slid her chair back, stood to her feet, and grabbed her drink. The others meekly followed suit.

Their host and his round assistant held their goblets high and intoned together: "We swear allegiance to our Great General and to his Kingdom which he protects. One royal people we, with gratitude and devotion, our King we serve." The four children, following their lead, lifted their cups up and clanged them together, spilling some of the liquid over the sizzling meat.

"The meat's been blessed proper, now," chortled the dwarf, who had managed to refill his cup. Quickly pulling out a dangerously long dagger from his belt, he began slicing slabs of venison as easily as if he were cutting butter.

"Don't forget—begin with the oldest," directed Slimgilley from the head of the table.

"Of corse, of corse, sor. I've not ever forgot that yet, have I?" he retorted with surprising tartness.

"That's true, very true, my dear Flaggon. And may I say on behalf of the five of us—and I'm certain I speak for all—how succulent your bread smells. I believe you outdid yourself on the vegetables as well." Slimgilley now appeared to be intent on mollifying the dwarf who was slicing the meat furiously, muttering blackly to himself.

Taking his cue, Jotham spoke up. "The meat looks delicious too!" Taking a sip from his cup, he choked, took a deep breath and went on bravely, "And . . . ahhh that is the most . . . interesting drink I've ever had in my life!" With a sly expression in Bart's direction, Jotham suggested innocently, "Bart, why don't you try it? I'm sure that you'll love it."

As their hosts turned expectantly toward Bart, Jotham slipped his goblet under the table. Carisa saw the sly movement and glared disapprovingly. Jotham merely smiled.

Bart raised his cup to his lips and took a sociable swallow. Suddenly his face grew white, then a blazing red, his eyes widening in dismay. Swallowing hard, he gasped, madly blinking the water from his eyes. Glaring at Jotham, he whispered hoarsely, "Yes . . . Flaggon . . . it is really very . . ." He wiped his eyes with his sleeve, took a breath and continued, ". . . ah, unusual. Jotham's right—I've never . . . had anything like it!"

71

The cook fairly glowed with pride. "That's me own special, family brew, sor. I learnt it from me fadder. He always said, 'Flaggon, me boy, it will make a real dwarf of ya!'" He handed a plate to Jotham, then to Carisa, Bart, and finally to Abe, following their birth order perfectly, even to the correct priority between the twins—a secret about which Bart was almost obsessive. The four eyed each other, arching their eyebrows questioningly.

Their tall host nodded approvingly at Flaggon, then spoke to his guests, "Please eat heartily. It is our custom when at table to keep conversation to a minimum, the better to enjoy the repast. After we've partaken, you may ask whatever you wish."

The children found that their appetites had not been affected by their reduction in age. If anything, it seemed to have increased it. Bart poked Carisa after she had taken a third helping. "I guess you're not worried about your figure anymore, are you?" he whispered.

She gave him a return jab in the ribs, stuck her tongue out at him, then smiled in surprise. "That felt good! You'd better watch out, Bartey; I can beat you up again, you know."

He snorted, "Fat chance! You're still just a skinny little kid."

"You should talk," Carisa muttered.

Slimgilley looked up over the rim of his cup, his lips set in a thin, disapproving line. "Where is that cat, Flaggon?" He inquired.

The dwarf swallowed quickly. "I just saw him walking away from his bowl a little strangely like. I believes Orion must be hiding from the guests as usual, sor."

The tall monk reached down and placed a bit of venison in the bowl on the floor. "He loves venison, I'll give him just a bite. Can't be spoiling him now, can we?"

Flaggon nodded approvingly, raised his cup and drunk a deep, hearty toast to the unsociable cat.

Their meal culminated with a delightful strawberry truffle. After effusively praising the highly sensitive cook, the children drew their chairs over to the fireplace where Slimgilley was sitting in a well-worn overstuffed chair, smoking a long clay pipe.

"Come, come now. All who come here have questions; I'm certain you are no exception. Most have worn my ear off by now with their infernal interrogatives. Let's get it over with, shall we? I must say, I certainly expected more chattering than this from four harlequins."

"Where are we?" Carisa was the first to speak.

"As I stated in the cavern," he answered gravely, "you are in the land of Issatar and you came here on command of the Great General himself. When he calls, you must answer. It is a great honor to be called, but a greater honor to be chosen."

Jotham leaned forward and inquired impatiently, "Called for what? How'd we get here? And how long are we going—"

"Slow down, Mr. Jotham. One at a time, please. I can't very well be expected to keep my thoughts straight if you insist on assailing me with a barrage of questions." He took a long draw on his pipe to compose himself. Flaggon, who had been putting the plates away, sat down attentively at the table behind them.

Through the floating rings of smoke, Slimgilley looked at them closely. "You are called to be Paladins, aren't you?"

There it is again! What does this guy know about us? Jotham mused. *And why are we "to be" Paladins?* His list of questions was growing longer by the minute.

"As all Paladins, you've been summoned to undertake a mission, of course." Drawing his long fingers together in the shape of a steeple, he pensively pressed the tip to his wide lips. He blew a puff of smoke, then pulled out the clay pipe from between his teeth, staring morosely at the ring spinning lazily toward Jotham. "Regarding its purpose I cannot answer, for it is one to which, in the Great General's wisdom, he has decided not to make me privy. How you arrived here, I also do not know."

Flaggon jumped in as Slimgilley cleared his throat. "Me master wouldna know about such matters," he explained, puffing his chest out proudly, "as he is a Messenger, not a Caller. There are as many entrances to Issatar as there are exits." He began rushing his words to avoid Slimgilley taking over the dialogue. "And regarding the length of your stay that depends whether you meet with success—"

"Flaggon!" the nasal tone interrupted sharply. "Methinks you forget your station. The ale has affected your judgment and your tongue."

"What about our parents?" Bart interjected with an uneasy glance toward Carisa. "They'll be really worried."

Their host drew deeply from his pipe and gazed above their heads in a mysterious manner, affecting a wise and knowledgeable air. "You need not concern yourself about matters in the outer-world while you are here.

Though travel between the various planes is not uncommon, in Issatar—or the 'inner-world,' as the Instructors are fond of calling it—events do not intersect with those out there."

Carisa looked at him with a confused expression which transformed quickly into suspicion. "What does that mean? Have you kidnapped us?" Her voice was getting higher with each question. "You'd better be careful," she said, anger rising in her eyes, "my father knows some important people. If you hurt us—"

She was interrupted by two sounds: Slimgilley's pipe hitting the stone floor, and from behind her, a goblet spilling its contents on the table as it slipped from Flaggon's startled fingers. Slimgilley sprung up and stood in front of the children, his face ashen, his mouth contorting as he strained to convey his dismay. "A-a-ah! A-a-ah!" he choked, incapable of articulate speech, shaking his fist through the sheer impotence of his throat and larynx. "Why, how dare . . . never have I . . . I. . . ." He began to sway, and Flaggon lunged toward him but lost his balance and landed on top of his master as he collapsed back into his chair. Due in no small part to Flaggon's added weight, the armchair flipped backward, somersaulting the gasping monk onto the hearth.

Huffing loudly, the dwarf bent over, lifting Slimgilley from the floor and placing him back in his chair. With ferocious energy, Flaggon swept up the scattered tobacco leaves into his hands, throwing them into the flames, and glared reprovingly at Carisa.

"I believes miss, that ya does owes us an apology. Like you, we be in the services of the General. An' I don't mind sayin' so, we has served long, bravely, and well, I might add. I would gladly defend me master's honor personal-like, but I has sworn not to take up arms against a lady." He spun away, his shoulders shoved back, and a wounded expression etched along the baggy pouches of his eyes.

Carisa's lips quivered at his harsh words and at the sight of the slumped form splayed across the chair in front of her.

"I really didn't mean . . . I'm very sorry if I offended you. It's just that this is all so . . ."

She looked back at Flaggon who was grunting emphatically while busily engaged in cleaning up the spilled liquid on the table. He ignored her apology as he vigorously wiped the surface, refusing to meet her chastened eyes. Sensing her dilemma, yet unable to resist the opportunity to poke fun at her, Bart walked over and rested a patronizing hand on her shoulder. "Yeah, you'll have to excuse my sister—she gets carried away sometimes, especially when she hasn't gotten enough sleep." He hesitated, searching for a clever explanation to repair the damage. "Plus," he continued, "she's just not used to being in new places." He patted her head. Carisa glared at him. Ignoring her discomfiture, he went on. "And to tell you the truth, she gets kind of tense when she eats out. She's just not accustomed to such . . . excellent food and drink." He was now standing directly in front of her.

Carisa pinched the back of his arm. "You'll pay for this," she whispered. Bart's smile only grew wider. It was clear that Flaggon was beginning to thaw. Bart reached back and pulled her forward. Too embarrassed to struggle, she stepped up next to him.

"Right, Car? It was the food, wasn't it?"

She threw a chilling glance at her brother. "Yes . . . I . . . don't know anyone who can bake bread like you . . . and that punch . . ." she let out a sigh, beginning to enter into the role. "If you could give me the recipe, I'd love to give it to my mother."

The dwarf's face was now glowing. "Anyway," she continued, "I apologize; you've both been very kind. I didn't mean to hurt your feelings."

Flaggon, now almost bursting, walked up to Carisa and presented her with a short but extravagant bow. It was obvious he missed having a hat to sweep dramatically into the air, but he made do surprisingly well. "I accepts your apology and extends forgiveness. And if I said anythin' not fittin' to a lady, I humbly begs your pardon." He straightened the leather belt around his belly and bustled over to the table.

Slimgilley had been slowly regaining his color along with his composure and had even nodded magnanimously—once—during Flaggon's speech. At its conclusion, he exclaimed with strained heartiness, "Well now, that's that. I believe this calls for another toast! Reparation of strained relations . . . making peace and all that."

Several more rounds followed in which the four children kept taking cautious and dutiful sips of their punch while their eccentric companions waxed eloquent about the history of Issatar and their bold exploits. After another hour, Jotham had begun to feel so tired that he thought he might easily fall over into the fireplace.

Slimgilley was cut short in midsentence when he saw Abe begin to nod. "Ahhem," he cleared his throat loudly, jerking Abe's head to attention.

75

"Flaggon, you've run on again and wearied our guests. Quite inconsiderate of you, I must say. They have had a long day, and they will need to be well rested for tomorrow. Show them their accommodations and don't dawdle."

The dwarf ushered them into an adjoining bedroom with a small window facing east. Four places had been prepared for them on the floor. Their beds consisted of rough, gray woolen blankets stretched over thick mattresses. Feeling his, Bart exclaimed, "It feels like straw in here."

The others dropped down on their mats, feeling the dried shafts skeptically. Jotham lay down and stretched his tired muscles. He sighed contentedly, "It's not too bad, guys. It's kinda like being outside camping, except a lot drier."

Carisa glanced over at Jotham who was looking very comfortable under the covers. "Jotham, I can't believe you're going to fall asleep! We need to figure out what we're going to do."

Jotham opened one bloodshot eye. "Slimgilley told us we would be given our instructions tomorrow. There's nothing we can do till then. It sounded like we might even be meeting the General, or King—whoever he is."

"It sounded like he was both," Carisa said.

Abe took off his shoes and tossed them into a corner. He slid under the wool blanket. "He called us Paladins!" he muttered in a sleepy voice. "How'd he know the name of our club?"

"Yeah. And how did the dwarf know who was the oldest?" Bart added.

Jotham yawned, "I don't know; they seemed to know lots about us," he rolled over, "but let's talk about it tomorrow."

Carisa pressed, "But, Jotham, aren't you even a little scared? How are we going to get back home? And what about our parents?" She prodded him with her foot. "Wake up! What are we going to do about that psycho who was chasing us?"

Bart leaned next to her on one elbow. "It's going to be all right, Carisa. I don't think we have to worry about him right now. I don't know what's happening or how we're gonna get out of here, but—I can't explain it—I really think we'll be okay."

Carisa edged close to her brother. "I just want to be sure we never see that horrible man with the gun ever again."

Bart grinned at her, "Relax, Car, when we get back we'll probably all be in college and our memories will be erased so we won't even remember this ever happened."

Carisa's mouth dropped open." What? . . . Miss our last months of high school? That would be awful. We wouldn't even get to go to our Senior Prom!"

Bart rolled over on his back. "Well, if we return like we are now, it's going to be a long time before any of us goes to a Prom."

"Oh no!" Carisa wailed. "I'll have to go through ninth grade again!"

Jotham stirred, "Don't get so upset," he mumbled impatiently, "he was only kidding. . . ." Sitting up suddenly, he turned toward them, a strange light in his eyes. "Bart, I . . . have that weird feeling too . . . We're going to be fine. . . ." He smiled at Carisa. "Actually, I'm kind of excited! I've got a hunch this is going to be the Paladins' greatest adventure ever." He lay back on his mat. "As long as we don't wake up and find out it's just been a dream."

Carisa laid her head down and closed her eyes, a small, tired smile replacing the lines of worry on her face. Jotham's excitement was contagious. Despite her concerns, she had to admit that a tingling of reckless anticipation was beginning to stir inside of her. It had been a long time since she'd felt that way—five years, to be exact.

The last image in her mind before falling asleep was that of Jotham with his ludicrously oversized biking clothes rolled up at his wrists surreptitiously emptying his punch into the cat's dish at dinner while their hosts' backs were turned.

Although exhausted, Jotham's mind was racing. He struggled to clear his head of the clamoring thoughts that were now keeping him awake. Questions were spinning around his head like a loose flywheel. After several long minutes he finally began to feel drowsy and began to doze. Instantly, he was wide awake. The hairs on his neck tingled, and cold sweat broke out on his forehead. There was a strange weight on his chest. He was suddenly terribly aware of the distinct contours of individual fingers pressing on him.

His eyes flew open.

At the foot of his bed stood a figure bent over him, dressed as a knight. He was blazing like fire. Slung along his thigh was a huge broadsword. Jotham drew himself up on his elbows, his eyes darting around the room to warn the others.

He sucked in his breath. . . . The room was empty! He was alone with the ghostly apparition.

Chapter Eleven

Jotham, his eyes wide with terror, stared up at the golden knight. Over his suit of armor he wore a brilliant, white tunic with a purple border. Embroidered on his chest below his right shoulder was a roaring lion rearing back on its hind legs, wearing a golden crown with three ornate prongs. Over the knight's left breast were embroidered several rows of minute characters that Jotham was unable to decipher.

His hair was long and black and streaked with bands of white. But it was his face which arrested Jotham. There was something indescribably beautiful yet unsettling about it. There was such an inflexible, almost ferocious, goodness in his appearance that it terrified him. The knight moved closer and was now looming directly over him. Jotham could make out the exquisite, fine links of golden mail covering the knight's blunt fingers, which were outstretched over Jotham's head. His shining muscular arm was motionless; his large hand was trembling slightly.

The knight stared down at him intently for several long seconds, and as he did, Jotham looked into the depths of the most unusual violet eyes he had ever seen. A hint of humor now softened their corners. However, Jotham remained frozen in breathless fear. What terrified Jotham was the expression of fierce anger on the knight's face.

Then he understood.

The knight had a scar that ran down from his forehead, across his left eyebrow and down over his high cheekbone. The wound had healed, twisting the lips slightly, leaving behind an expression of hostility. Somehow, it made the knight's beauty all the more compelling.

After an interminable silence, the stern visitor opened his mouth to speak. "Do not fear, young squire. I am come to you, in the name of the Great General. My name is Warrior." His voice had a timbre like that of a stringed bass.

If Jotham could have moved, he would have thrown himself on his face and grabbed the knight's ankles in awe and reverence. Looking deep inside Jotham, a fire of understanding exploded in Warrior's eyes. His nostrils dilated as harsh indignation swept over him.

"Stand up!" Warrior shouted his command, steel in his voice. "I, like you, am in service to my liege lord. We give glory alone to him. He alone gives honor to us." He impatiently withdrew a scroll from the folds of his tunic. "Prepare to receive your commission."

Jotham brought himself erect on legs that shook like those of a drunken sailor. Warrior reverently unfurled the parchment. As the knight looked down to read its contents, Jotham noticed for the first time the circlet of gold glowing on his black hair. It was curiously etched with leaves, thorns and roses. In the very center was a white stone inscribed with an elegant letter "M."

Warrior spread out his legs resolutely, drew back his head and began to chant in a richly textured voice, "Thus says our liege lord:

You, Jotham, are this day commissioned
Into the army of Justar the Great General.
Special commission is also hereby granted
Into His Majesty's select order of Paladins
As warrior priests to battle his mortal enemy, Ghnostar.
Ultimate rank shall be contingent
On obedience to your orders
And fulfillment of your vows.

You are hereby given command of a band of three.
You shall lead by service and example.
Authority is hereby delegated to you.
Lead well, they are to be on your heart,
Not under your feet.
Permission is expressly given
To enter the Great General's palace,
At which time your mission
Will be more fully revealed.
You will then be fitted for battle.

The knight's sculpted face flamed, and his deep resonant voice, as it rose and fell in measured cadences, was almost hypnotic. Jotham was startled when Warrior snapped his feet back together and declared, "Truly, truly these are the words of Justar the King." Then, rolling up the scroll, he handed it to Jotham. "Present this for safe passage."

Thrusting his arm upwards in a fierce salute he shouted: "Hail Justar! Hail to the one true King!" Striking his chest with the flat of his clenched fist, he declared, "Paladin, I salute you!" then vanished.

Jotham was stunned; his pulse was racing. Warrior's parting words were almost intoxicating. He took breaths in short, shallow gasps and wiped the perspiration from his face. He looked at his arm. It felt odd. He rubbed his biceps with his free hand. Although the material was still loose, it felt a little more taut against his skin.

As he lay back on his pallet, he was surprised to notice that there were once again three other beds in the room. His band was present and account-ed for. He strained to comprehend what had just transpired. Events were happening too fast. He felt exhilarated and dizzy, excited yet afraid. He could barely believe what had just occurred. The only thing which con-vinced him that he had not dreamed the encounter was the thick vellum scroll in his hand.

Jotham cradled his arms behind his head and released a deep breath. Warrior's message brought back the conversation around the fireplace. Jotham was convinced that this extraordinary commission was directly related to what Slimgilley had told them hours earlier.

Their tall host, pipe clasped firmly in his teeth, had grown loquacious with the warmth and the ale. He had rambled on for hours. Though Jotham's head felt woozy from exhaustion, he had been fascinated by the incredible tale.

The thin, monkish figure had spoken quite at length about some crea-ture called Ghnostar. *What had he said?*

The words came back in a rush. "Ghnostar is a cruel and wicked one, he is. Some there be who jeer at him, calling him old Two-Head (behind his back, of course), but I have seen what he can do. I hate him, but I do respect his powers. I stopped mocking long ago. In my limited experience, I have come to believe that those who do the loudest laughing are those who do the fastest running when the battle is well and truly joined. Our Teachers are always reminding young Paladins of the important truth that in hand-to-hand combat, age and experience will inevitably defeat youth and zeal—every time."

He removed his pipe and looked at the floor with a pained expression. "If I may be so bold as to offer a bit of humble advice, I would say beware of overconfidence. Treat it like the plague. It is one of Ghnostar's favorite ploys. 'Respect him my boy,' my dear mother would always say, 'but you need not fear him—that's the ticket.' She was a fierce warrior, she was . . ."

His voice trailed off for a moment, then he blinked repeatedly and blew a cloud of smoke toward the children. "Ahhem, well, in any event, as I was saying—"

Carisa interrupted, "But who is Ghnostar?"

"You will find out soon enough, I warrant." The pipe was returned to his teeth.

"He sounds scary," Abe interjected. "Does he live around here?"

"What does he do? Why do we have to worry about him? . . . Please, can't you tell us anything more about him?" Carisa pleaded.

Their host rather quickly relented. "As I tried to make clear at the outset, I am not a Teacher; I'm only a humble Messenger. I expect that Justar will probably have me defrocked for speaking beyond my station—I will expostulate, however, very briefly. . . ." He held both palms up. "But only because you insist." Then he spoke in a conspiratorial whisper, "Ghnostar is Justar's implacable enemy, and therefore, ours as well. He hates us only a little less than he does Justar."

"But why?" asked Carisa.

"It's not personal, mind you," their host continued. "He simply wants to kill anything that is in any way related to Justar in order to avenge his humiliation."

"Humiliation? What do you mean?" she interrupted.

Slimgilley stared at her, impatience brimming in his eyes. "If you would stop disturbing my explanation, I think your curiosity would be satisfied," he muttered sullenly.

Jotham encouraged him to proceed, warning Carisa with a sidelong glance.

"Ghnostar is a huge, two-headed dragon. Two rows of horns grow out of his back all the way down to the end of his scarlet and green tail. It is blunt now, ever since the battle of Baracrux. That was the great battle where Justar defeated Ghnostar's special forces. It was during this final campaign that the Crown Prince—may his memory be blessed—lost his life. As punishment and as a perpetual reminder, before throwing him into the dungeon deep, Justar clipped his wings and sliced off the poisonous barb on the tip of Ghnostar's fearsome tail. Hence the phrase, 'the sting's been wrenched, the flame's been quenched.'"

Carisa jumped in before Jotham could stop her. "What does that mean?"

Slimgilley glanced around suspiciously then lowered his voice further. "It is *also* wise to speak very carefully about these matters. Ghnostar has been known to appear where his name has been spoken brashly. He is not to be trifled with, I tell you. He does not suffer fools lightly. It is best not to speak of him overmuch, and certainly, never carelessly."

He'd retreated into an uncertain silence.

"But what about that quenched thing?" Carisa whispered.

Slimgilley stared for several seconds at the darkness outside the window. "Another way our children learn about that is with this rhyme: 'When the dragon's sting was blunted, his stinging fire was stunted.'" Their host shrugged. "Though very simple, it does help the little ones remember. I shouldn't say any more, but I will only add that Justar implanted iron rings in the dragon's nose. Maybe that's what turned off the flames, we simply don't know. In any event, the rings were used to hook Ghnostar to an unbreakable chain for 100 years. It has never been explained to my satisfaction exactly how he escaped. But I can tell you that he despises Justar and has been his mortal foe ever since."

The three oldest Paladin's eyes were riveted on their host. Abe's were now closed, and his head slumped against Carisa's shoulder. She stared at Slimgilley dubiously. "You aren't just trying to frighten us with monster stories, are you?"

Jotham tensed, but to his surprise, Slimgilley remained calm; the only noticeable response was a slight quiver to the clay stem in his mouth.

He inhaled deeply and continued. "I thought the same when I first heard about him from my grandfather." His eyes grew misty and vacant. "He was a wonderful grandpa. It's been centuries, but I still miss him terribly. . . . Do you have . . . ?" He began, then stopped, clearing his throat loudly and furiously blinking his watery eyes.

"My apologies. It was inconsiderate of me to burden you with my, ahhm, personal feelings. Completely out of character, I can assure you. It must be Flaggon's blasted ale." He picked up his goblet which had been growing warm by the fire. He swirled the amber liquid, stared into it as if seeing it for the first time, then took a huge gulp. Smacking his wide lips, he continued. "Of course, it goes without saying, I am certainly *not* trying to frighten you. That would serve no purpose, now, would it?"

He rubbed the bridge of his hawk's nose with long tapered fingers. "I was explaining why Ghnostar hates our King and why it is the better part of wisdom to respect his powers. Fortunately, Ghnostar himself does not appear often; it is his special forces we generally must contend with."

That had caught Bart's attention. "Who are they?"

"They are deceptive and odious creatures. They are known as the Ghargakons, or Ghargs, for short. They fly in packs and can occasionally change shape. Most of the time, however, they retain their true and disgusting form: huge bats of varying sizes with tails like those of monkeys. Some have the appearance of swine, others resemble foxes, while others can only be described as monstrous." Their instructor coughed, took a thoughtful sip, and continued, "They can also make themselves invisible. Fortunately, they can remain so only for brief periods."

Carisa looked anxiously about the room. "How can you tell where they are?"

"Don't worry," the tall Messenger-turned-Teacher snorted, "the smell generally gives them away, but if they do take on human form, the brand on their left palm is how you can pierce their disguise. That cannot be hidden."

"What does it look like?" Jotham asked.

"As is common with our enemy, it is precisely the opposite of King Justar's sign. Ghnostar is notoriously uncreative—he can mimic but never create. It is a three-pronged crown, but in the inverted position."

"Upside down?" Abe, who had roused himself, asked.

Slimgilley nodded, sending a plume of smoke toward the rafters. "Yes . . . and it's blood red."

Chapter Twelve

The smell of his mother's blueberry pancakes roused Jotham from a deep sleep. His mouth watering, he stretched and rubbed his eyes, preparing to go downstairs for breakfast. He squinted, looking for Plato perched in his usual place above his bookshelf. There was no bird and no shelf. Stone walls enclosed him in a simple room with three slumbering companions. In a dizzying rush, the astounding events of the prior day came flooding back.

He strained to remember each word spoken by his ethereal visitor, but some were already beginning to fade. He wished he could freeze-frame each second and replay it for himself, and the other Paladins as well. A proud warmth flowed through him as he recalled the statement about his selection. It felt good to be chosen. He just wished the others had been listening in.

From the one small window he could see that the dawn had begun to paint the sky a light gray. In his hand, he still grasped the scroll. The early light was insufficient to enable him to decipher the script, so he got up to hunt for a lamp.

He walked quietly into the living room and lit a thin stick from the embers in the fireplace. Carrying it back into their bed chamber, he used it to light a candle on the stand next to his bed. Sitting down on a low three-legged stool, he unfurled the scroll and read the words that Warrior had declared the night before. His chest burned with the honor of his commission. One of the sleepers stirred. Jotham hastily rolled the scroll up; as he did so, his attention was drawn to thick bundles at the foot of their beds.

Before he could step over to examine them, Bart began to mumble. His body twitched; then his eyes blinked open. He stared up at the candle blankly. "Sir? W-where . . . ? Don't . . ." The look of confusion gradually melted as his eyes focused on Jotham, who was glancing over at him with amusement.

84

Jotham covered the scroll with his hands. "What were you dreaming about? It couldn't be anyone I know. I don't think I've ever heard you call anybody 'sir' in your life."

Bart looked at the candle sheepishly. After a moment's thought, he stated in a quiet voice, "I thought it was a knight."

Jotham's eyes widened. "Did you say a knight?"

Bart nodded. Carisa's tousled head was raised, and her attention was fixed on him.

"You're kidding, Bart," she exclaimed. "You won't believe this, but I dreamed about one too."

Abe sat up groggily. "Yeah, I think I did too," he said, looking at a scroll in his hands, "but I don't think it was a dream."

The others stared at him in astonishment. Carisa and Bart began fumbling around their covers and soon located theirs. The three hurriedly gathered around the candle to inspect them. They appeared to be identical. They were made of thin leather and had the texture of thin poster board. A large, red wax seal, with the emblem of a roaring lion, secured the scrolls. Each of the stamped impressions was cracked across the middle.

After inspecting their parchments, they each described their encounter with the glowing messenger. It was clear that they had seen the same visitor, and except for the leadership clause which was unique to Jotham's scroll, each of the messages Warrior had delivered was identical. Jotham was gratified to hear that the other Paladins had been verbally advised about his position in the band. Whatever their adventure chanced to be, he would be in charge. He thought the choice had been well made.

"Something tells me we're gonna see him today," Bart said.

"See who?" Abe asked.

"That King . . . you know, Jestar."

"King Justar," Carisa and Jotham corrected him simultaneously.

Carisa looked at Jotham with a troubled frown. "How will we know how to get there?"

"I'm sure Flaggon or Slimgilley will know how to find him."

Abe had noticed the parcel at the foot of his bed and crawled over his sleeping pad to inspect it. "Whoa!" he shouted, "Whatever's in here is really heavy." He uncovered the bundle, then stood up, holding out in front of him a simple white tunic with purple border. "Hey, check this out guys— it's just like Warrior's."

He swiveled his hips and took a few mincing steps toward the others. "Just what I've always wanted—a dress," he said in a melodramatic falsetto.

Jotham and Bart launched their shoes at him. Abe ducked behind his tunic. Peeking out from around the armhole, he laughed, "Naa Naa, you missed me."

Carisa snorted in disgust and picked up her parcel. "I think Justar made a big mistake. He should have put *me* in charge. You guys are so immature; you never know when to be serious."

Ignoring her, the boys scrambled to look over their new garments. Jotham lifted up a pair of leather sandals with extremely long thongs. "What in the world?" he muttered, as the ends of the thongs dragged on to the floor.

"They're to wrap around your legs, dufus," Carisa explained.

Jotham grunted and began strapping them on.

The loudest exclamations were reserved for the dense, finely linked suits of mail that completed their gear.

Carisa ran her hands over the supple gray links. "I can't believe how soft it is. You'd never believe it was made out of metal!"

Jotham traced his finger over the embroidered lion on the chest of his tunic; it had the weight and texture of real gold thread. He was puzzled to notice that the names of his three friends had also been embroidered in gold letters over the left breast.

Strangely, the others only had his name on theirs. He picked up the thick leather belt which completed his attire. The pouch which hung from it was empty except for a few flints.

It was Carisa who discovered that they also made ideal containers for their scrolls.

Bart, pointing to his belt, walked over to Jotham, "I figured it out. You know what these metal clasp-like things are for?"

"What's that, Sherlock?" Carisa inquired, crossing her eyes and looking down her nose at him, a perfect picture of rank stupidity.

"They're for our swords!" he exulted triumphantly.

"All right!" Jotham exclaimed.

"But where are they?" Abe asked looking under his mattress.

"It's standard practice for the King to give them to his subjects when they are knighted," Bart responded, pretending more certainty than he actually felt. Chivalry was a hobby of his, but he actually had no idea how swords were bestowed on anyone.

Carisa slipped the tunic over her suit of mail. It fit perfectly. "How do I look?" she asked the others, looking down at herself. Bart and Jotham didn't hear her. They were prancing about the room, waving imaginary weapons at each other. Jotham lunged, shoving his fist into his adversary's stomach. Bart crashed theatrically to the floor, landing heavily on Abe who was trying to determine which was the front of his tunic.

"Oww. Get off my legs—you weigh a ton!" Abe complained, shoving Bart on to his side. Bart rolled over, letting his head slump to the side, pretending to be coughing up blood.

Carisa looked disapprovingly at her brother. "Can't you boys stop playing around?" She spun around showing off her attire. "What do you think?" she again inquired.

Bart opened one eye and gave her a long cool stare. "I think you look like a dopey girl trying to dress up like a soldier from King Arthur's Court."

Carisa dropped down, pinning his arms to the floor. "Dopey . . . *right!* She began tickling him under his arms. "At least I'm not the one lying on the ground with drool all over my chin."

"Stop it ple . . . Carisa . . . Please!" he pleaded, writhing away from her merciless fingers.

She jumped to her feet. "Sto-op it, ple-ease," she imitated him in a high-pitched tone. "Who sounds like a dopey girl now?"

When they eventually emerged from their room in their new attire, the red-bearded dwarf stopped bustling about the kitchen. He glanced at them momentarily; then returned to his duties. "Now you looks like proper knights," he remarked matter-of-factly.

"Uhh, humm," sighed Abe, who'd walked up to smell the bread.

"Let's take a look at yore pilgrim's scrip," Flaggon asked.

Abe gave him a blank stare.

Flaggon pointed impatiently at the leather pouch hanging at his waist. "I'm referin' to yore wallet there, young sor."

Abe untied it and Flaggon looked in. He pushed aside the scroll, and nodded. "Good. They remembered the flints. Last time we had to give up a pair of our own."

Slimgilley's seat at the kitchen table was vacant. Flaggon explained that he'd been called away on an unexpected errand and was unsure when he would return. The bald cook removed a large loaf from the stone oven and placed it on the wooden tray in the middle of the table. Milk was poured from the pitcher, and Flaggon sliced open the bread with a flourish.

Steam poured out, the delicious smell of cooked blueberries, apples and raisins filling the air.

"Sweet bread," explained the dwarf with a shrug.

Stuffing his mouth with a warm handful, Abe's eyes widened with delight. "Ith wommerful."

Flaggon sighed contentedly, lifted a cup, and inclined his head in Abe's direction, acknowledging the compliment. He stopped before taking a drink. "It's our custom-like to make a toast before indulging, sors and lady."

Carisa frowned and glared at Abe whose cheeks protruded like those of a squirrel preparing its winter stash. Abe nodded.

As they picked up the frothy cups, the Paladins tensed—not sure what their contents would be. The cook's eyes were inscrutable. "You has fresh milk, though can't says as I understands it," he muttered loudly to himself.

After Flaggon toasted the Great General and his guests, the meal began in earnest. As if compensating for Abe's uncouth conduct, Carisa took several dainty bites. Wiping her mouth carefully with a napkin, she smiled at the dwarf who was spreading butter over his bread. "It is *delicious,* Falag—Falg—Glaff—" she stopped, her face turning a beet red, "—um—sir."

"It's *Fla-ggon,*" Abe intoned, as if instructing a kindergartner.

Her brown eyes flashed, but she continued undaunted. "We'll never forget our first breakfast in Issatar, will we boys? *Flaggon,*" she said it with emphasis, "you are a marvelous cook!"

Flaggon's eyes grew watery with delight. His chest seemed to puff up like a balloon.

The others mumbled their agreement. Jotham emptied his cup and patted the pouch which hung from the leather belt. "Flaggon, last night I had—I mean—we had a visitor. It was kind of a dream . . . but not really one, if you know what I mean?"

"Certainly, sor," responded the dwarf, the corners of his eyes narrowing. "Actually, you be the visitors. Warrior comes only to our most important guests. He be the Great General's chief Messenger."

"Good, you know him then," Jotham said with relief. "I think we're supposed to go to Justar's castle today to receive our . . . um . . . instructions. Could you show us how to get there?"

Flaggon dropped his bread on his plate, jumped down off his seat, drawing himself to attention. "At your orders, sor. If I may say so, I were already plannin' to accompany you gentlemen . . ." he bowed his head toward Carisa, ". . . and the lady, today."

"Thanks, Flaggon. Can we leave right away? The sooner we find out what we're doing here, the sooner we can get back home."

After the table was cleaned off, Flaggon put a thick forefinger to his lips, winked slyly and walked over to the fireplace. Standing on the tips of his toes, he pulled out a loose stone, setting it carefully on the mantle. Grunting with the exertion, he thrust his arm into the hole and slowly pulled out a long wad of oily cloths.

"I jus' don't knows why he puts it so high," he grumbled as he unwrapped the greasy strips from a glittering short scabbard and sword. "I told him and told him, it were a mighty inconvenience." He strapped on the sword, continuing his complaint, "But, no, he wouldna' listen. I be only a dwarf after all . . ." He beckoned them to follow and was still muttering as he closed the sturdy front door behind them.

The Paladins found themselves outside a whitewashed cottage. It had a dark peat moss roof rounded at the eaves like the corners of a well-made bed. The cottage had a small lawn with a purple beech tree in the center, surrounded by the bright trumpets of daffodils and narcissi. While a beech hedge set off the whole affair very neatly. The heavily planted beds leading from the stone porch were a delight of color and scent. The happy chirping of robins and chickadees filled the air as they made their way into town. It was a warm summer day. The sun was already high in the deep blue sky, and there was a gentle breeze blowing.

Flaggon motioned for them to head down a narrow cobblestone path. Picturesque cottages with tidy yards pressed in on both sides. Most had flower boxes with a riot of colorful plantings setting off the starkness of the white walls.

Carisa nudged her brother, "Toto," she said breathlessly, "I have a feeling we're not in Kansas anymore. . . ."

"Why, Dorothy, how perceptive," Bart responded. "I *do* think you're on to something. . . ."

The dwarf turned an angry stare at the twins, his finger against his lips. "As me master says, it would be 'the better part of wisdom' to keep quiet as we go through town. An', please lets me do the talkin' to any passersby."

He rested his hand briefly on the broadsword at his waist, running his fingers over the worn leather strap which hung from the ornate hilt. Bart stared at it enviously.

Soon, the row of cottages gave way to a narrow street hemmed in on both sides by ten foot high whitewashed walls interspersed with occasional wooden doorways. Above their heads balconies with voluptuous streams of multi-colored blossoms cascaded over the wrought iron fencing.

The town was surprisingly quiet. They walked without conversation. The soft slapping of leather against stone bounced off the high walls as they went in a downward sloping direction. They passed very few townsfolk; however, when they did, they all seemed to be heading in the same direction. As they walked by, suspicious glances were cast out of the corners of darting black eyes. One villager, a rather heavyset, older woman, drew her skirts around her in a demonstrative gesture of disdain as Flaggon trotted past.

Carisa, unable to restrain her curiosity, ran up to him. "Why are the people so mean to you?" she whispered.

He kept walking at a quick trot, not answering for several moments. Carisa was about to repeat her question, when he cleared his throat and said, "The Ursa Majorians—that's the name for those as lives here—thinks all dwarfs be inferior. They believes they be better than anyone as doesn't look same as them." He shook his bushy beard in disgust.

As they approached the heart of town, they began to hear faint sounds of music, shouting and laughing, which were quickly growing louder. Soon, the harsh voices of hucksters selling their wares and children shrieking in delight made it plain that they were heading toward some kind of festive gathering. From the general din, it was apparent that a huge crowd had assembled. Now and again, a piercing bugle blast, the high piping of fifes, and thumping of drums punctuated the confused noise. Making a last sharp turn through the winding streets, they found themselves in a large open area, walking on a path that led around the town commons.

The park was quite large. Over the several acres of grass spread out in front of them, two pair of large pavilions had been placed at either end, while a dozen smaller colorful tents were scattered about in the middle. Several thousand gaily attired villagers were meandering about, enjoying the festivities. Gymnasts and jugglers were surrounded by crowds loudly applauding their clever tricks. A dancing bear was chained to a heavy post, while his master strummed a waltzing tune on a small guitar like a ukulele. Hawkers were strutting about endeavoring to part silver from their respective owners. All around them the smell of frying fish, fresh bread, baked apples and roasting pig wafted deliciously toward them. Despite their satisfying breakfast, Jotham's mouth was soon watering.

The dwarf pressed on, seemingly oblivious to the festivities. A fanfare of trumpets pierced the air. It was repeated three times; and with each blast, the hullabaloo increased. An expectant tension filled the commons with an electrical charge. Much of the attention appeared to be drawn to an elevated platform in front of a large, russet and yellow striped pavilion in the middle of the grounds. It was flying colorful pennants at each corner. A short, fleshy man emerged and waddled up the stairs to the dais where 12 ornate chairs sat empty. Overcome by curiosity, Jotham hurried ahead toward the crowd, which was massing in front of the raised platform.

"Young sor . . . come back! Come back!" Flaggon yelled.

The dwarf's bellow was drowned out by the noisy chaos of the throng. Soon, Jotham was caught up in the irresistible press of hundreds of milling bodies.

The man who stood on the platform wore a circular, scarlet silk hat with a gold braid around the brim and a tunic of the same color. His pantaloons were puffed out to below his knees, and a gold clasp held up his white leggings. A broad sash, also of embroidered silk with a large gold medallion in the center, sloped across his rotund chest, ending in a bow which rested against a broad thigh. He reminded Jotham of a red penguin—an extremely self-important one at that.

Jotham felt an annoying series of sharp pricks against his calf. He turned in irritation and saw a child of about six staring at him. The little boy wore a light blue tunic, which looked to be several sizes too small, and a small leather cap on his round head. He fit into his clothes like a chubby little sausage. His fair hair was cut in straight bangs over small piggish eyes. One hand was holding the edge of his mother's white apron. In his other hand, he grasped a well-sharpened, wooden sword.

The boy pointed at Jotham with a suspicious stare. "Mama, look at him. Who is he? Is he one of the bad people?"

The plump, middle-aged woman eyed Jotham suspiciously and drew her son into the folds of her voluminous dress. Jotham stood there opening and closing his mouth, unsure what to say. He suddenly felt extremely conspicuous and a little foolish. He wanted to run, but decided quickly that running would probably be the least advantageous course to take.

She looked him over sharply. Jotham attempted a weak smile at the tow-headed boy who was now smirking and crossing his eyes at him. Reaching a quick conclusion, the round-faced woman yanked her son behind her. "We must hurry on, Aliah. No, I don't think he's one of the bad ones. He's a dim-witted mute playing the part of a soldier. Haste now boy, I don't want to miss the mayor's speech." She trundled him quickly away, shoving aside the unfortunates in her way.

Jotham turned around to look for his companions but could not see them anywhere. He was now pressed in on all sides by the large crowd which surrounded the platform. There was something oddly repulsive about the crush of bodies. Slowly it dawned on him. There was an oppressive sense of fleshly indulgence in the atmosphere. A flaccid weakness in the villagers' faces and a lethargy in their eyes testified to a long-term surrender to it.

Another, more lavish, fanfare pealed forth from the striped pavilion behind Jotham. He turned toward the sound. The 12 chairs on the dais were being filled by six men and six ladies all dressed in an extraordinary, extravagant display of colored silks, feathers, flashing gems, and gold jewelry. By their high foreheads and aquiline noses, it was apparent that they were high-born personages; but there was a dissolute softness around the eyes which contrasted unfavorably with their strong features.

"Gentlemen and ladeeth, free born and thervanth," the mayor addressed the milling mass in a lisping voice. "Honored gueth and dithtinguished nobility," he turned and presented the twelve with an elaborate bow, "welcome to our moth joyful and auguth thelebration—the anniverthary of the Holy and Blethed Truthe. It ith a day to commemorate the withdom of our forefatherth, and rejoith in the prothperity their clear thinking hath brought." A tumultuous ovation erupted from the gathered villagers. Hats were scattered into the air like confetti. The nobles seated on the stage glanced smugly at each other.

The mayor held up his hand. "But let uth not forget, it ith of courth altho a day to give thankth to the, umhh, Great One himthelf for hith—ah—many blethings, which he hath tho kindly lavished on uth."

He winked broadly at the crowd. "What would we do without hith mithguided interferenth?" Snickers and jeers rose up from the crowd. "All for our own good—of courth!" He hesitated, poised to deliver the punch line. "Ath we all know . . . Juthtar knowth betht!" The throng dissolved into gales of laughter. Clearly the mayor envisioned himself a marvelous comic; the villagers obviously agreed.

"Hooray forsha Old Man onsha hill!" a drunken shout interrupted the

92

mayor. Derisive applause broke out around Jotham. The nobility, their faces inscrutable, clapped politely. "Now, now," the rotund mayor chided mildly, "leth not forget the moment of thilencth in the General'th honor." He removed his hat and placed it perfunctorily over his breast. Many of the townspeople ritualistically followed suit, then virtually in one motion, again covered their heads.

The mayor held up an ornate horn which had been handed to him by an attendant. "Well, that's that. . . . We can thertainly never be accuthed of being ungrateful." He unscrewed a plug from the small end of the horn and held his finger over the opening. Excitement began building.

"Good people of Ithatar and of our wonderful, incomparable Urtha Majoria, I offer you all a toatht to declare our bithentennial thelebration offithially open." He removed his finger from the tip of the horn and held it aloft, as a stream of red wine poured into his open mouth. He guzzled several mouthfuls, and as he did the crowd let loose a deafening roar, the ground trembling as thousands of feet stomped their approval. The mayor wiped a sleeve across the droplets on his double chin, then waved both arms in the air. He turned, but the guests of honor ignored his obsequious bow as they strutted off the stage.

As the assembly began to disperse, Jotham felt a hard tug on the sleeve of his tunic. He looked down on Flaggon's hot, flustered face, his dark eyes sparking with anger.

"Come, come sor, I instructed you to follow me." Flaggon's voice quivered with indignation. "You are in serious danger here. It is never wise to go off alone. No good can ever come of it. . . . No good at all. We must leave immediately."

His grip did not loosen on Jotham's sleeve as he dragged him from the festivities, guiding him toward the far edge of the green. Jotham yanked his arm up to try and disengage himself from Flaggon's grasp.

"I forgot, that's all," he objected defensively. "I saw the crowd and I just wanted to find out what it was all about. I didn't mean to do anything wrong. You don't have to make such a—"

"Stop! Stand and declare your business!" A harsh snarl along with an oddly familiar stench cut Jotham off.

Behind them stood a grizzled soldier dressed in a greasy shirt of mail. A battered breastplate covered his rotund stomach. Much of his face was obscured by a sinister helmet with nose and curved side pieces. It was rounded at the top and sloped down to an upward curve behind the neck. Though his eyes were in shadow, Jotham could see thick lips pulled back in a snarl over his stained teeth. In his hands, he held a spear with its razor point steady, aimed directly at Jotham's throat!

Chapter Thirteen

Another soldier, a superior—judging by the red feather flowing jauntily from his headpiece—strode up behind Flaggon, his cruel eyes snapping. With a cold sneer on his handsome face, he drew his sword deliberately and pressed it purposefully into the dwarf's lower back. His dark eyes gazed lazily with the confidence of status. Flaggon grimaced as the point cut into his flesh. Refusing to give his enemy satisfaction, he drew his chest out, pursed his lips tightly and held his position. Flaggon's eyes flashed a clear warning to Jotham. They both turned to face their new threat.

The dark-complexioned soldier now standing behind them—not to be outdone in savagery—shoved his spear into the back of Jotham's neck, drawing blood. Jotham grunted, instinctively taking a half-step forward. He felt a warm trickle seeping down his neck and onto his tunic.

"Steady there, tall one," warned the captain, swinging the sword point toward Jotham's face, burning him with killer eyes. "Sirrah, what have we here? Insurrectionists, I'll wager."

"My thoughts exactly, my captain," the paunchy guard agreed. "I've been a keepin' my eyes on these two for hours, sir," he exaggerated. "I apprehended them for their suspicious converse and attire. I present them to you, sir, with my compliments." He drew his spear back and hit the ground with the end of the wooden shaft. He stood at attention, his right arm holding the spear rigidly at his side, angled away from his body.

"Well done, Braxxon. At ease." The red-plumed soldier gestured menacingly at Flaggon's thigh. "That, little knave, looks suspiciously like a sword. What say you to the charge of insubordination and disturbing the peace? You are, after all, carrying military weaponry." He grabbed Flaggon's beard, yanking his head up as he spoke.

"Speak up now, short one. I know your type, and I will have none of the cheeky truculence so common in those of your ilk."

During the captain's monologue, Flaggon had begun insinuating a silly smirk on his face, which grew increasingly wider as he spoke. Jotham stared at him incredulously.

The soldier's face grew red with indignation. "Do you find humor in what I say? I'll teach you proper respect, by the gods!" He drew back his hand.

Flaggon sniggered, rubbing his hairless dome, then worrying his red beard.

The captain slapped the dwarf's face resoundingly. "You insolent gnome! I will flay your skin from your bones!"

Blood began dripping from Flaggon's lip, but he ignored it, bowing deeply, affecting a posture of profound servility. He placed his hand carefully above the hilt of the sword hanging from his belt. "Ahh . . . if you will . . . ahh, permit me sor, I'll show yore excellence that . . . we means no harm and poses less danger. No, sor, we certainly does not."

"Easily said, corpulent midget, but you had better have means to establish your veracity or I will see you roasting on a spit!"

Flaggon, continuing to smile broadly, pulled the sword up by the strap attached to the hilt. As it came out the blade remained hidden in its sheath. The soldiers' mouths dropped open. "Ahh . . . you sees good sor, we are but humble members of a travelin' circus and do but plays at the fine arts of warrin'." He bowed as deeply as his round stomach would allow, scraping the grass with the hilt. "With me stature I can barely swing a loaf of bread much less a fine blade like yores." He pursed his lips deprecatingly. "We've merely stopped for the fortnight to help . . . ahh, celebrate the festivities."

The captain, reluctantly convinced, turned his attention to Jotham, "And what are we to make of this youngster's subversive garb? Surely you are aware of the prohibition against donning military dress by the citizenry?"

He waved his sword in Jotham's face then pressed the point against the metal links on the sleeve of his forearm. "My blade is convinced that your attire is real enough. Declare, squire, or it will be the worse for you. What proof do you have of your companion's protestations?"

Jotham's face blanched. He had assumed Flaggon's quick thinking had saved them. He began ransacking his mind for some satisfactory explanation. As the point pricked him on his elbow, he had a flash of inspiration. Adopting a similar lighthearted expression as his bearded guide, he inclined his head respectfully and pulled up the mail covering his arm. Underneath was the bright colored material of his bicycle suit.

96

"Sir, as he said, I'm actually a jester playing the part of a soldier." Jotham spread out his hands, smiling harmlessly. "You see, I don't even have a sword."

The red-plumed soldier stared at Jotham, his eyes narrowing. "Hmph! You speak poorly . . . even for a jester." The captain looked at Jotham quietly for several seconds. A bead of sweat ran down the middle of Jotham's back. The captain grudgingly sheathed his sword. "All right then, begone, the both of you, and take care how you act. I've drawn and quartered many for less." He spun on his heels and marched away. "Braxx, come with me."

With obvious reluctance the grizzled guard released his prisoners, but as he passed them he threw a dubious glare in Jotham's direction, "Hah! If you be a jester, then I'm the Queen Mother! If ye be not rebels, I'll take a bath in the river." Making sure the captain's back was turned, he poked Jotham in the stomach with the butt of his spear, then leaned over breathing garlic and cheap wine into Jotham's face. "Watch your step, you seditious pup. I don't like the looks o' you one bit. Take care, or I'll grind you and your little midget friend into the dirt like the filthy scum you are!"

Flaggon's eyes smoldered.

Jotham's skin crawled as he wiped the soldier's spittle off his cheek. The two remained in place until they were certain the guard had lumbered away for good. With a jerk of his forefinger, Flaggon signalled Jotham to follow him quickly.

They veered away from the commons and soon left the revelry behind. Then, taking a footpath along a stream, they headed into the woods and found the rest of the band waiting nervously next to a green pond. Abe was tossing pebbles into the slimy water while Bart and Carisa sat despondently on a hollow log, staring blankly at the surface. When they appeared, the three Paladins jumped up and ran toward them. Jotham could tell by the sparks in her dark eyes that Carisa was ready for a fight. However, to his great relief, before she had a chance to launch her fusillade, Flaggon headed her off with a wave.

"There's no time for that, m'lady; we be late as it is. I'm certain yore captain will be glad to explain everythin' on the way." He looked at Jotham's chagrined countenance, and a hint of sympathy softened the dwarf's stern expression. "He's done learned a valuable lesson in followin' instructions, I believe. 'Tis one you'd be wise to learn yoreselves."

Carisa looked frostily at Jotham but bit her tongue, marching stiffly in the lead alongside Flaggon. Jotham felt the sting of her unspoken indictments slashing him as they walked in silence.

The sun scorched them as they made their way up the steep mountain path. There was little breeze and no shade. The climb was exhausting. After two hours of a trudging steadily uphill, they pulled aside to rest by a winding stream. The Paladins, hot and sweaty, gratefully dropped down on the sparse grass. A large stone had long ago rolled into the stream creating a small, clear pool. The water flowing around its base bubbled gently, giving quiet voice to its successful course around the rocks. The four plunged their faces into the cold pond. Bart doused his whole head while Abe squirted a thin stream of water from his mouth toward the opposite embankment.

Flaggon knelt on one knee and took one handful at a time. "Ahem. Young sors and miss, not to be repetitious, but it is the better part of wisdom to always be cautious, even when takin' some refreshment." He gazed with obvious disapproval at Abe who was now lying on his stomach, cooling his forehead in the stream. "You have much to learn. As yore captain here has discovered, this is no game."

Carisa had pulled her hair back in a ponytail and was drying her flushed cheeks with the sleeve of her tunic. Ignoring Jotham who had sat down next to the dwarf, she stood with her hands on her hips facing Flaggon. "What I want to know is, when are you going to to tell us how we're going to get home?"

Flaggon opened his mouth, but Carisa continued her barrage. What had seemed like an exciting adventure at the beginning of the day, had quickly lost its romance during the hot trek up the mountain. Questions had been simmering inside her for hours, and once the lid was off, they spilled out furiously like lava.

"What are we doing in this place? What does Justar want us for and whatever it is, why can't his soldiers do it? Why drag *us* into it?" Her eyes grew red as she fought to hold the tears back. She had to stop when her voice broke.

Flaggon nodded his head sympathetically as if fully expecting this outburst. He held up a finger calmly and said, "Hold on, m'lady, while I take a drink from me bota." He unstopped the leather bottle and took a long pull. "Got's to whet the old whastle, as me granddaddy used to say." He broke off a hunk of bread and sausage, took a huge bite and after chewing deliberately, swallowed and gave his response.

"Good questions, those, though I has to warn ya, those I canna' answer I leaves to me King to explicate in his time and his ways. But first, I suggests m'lady that you sit and conserves your energy for the rest of our climb, whilst I talk." He drew his bushy eyebrows together and ran his fingers through his thick, red beard. "Now let me get me thots in proper order." He sat on the ground cross-legged, his eyes growing momentarily distant. "Many, many years ago, the Issatarians were known far and wide as mighty warrior monks."

Bart held up his hand apologetically. "Sorry to stop you, Flaggon . . . But you just reminded me about something Warrior said. Do you mind?"

The dwarf took a deep breath, his cheeks puffing out like those of a red bearded chipmunk; then he let it out slowly. His eyes flashed.

Despite Flaggon's reaction Bart pressed on, "Warrior told us that we were being commissioned as warrior priests. What's that? Is that the same as warrior *monks?*"

"Yes, they be the same. Some says it were wrong of Justar to puts them two callin's together. I just ignores 'em. What the King does is his business and I just tells 'em my callin' is to obeys me lord, not be meddlin' and worryin' in affairs beyond me. All's what I know—since I'm jest a warrior meself—is that priests has some kind of power, kind of magical, which Justar gives only to them." He rubbed his large red nose thoughtfully, his leathery face wrinkled in concentration. "It's got to do with speakin' words—there's more to it than that—but me granddaddy never told me, and I never asked."

Flaggon held up a stubby forefinger in quiet warning and took a long, hard pull from his bota. Further questions were obviously not welcome.

"Let me see . . . as I was sayin' . . . the peoples was famous. The nations trembled at them. They were 'holy terrors,' granddaddy used to say—the men as well as the ladies, mind you. Some of the women, I hears tell, were the bravest fighters. It's hard to believe it looking at them now." He opened his mouth to catch another amber stream from the opening in the leather bottle. Wiping his mouth with relish, he continued.

"As soldiers, they conquered many nations in the name of Justar the true King, and as priests they taught the peoples to loves and obeys him. But battlin' and priestin' is hard work and there come a time when they got tired of the fightin', the disciplin' and the rigors of the soldier's life. They had a council and a concordat was reached in which they decides to arrange truce with Ghnostar—the King's sworn enemy."

"But what about Justar, what did he say?" asked Carisa as she bit into a piece of cheese.

"Nothin'. That's the strange part. He knew of the conspiracy but he let the nobles go their own way. I s'pose he figured he'd warned them enuff about the Enemy's sly tricks and that if they wanted to ignore him, it was their decision. That's always been Justar's way. If it were up to me I would have strung them clever nobles up by their soft, lily white heels. But he didn't, the truce was signed and hostilities ceased." He took a drink, scowled fiercely and spat it out on the ground in an extremity of disgust.

"Ceased, that is, if you believe what Ghnostar and them pompous nobles says. They're dupes, the lot of them: soft in the head and soft in the body. Ghnostar talked them into surrenderin' their swords. Broke them all in a big ceremony he did."

"Their swords?" Bart asked incredulously. "They gave up their weapons?"

"Yah, every blasted one of them! Me granddaddy was there. He said to me, I recall his words exact: 'Glonney' he said—that's what he always called me—'Glonney, I never seen such a public display of utter stupidity in me life; they was acting like dumb-fool sheep. It was disgustin!' Those were his words. The warriors, most of them, except for the rebels of course, also gave up their suits of armor. And they had to swear an oath."

"What was that?" Carisa asked.

"They had to swear never to refer to Justar as King or put on their warrin' garb. It was considered disruptin' the peace. Can you believes it? Seems to me its high time their peace was disturbed."

"Wow, so that's why the guard almost arrested me this morning!" Jotham exclaimed, looking down at the fine metal links covering his arms and legs.

Flaggon jerked himself up, his face mottled and his dark eyes blazing. "The idiots be convinced the war is over! Jotham, sor, you heard them congratulatin' themselves on the prosperity brought by the truce, but it's a lie I tells you!"

Flaggon threw back his head and bellowed, "He's a liar! Ghnostar is a filthy liar!" The wild intensity in the dwarf's eyes frightened the Paladins. Flaggon continued, in a voice that was almost a shriek, "The truce is a rotten evil trick!" His voice cracked and his eyes grew red. Shaking his fist in the air, he screamed the words: "It's a lie!"

100

He stood clenching and unclenching his fists in a fit of frustration. The Paladins held their breath. All that could be heard was the sounds of the gurgling brook and Flaggon's harsh panting.

Speaking softly to himself, he murmured, "And I don't knows why he lets that dragon be! . . . He's the King! . . . I just don't und—" He caught himself, glancing at the Paladins, his red eyes brimming. He coughed, cleared his throat, then took a deep breath. "I apologize for the shoutin' . . . it's just that sometimes it does feels so nice and peaceful-like I'm almost tempted meself to believe them fancy speeches about 'peace, peace.' But it's not the truth . . . I knows better. So, sometimes I just has to shout so's I don't forgets it."

While the others had been staring intently at the dwarf, Abe had been throwing stones across the water. He took aim at a flower several yards away and tore the gold blossom apart. He turned his head to look at Flaggon. "What I want to know is, how you did that trick with your sword? On the way up here, Jotham told me you pulled the top off like a magician's trick."

Flaggon gave Abe a hard look. "It weren't magic, I can assure you. It were something Master Slimgilley come up with. I push this little knob-like thing here on the side and the hilt comes off. It weakens the sword a bit, but it's saved me skin more'n once, so's I think it's a fair bargain."

Abe came over to look at it, but Flaggon placed his hand over the hilt, quickly tied the loose wrist strap around the crosspiece and turned away abruptly. "It's high time that we be on our way."

For two more hours they trekked up the barren face of the hill, the path becoming slightly narrower and much more frightening as they wound their way up. The edge of the trail now fell away abruptly down to rocky outcroppings hundreds of feet below.

The four Paladins walked single-file, hugging the craggy, red clay mountain. Flaggon seemed unconscious of the danger. He swung his staff and whistled as if he were strolling in the park.

At their next stop, after pouring some water over his head, Jotham pulled Flaggon aside. "There's something else I just don't understand. Why were the people of Ursa Majoria so disrespectful of Justar if he is the true King? Didn't Slimgilley say that the prince died in a big battle against that dragon? If the King's son gave his life trying to protect them, why do they make fun of him?"

"Sor, that there is the sad thing. After the truce, that wicked serpent placed some kind of spell on the people so that now many actually believes

Justar is the one who is not to be trusted. Some (when they're in their cups, mind you) even says Prince Gabriel was to blame for the battle. And they goes so far as to say—and it hurts me to repeat it—that he deserved to die for attacking the dragon. The spell's so strong, they believes more what Ghnostar tells them than what Justar's Messengers says."

Looking up at the position of the sun in the cloudless sky, Flaggon motioned for them to continue their dusty walk up the mountain.

"They've all lost any notion of battle," Flaggon continued, talking over his shoulder at Jotham, who was keeping pace behind him. They're more like fat cows instead of warriors. Easy pickin's for the dragon, I says. You can't convince them that old snake is still up to his wicked mischief, stealin' away and imprisonin' people when their guards is down. Master Slimgilley has done his best. I tells him to save his breath, it's like talkin' to stupid cows as gots no ears or brains." He brandished his staff in the air. "Worse, actually! The peoples, from the nobles down, just laughs and goes on feastin' and pleasurin' themselves."

Jotham dodged a wave of Flaggon's staff. "Doesn't anybody listen?"

"Haah! . . . Hardly! The mothers (Justar forgive 'em) suckle their children on lies. They puts them to sleep with an asinine poem—forgive me language, sor—I hates to even repeats it, but it goes somethin' like this:

If we leaves Ghnostar alone
Then we will no longer moan.
If we choose to let him be,
He will let us all go free.
Yes, we're at peace

They repeats that stupid last phrase three times, then they ends by singin':

All hostilities has ceast.

Flaggon's face was red by the end of the little ditty. He uncapped his bottle, and took a long drink from it, washing the unpleasantness from his mouth.

"The children also have a silly game where they chase each other chantin': 'Igno-ore him and he'll igno-ore yo-ou' . . . I says it's not silly at all; it's plain dangerous." He shook his head furiously then angrily strode on, mumbling to himself. The others followed and bumped into each other when he stopped abruptly and growled gruffly to himself, "We were once known as a nation who sang. To think that dragon has stolen not only their courage but their songs as well. It's enough to make one . . ."

Jotham was unable to hear the rest. After that, Flaggon refused to speak another word.

Their legs were growing numb with weariness, and their faces were caked with dust and sweat by the time Flaggon gestured with his staff at a turn in the road. "It's on the other side of the bend, sors and lady. Step lively now; remember you are Paladins. But don't expect me to linger. I hates farewells." Pointing at Abe straggling behind, he told Jotham to wait for him; then, walking briskly on ahead, he disappeared around the bend.

A minute later, when the four turned the same corner, they were confronted with a huge iron gate with tall spikes piercing the sky. The Paladins' hearts dropped. Their bearded guide was gone!

Chapter Fourteen

The immense gateway was constructed of polished, marble blocks; its towering iron gate was bolted into the rose-colored stone with thick metal bands. It looked as though it could withstand a stampede of elephants. On either side, a thick wall extended in undulating curves as it followed the contours of the mountainous terrain. There seemed to be no other entrance to the castle, as far as they could see. The meandering wall curved gracefully, surrounding a turreted castle which gleamed a creamy rose-white, looming above them approximately 70 yards away. A large purple banner snapped regally from the topmost of its seven spires. The exterior wall had an aura of great age, as did the castle itself, but surprisingly, there were neither cracks nor moss on its smooth surface.

From behind the gate they could hear the sounds of water playing on stone and gentle voices blending delightfully, accompanied by the mellow strumming of stringed instruments. Occasional laughter broke through the lilting strains. It made the Paladins smile and want to sing along. They pressed their faces to the iron bars searching both for the source of the music and their vanished guide. There was a momentary lull in the singing. Then, a faint jingling and the methodical clip clop of horse's hooves caused the four to draw back from the gate.

Carisa glanced over at Abe and motioned for him to adjust his disheveled tunic. Following her lead, the other two slapped the dust from their clothes and ran their fingers quickly through their hair, trying to prepare themselves as best they could. From a dip in the stone path leading down to the castle they could see downy, white feathers approaching, bobbing in mid-air. Carisa squinted her eyes, mystified by the strange apparition. As it came closer she began to make out the tip of a tall lance to which the jaunty plumes were affixed.

With a stately grace, the scarlet and white streamers on the helmet of a knight dressed in a gleaming silver suit of arms emerged over the top of the knoll. He was astride a muscular war horse, splendidly white except for splashes of black between keen flashing eyes and on each foreleg. She pranced proudly, snorting and tossing her silky white mane. The disdainful toss of the horse's neck and mane caused Jotham to look at Carisa. He smiled to himself as he glanced at her long, thick hair.

A medium-sized shield was slung from a hook on the knight's saddle and on it was emblazoned Justar's coat of arms. Bart observed that three gold crowns were in the top left corner which, he recalled from Glumpuddle's books on heraldry, was the "dexter chief point." "It is the most important section on a shield," Glumpuddle had explained to him. It was on a field of white intersected by a crimson band. Inscribed on the bottom right corner was a severed serpent's tail.

Unable to restrain his studied expertise, Bart whispered to Jotham, "Interesting that the shield is 'party per bend,' don't you think?"

Jotham glanced sideways at him. "Wha-at are you talking about?"

"The coat of arms. The field is divided into two equal sections with a band running from the dexter chief to the sinister base."

Jotham squinted at him incredulously, but before he had a chance to respond, the silver knight reached the gate. With no discernible direction, his horse executed a masterful half turn spin and came to a standstill, muscles quivering. The knight removed his helmet, holding it in the crook of his arm. His shoulder-length hair was blond; his age, indecipherable. Through the gate his light brown eyes leveled a cool, dispassionate gaze at the four Paladins standing nervously shoulder to shoulder in front of him.

After staring quietly at them for several moments, he slid his lance into the two rings on his saddle, removed his glove, and held his hand out toward them. "State your business and proffer instruments of safe passage."

Jotham looked blankly at the others. He felt utterly foolish and inept. With a questioning glance, he turned to face the knight who was gazing at him impatiently, his face hardening.

"Come, come this is no time for child's play, the royal protocol demands authorization, and I am sworn to obtain it from all alike, whether friend or foe." A frosty chill gathered like storm clouds in his eyes. "Present them now or be run off the King's domain at the point of my lance!"

Bart suddenly understood. He quickly began untying his leather wallet. "Hurry, he wants to see our scrolls!"

Jotham pulled his out first. He passed his through the bars to the warrior who took it with his ungloved hand. Unrolling it carefully, the knight nodded as he read, a slight smile softening the stern line of his mouth as he glanced at Jotham. The others handed him theirs. When he was finished he slipped them into a large pouch. After scanning the remaining scrolls, he nudged his horse gently with his knees. The mare took several stately paces backwards; and as she did so, the knight replaced his helmet and glove. He slapped his hands together loudly and shouted, "Open wide in the name of Justar the King!"

The gate swung open like a swan gliding over water, and as it did, the white steed reared on its back legs, its forelegs flailing. The knight struck his broad chest with the flat of his clenched fist declaring: "Enter, Paladins!" The war-horse pawed the air and whinnied loudly as she jerked her large head up and down, causing the bit and bridle to burst out in its own jangling salute.

The four nervously followed the prancing animal down the hill and on toward the palace. On their left they passed by a walled garden from which they could see water splashing from a tall fountain. Voices could also be heard joined in a melodious sonnet. Beautifully manicured grass surrounded the castle. Carefully trimmed hedges and strategically cultivated bushes and flower beds lent the grounds a sense of peaceful repose.

Justar's castle seemed to drink in the sun's warm rays, reflecting them back in pearly beams. Large, spacious balconies and ornate, leaded-glass doorways spread across the upper stories. Elegant and intricate carvings decorated the exterior of the building. The tall, narrow window on the lower story provided a symmetrical counter point for the balconies above. It was a beautiful building, perfectly balancing beauty and grace.

They crossed a wooden drawbridge, their deliberate steps echoing hollowly underneath, walked through a tall arch, then into a large receiving area. The archway was fantastically engraved with wild beasts cavorting among garlands of flowers and grapevines, interspersed with seven coats of arms. On both sides, they were flanked by two eight-foot stone statues of lions clawing the air majestically.

The knight dismounted and handed the bridle to a page who had appeared on silent feet. As his horse was led away, he held up his hand motioning for the Paladins to sit on a mahogany bench resembling a sumptuously carved church pew. As he strode away, his armor clanked dully off the tapestry covered walls. After he turned a corner, the sounds of metal against stone retreated until all was silent. After a moment they heard a heavy door opening ponderously and thudding shut. It sent reverberations through the stone floor.

Abe looked apprehensively at the others who were deep in thought. His palms were sweaty. He rubbed them together nervously. "What do you think Justar will be like?" he asked, anxious to break the tense silence.

"It sounded like he's pretty old. He might be kind of like our grandpa, except with a long beard," Carisa suggested.

"Naah," objected her brother, also glad to relieve the tension. "I'll bet Justar is really big, really muscular and tall. You know, sort of like a huge NBA center."

Jotham looked askance at Bart, shaking his head in disbelief. "Do you remember what Warrior looked like? He didn't look like any football or basketball player I've ever seen, and I don't think his leader would look like one either."

Though intent on feigning confidence, Jotham was terrified. He felt suddenly small and weak and completely overwhelmed. He was this group's leader! What could Justar expect of him? He was only a kid! (although he had no idea how old he really was now).

And why are we so stinking little if we're supposed to fight some battle?

Unbidden, the memory of the ordeal at Trisha McCauley's house, now seemingly eons ago, flashed through his mind. He cringed at the recollection of that humiliating affair. Once again he was overwhelmed with fear and embarrassment at his own inadequacy. The same desire he'd had outside Trent's door began rising inside him: he wanted to bolt and get away as fast as he could.

Before he could act on the impulse, the shuddering of the floor beneath him indicated that the heavy door was being opened once again.

There was silence for several long seconds. Then, the sound of sandals could be heard slapping slowly toward them. Hearts pounding, the Paladins stood up as one. Then, from around the corner came the reassuring shape of their friend Flaggon and beside him, walking somberly and looking less tall than before, came Slimgilley, their host. Both were now wearing white tunics with a gold border.

"Mr. Slimgilley!" Abe exclaimed. "How'd you get here?"

"Flaggon! Where'd you go?" Carisa ran up to him and threw her arms around his shoulders. The dwarf's face turned a deep red.

Slimgilley cleared his throat and pulled his elongated body and shoulders back so that he resembled a long bow. "Ahem . . . my King has appointed me to bring you into his throne room."

Flaggon's leathery face was creased with a toothy smile. He gave them a broad wink, then held his stubby forefinger up to his lips.

"I—we that is, had business with the King," he whispered, raising his eyebrows importantly. "But mind now how you act, you are in one of the castles of the Great General! 'Tis a great honor and one not to be taken lightly."

Slimgilley nudged the dwarf with a bony elbow. "Aren't you supposed to bring something?"

Crestfallen, Flaggon bowed hastily, and bobbing his head, hurried down the hall. Slimgilley looked them over carefully. He straightened Abe's tunic and adjusted Bart's belt. When he was satisfied with their appearance, he gestured for them to follow.

As they turned the corner and approached an imposing, studded door, the silver knight stepped sideways, planted his legs wide and pulled out his sword. Its hilt was at waist level, flat side toward the Paladins.

"The Great General bids you enter," he announced.

"Do we all go in together?" inquired Carisa, looking anxiously at Slimgilley.

"Yes, Justar wishes to speak with the entire band."

As he stared up at the massive doorway, Jotham was crushed by the terrifying realization of their puny smallness, their foolish attire, and the total inappropriateness of their condition. He drew back overwhelmed. Unable to hold back any longer, he voiced the question which had been gnawing at him since Warrior's commission. "But why are we so young? If we're here to fight, why have we turned into weak little kids?" His voice wavered and cracked.

Slimgilley looked startled. "I did not know . . ." He pressed his lips into a wide, narrow line. "I see . . . I see. Ahhmm." His eyes began to glow with understanding. "Yes . . . well, the King has many ways, and not all comprehensible to one in my humble position." He rubbed the bridge of his nose, "But if I were to offer my most modest opinion, it may have somewhat to do with a little saying we repeat to our children: 'When you are weak with no strength to seek, make his name your song and you'll be strong.'"

Slimgilley levelled his gaze at them. "The King pays special attention to the feeble—that's one of the reasons Ghnostar rose up in rebellion, or so I've been told. He loathes the weak. In any event, the King has a special place in his heart for children in particular." He rolled his eyes and shook his tousled mane. "Can't say as I comprehend his predilection myself. They drive me to distraction, present company excepted of course." He held out his hands. "Be that as it may, some suspect that Justar particularly enjoys using young ones to show up that wicked dragon, who prides himself on his great strength."

"But why—?" Jotham began. He was interrupted by the huge door opening before them.

The Paladins entered the great room together with Slimgilley keeping a discreet distance behind them. Their mouths fell open in astonishment. The square room was about half the length of a football field in both length and width. Along the back wall were 12 imposing, stained glass windows depicting dramatic battles. Between each were gorgeous tapestries in brilliant hues. They stretched from floor to ceiling and were lavishly embroidered with animals of every variety in breathtaking scenery. The artwork was so exquisite and so intricate that they seemed to be more like photographs than cloth and thread. They pulsated with life.

The vaulted ceiling about 30 feet overhead was elaborately carved and painted—a panorama of festivities in which people and creatures were romping about in joyful celebration. In the center of the vast mural, a smiling Justar was surrounded by small children holding hands and dancing in circles, as young animals frolicked around his throne.

A thick strip of purple tapestry lay on the floor, intersecting the huge room. Along each side, at attention, was a phalanx of hundreds of knights in full array. They were resplendent in gleaming suits of armor of gold, silver and bronze. These mighty warriors held tall lances at their sides, shafts to the floor, angled away from their bodies. Something about their presence made the knees of the four children grow weak and trembly. The sheer weight of the knights' splendor was so heavy, it almost drove them to the floor.

The knights' faces held the same fearless, almost ferocious intensity as Warrior's. A shiver ran through Carisa as she walked past. She tried not to look at them, but her eyes kept being drawn to their exquisite suits of armor. There was incredible variations in their styling and accents. Apparently, uniformity was not of great importance to the Great General. As her gaze strayed up from a glittering breastplate, she was shocked to see that this knight was a woman. Looking at the glowing soldiers more carefully out of the corners of her eyes, she began to realize how many of them there were. Their faces held that same wild boldness and tenacity as the men's. An aching thrill of longing flashed through her. She felt suddenly flushed and her pulse quickened.

On the raised platform in front of them sat seven thrones, empty except for the largest one in the middle. It was stunning in its golden symmetry and simplicity. Along its curved top, 12 gems shone, each the size of large brilliant walnuts, except that the star sapphire in the center was twice as big, radiating a rainbow of indigo beams. Three ornate posts rose from the curved back of the throne. From each shone a resplendent diamond as large as Warrior's fist. It was crafted ingeniously to appear as if the King were seated in the center of a gorgeous crown.

As the Paladins approached, their attention was riveted on the King. He was dressed in a tunic which resembled theirs, although from the chest to the knees it was covered by rows of writing which Jotham surmised were names. He wondered fleetingly if his was included. The King's hair was a pristine white and fell in thick locks to his shoulders. His beard was of the same color. He appeared neither old nor young. There was both the fire of youth in his eyes as well as the stillness of many years. They were indescribably beautiful, a golden hazel, dusted with flecks of green and blue. It reminded Jotham of the sun sparkling on emerald ocean waves. On his head rested a simple three-pronged gold coronet, encrusted with a band of diamonds along its edge.

Gazing into his face, they were transfixed. His eyes sparkled with such joy and delight that it made Jotham want to burst out in tears and laughter at the same time. Jotham was torn between wanting to hide and wanting to run up the steps to fall at Justar's feet. The longer Jotham looked into those golden eyes, the more confused he became. He tried to look away but couldn't. A heat seemed to be entering into him and melting him inside. He could neither move nor speak. Tremors ran up and down like electrical currents through his body. Strangely, he felt his right hand begin to shake uncontrollably.

Suddenly, his knees gave way and he found himself on his face before the King. The three others fell prone next to him.

From behind came the searing clang of a sword being unsheathed and the silver knight's voice: "Justar, your Paladins salute you!"

110

Chapter Fifteen

The silver knight's commanding voice resonated off the granite walls and imparted strength to their bodies. Still lying prone, they were able to lift their heads and look up at the Great General. Justar's face was aflame with delight. His smile glowed, almost blinding in its brilliance.

He lifted his hand, raising his scepter. It was three feet long, solid gold, with two rows of gems spiraling up the shaft. At the top was a curiously engraved knob. As Justar inclined it toward them, they could see that it was the gentle face of a lamb. On the opposite side was the open mouth of a roaring lion.

"Stand, my Paladins!" The King's voice rang like the penetrating peal of a cathedral bell, entering into them and causing them to vibrate. Whereas his representatives had spoken with firm authority, Justar's voice was absolutely distinct—it had the undisputed quality of majesty. It seemed to contain the mighty resonance of the oceans and the terrifying ferocity of a savage beast on the prowl.

The four found themselves on their feet facing the King. It felt to Jotham as if he had been lifted from the floor by an unseen hand. Justar had spoken and his body had responded, although there had been no apparent decision on his part to obey.

Jotham felt conflicting emotions. He was at once drawn by an irresistible urge, yet repelled by a stark terror. It was as if a mighty Bengal tiger were looming before him ready to spring, its impassive face gazing silently at him, its luminous eyes compelling him to approach.

Oh God, help me. Who is this King? Jotham moaned to himself. Immediately, a warm flood of reassurance poured through him. He was aware that it was emanating from beyond Justar. A strong, gentle voice, which he recognized immediately as the one he'd heard in his high school cafeteria, whispered inside him: "All is well. You can rely on the King as

111

you rely on me." Though partially comforted, Jotham was certain this powerful King was still to be feared.

King Justar rose from his throne and walked down the stairs holding his scepter toward them. Instinctively, Jotham knew what to do. He took a step forward and placed a kiss on the face of the lamb. As Jotham's lips brushed the scepter, a surge of power pulsated through his body. At the same time, his muscles and bones grew hot, and strangely, felt like they were expanding. The trembling in his hand grew stronger and spread up into his arm. He glanced in embarrassment at the others. He was surprised to see that Carisa's entire body was shaking. Yet she seemed completely unconcerned and at peace. Bart and Abe were standing motionless next to her.

He watched Carisa kiss the lamb and was amazed to see a light encircle her. As it enfolded her, she appeared to grow several inches and age by as many years. When the same thing occurred to the other two, Jotham realized that Justar was releasing his power into them. He glanced down at his arms and noticed that his wrists were now exposed. He quickly unrolled the folds of the cycling top, lengthening the sleeves by another pleat.

The Great General retracted his scepter and from within his tunic removed four scrolls. They were parchments like the others, but these were secured with a wide purple band. "You have been called and granted authority to come before me. Prepare now to receive your commission."

The Paladins felt suddenly light-headed—nearly intoxicated. The room seemed to be drenched in perfume. With every word from the King's mouth, a delightful fragrance was released. The smell of hyacinths, roses, jasmine, and honeysuckle flowed around the Paladins, combining delectably with orange blossoms and cinnamon. Beginning with Jotham, King Justar handed each of them a scroll, which they placed in the pouches hanging at their waists.

"I have chosen you to go on a mission for my royal honor. It has been given you the task of conquering four strongholds taken captive by the forces of my enemy, Ghnostar. You are to reclaim them, in my name, setting free those imprisoned under his dread dominion."

His scepter lightly touched their heads. "I hereby also anoint you into the priestly order and sanction your use of my name."

He turned the scepter so that the lion's head now faced them, inclining it in turn so that it rested on their lips. There was a faint sweet taste then their lips began to tingle and burn, almost as if a hot pepper dipped in honey had been placed on their mouths. Jotham felt his entire face flushing with the prickling warmth.

"You now go for me," Justar continued, "and represent my interests as my select emissaries. You may speak now for me, and to me, for others." He turned his head, lifting his hand in a commanding gesture. Immediately, Flaggon materialized, cradling four weapons in his outstretched arms.

"You are heading into battle. Ghnostar's army is well-equipped, so you must be prepared for war. You go to deliver; they will come to destroy." Justar's eyes began to glow with white-hot passion. It seemed to the Paladins that as he continued speaking, they were being showered with sparks of fire that cascaded from him.

"Be alert and on guard! Though all around you there may be shouts of 'peace, peace,' heed it not. It is deception. Make no mistake, yours is a battle to the death. You have been called into a contest where no quarter will be asked or given. Hence, I present you with your weapons of war."

Standing in front of Carisa, the King held out to her a crossbow with a sheath containing over a dozen razor sharp metal bolts. She took them and strapped them over her shoulder. As she did, her eyes met the King's, tears of pride sliding down her cheeks.

"Hold out your hands, my dear," King Justar commanded in a gentle whisper. He rested his palms lightly on hers and then withdrew them. Carisa stared down at her open hands, which felt as if they had been infused with fire. "I give you mercy." She looked up at Justar questioningly. Without saying a word he put a crystal vial in her hands. Then placing his hands over hers, he closed her fingers around the fragile, green container, smiled and said, "You will heal in my name."

Bart was given a long bow, approximately five feet tall and a quiver, from which protruded a score of lethal arrows. He took the quiver and slung it across his back. Justar placed his hands over Bart's eyes and then touched his ears, declaring, "To you I grant discernment. You will have eyes that see and ears that hear."

A sad smile came across Justar's face as he handed Abe a long-handled battle ax with a strap to sling over his neck. Abe tossed it from hand to hand. Its weight and balance felt good to him. Unexpectedly, Justar placed his arms around Abe's shoulders and hugged him tightly. He whispered something in Abe's ear; then placed one hand on Abe's chest. "And you . . . you will feel what I feel."

Nodding to Jotham, the King handed him a long, black bull whip with an ornate ivory handle. Justar extended his hand, placing it on top of Jotham's head. An electric tingle sped through his body, followed by a gentle sweetness which settled over him. Jotham's right hand grew still.

"I give you authority. You will lead in my name," he told him.

Jotham's heart swelled with excitement, and his face flushed. The compassion in the voice of the King touched something that Jotham had closed off when his father had left home. He felt torn. He wanted to openly accept the King's blessing, but there was a stubborn guard in his heart that refused to budge.

Then out of the corner of his eyes he looked at the others standing by his side and a wave of protectiveness swept over him. His chest suddenly felt very heavy, and his eyes stung. As the pressure in his chest increased, a resolution welled up inside him. He took a solemn vow: *Justar, you are my King, I will serve and follow you—to the death.*

Somehow, Jotham knew that King Justar had heard and accepted his oath of allegiance. Although the tightness was lessening, he wished the resistant barrier would disappear as well. It was keeping him at a distance from his King, but there was nothing he could do to take it out of the way.

The Great General's melodious voice drew Jotham's attention. "Children, if you are willing to take me as your King and serve me faithfully, then I will give you your heart's desire." They each knew, immediately, what that would be: a safe return home.

Carisa began sobbing softly next to him. Other than her quiet cries there was a total stillness in the imposing hall.

Jotham dared not lift his head; then he heard Justar's voice whispering inside him: *Jotham, know this—I am for you—I have chosen you; confide in me.* There was a smile in his voice.

The gracious words entered Jotham's mind but bounced back off the barricade around his heart. He heard them but was unable to feel their full weight. A paralyzing sense of unworthiness settled over him. *No! It can't be! I'm nobody . . . just a stupid kid. Justar doesn't know who I really am. . . He wouldn't say those things if he really knew."*

Cold beads of sweat broke out on his forehead.

With a solemn, penetrating gaze Justar looked over the small band, their weapons in place. "Mark well, these are mighty instruments of war. They are granted to you both for blessing and battle. Now kneel to receive your battle swords. With them your armor is complete."

Flaggon again approached, their swords lying on his arms. The four knelt down on one knee and bowed their heads. Their King placed a gleaming broadsword in each of the Paladins' outstretched hands.

"I present you with your swords for battle. They are strong and true. But place not your trust in them, rather in he by whom they are bestowed." His voice flowed over them like honey. "Use them boldly and obediently, and with great courage. Do not fear—I will go with you."

An expectant hush settled over the room as the Great General stepped backward up to the dais. Then, in a voice soft as fresh as snow—yet as sharp as crystal—he inquired: "Paladins, do you choose to fight for me?"

Their throats finally free, the four exclaimed in loud unison: "Yes, our King, for you we will fight!"

Jotham lifted up his face to look at the King, but when he raised his eyes, Justar and the castle were gone! He looked around and saw the others kneeling beside him by a small brook at the foot of a rocky mountain. On the grass in front of them were small shields embossed with Justar's scepter: the face of a roaring lion, its mane flowing into the shape of a lamb's head. Their swords were sheathed at their sides.

Something pungent shocked Jotham into alertness. His nose wrinkling in disgust, he jumped to his feet. A revolting smell like rancid meat was winding its way toward them on the warm breeze.

He looked around wildly.

It was the same stench he remembered smelling at Trent's house. He pulled out his sword and spun around, fear rising within him like a cobra's head.

Chapter Sixteen

Bart and Abe gaped at Jotham. Carisa remained motionless, a slight smile on her lips. Her natural inquisitiveness seemingly blunted by the dramatic events which had just transpired. There was a sweet vacancy in her face as though she had recently awakened from a delightful dream that she was still intently savoring.

Bart looked quizzically at him. "What's up Jo? Where are we? How did we . . . ?" His eyes narrowed, and he turned to peer at the mountain. "Did you guys hear that? It almost sounded like . . . a voice. It was weird, I couldn't make it out, but it seemed like it was giving a warning."

Jotham and Abe shook their heads. They could hear nothing, but the odor was becoming more repulsive. The brothers stood next to each other, looking at the path which disappeared in a bend less than 100 yards away.

"Whadda you think it is?" Abe asked, his fingers pressing his nostrils shut.

Jotham stared at the winding path. "I'm not sure. All I know is that last time I smelled something like this it was bad news."

A breeze blew toward the mountain. Jotham sniffed the air again. "It seems to be getting a little better. Maybe it's only a dead animal or something up ahead."

"Can I bweethe now?"

"Go ahead, it's safe, you wimp," Jotham grabbed his brother around the shoulders and kicked his feet out from under him, sending Abe sprawling on the grass.

Bart glanced at them and then at himself in surprise. "Hey, we've gotten bigger!" he exclaimed, raising his arm and looking in relief at his sleeve, now riding above his wrist. "I was worried I'd be stuck forever as a little squirt."

"Come over here you guys, look at this," Carisa called to them softly, holding up a strip of cloth she had found inside her scroll.

They gathered around her and ran their fingers over the material. It was fine, white linen torn from a larger piece. Sprinkled liberally over it were rust-red splotches. Jotham placed it up to his nose. It reminded him of the smell of old iron.

Carisa stared pensively at the cloth, awareness dawning in her brown eyes. "I think it's dried blood."

"Ughh. You're kidding!" Abe exclaimed, tossing it back to her.

Bart broke open his scroll. "Let's see if we have them too!"

The three others found similar strips in theirs. Carisa sat still, gazing quietly at the linen, then at the shield at her feet. Her fingers gently stroked the expensive material.

"What do your scrolls say?" Bart asked, unrolling his parchment. "Check to see if they're the same as mine."

As he began to read, the words: *Go to the mountain! Go to the mountain!* rushed into Jotham's mind and began an insistent clamoring. He tried to ignore them, unfurling his scroll and reading along silently. Their scrolls read:

Paladins, King Justar salutes you!

To battle you have been chosen;
For battle you have been born.

Fear not, mighty warriors brave,
My power before you goes to save.

I am with you, in darkest night;
My presence yours, be strong and fight.

On your way, my words obey,
Read them faithfully day by day;
Then ev'n the darkness will be bright,
For, you will see, they give you light.

If you choose to fight as one,
I grant to you, your battles won.
Promised victories are hereby sealed,
If you place your trust in me your shield.

117

I sent my Prince to take my name,
And earn great honor and acclaim.
So send I you under my name,
To gain a crown of joy and fame.

You go as priests to speak for me,
Showing mercy to one and all.
You go as warriors to fight for me;
No mercy show to those who fall.

You are called as lambs to be,
Bold as lions, set captives free.
Fulfilling promise of ancient lore;
A band of four goes off to war.

Henceforth emblazon'd on your shield,
The symbol of my power you're called to wield.
With fearsome charity serve your lord,
And bright will be your great reward.
Giving honor ev'n as honor bound,
With eternal glory you shall be crowned.

Jotham stared at the words on his own scroll. He gingerly placed his fingers over them. The letters were unlike anything he had ever seen. They seemed to have an inner life of their own. The script had a slight glow around the edges, and as his eyes focused on each sentence, they appeared to levitate off the parchment. He touched the words with his fingertips. They pulsated lightly.

Jotham looked away toward the mountain which was again pulling at him.

Bart replaced his scroll and linen strip in his wallet. "A band of four goes off to war,'" he quoted. "Sounds good to me." He swaggered a bit as he tossed Justar's shield over his right shoulder.

Abe smiled, relishing the solid weight of his battle ax. "I like that 'bold as lions, set captives free' part." Swinging his ax in wide arcs around his head, he yelled, "Look out—here come the Paladins!"

"Cool it," admonished his older brother, feeling a little giddy with excitement himself. "From what Flaggon told me on the way to the castle,

Ghnostar's been pretending that he's stopped fighting to trick the people. Kinda' like when we run three running plays, setting up the other team for the long pass. He's convinced the people that as long as they let him alone they don't have anything to worry about; and when they're nice and relaxed, he grabs them."

As Jotham was speaking, he'd tried to suppress the command which was echoing more and more emphatically in his mind. At the same time, the rancid, burning smell returned. Anxiety began whirling inside him. Something terrible was happening around the bend, and it was his responsibility as leader of the band to speed the others into quick action.

Jumping to his feet, he shouted, "We need to go to the mountain right away and help someone in trouble!"

Carisa stood up, a troubled expression on her face. "What's the matter, Jotham? Who's in trouble?"

"I don't know, I just have this feeling that something is going on over there and we need to go there quick. . . . Come on we've got to hurry!"

Bart looked at him skeptically. "Hold on a minute. We're supposed to go and free some castles that Ghnostar has captured. I'm not sure that heading toward the mountain is the right direction." He pointed to a range of gray hills south of them. "If you look over there, you can just see the top of a tower over that summit."

Carisa nodded her head. "You're right, Bart. I think we need to head toward that castle."

Bart was looking at the mountain, shaking his head; he had a vague premonition of danger. Abe was clearly undecided.

"Fine!" Jotham snapped. "If you guys don't want to help, you can go on ahead. I'll go by myself!" Turning on his heels, he strode angrily toward the winding trail at the base of the mountain, shouting over his shoulder: "I'm not going to stand around arguing . . . but remember, Justar did make me captain!"

"But didn't the scrolls say we should go as one?" yelled Abe at his brother's retreating back.

"Yeah, they did," Jotham yelled back. "So get moving!"

Abe shrugged his shoulders and began following his brother.

Carisa huffed, "We *are* supposed to go together, but I think Justar meant we should agree on where we're supposed to go, first." She followed Abe and Jotham, her teeth clenched in anger. "I just knew choosing him to be the leader would go to his head."

Coming up alongside Abe, she said, "Your brother's too stubborn for his own good!"

Abe grimaced, "That's what Mom thinks too."

When they turned the bend, they saw that Jotham was heading into the mouth of a large cave.

"Wait up, we're coming with you," Bart yelled.

Jotham kept walking into the opening. Without turning, he waved his arm in an imperious gesture, demanding the rest to hurry and catch up.

The three began running toward the cave. As Abe lowered his head to step into the cold, damp interior, it almost seemed to him as though he were walking into a monster's open mouth; his skin prickled at the thought.

The Paladins stopped to listen; the melancholy plip plop of drops falling into icy pools was the only sound in the dark interior.

Abe put his hand over his nose. Carisa edged over toward her brother and whispered, "Be glad you can't smell. It's like something's been dead in here for a long time, and it's big!"

"Hey, I found a torch!" Jotham yelled, grabbing a club from a bracket on the wall. It was as thick as Justar's scepter and its tip was daubed with pitch. Removing the flints from his pouch, he struck them until a spark ignited the torch. A yellow light flared, illuminating the recesses of a large cavern. Gray stalactites hung from the ceiling 40 feet above their heads, and in several places stalagmites had merged with the formations from above, creating a pantheon of glistening pillars. The trail led between the misshapen forms, like grotesque sentinels guarding their path.

"We should be ready for anything," instructed Jotham, as he unsheathed his sword.

"Oh man, I don't know about this. . . ." Bart muttered, his sword at the ready, a dreadful fear chilling him.

The torchlight created eerie shadows and reflections among the wet calcified stone. Occasionally, Bart thought he detected reflections of amber light along the side walls. They disappeared as soon as they caught his eye. His heart began to race with apprehension. He clutched his sword. His knuckles were white.

Jotham came to a fork in the path and hesitated. After walking a few paces down one, he turned back and did the same down the other. "Shhh," he ordered. "I think I hear someone this way." Holding the smoky torch in the right-hand opening he yelled, "Is anyone in here?"

"No one but us bloodthirsty goblins," intoned Bart under his breath.

"Be quiet!" his sister hissed.

Taking several steps forward, Jotham called back to the waiting Paladins. "Follow me—I'm sure I heard someone in here—but be careful and stick together." The polished steel of his sword sparkled, bouncing prisms of light off the walls on either side. The tunnel was almost wide enough for the band to stand shoulder to shoulder.

"How's the smell?" asked Bart to Abe who was walking in front of him.

"Worse—like a toilet overflowed in here."

Carisa motioned for them to catch up to her. "If we get separated, we'll be in big trouble." She slipped on a slimy patch on the ground. "I wish Jotham would go a little slower."

"That's his normal speed," commented the younger brother. "He always walks like he's in a race."

Stepping over a slick puddle, Bart grumbled, "Yeah, but he's the only one with a light."

As they progressed deeper into the tunnel, they began noticing round holes in the base of the tunnel walls, each approximately two feet in diameter. The temperature was dropping noticeably, and their footing was growing increasingly more precarious. Abe and Carisa were counting the strange openings, so they didn't notice that Bart had fallen behind. They had counted 17 so far.

Bart was the first to hear it: a soft scraping sound, like that of a limp body dragging heavily on the ground. He twisted his head but was unable to see anything in the darkness. The sword in his hand felt clammy and very heavy.

His scalp began tingling. He continued walking, more quickly this time. The sound was closer. He was almost certain that it had now been joined by others. Jerking his body around to face whatever was behind him, he stopped. His pulse was racing out of control. The sluffing came to an abrupt halt.

Peering into the blackness, he inched backwards toward the rest of the band. His hand on the sword hilt was now slippery with sweat. Again, he could hear the dragging sounds, and they seemed to be speeding up.

"Something's following us!" he yelled, his voice trembling. He turned and began running toward his companions.

The torch several yards ahead spun, heading back toward him. As the luminous halo came closer, angry snorting and hissing began filling the tunnel.

Bart's blood froze.

The torch had revealed their pursuers.

He heard a scream of terror careening down the walls of the passage—then realized it was coming from his open mouth.

Staring at him was a mass of amber reptilian eyes in a tight cluster on the path behind them. The torchlight was dancing madly in scores of large, hungry eyes. From the round hole closest to him, the head of another huge, horned lizard was slithering out of its den. Its long, forked tongue flicked wickedly at him, venom dripping from its snout.

The hair on the back of his neck stood on prickly ends. Cold shivers raced down his spine at the terrifying sound of grinding teeth and snapping jaws; razor-sharp fangs were being honed for a frontal attack.

He took a step backward. His foot hit something solid.

He screamed again.

Chapter Seventeen

Bart was about to swing his sword around when he realized he'd bumped into Abe, who was planted directly behind him. Abe didn't respond. His body was rigid, hypnotized by the lizards' ominous glares. His sword dangled from listless fingers.

Jotham ran toward them holding the torch high. The hissing grew louder and more threatening. The flame revealed a dozen milky-green lizards about 15 feet in length. Twin rows of sharp pointed horns ran down the length of their backs, ending at the tips of swinging, pallid split tails. They were cracking their dripping fangs together, emitting hoarse growls and furious hisses. Their menacing catlike movements and synchronized sweeping of their lethal tails was mesmerizing.

As Jotham stared at them, a terrible power began to overcome him, rendering him defenseless.

Suddenly, he knew what was happening. "No!" he screamed, as he jerked his face away. The words ricocheted off the tunnel walls like a spent cartridge. The lizards had been holding him fast with their yellow eyes. Their unblinking, pink-lidded gaze, combined with their slithering, sensuous approach was a hypnotic stratagem to lure their prey into waiting jaws.

The monsters came to an abrupt halt. Abe and Bart blinked; their eyes grew suddenly wide with horror. The huge lizards were within inches of their legs. Abe jumped back convulsively, knocking the torch from Jotham's hands. It hissed as it hit the cold, slimy stones and went out. Thick darkness came crashing down on them with the force of an ax-head.

"Abe!" Jotham shrieked as the torch rolled, striking Bart's heel.

Bart leaped forward, his sword cutting the air in wide arcs as he bent down, fumbling madly for the torch. Carisa grasped frantically for her sword. Jotham felt the heavy leather coil at his side. With a quick tug he pulled the whip loose.

"Move back," he ordered, making room for his whip. He snapped it in the direction of the nearest reptile. There was a loud popping sound and a brief flash of light. The shuffling of retreating claws and low growls confirmed that he was holding them at bay, at least temporarily. He snapped it again, but it was awkward; the low ceiling made it difficult to deliver a strong blow. There was another dull explosion, and again the reptiles were driven back.

Bart continued his desperate search for the wooden handle. His fingers were now covered by cold slime.

"Ouch!" he exclaimed, making contact with the hot end of the torch. "I've got it!"

As his fingers closed around the wood, he sensed, rather than saw, sharp teeth lurching toward his face from a side opening. He jerked back, but not before a sharp fang sliced across his eyebrow and cheek, peeling the skin to the bone. He screamed in pain and felt the muscles in his face grow immediately numb.

"Bart! Are you okay?" Carisa cried out.

"Yeth," he slurred, his lips unresponsive.

The sounds of hissing drew nearer. Carisa felt a menacing tendril lick at her calf. She swung her sword, felt its edge bite into leathery hide, and heard an angry snarl of retreat. Another lizard made its attack, leaping up at her chest. Its snout hit her shield, but its claws scratched sharply along the mail covering her forearm, slashing her wrist as they slid down her hand.

Sparks were showering in all directions as Bart tried desperately to set fire to the torch with his flint.

Finally, the flame caught and light exploded into the passageway. A reptile less than a yard from Jotham's leg drew back, its jaws still open for the bite. Jotham swung down, slicing its tongue off. The thin forked string of red muscle flopped and twitched on the cold floor. Another reptile thrust its snout out of the closest hole and greedily swallowed it.

Jotham took the torch from Bart's hand, grimacing at the sight of the blood streaked across his friend's face. Bart's back was to the other Paladins as he swung his sword in vicious swaths, holding back the next charge. Jotham motioned for Abe to take the torch.

"It's my fault," Jotham panted. "You take the torch and lead the way; I'll stay here with Bart and we'll use our swords to hold them off. Hurry! And keep your shields up."

Abe made a sound as if he were going to argue. Jotham cut him off, thrusting the light at him.

"Go!" He commanded through gritted teeth. "There's another room up ahead, now move!"

Abe and Carisa took the lead while Jotham and Bart, their swords jabbing and slashing, felt their way backwards. The pallid monster in the lead was clawing its way boldly toward them, its long split tongue flicking possessively closer, already seeming to revel in the salty taste of their blood. Their feet slid on the slick floor as they inched away from their pursuers.

A long, thin tongue darted out at them again. Jotham swung his sword but it was withdrawn before he could connect. The lizard's eyes seemed to narrow with increased confidence. It grew dangerously still; then, without warning, it sprang forward, its ravenous jaws closing in on Jotham's face. He smelled the fetid warmth of decayed flesh and saw large yellow curving spikes slicing toward him. Taking a half step back, he blindly thrust his sword up and under the creature's lower jaw.

There was a sound like hard leather being struck; warm spittle sprayed his cheek, but his sword was unable to penetrate the scaly hide. However, the lizard pulled back, rearing its head, snorting and growling deep in its throat. The other lizards joined in, hissing and roaring their obscene contempt.

"What's with your sword?" Bart cried.

"I don't know." Jotham was groping backwards and feeling its edge with his thumb. "It felt really sharp before. It's somehow lost its edge!" He grabbed Bart's arm, "Next time use yours."

As he was speaking, a cluster of lizards in the front of the pack began to charge forward. Their eyes filled with yellow hatred, intent on finishing off their quarry.

"Bart! Jotham! Get in here!" yelled Carisa several yards behind them.

Jotham looked over his shoulder and saw Abe and Carisa waving at them from a large entrance. "Come on!" he yelled at Bart who was preparing to swing at the onrushing creatures. "Let's run for it!"

They turned, racing toward the torchlight. The sounds of panting and claws skidding along the slick floor followed them, moving with increasing speed.

"Hurry!" yelled Abe. "Follow me!"

They ran up alongside Abe and Carisa as they entered a large cavern. The air was considerably cooler. Up ahead they could hear a deep rumbling; behind them the growling was becoming frenzied.

Abe swung the torch around the cavern. "I see light ahead!" he yelled.

The four began to run toward the flickering light and the rumbling noise.

Carisa's eyes widened in horror. The furious hissing sounds were now coming from around them as well as behind!

"Swing the torch over here!" she shouted.

The jerking flame illumined snarling, salivating snouts protruding from rows of circular holes at irregular intervals along the wall of the cavern. They were in the middle of the voracious reptiles' central den, and the mammoth lizards were surrounding them.

They were trapped; there was no place to run.

Carisa shrieked as two beasts with lidless eyes slithered beside her.

Jotham and Bart jumped toward her, jabbing their swords at the startled creatures. Bart's sword made contact first, slashing across the monster's open snout, while Jotham struck a blow across the horns on top of its head. Despite their dullness, their swords partially penetrated the tough hide, leaving narrow rivulets of dark blood on the pale skin.

Undaunted, the beasts snapped and growled even more furiously. Six more were now drawing near from behind. They moved forward tenaciously, like hangmen intent on pulling the noose tight around the helpless necks of the condemned. As if by mysterious command, the creatures stopped running and began to plod toward them, a scornful gleam in their glistening eyes. They appeared to be enjoying the Paladins' fear as much as the prospect of their impending meal.

"Have your swords ready," Jotham cried.

"Move in close! Carisa, stand next to me. Bart, you and Abe stand behind us." They formed a tight, defensive square, swords pointed in all directions.

Abe, his back to his brother, swung his torch toward the row of lizards in front of him. They backed away. Less than ten feet behind the threatening creatures, Abe could see light reflecting darkly off rushing water.

"There's a river back here," he hissed. "That's where the noise is coming from."

Jotham looked quickly over his shoulder.

At that moment, the largest lizard, almost 20 feet long, reared back its huge snout, hissed like a boiling kettle and lunged at the Paladins' tight formation.

Carisa was ready. She had been fitting a sharpened steel bolt into her crossbow with shaking fingers. As the beast charged, she drew in her breath, closed her eyes and released the catch, sending the arrow hurtling down at the lizard's head. The bolt slammed into its snout with such force that its point erupted out through its throat, plunging the arrow's metal tip deep into its soft underbelly. A bellow of pain pummeled its way around the cavern. Those nearest the flailing reptile flung themselves upon it in a bloody orgy.

Jotham looked at Carisa in surprise. "Nice shot!" he yelled.

"All right!" he shouted to Abe who was holding the lizards behind them at bay with his torch. "We're gonna make a run for it, but wait for my signal."

Jotham jabbed at a fat reptile with blood smeared on its open snout. "On the count of three, we're going for the water and swim like crazy. Let's hope they don't follow."

Carisa nodded and grabbed his hand.

He began quietly, "One . . . two . . ." Then with a wild yell, "three!"

Abe thrust his torch at the thin line of beasts between them and the water. Jotham and Carisa spun around, running behind Abe and Bart who were swinging their swords in front and to the sides. Caught by surprise, the lizards drew aside, unwittingly making an opening for their escape.

Bart and Abe were the first to plunge into the water. When Abe jumped in, he had the presence of mind to make sure that he was holding the torch high. Carisa and Jotham followed close behind.

The water was so cold it sucked the air from their lungs as if they'd been punched in the stomach. Their entire bodies went instantly numb.

Up ahead Jotham saw that Bart had grabbed onto a rock and was straining to hold on. As Jotham spun past, Bart lost his grip and slipped backwards into the water. Their arms and legs were deadened, their chests painfully constricted; the current carried them relentlessly toward a narrow opening.

"Watch your heads!" Jotham screamed. His words were lost in the rumbling of the frothy current.

Abe plummeted through first, holding aloft the light, followed by Carisa close behind. As he was dragged into the tunnel, the low roof stripped the torch from his hand. It fell into the cold, dark water with a heart-breaking hiss, plunging them into total darkness.

The current's speed began increasing, and the thundering became a deafening roar. The walls of the narrow channel began to shake. The Paladins were tossed head over heels as the water spun them about, their arms and shoulders scraping against the rough rocks.

Careening around a bend, Abe saw a light. His jaws were so numb he was unable to cry out. It wouldn't have made any difference—the roaring was now so intense a stick of dynamite could have exploded undetected. The force of the stream pulled him under, throwing him against the submerged boulders. Abe was flung sideways. He twisted his body away from the jagged outcroppings along the edge of the channel; then without warning, the bottom fell out and he was screaming as he dropped through space.

Seconds afterward, Jotham also saw the light ahead, and Carisa's head bobbing in front of him. Then it disappeared completely. Before he had time to yell her name, he was propelled through a narrow opening into a blinding light. He shut his eyes and immediately felt himself falling, surrounded by a pounding torrent of water, hurtling downward at terrifying speed.

Chapter Eighteen

Their free fall was finally broken by a small pool of blue-green water that seemed to have no bottom. As Jotham plunged down, down, he heard a muffled crash above his head. He began kicking and flailing his numbed arms madly in a desperate attempt to stop the momentum of his descent. Slowly, he began to thrust his way upward, the weight of his armor pulling at him like a leaden anchor.

Finally his face emerged. He opened his mouth and took in a huge, rasping gulp of air. His chest and arms ached with pain and exhaustion. Several yards ahead of him, Carisa and Abe were dragging themselves onto a grassy slope surrounding the small lake. Jotham's listless arms struck the water with little effect. He forced his spent muscles to pull him toward his companions. Finally, he felt slick weeds slapping at his feet. With a few more feeble strokes he was at the edge, clawing up next to Carisa, who was on her stomach, gasping for air. Abe lay on his back, his face white, his lips blue and his chest heaving.

Hearing a loud sucking breath behind him, Jotham turned to see Bart's red face streaming up out of the water.

"You can make it!" Jotham yelled hoarsely. The muscles in his face felt deadened with the cold. Bart's long arms made better progress than Jotham's, and soon he was at the pool's edge. Jotham reached out to grab his friend's hand and pull him out of the water.

Within minutes the exhausted Paladins were lying on the soft carpet of grass, letting the hot afternoon sun warm their fatigued bodies. Jotham's muscles were shaking. As he lay on the ground, a stupor crept over him. Before any of them were able to utter a word, they had all fallen asleep.

When Jotham opened his eyes, his clothes were completely dry, but he was nonetheless shivering with cold. The sun was setting and a cool breeze had arisen. He stretched his muscles, stiff from lying face-down on the ground. After rubbing some of the soreness out, he felt a dull ache in his stomach. He was famished.

"We've gotta find a place to spend the night and something to eat too," he informed the others.

Carisa was up on one elbow staring at a clump of trees. "Orange blossoms! I thought that's what I was smelling!" She jumped to her feet, wincing at the pain in her arms and back. "I could eat a bushel!"

She glanced over at Bart, who was rubbing his right cheek groggily. It was swollen and streaked with a large purple and dark red bruise. A circle of yellow was also forming around his eye. A jagged cut arced in an ugly red crescent from just above his eyebrow to the top of his lip, which was swollen and severely misshapen.

She gasped and fell down by his side. "Oh Bart . . . Bart, your face!"

Icy fear congealed Jotham's stomach as he walked over. Carisa glared up at him. "Look at what you did! It's your fault! If you hadn't been so stupid and stubborn back on the path, this never would have happened!" Her eyes overflowed with angry tears as she wiped her brother's warm forehead with the edge of her tunic.

Jotham looked helplessly down at the two. His cheeks were flushed with shame. He knew that Carisa was right. *Way to go, idiot! You almost got your best friend killed!* He gazed miserably at Bart's mangled face, wishing it had been himself. Jotham cleared his throat, but the words stuck to his tongue. He knew that if he started to say what he really felt, he'd start crying himself. Finally, he was able to croak out: "I'm sorry, Bart. . . . I should have listened to you guys."

At the sight of Jotham's reddening face, Carisa softened momentarily. But when she looked back down at her brother, her eyes again hardened into angry knife points. "Yeah, you were wrong! And Justar was wrong too for putting you in charge!"

Abe ran up to them, his pouch and hands overflowing with peaches, oranges and cherries. "Come on! There's a cottage up ahead and it's empty! And the fruit is delicious."

Carisa helped Bart to his feet. He stood, swaying slightly. His face was ashen and his one open eye was glazed. She placed her arm around his waist and walked past Jotham, ignoring his outstretched hand.

The cabin was made of cedar logs and smelled as though it had been recently cleaned. On the table was a note of welcome. It invited any and all weary Paladins to make themselves at home and was signed by their friend Flaggon. The table was set for four, and in the center was Flaggon's unmistakable contribution: a large, round loaf of fresh oatmeal bread with a bowl of honey beside it. A kettle of stew was bubbling over the fire in the flagstone fireplace. The smell sent a sharp pang through Jotham's stomach.

Carisa led Bart over to one of the four beds that had been prepared for the cottage guests. Bart fell back groaning. The inflammation in his face was getting worse. His right eye was now swollen shut. Streaks of vermilion and black had turned his face into an evil mask.

"He has a fever," Carisa muttered to no one in particular, feeling his forehead. "Abe, please bring some water." Noticing that Abe was eating out of the ladle, she added caustically, "Bart needs some food *too,* you know."

He filled a clay bowl and brought it over quickly along with a cup of water. Stung by her anger yet hoping to conciliate her, Abe murmured, "Be careful—the stew's kind of hot."

She nodded coolly.

Abe and Jotham sat down at the table and began wolfing the stew and bread, the tense silence broken only by the scraping of metal spoons against clay. While they ate, Carisa gave small spoonfuls to her brother, who swallowed painfully. Although she looked famished, she refused to take any for herself. The stiffness of her back and abrupt movements spoke volumes. Her unspoken rebuke drained all their pleasure from the meal.

After several minutes, Jotham walked over beside the bed and sat down, tentatively, on its edge. "Carisa?"

She refused to answer.

Jotham continued, "Maybe . . . Well, I was wondering if you could try the bottle Justar gave you."

"What bottle . . . ?" Her confused gaze looked past him, then focused into a point over his shoulder as understanding came. She looked at the wallet at her side, and her eyes widened. "Of course . . . Yeah. You're right!" she gasped. She fumbled inside, then pulled out the green crystal cruse. "I should have thought of it myself," she murmured, trying to cover her embarrassment.

Abe brought some cloths from the kitchen, and Carisa poured a tablespoon of the red liquid onto a strip. The fragrant smell of perfumed olive oil mixed with other spices wafted up around them. She dabbed it on Bart's wound. With another cloth that she had moistened with cold water, she wiped away the sweat on his flushed face.

Bart opened his eyes and attempted a lopsided smile. "Feels good . . ." His eyes closed and very quickly the sounds of deep, rhythmic breathing confirmed that he had fallen asleep.

Without saying a word, Carisa walked over to the table and grimly finished two bowls of stew and several hunks of Flaggon's brown bread.

Jotham remained sitting by his friend. He placed his hand on Bart's forehead and nodded, but waited till Carisa was finished eating before saying, "The fever's broken."

Carisa jumped to her feet, hurrying quickly to his bed. Jotham stepped back and sat down next to Abe on the third bed. It was apparent that Bart's temperature was near normal. The swelling and discoloration had also greatly improved. However, an ugly reddish black circle still surrounded his right eye.

"Thanks for reminding me about the bottle," Carisa murmured flatly, glancing at Jotham. She again wet the cloth with water and laid it on Bart's forehead. She sat down, her back to the two brothers.

Jotham pointed to the remaining bed. "You'd better get some rest, Abe; you never know what's gonna' happen tomorrow." He glanced at Carisa's stiff back. "If you want, I can stay up with Bart," he offered.

"I'll be all right," she responded dabbing at Bart's eye with the cloth.

Abe and Jotham lay down. Although he felt weary, Carisa's hostility and his own remorse had driven sleep from Jotham. The coarse woolen blankets were unable to overcome the chill which permeated the room and had entered into him. It had apparently affected Abe similarly. Unable to lie quietly any longer, Abe leaned over the side of his bed and reached for his battle ax. He tossed it from one hand to the other, testing its balance.

Abe ran his fingers over the handle, again noticing the symmetrical row of holes running along its length. They were all the same size, except for one at the end which was twice as large as the others. The handle was a hollow tube and resembled a flute. Abe lifted it to his lips and blew tentatively into the largest hole. A rich, woody tone filled the cabin. He had played a recorder at school, off and on (although mostly off), but he was soon improvising a lilting folk melody which Jotham had never heard. The tune seemed to be perfectly suited to the wild promise and danger of their surroundings.

Jotham looked over at his brother who was blowing into the ax handle, eyes closed, and his forehead creased in concentration. He let the music simmer warmly over him, delighted by its sweetness, yet awed at his sibling's unexpected virtuosity.

"Not too shabby, guy," he said.

Abe kept playing.

His curiosity overcame him and Jotham asked, "Where'd you learn to play like that, man?"

Abe opened one eye, raising both eyebrows, looking as mystified as his older brother.

The haunting throatiness of the instrument comforted Jotham, cleansing some of the shame that had seeped into his bones like a winter's sleet. He slowly began to relax as Abe drew from the instrument a soothing lament. He was playing it like a master, making it weep and brood and exult in turn. Soon, Jotham had fallen into a deep slumber. Shortly thereafter, Abe laid the ax down and also fell asleep.

They were sleeping so soundly that neither heard Carisa quietly whisper Jotham's name, nor see her tiptoe over to his side, hesitate a moment as she looked down at him, then return to her bed.

* * * * * * * *

Well past midnight, the sounds of rhythmic breathing and the occasional crackle and pop from the fireplace were all that could be heard from inside the cottage. The only light was cast by the dying embers. From its feeble glow, had the Paladins been awake, they would have seen two leering faces pressed against the glazed window panes; their hairy, grotesque pug-snouts contorted in a mask of raw hatred. Their red eyes were focused on the ax lying on the floor near Abe's bed. Their claws, gripping the cracked, wooden sill, shook. They snorted disgustedly, gargling and snapping at each other for several minutes. Finally, after an angry bark, one of the creatures abruptly spread its leathery wings and lurched upwards, landing heavily on the roof. The other soon followed, huffing resentfully.

Throughout the night, they raked the dark sky with their wicked eyes, sniffling and cackling, flapping their veined wings and hopping impatiently from one taloned foot to the other. Their blunt, hairy tails twitched spasmodically while they waited. As a thin, grayish light began spreading over the distant hills, they began gleefully to chatter and snigger. Against the horizon, they could see the silhouettes of seven bat-like bodies with large bulbous heads approaching at breakneck speed.

Chapter Nineteen

Carisa struggled to open her eyes. She felt like her eyelids had been glued shut. Something horrible was happening to her brother, and she was helpless to prevent it. Her head and neck were being held back by a terrible weight. An awful force was holding her against her will, and she couldn't break free.

Her eyes flew open. "Bart!" she screamed.

Her heart was throbbing uncontrollably. With terror-filled eyes she made a sweeping survey of the room. She lay back with a flood of relief when she saw her brother and the others stirring next to her.

"Hey, what gives?" Bart inquired, blinking bleary eyes and yawning loudly. Carisa looked intently at him. All that remained of his injury was a dark reddish blotch under his right eye. But, when she looked closely she noticed a cloudy film across the pupil.

"I had a terrible dream that you were being kidnapped by two huge bats. They were pulling you up into the air with long, disgusting, hairy tails; and at the same time, the biggest one was scratching you in the face with his claws."

She shuddered at the memory. "I couldn't do anything. I was paralyzed, like a statue or something. It was just horrible."

Bart swung his legs over the side of his bed and gingerly got to his feet. "Sounds like you were dreaming about Ghnostar's gang." He looked over at Jotham, "What were they called?"

"I think Slimgilley called them Argaks, or Kharks."

Carisa broke in, "No . . . that wasn't it. . . ." she thought briefly, "Ghargs! That's what it was. They sound as ugly as their names!"

Bart sat down at the table, cut off a large slice of bread and generously spread honey over it. He began taking huge bites. Abe got up and poured him a cup of frothy milk from a clay jug.

"Tastes like it just came from old Daisy this morning!" Bart said smacking his lips. "Where'd it come from?"

"It was in there," Abe answered, indicating a stone cupboard recessed into the wall.

"How are you feeling?" Carisa asked looking into her brother's eyes.

He stretched his face and jaw muscles, testing the wound. The thin, red welt was now only a barely discernible curve across his cheek. "Fine . . . really! Whatever's in your bottle is really potent! I'd like to take it with us and market it back home. We'd be rich!"

Carisa was unconvinced. "You sure you're okay?"

Bart rubbed his cheek. "Everything feels like it's back to normal." He blinked his eyes, then turned his head slowly, scanning the room. "Everything—except my right eye." He covered his left eye. "You look blurry, but I'm sure it'll be okay soon."

Abe sat down next to them at the table, Jotham following behind. "At least now that you're back to scheming about getting rich, I know you're back to your old self," Carisa said, patting her brother on the head. Jotham sat down and cut two pieces of bread, handing one to Carisa.

"Thanks," she said. Her eyes met his momentarily, then swerved hastily away.

Jotham decided to walk through the small opening afforded by her response. "Carisa, did you hear anything strange last night?"

"No, not really. All I remember is that weird dream."

"Were we in it too?"

Carisa stared at the milk jug, a sly smile creasing her face. "Yeah, you both were." She looked at him out of the corners of her eyes, "Although not terribly impressively, I should add."

Feeling like a prisoner stepping toward the guillotine, he asked: "W-what were we doing?"

"You and your brother were dancing."

Jotham's face went red.

"You're kidding!" Abe exclaimed. "Please don't tell me it was a polka—I hate that weird dance."

Jotham released a grateful sigh, for once delighted to have his younger brother cutting in.

"Actually, I think it was some kind of a jig," she answered, her face becoming serious. "It kind of reminded me of a Scottish folk dance. Come

135

to think of it, you weren't hopping around in kilts, so maybe it was Irish." She grinned at Abe, picturing the scene in her mind. "You were playing your ax-flute thing, though, and you know," she looked pensively at him, "it was driving those bat-monsters crazy. It was totally amazing."

Bart couldn't resist the opportunity. "What's so amazing about that? Last night it was driving me crazy too! If I hadn't been so sick I would have stuck a sock in the end of that thing."

"Don't pay attention to him, Abe," Carisa said. "He loved it, he's just too much of a macho-guy to admit it."

She scowled at her brother. "Bart, I think you've got a congenital defect that keeps you from being able to say nice things to people." Carisa patted Abe's shoulder. "Anyway, *I* thought it was really beautiful! I never knew that you'd learned to play so well."

Up on the roof, the nine Ghargs were scuttling about. They had perched themselves in a ragged line along the rounded crest of the peat moss roof. The largest bat, clearly the leader, was distinguished by a wispy, reddish brown beard, which formed a thin point in the middle of his barrel-chest. He was an obscene mutation: part goat, part monkey and part bat.

There was strong disagreement among the malevolent band. The insubordinate creatures seemed to hate their leader only slightly less than the cabin's occupants and were opposing his directions. The bearded bat suddenly shrieked in a frustrated frenzy. The other eight snorted in surprise, leaping into the air, their wings slapping loudly against each other.

Bits of dried grass and twigs drifted down to the Paladins' table. A clod of dark moss dropped into Carisa's glass. It was followed by piercing grunts and squeals. A deathly quiet settled immediately upon the four Paladins below.

Carisa jumped to her feet, gripping the table with shaking hands at the crescendo of angry snorting and growling overhead.

Jotham leaped up with her. "Ghargs?" he asked. Carisa looked fearfully up at the ceiling, her face ashen, her brown eyes wide.

She nodded her head numbly.

The others grew rigid as fear bore a hole through them.

The noise that followed filled them with dread, draining them of clear thought—it was the tearing sound of moss being ripped from the roof.

Curved, yellow talons slashed through it directly above their table.

The sickening oily stench, which now seeped through, was all too familiar. Jotham felt his stomach lurch.

The crash of splintering wood from the window behind them wrenched them free from their paralysis. They spun around to see a wrinkled snout quivering as it sneered at them through the broken shutters across from their beds. Deep in its throat, a contemptuous chortle burst out as the Gharg clambered through the smashed window. At the same moment, the Paladins heard the crunching sounds of the front door beginning to splinter. It was being scraped and struck repeatedly by sharp claws.

A palpable horror draped itself over them like a suffocating shroud. Panic began to well up inside the Paladins like a black geyser.

Carisa, undone, fell to her knees grabbing at Bart as she fell; then, covering her face, she began to sob convulsively.

The sight of Carisa sinking to the ground checked the crushing wave that also threatened to smash Jotham down to the floor. Hot rage rose up in his chest, and he ran toward the window, feeling for his sword. The only metal his fingers touched was the chain mail.

He came to a dead stop.

He'd left his sheath and sword underneath the bed farthest away from the window. He made a grab for the closest weapon, the whip which he'd left on the bench. He charged at the Gharg whose head and upper body were now squeezed through the window and into the room. With a lunge, Jotham snapped the whip toward the creature's bulbous head. There was a smack, a sharp explosion and a cloud of pink and orange flame followed by the sounds of bone and flesh spraying the floor and wall.

The explosive blast instantly brought the coordinated attack to a halt. When the smoke cleared, all that was left of the intruder was a greenish-black smear on the wall and several scattered pieces of charred flesh.

Jotham stared incredulously at the whip in his hand. A thin wisp of white smoke rose innocuously from its tip.

Bart had his arms around his trembling sister, who was staring incomprehensibly at the window. Soon, the sounds of snorting and the scrambling of claws could again be heard above them.

Bart, his face ashen, squinted at the roof. "Carisa, in your dream Abe's music drove the bats wild, right?"

"Y-yes," she whispered.

There was an odd light gleaming in his eyes. "Maybe your dream was really a message."

"What do you mean?"

137

"I'm not sure. . . . It's just a hunch." He turned to Abe. "Grab your ax and start playing for all you're worth."

Abe ran over to his bed and picked up the ax. Before putting it to his lips, he quickly wiped off the bits of burned residue, then began to play a fearless Highland fling. As the music danced its way through the thatched roof, the clawing ceased and was replaced by a hissing and snarling, followed by the wild scuttling of claws.

Abe's fingers froze.

"Keep playing," Jotham ordered, staring intently at the shaking beams and the confusion overhead.

As the pulsating tones filled the cottage, a heavy thud was heard on the path leading to the front door, followed quickly by another, then another. Odd flapping sounds were mixed with gagging and rasping coughs. The creatures seemed to be congregating in the front yard.

Bart slid over to the window. He peered carefully around the corner of the broken pane.

"What in the . . . ?" he asked in disbelief.

He drew in his breath, but didn't move. He was transfixed. The others stared at him, fear again beginning to grip them. Slowly, Bart's shoulders began shaking.

"Come over . . . here," he gasped, "you won't . . . believe this."

Jotham ran up to him. What he saw amazed him. Five Ghargs were stumbling around on the grass, staggering, tripping and blundering into each other. Two others were hunched over by a tree coughing violently. The music had apparently made their foes helplessly drunk.

The Paladins laughed at the comical sight. Two larger Ghargs careened off the roof and landed on their heads in the bushes along the path. They emerged completely disoriented. The Paladins giggled as their fearful enemies weaved and staggered on the lawn, their eyes spinning, mouths open in wide, inane grins. A tall, thin Gharg with baboon arms extending down to its calves, began walking in tighter and tighter concentric circles at an increasing angle, until it fell headlong into the flower bed. It lay motionless, groaning loudly. Slowly, it raised its hairy head, began to cough, then retched on the begonias.

The largest Gharg attempted a more dignified retreat. It flapped its veined, translucent wings, spun crazily into the air and thudded head first into a low tree branch. It crashed to the ground where it remained in a sitting position, its head bobbing foolishly back and forth.

After flapping their wings ineffectively, the creatures decided to wend their way into the forest on foot. Soon the front lawn was cleared of their attackers.

When the last one was out of sight, Carisa lowered her head. "I'm sorry for falling apart, guys. I was just . . . so scared . . . I thought those lizards were the worst, scariest things I'd ever seen in my life. But these . . . these Ghargs—they're awful!" She choked down a sob and stared at the floor. "I thought we were all going to die."

"Hey, it's okay," Bart consoled her, patting her bowed head. "We guys understand, don't we? After all, girls are the weaker vessels and all that. Right?"

Carisa's shoulders drooped further.

"Cut it out," Jotham snapped.

"I was only trying to make her laugh," he protested weakly.

Jotham ignored him, placing a hand on her arm. "Carisa, don't feel bad. To tell you the truth, I almost lost it myself."

He glanced toward Bart, glaring daggers at him. "I betcha if we could get your brother to give us a straight answer, he'd admit it too." Bart averted his eyes and sheepishly draped his arm around her shoulders.

"Sorry, Car . . . Jotham's right," he admitted.

Jotham looked up at the roof thoughtfully. "When they were coming through the ceiling, it was like my mind went totally blank." He stopped, then continued. "You know guys, I'm beginning to think that Ghnostar's troops are trained to use fear on purpose: it's like they want to hurt us not only physically but mentally too. If you think about it, they could have burst in all together. I bet they just plain like scaring their victims to death."

Carisa nodded her bowed head. Jotham wished he had the courage to place a comforting hand on her soft hair. "You don't have anything to be ashamed of, Carisa."

She slowly looked up at him, a grateful smile on her lips.

Abe was standing by the window and was the first to see it: a figure clothed in white approaching from the shadowy forest. As the man walked out into the light, Abe was surprised to see him bring his hands together. He was clapping. As he drew closer, Abe realized that it was a young man, sturdily built, with no sword, but over his shoulder he could make out the burnished tip of a tall javelin.

Abe blinked.

For a moment he'd been almost certain he'd seen the weapon convulse.

He squinted his eyes trying to get a clearer view through the shadows, but he could detect no further movement, if there had been one to begin with. The figure stopped and gave a loud yell.

"Hail Paladins!"

Abe waved the others toward him.

They looked out at their visitor standing on the path which led to their cabin. His tunic shone, bathed in sunlight.

Chapter Twenty

To escape the unpleasant smell that lingered on their front lawn, the Paladins decided to meet their visitor on the grassy knoll behind the cottage. Jotham opened the door and motioned for him to go around the back.

With the Paladins gathered warily around him, he introduced himself as Abner, a Messenger Paladin. He wore the same white tunic as theirs, except that his had an orange border. On his left shoulder, Justar's emblem was proudly embroidered.

Abner had long, black, curly hair which fell to his shoulders. His dark brown eyes were ringed with thick lashes. He appeared to be a few years older than they and had a husky, athletic physique. Judging by the size of his biceps, Jotham concluded that he would be a tough opponent. And to top it off, he had a brilliant smile which caused his entire face to glow.

Jotham was suddenly painfully aware of Carisa standing next to him. Uncharacteristically, she hadn't said a word since the new Paladin had arrived. He looked at her out of the corner of his eye. She appeared to be stunned.

A pang of jealousy lanced through him.

Abner's dark, smiling eyes seemed to be fixed on her as if she were the only person in the universe.

Carisa's conclusion was more specific: Abner was quite simply the most handsome young man she'd ever seen. He reminded her of how the virile young King David must have looked. Carisa felt her face begin to blush. Her chest grew heavy, and her breaths came in short bursts. She drew back a little, creating a safe buffer between them.

"I applaud your victory!" he declared, clapping his hands together and looking at each of them with warm approval. "You delivered the enemy's forces a sound defeat. I congratulate you in Justar's name. Take courage from your victory; you have shown great resourcefulness. Though you may feel weak, have confidence, you are stronger than you think."

His dark eyes rested on Bart's face. "I see you have already tasted the sting of the enemies' claws." He placed himself directly in front of Bart, touching the scar lightly with his fingertips.

"Paladin, bear your battle scar proudly. It is a badge of honor."

Although flattered by Abner's gracious words, thinking back over the frightening incident, Bart felt that it was actually more like a badge of stupidity. But he kept his peace.

Abner turned quickly, his smile flashing confidently, then resting pointedly on Carisa. Uncomfortable butterflies began stirring inside of her. "Justar has sent me to deliver further instructions: to be more precise—clarifications—about your first mission. Despite certain difficulties thus far, Justar is, nevertheless, pleased with your excellent progress. He understands that these problems are attributable to youth and inexperience and so has sent me to assist you in confirming the battle strategy."

He placed his hands warmly on Jotham's and Bart's shoulders and drew them toward him conspiratorially. "I remember my first battle," he said as he gazed away to the hills in the distance. "It was many years ago, but I will never forget it! It was both a frightening and a wondrous thing. There is nothing like the thrill of castle walls crumbling and the enemy routed . . . I envy you Paladins!"

His eyes flashed at Carisa, "The only thing better than the heat and excitement of battle is the dancing fire in the eyes of a beautiful woman." He lowered his arms and took Carisa's hands in his.

Her cheeks began to burn in earnest. She didn't know whether to be flattered or angry. His eyes had touched something inside that frightened her. She was used to being in control, but this was very different, and part of her was excited by the shift. It was clear that Abner knew he'd gained the upper hand and was enjoying it. The way he looked at her told her he was used to winning.

Jotham's jaw clenched. He imagined how gallant Abner would look with a smashed nose and a mouthful of splintered teeth. He seethed in silence.

Unconcerned about the rising tension, Abner pulled out a scroll from his belt. It had a wax seal with the imprint of a crown on it. "Let me read your orders:

Paladins, greetings!

On the eve of battle, I say this to you: do not look back;
but rather when you approach, go up through the back.
Use the weapons I've bestowed, with great caution and great care,
As you assault the dreadful enemy's lair.
Not in concert, but one by one they must be cast,
For their potency must needs last.

Ghnostar's forces are trembling before you.
They fear you, so do not fear them.
They will fall away like dry grass blown by the rushing wind.
They are cowards and cannot stand against your might.

Have confidence in your weapons!
Have confidence in what you've learned.
Be strong and take heart, for inside of you is a lion's heart.

Now rest and prepare for the morrow's test.

My messenger, Abner, speaks for me.
Receive his words and his gift;
It will render your armor complete.

When Abner finished reading he saluted and shouted, "Long live the true King!" There was a flicker of mocking humor in his dark eyes as he watched the Paladins awkwardly seeking to follow his lead.

He handed the scroll to Jotham, then turned to Abe with a wide grin, showing his white, even teeth. In one smooth motion, he reached over his shoulder and thrust the rounded end of a javelin at Abe, in mock assault. It grazed Abe's stomach, but was expertly restrained, coming to rest lightly against his tunic.

"Justar gives you this weapon as a reward for the wise and courageous use of your battle-ax. It will more than adequately replace what Justar first gave you. *That* was a weapon for a child." Retracting the shaft, he spun the javelin with an impressive flourish. "*This* is for a warrior."

Abner was now holding the javelin in front of him, on open palms. *"Abraham,"* Abner continued, "Justar wanted me to personally assure you of his recognition of your bravery and of his confidence in your continued signal accomplishments. But beware, the enemy has taken notice of your exploits. Always be on guard, they would like nothing better than to see you fall. They have a saying which would behoove you to remember: '*Corruptio optimi optima*—the corruption of the best is the best'." There was a strange light in his eyes as he quoted these words.

The older Paladins waited with eagerness for their messages of approval, but were deflated when none were forthcoming. The three were unable to stifle a surge of jealousy at their youngest companion's commendation.

Abe bowed his head humbly, then reached to take his new weapon. With a wide smile Abner drew it back, gesturing an empty hand for Abe's ax in exchange. Abe tossed it jauntily at the dashing Paladin and bit his lip to stifle a pleased grin when he received Abner's sturdy spear. An exciting, intoxicating strength coursed through him when he touched it. It was solid, intricately carved, with a curious red seam running from top to bottom and a wickedly sharp, polished brass tip. As he grasped it with both hands, a powerful, wild boldness seemed to flow into them.

"You feel it, don't you?" Abner inquired, staring at him solemnly for several moments. "I knew you would!" He slapped Abe on the shoulder.

"That is both a sign and token of a true warrior. The war staff has inherent power, but it can only be released in response to the power of a man of war." He slipped Abe's ax into his own belt. "It will serve you well."

Carisa stepped forward. There seemed to be no more need for a buffer. "Would you stay for lunch, Abner?" she offered hospitably. "I'm sure we have plenty of stew left over from last night."

Abner's smile again flashed brilliantly, enveloping her in a warm glow. Carisa felt her pulse quicken with a rush.

He reached out and gently took her hand. Her throat grew tight. "Any food from these hands would be a feast! But I'm afraid I must decline. Upon my honor, I have another urgent message, which I am pressed to deliver." He bowed low and kissed her fingers.

There was a delirious melting in her chest. Her knees trembled.

Jotham's fingers were aching to grab his whip and land a crisp blow on Abner's curled mane. A more violent image burst upon him: the messenger, face first on the ground, and Jotham on top smashing Abner's mouth into the rocky soil.

Turning to the others, Abner pointed east toward the hills swathed in gray mist. "Yonder lies the stronghold of the enemy, and there will be the path to your reward." Then, striking his chest with the palm of his hand, he declared, "Rest well, Paladins, for tomorrow is your day of glory!"

Instead of shaking the others by the hand, he grasped each of them firmly by the forearm, gave Carisa a deep, disconcerting look, spun on his heels and began running with sure, compact strides into the forest.

Carisa's head was spinning. She felt as if she'd just stepped off a carnival ride. Abner's eyes and smile had entered into her, but like a thief, had taken something with him. She didn't know whether to laugh or cry.

Bart stumbled over to his sister, placing a languid arm on her shoulders. "My, my, I wonder who made the deepest impression on whom?" Then, falling to his knees, and clasping her hand to his heart, he intoned breathlessly, "My darling, your beauty has smitten my heart! I will die unless I see the dancing fire of love in your eyes."

Carisa yanked her hand free and made as if to give him a resounding slap.

He cowered, gazing up at her theatrically, "One blow of your lovely hand, and I will be forever yours." Bart raised his hands to her, sighing profoundly. "Your anger, my sweet, is sweeter than the love of a thousand others."

"Boys!" she snorted angrily, tossing her head in disgust. "You wouldn't know what romance was if it bit you on the leg." She strode angrily toward the cottage.

"Mercy, my fair lady," Bart moaned, clambering after her on his knees.

"Give it a rest," Jotham ordered, wishing he could find something to hit. He thought about taking his sword and attacking a tree but decided against it. Instead, he opted to kick a stone in the path. It was not a wise choice. The stone was the protruding tip of a submerged rock. His toe exploded in a spasm of agony. He stumbled, but just managed to catch himself before falling on his face. Mercifully, Carisa had flounced haughtily into the cabin and didn't appear to have noticed.

They decided to spend the afternoon swimming in the river and dozing on the grass in the warm sunshine. At supper that evening, they discovered that the stew was even better than the night before. They cleaned out the kettle, consuming the remaining bread in the process. The sun and the water had clearly improved their appetites.

Lying on their beds after their filling meal and listening to the tree frogs and crickets chirping outside, Jotham remembered Abner's scroll and pulled it out of his pouch. He glanced over at Bart. "Abner said he came to help us with strategy for tomorrow's battle, but he didn't really say anything about it. Did he?"

"Yeah. He left pretty quickly. I was kind of expecting some kind of council of war. Weren't you?" Bart noticed the scroll in Jotham's hands. "Seems like there was something in the scroll he read about how we should attack."

By the light of their oil lamp, Jotham reread the instructions in the parchment. "You're right. I'd forgotten this line here about how when we approach we need to 'go up through the back.' I guess there must be some doorway at the rear of the castle."

"What was that line about using our weapons carefully?" Carisa inquired.

"Hey, you do have a voice!" exclaimed Bart, smirking at his sister sitting alone by the fireplace. "I was beginning to think that the ax wasn't the only thing Abner took with him when he left."

Carisa launched a frosty stare in his direction.

"Just ignore him, Carisa. If you get mad, you'll just encourage him," Jotham urged in what he hoped was a disinterested manner.

Bart rolled his eyes at him. "Speaking about getting mad, seems like there was someone else today looking pree-tty upset. For a moment—"

Jotham reached over and grabbed the neck of Bart's tunic, pulling Bart's face close to his. Jotham glared ominously at him for a moment, his eyebrows lifted in dire warning, then released him. Bart decided that silence, at least temporarily, might truly be—in Slimgilley's words—"the better part of wisdom."

As if there had been no interruption, Jotham continued his review of the scroll. "According to these instructions, we have to use our weapons 'with great caution and great care.' Then, it goes on to say that they're not to be used 'in concert, but one by one.'"

Abe, not wanting to be left out of the strategic planning, interjected his opinion. "I guess that means we're supposed to walk up to the back gate in single file and then let loose with our weapons one at a time. Right?"

"Sounds kind of like that to me," Jotham answered. He glanced over at Carisa, who was sitting by the fire, her chin cradled in one hand. The beautiful, dark veil of her hair was flecked with a shimmering glow from the

146

flames. There was a soft, golden fringe around her face. Her beauty made his throat ache. He fought to not look at her softness, the way the firelight danced and shimmered on her skin. The pulse in his throat began to throb painfully. He tore his eyes away.

Bart had seen him staring. "How about you, Carisa? What do you think?"

She didn't respond. "Jo, I'm afraid she is no longer with us. She's in dreamland with her dreamboat."

Jotham shook his head at him in disgust. He rolled over, his heart heavy in his chest. He had lost Carisa before he'd even won her. As he finally succumbed to slumber, his last conscious thought was of Abner's flashing white teeth which elongated slowly into beautifully dangerous, ivory spears.

Darkness had settled deeply upon the cottage. At midnight there was a blood-red flash which momentarily lit the Paladins' quiet forms.

No one moved.

It was followed by another.

Something horrible and menacing permeated the light. But the Paladins remained asleep. Soon, an unnatural reddish glow was oozing out from underneath Abe's bed. The red vein running along the edge of the war staff began to glow and expand as if an artery had burst and was hemorrhaging internally. Soon, the rod turned ruby-red and shone eerily. Insidiously, it began to pulsate in deliberate, undulating waves from the end of the shaft toward the brass tip. When the ripples of current settled in its sharp point, the brass head slowly opened and a flickering pronged tongue began smelling the air, in quick darts.

After a series of shivering convulsions, the staff metamorphosed into a sinuous adder, its scales a deep crimson hue. Silently, it began slithering toward the post at the foot of Abe's bed. It wrapped its coils around the leg, insinuating itself upward, until its scaly snub nose was inches from Abe's feet. It opened its mouth exposing two curved fangs.

It moved closer.

Abe twitched.

The adder froze, waiting in utter stillness. When there was no further movement, gently it pressed its two fangs into its victim's right heel. A spasm of pleasure rippled through the serpent's marbled skin; then, just as gently, the barbs were withdrawn, dripping yellow venom onto the blanket.

The silent attack was repeated on each of the other sleepers. Slipping down, away from Bart's pierced foot, it eased its way back under Abe's bed, grew cool, then still.

Darkness once again closed itself around the unsuspecting, poisoned warriors.

Chapter Twenty One

Jotham saw himself locked in a desperate struggle with the huge oak tree, which was writhing in serpentine movements. He pulled out his sword, and the oak instantly became a monstrous snake which spit and hissed at him. Before he could swing his arm, it wrapped itself around him in sensuous, merciless coils, squeezing the breath from him. Suddenly, he had the terrible sensation of falling from a precipice into a bottomless pit, carried down by the reptile's irresistible weight.

He awoke with a painful gasp when his head hit the floor.

Meanwhile, Bart coughed and groaned, flailing his arm as if to keep an attacker at bay. "Be quiet . . . Get away!" he moaned, rolled over, then dropped off the side of his bed, only a few feet from where Jotham lay.

The heavy thumps on each side of her woke Carisa. She looked down groggily at the two forms groveling face down on the floor. Jotham lifted his head and tried to focus his bleary eyes. Everything looked double. His eyes stung. He rubbed his nose and felt a sticky warmth on his fingers. They were covered with blood.

Carisa stared stupidly at him, trying to orient herself. She couldn't quite remember where they were. She had been startled out of the throes of a nightmare she couldn't recall and felt terribly thirsty and angry. "Jotham, you're bleeding," she managed to wheeze out in an accusatory tone, as if affronted by the stains on his tunic.

"No kidding," he snapped back, stumbling over to the bucket of water in the kitchen area, holding his head back.

Carisa felt a wave of nausea rising up inside her. Jotham's impatient response had triggered a rush of emotion, but she was so confused she didn't know whether to get up, punch him, scream or cry. Instead, she rolled into a miserable ball, holding her arms tightly around herself. She whimpered, tempted to cry out for her mother. Grimacing, she struggled to keep the contents of her stomach down.

Bart clambered painfully back into his bed, moaning softly. Apparently he didn't feel much better than his sister.

Abe squinted his eyes at the early morning sunlight streaming into the cabin through the broken window. He threw his arms over his face to block out the brightness. "Leave me alone," he muttered. "Just leave me alone."

"Shut up, Abe," Bart grunted, pressing his hot face into his pillow and covering his ears with both hands.

Jotham walked back to the three reclining figures, his face and hair damp. A few telltale pink splotches still remained on the front of his white tunic. "Stop laying around, it's time to get up and do our thing." He kicked the leg of Bart's bed. "Get up! You've overslept enough as it is."

The three dragged themselves up, muttering and complaining. Jotham was so intent on establishing his authority over the resistant band that he failed to take notice of a strange commonality of symptoms: they were all limping on inflamed heels, and they had dark red circles around their bloodshot eyes, resembling the haggard look of escapees from a prison camp.

He was also consumed with memories of Abner, a seething resentment toward Carisa, and to a lesser degree, toward the two others who were beginning to drag on him like heavy iron weights. He imagined himself walking out the door and into the forest alone. The freedom, quiet and solitude beckoned to him.

"So what are we going to do?" queried his brother, testily.

Jotham resisted an impulse to hit him and tell him to grow up and figure it out for himself. With concerted effort he held his tongue and stated, "Whoever is hungry can eat some fruit for breakfast, and then we'll head toward the castle. Abner showed us the way . . . You do remember, don't you?"

Abe shrugged, slumped down at the table and poured himself some water. After taking several long drinks, he dropped his head heavily on his arms and mumbled, "I don't want to go out. I don't feel so great. The stew must have fermented or something; I think I have a hangover."

"Don't you wimp out on us," Jotham barked. He looked around at the others who were shuffling about the room like zombies.

"None of us feels too terrific either. But our instructions were clear. We're supposed to go out today, and so we're all gonna' go!"

Giving orders felt good. *Maybe being the captain won't be so bad after all,* he told himself. *I'll shape up these lazy bums and we'll kick some butt today.* With a rush of adrenaline, his competitive juices began flowing. He almost felt normal—if it weren't for his burning eyes, the dull headache, and the annoying pain in his foot.

None of the Paladins had much appetite for fruit, so after filling their water bottles they made their way out the cabin. Looking for the path which headed south, Jotham, who already was several impatient yards ahead of the others, stopped and turned around abruptly. "Is there anything we've forgotten?" he asked with a confused expression. The three looked at him dully.

He snorted, "Thanks for your brilliant assistance. Remind me not to ask for your help again."

As he began striding down a foot path into the woods, Carisa's raspy voice interrupted him, "Wait!"

Again Jotham stopped, waiting in tense impatience.

"Didn't Justar say something about reading his instructions, 'every day' or 'day by day,' or something like that?" She rubbed her hand over her eyes as if concentrating was too painful for her.

"She's right," Bart concurred glumly, sitting down on a rock next to the path. "Besides, Abner—"

"Come on, get up you lazy jerk!" Jotham interrupted him. The mention of his competitor's name caused his blood to boil and threw him into an irrational fury. "You're just looking for an excuse to take a rest," he snarled. "And besides, there's no need to read the scrolls again. We read them already." He strode into the woods in a black rage, waving them to follow him.

"Is this *deja vu* or what?" Bart muttered. "Didn't we do something like this once before? . . . It didn't turn out very well, if my memory serves me." He fingered the faint scar on his cheek which had begun throbbing again. He slumped back down in a heap. "I just want to go to sleep," he moaned.

Carisa nodded her head sympathetically.

"In fact," he continued, "I don't know why we're even doing this. I think we just ought to find our own way back home and forget this insane battle stuff."

His sister dropped to the ground next to him. "I think so too."

Abe was clearly torn. He turned toward them and then looked at his brother whose back was barely visible through the trees. "Come on, guys.

151

You know the only way for us to get back home is to do what Justar said."

"Big deal! What does *he* know?" Bart grumbled. "If he wants to battle Ghnostar so badly, let him do it."

"I'm sure Justar knows what he's doing," Abe responded. "Plus, if we don't follow Jotham, who knows what worse mess we'll all wind up in. We might never find our way back home then."

Carisa stood, pulling her brother up by his tunic. "Come on, Bart," she agreed unhappily, "Abe's right. We don't have any other choice." She looked down at her leather pouch. "I don't think we have to worry about the scrolls either. Abner's instructions were pretty straightforward." She jerked her thumb in Jotham's direction. "Let's follow him before he gets us all hopelessly lost."

It was a hot, humid day. The warm air stuck to them like moss. After the Paladins traveled several miles in a southeasterly direction, their tunics were damp, and their suits of mail dragged at them like a thick chain. Sweat stung their eyes. The dense foliage blocked most of the sunlight, trapping the humidity underneath its canopy and magnifying the heat.

They came to a fork in the path. Jotham stood indecisively looking down paths which meandered into identical shadows.

Bart came huffing behind him. "Which way, fearless leader?"

Jotham evaluated the options. "I think that's the route." He was pointing left.

"Why?"

"Well, which do *you* think is the right way?" Jotham fumed. He was tired of the walk and of the Paladins' insubordination; Bart's notoriously bad sense of direction provided the perfect opportunity for Jotham to vent his frustration.

"I'm not sure," Bart said, his voice growing hard. "I just think we need to vote on it. Last time you rushed ahead we got into big trouble, and it's not gonna happen again."

Jotham's cheeks flamed; he opened his mouth, but then closed it, defeated by Bart's inescapable logic, and awaited the consensus.

Carisa stared at the path on the right and noticed a small animal scurrying toward them. Catching wind of the Paladins, it slid to a startled stop. The little animal stood up stiffly on its hind legs, its nose twitching suspiciously. It looked like a snowball with two dark eyes. After several seconds it dropped down on four legs and raced back the way it had come.

"I think we should follow him," she concluded.

Jotham sputtered. "That's insane. . . ."

"He's got to have more sense than you," she struck back. "At least he won't take us to a bunch of lizards!"

Her words sliced him like shards of glass. He wanted to grab her by the shoulders and shake her. Abner's grinning face flashed before him. He squeezed his lips closed and choked down his fury. The two others also opted for the path on the right. His jaw set, Jotham turned on his heel and led the way, his fists clenched in anger. Quickly, the footing became more treacherous. They were now having to clamber over rocks and tangled roots.

"What I wouldn't give for my mountain bike," panted Carisa.

"The way I'm feeling," Bart said, "I'd probably just flop over the handlebars and do myself and my bike some major damage."

Carisa looked at the scrape on her palm she'd gotten tripping over a fallen branch. "I just hope that our bikes are okay where we left them. I saved up for a whole year for mine."

"I'm just hoping that that crazy maniac didn't run over them with his stupid van," Abe muttered glumly. Pursing his lips in a tight line, he asked, "Who do you think that guy was, Bart?"

"I dunno. Anyway, he got what he was after, so I don't think we have anything to worry about. He's got to be long gone by now."

"Hurry up!" Jotham yelled, "We've got to stay together."

After a long, uphill climb they finally emerged from the woods and found that their path was leading them toward a broad, grassy plain in the opposite direction from the gray hills.

"Good choice, Paladins!" Jotham snorted sarcastically. "I told you this was the wrong way." He dropped down on a rock, wiping the matted hair out of his eyes. "Let's stop for a drink. But we're only gonna take a short rest since we've already wasted too much time on this stupid rabbit trail."

The correct path, which they were able to locate without difficulty now, proved to be much less forbidding. After a brief stop to drink and finish the fruit they'd brought with them, they trudged downhill for two more hours. The trail finally led them through the middle of the crest of southern hills into a valley enclosed by rugged bluffs. And in the exact center, surrounded by a watery moat was a turreted castle about 100 yards away. And behind it, leading up into the hills was a dense forest.

The castle was angular, with six high, thin towers of various heights. It was constructed in a circular pattern, with ramparts jutting up from the outer wall. There was a fortified causeway in front, leading to a tall wooden door with large, black metal rivets. At the back, they could also make out a less obtrusive entrance that was open. It had a smaller causeway and was flanked by two small huts.

"Get down," Jotham hissed. They lay on their faces, their bodies obscured by the tall grass. He glanced darkly at Bart, "And whatever you do, don't sneeze!"

Two guards were emerging from the huts. They stretched lazily and looked down at a parchment one of them held in his hands. Shielding their eyes from the afternoon sun, they stared out into the valley in the Paladins' direction.

The four stiffened as the soldiers' gaze raked their hiding place.

After conferring briefly, they walked into the castle through the open door. It clanged shut behind them with a sound of mocking finality.

Bart stared incredulously at the thick, gray-white walls. "We're supposed to take this castle, by ourselves, with these weapons?" He pulled out an arrow, fingering its thin shaft, and shook his head in dismay. "I think this is a very bad joke."

Carisa placed her crossbow in the grass in front of her. She looked at it dubiously.

Abe got up on his knees, taking aim with his javelin. "We can do this! These are not your basic weapons. Remember what happened to that Gharg when Jo whacked him with his whip? These are potent, guys. They've got special power like explosives or something. Like Abner's message said, we've got to have confidence in our weapons!"

"Yeah, right—*Abner* . . . I remember him," Jotham responded, unable to keep the jealousy out of his voice.

As Abe had spoken, a warning flared briefly in Bart's mind. Something was out of place; he couldn't put his finger on it. His head was in a fog; he just couldn't pierce through the confusion.

"You're right, Abe," Carisa conceded. "Justar wouldn't have sent us out here if we weren't properly equipped."

Jotham waved for them to gather around him. "Let's crawl over to the back," he whispered, "then we'll attack like the instructions said: one by one. . . . I'll be the first one up." Without waiting for their assent he started crawling quickly toward the castle.

The tall grass had fine thorns that scratched at their skin and clothing. Jotham, in the lead, suffered the brunt of its pricking and slashing. He felt like he was being attacked on all sides by fierce, diminutive swordsmen. It reminded him of Gulliver being assaulted by the Lilliputians. He lowered his head to protect his face and eyes.

As he crawled, he tried to recall what had been tugging at the back of his mind. There was something that just wasn't right. He'd sensed it since Abner had left, but he had been frustrated in his struggle to make sense of it. It was as if he were staring at a painting, knowing that something was either terribly askew, or absent, but unable to decipher what it was. An insistent voice was nagging at the recesses of his mind, but strain as he might, he couldn't make out its meaning.

The small column came to a halt within a few yards of the guards' huts. The moat, on this side of the castle, looked to be about ten feet wide. Jotham stretched out the black leather whip in front of him, measuring it. He estimated it was about eight feet long. Since the causeway had been left down, Jotham knew there would be no difficulty in approaching close enough to strike the gate with his weapon. It loomed in front of him, easily twice his height.

"Everybody all right?" he inquired, peering at his troops. For the first time, he noticed how haggard they looked. Their skin was sallow and their eyes were a salmon color. He hoped that the battle would be over quickly. His band didn't appear to have much reserve strength for a protracted encounter.

"If any one has some final words, speak now or forever hold your peace."

"Good luck, Jo," Abe said.

Bart slapped him on the back, "Give 'em heck," he added.

Carisa stared quietly at him with bloodshot eyes. Her throat constricted, but she made no sound. There were words massed behind those long lashes; but for the first time, she was apparently at a loss for what to say to him.

Jotham winked at her, poked his head above the grass and ran toward the gate in a crouched position, his whip coiled loosely in his right hand. He stopped when he got to the huts, looked inside, then ran lightly onto the wooden causeway. About six feet from the barred entrance, he planted his feet, drew back his arm and whipped it forward.

There was a dull popping sound and a small burst of smoke. When it cleared, the door was intact. The only evidence of the attack was a black smudge on the wood. Jotham took aim and struck again, with similar result. With each swing the explosion decreased, until all that could be heard was the futile sound of leather slapping on solid wood.

Bart, by this time, was standing near the guard huts. "Let me give it a try," he offered, holding his taut bow at his side. There was a steely determination in his face.

"Back up," he said, taking aim at the round rivet in the middle of the door. He released the shaft, and it struck dead center. There was a splintering sound, and the Paladins gaped as the arrow fell in pieces on the planks. The metal tip bounced and dropped at their feet, broken and bent.

"This is not good," Bart remarked, fear rising in his eyes.

Abe stuck his head out of the hut nearest them, "I'm gonna give it a shot. I think my war staff should do it." Carisa stepped out of the other hut, crossbow in hand.

Bart looked over his shoulder at the castle keep, the strongest part of the fortress. "I don't know, something tells me that we should leave now."

"Yeah, something's not right here; maybe we ought to go," Carisa concurred.

Jotham didn't know what to say.

Abe's stared at them incredulously. "No way, man, I'm not going without using my weapon! Feel it—it's vibrating. It's like it wants me to launch it. . . . Like you said, Jotham, we were told to fight today, and I'm gonna fight!"

Without hesitation, he ran ahead and lunged forward, releasing the javelin in a mighty thrust. It struck high up at the top of the door where it stuck fast, its shaft quivering. There was the high pitched fizzling sound of gas escaping, then an earsplitting shriek followed by a sharp explosion. The top of the door blew off.

"I told you. . . . I told you!" Abe was fairly dancing in excitement. He ran to retrieve the javelin from where it had fallen.

The rest of the band were quiet, staring at the large gate. A foreboding silence, along with the dark blotch of smoke coiled itself insidiously around them. Dread and a nameless terror began to choke them.

Abe stared at them in dismay. His arm was bent back ready for another toss.

Suddenly, the dense quiet was broken by mocking laughter. When the smoke cleared, an ugly, wolfish face was peering out from the edge of the charred hole. Soon there was another, then another. In a matter of moments, there were over a dozen Ghargs cackling at them. Although they were approximately half the size of the creatures they had battled at the cabin, their identity was betrayed by their veined wings and thick, twitching tails. Their faces were longer and thinner; and when they hissed, a barbed comb spread out like a fan around the back of their heads. It was a sinister backdrop for faces glistening with pure evil.

The Paladins' minds were spinning.

They stood frozen in terror.

Before they could act, the creatures launched themselves en masse. The Ghargs plummeted toward them, their wings beating furiously. They flew directly at the Paladins' heads, talons exposed, aiming for their eyes.

At the last moment, the four warriors dropped to their knees, covering their heads with their shields.

Razor claws raked the air inches above them. Steel rang as talons grazed the metal armor protecting them.

Their attackers, in loose formation, looped upwards. They were beginning a wide turn to circle back for another dive.

This time their attack would be better aimed.

Jotham was stung into action. "Stand in front of that hut," he barked at Bart and Carisa. "Abe and I will stand in front of this one. When I shout, 'Now!' drop to the ground!" He gestured wildly toward a field to their left. "Then, when I give the word, run like mad toward the trees over there."

The Ghargs were approaching swiftly in two groups. They were picking up speed, and this time, were flying much lower to the ground. The snouts of the five in front were drawn back wickedly, showing thin yellow fangs.

"Hold it!" ordered Jotham, standing at rigid attention.

The first formation was closing in.

"Wait. . . ."

They were now nearly on top of them.

"Now!" he roared.

The four Paladins fell flat on their faces.

One Gharg smacked into the hut on the left and two hit the one on the right. As they hit the stone, a wheeze burst from them like air expelled from a balloon, followed by a crunching of smashing bones.

The second column had a brief warning, and so was able to swoop up at a sharp angle. Two were unable to make the adjustment, clipped the pointed roofs with their wings and were sent spinning and shrieking into the moat where they immediately sank.

"Run!"

The four terrified warriors sprinted toward a copse of trees approximately a football field length away. They could hear the remaining Ghargs above and behind howling out their rage.

The trees were rapidly approaching. Jotham didn't dare look back.

His feet had never moved so fast. He could hear Carisa panting behind him.

Five more seconds and they would be under the cover of branches.

Bart was in the lead, running with his left arm holding his shield up over his head. Since it came from his left, he didn't see the blow coming. The swiftest Gharg had caught up to him, and with its powerful tail struck him a brutal blow on the head. It knocked the shield out of his hands, and he was sent sprawling, only 20 feet from safety.

He lay on the ground stunned. His left shoulder was throbbing from the fall.

The remaining Ghargs flew down, sending the Paladins diving into the grass. As the Paladins lifted their heads, several more attackers swooped down, striking them mercilessly on their backs and faces with their blunt tails. They felt like flexible clubs beating their heads and shoulders to a pulp. The enemy appeared intent on inflicting a bloody and utterly humiliating defeat on the Paladins.

Their ears were ringing, their thoughts scrambled. The salty taste of blood filled their mouths. Bart had received the harshest blow of all and was on the verge of losing consciousness.

Abruptly, all seven Ghargs spun upwards cackling in triumphant delight.

With the reprieve, Jotham shook his head clear. In a flash of clarity he remembered the steel weaponry which hung at their waists. He scrambled up on his knees and pulled out his sword.

"Follow me," he cried leaping to his feet, waving his sword in the air.

Carisa and Abe followed him. Jotham reached down to pull Bart up. Bart stood next to him on wobbly legs, a thin line of blood running out of his right ear. They huddled in a tight circle. Holding their weapons angled up in front of them, they formed a porcupine of sword points.

158

Recalling the dullness of their blades in the tunnel, Jotham muttered, "I hope these Ghargs have thinner skin than those reptiles did."

They weren't given an opportunity to find out. Confronted now by this spiny and dangerous organism, the Ghargs wheeled overhead chattering furiously. No longer able to reach their victims with impunity, they spat at their enemies below. Sticky, smelly droplets sprayed over them. Faced with serious opposition, the Ghargs appeared to be losing their confidence.

"Watch your eyes," Jotham warned, wiping the spittle from his cheeks.

Growing tired of this sport, the creatures formed several disorganized clusters; then, flying insolently over head, just out of sword reach, they flapped their wings derisively, lifted their tails and emitted a dense, oily cloud smelling of bile and rancid grease. The gaseous fumes caused the Paladins to gag and choke.

"Let's get out of here!" Jotham wheezed.

With eyes watering and noses running, they stumbled into the safety of the dense woods. As Jotham fell under a large pine, he unplugged his water bottle and poured the liquid over his stinging eyes. *What went wrong? I thought Justar said we would conquer!* Slowly the pain subsided and his vision cleared, but taking its place was the bitter memory of another shameful defeat—not at the hands of grotesque flying creatures—but one inflicted by a desperate and defiant young man.

Chapter Twenty Two

When the biting fog lifted, Jotham peered out from underneath his protective canopy. The malevolent band that had ambushed them was gone. Hearing the rippling of water behind him, Jotham motioned for the others to follow him into the dense growth. Throwing themselves down beside a small brook winding carelessly through the trees, they plunged their heads into the clear mountain water, soaking the stench from their hair and the stinging pain from their eyes. The deliciously cold mountain water refreshed as it cleansed them.

After shaking the water from his hair, Jotham turned over to lay on his back and stare up at the light filtering through the branches overhead. The others imitated him, but soon, all except Jotham had fallen into a despondent sleep. His mind whirled with thoughts of resentment and blame. He felt overwhelmed with confusion and frustration. He wanted to shake his fist and scream out his anger at Justar. They had followed his instructions to the letter and had been humiliated. It was by only pure chance that they hadn't been shredded by the raking by their enemies' talons.

Why? Why had this happened? Again, the feeling that he was forgetting something interrupted him; a disturbing contradiction had been tugging at him all day, but it still eluded him.

He was having a hard time thinking coherently; his mind was spinning in dizzying circles. He took another drink from the brook. As he rolled onto his back, an odd picture flashed before him: he was in a cage racing like a mouse on an exercise wheel and the bottom of the cage was littered with shredded parchments.

Papers . . . documents . . . the scrolls! . . . That's what it was! Carisa's words as they had walked out of the cottage leaped out at him. Justar had clearly told them to read his instructions every day. He vividly recalled his specific words: "On your way, my words obey." The rhyming made it easier to remember, now that he put his mind to it.

160

He'd been so jealous of Abner and so intent on demonstrating his authority that he'd refused to take Carisa's reminder seriously.

A sick dread that his pride had caused him to fail his friends again clamped down on his chest like a vise. Pushing his hair out of his face, he crawled over to sit against the trunk of a tree. Unclasping his wallet, he removed the top scroll; it was Abner's. He was going to toss it aside, but something made him stop and open it. His fingers were shaking as he unrolled it. The concluding sentence struck him: "Receive his words and his gift. It will render your armor complete."

A troubling memory stirred like the twitching of a cat's tail.

What was it that Justar told us when he handed us our weapons? The answer was immediate: *He told us to kneel and receive our swords and with them our armor was complete.* He now distinctly remembered how Justar had stressed the word *"complete."*

Was that the vexing contradiction that had been nagging? If the King had given them all they needed for battle, why would he have exchanged Abe's ax? Why the switch? Would their General change his mind? Had he been wrong? There had been something about Justar's wisdom and majesty, which rendered it impossible to even entertain those possibilities.

His heart began to race, and fear stalled his breath.

He fumbled inside his pouch, hastily unrolling the scroll Justar had given him at his commissioning. He was horrified at what he saw. It was blank!

Where were Justar's instructions? He turned the scroll over and over in his hands.

Then he noticed a brief phrase printed at the bottom of the parchment. It sent a shiver through him: "Do not draw near from the rear."

Shame now expelled the anger, and the cold flood of failure extinguished his resentment. They were only a few words, but he knew instantly that they had come directly from Justar. The lettering was exactly like the original. It floated lightly over the parchment.

Suddenly, it struck him!

He grabbed Abner's scroll, unrolling it furiously. In his haste he ripped off a corner.

There! That was what had been tugging at him!

The letters . . . they were stuck to the page! In comparison to Justar's they appeared flat and devoid of life. The scroll could never have come from Justar!

He scratched the back of his foot distractedly, suspicion beginning to seep into him like a chilling wind. His fingers felt a swelling that seemed to be infected. Lifting his heel closer, he noticed two odd reddish indentations. In his biology textbook he had seen pictures of snake bites. The marks on his heel seemed to be identical.

Thinking over their travels that morning, he recalled seeing Bart and Abe limping and rubbing their heels while trekking toward the castle.

Carisa too, he remembered.

Abruptly, his suspicion crystallized.

He leapt to his feet and quietly inspected the others' heels. The marks on each were identical. He looked down at the staff lying next to Abe. It was blackened and misshapen at the tip.

He nudged it with his toe. It was stiff and heavy.

Bending down, he picked it up cautiously, weighing it in his hands. Although it was made of wood, it had an unusual density. He examined the red seam. *It looks like a thick vein,* he mused.

He was startled when a picture of a snake flashed into his mind, bringing back the dream which had awakened him on the floor that morning. Somehow, he knew that this staff was related to their defeat; he simply had no way of proving it.

Justar, Justar please help me, he called out silently.

A strange tremor vibrated through the shaft.

He waited.

It quickly died out. When nothing further happened, he set the javelin down next to Abe and sat down. Pulling out his sword, he began to wipe it clean. Within moments his eyes had grown heavy and his head began to droop. He was soon fast asleep.

It was Bart's hoarse cry that awakened him.

Jotham's head jerked forward. Bart was staring at Abe, his mouth open.

Horror slammed into his chest like a fist. The staff, which he'd laid on the grass, was now swaying above Abe's head, glowing a brilliant red. Its fangs were bared and ready to puncture Abe's throat.

"No!" Jotham screamed. The adder stiffened, swiveling its head toward the sound. Gripping the sword hilt in his right hand, Jotham leaped to his feet and swung the blade down.

The now razor-sharp steel ripped the serpent's head from its body.

Abe scrambled to his knees, madly flicking the bloody head off his chest.

Carisa stared at it, as a dawning horror began to rise in her eyes.

The long tail on the grass was twitching and flailing violently. Jotham pierced it through with his sword. It ceased thrashing.

"Thanks, Jo," Abe gasped.

"What happened? Where did that snake come from?" Bart asked.

"It was Abner's war staff!" Jotham replied angrily. Wheeling toward Abe, he began harshly, "You never should have—!" but stopped short at the sight of Abe's burning face. He turned toward the others and continued, "Abner's *gift* was a little trick intended to get us all killed."

Abe was staring at the ground, too ashamed to look at the other Paladins.

Jotham described what he'd discovered on each of their heels and then explained the discrepancies between Abner's message and Justar's. As he spoke, he remembered another obvious clue. If he'd been listening more carefully instead of envisioning torturous damage to Abner's face, he realized he would have caught it immediately.

". . . It just hit me, in each of the scrolls Justar gave us, he told us specifically that if we fought as 'one,' he would grant to us, 'our battles won'." Jotham rubbed his forehead ruefully. "Abner twisted the words, instructing us to do just the opposite."

Bart threw a stone into the brook. "Sooo . . . you're sayin' that good ole boy, Abner, was a plant?"

Jotham nodded, pointing at the tail pinned to the ground. "Sure looks that way."

Carisa couldn't take her eyes off the exposed fangs protruding from the severed head. "That explains why we all felt so weak and sick today." She looked down at her fingers, remembering Abner's gallant kiss, and balled her hand into a hard fist.

While the others had been talking, Abe seemed to be withdrawing into himself. He remained silent, staring at Jotham with unusual coldness.

"There was one other thing we missed," Carisa continued through gritted teeth. "Maybe the most obvious, come to think of it. The whole point of what he said to us was to put our confidence in everything *but* Justar."

"You're exactly right, Carisa," Jotham agreed. "I can't believe I fell for it."

"Hey, Jo, he suckered us all," Bart said. "That dude was a pro."

"I'd like to see that pro just one more time!" Carisa muttered.

Jotham smiled grimly, trying to contain his satisfaction. "Perhaps you'll get your chance." He pulled his sword out of the ground and flicked the bloody tail and head into the brush; then, after wiping off the blade with a handful of grass, he said, "Everyone sit down."

They clustered in a tight circle. After a brief embarrassed silence, Jotham cleared his throat and spoke. "Carisa was right this morning. Justar did tell us that we should read his words every day. Carisa, I apologize for not listening to your suggestion before setting out. . . . I was wrong."

She looked away. "It's okay," she paused and then slowly replied, "and I'm really sorry for the mean things I said to you about Bart and the lizards."

He met her brown eyes; she smiled faintly. He stuck out his hand. "Friends?"

"Friends," she responded, giving his hand a hard squeeze.

Jotham looked around the group and grinned. "What do ya say we . . . ehh, take out our scrolls and read what they say."

Bart read his first, "A concerted attack will drive the enemy back." He stuffed the parchment back into his pouch. "Well, now we know what was wrong with our plan," he fumed.

"How about yours, Carisa?" Jotham inquired.

Her cheeks were pink. She had already read hers. Hesitantly, she handed her scroll to Jotham, who read it silently as color rose higher in her face. Looking over at her, he saw that she was biting her lip.

"It's okay—you don't need to read it out loud," he said, handing it back to her.

She shook her head. "No, you do it," she whispered.

Jotham read, "Don't be misled by a beautiful smile; it can disguise a heart of guile. Beauty may lay on the surface, but treachery goes down to the very bones."

Avoiding their eyes, she rolled it up and placed the parchment back in her pouch.

Jotham glanced over at his brother. Abe refused to look at him, but he unrolled his scroll and read, his voice flat, "Remember my child, your armor's complete. Surrendering your weapon means certain defeat."

"Yep," Jotham assented. He looked over at Bart, "I think there was really only one thing true in what Abner told us."

"What was that?" Bart asked.

"Justar wanted us to attack today. These instructions he gave us were meant to be followed this morning. If we'd read them like we were supposed to, we wouldn't be here now."

Bart nodded.

Carisa's face was averted. It was obvious she was fighting off tears.

There was an uncharacteristic forcefulness in Jotham's voice when he continued. It was so unexpected, it caused the three Paladins to look at him sharply. "I think we should catch the enemy by surprise. If we attack now it will be the last thing they'll expect."

Three pairs of eyes widened in disbelief.

"Now?" Abe exclaimed, in spite of himself.

"Yeah! Now!"

Jotham had already jumped up and was beginning to shake out his whip, removing clumps of grass and mud. After cleaning it in silence, he coiled and tied it firmly against his right hip.

"We've messed up Justar's instructions badly enough as it is; we're not going to make it worse by disobeying and backing out of the battle today. . . . Any arguments?"

None were forthcoming, so he crouched next to the others and gave them the battle strategy. The others cautiously agreed.

As they crept back through the grassy field, Abe's anger against his older brother continued to grow. Because he had no weapon, he'd been given no part to play in Jotham's plan of attack. It was clear to him that at least Jotham, and probably the others, regarded him as a fool for surrendering his battle-ax. Abner had made him look like an idiot, and Jotham had been all too happy to rub it in.

Jotham's tactless words had stung: "Looks like you'll be no help in the battle. So, just stay behind me, and I'll keep you out of trouble."

I know what he was thinking, Abe told himself, recalling the accusation brimming in his brother's glance. *As usual, I'm just a stupid little kid.* A deep resentment burned its way to the surface. *You've always thought you were so tough. Well, I'll show you!* he swore to himself.

You've always got to be the big hero. All you want to do is impress Carisa. Well, you just wait.

They looped around to the front of the castle, crawling toward the gate keep that guarded the walkway leading to the imposing wooden gate. On the planks of the door, a large two-headed dragon had been designed out of black metal rivets. There was a three-pronged crown on each head made out of silver. The image depicted the serpent with its tail intact; at its end was a wicked red barb.

About 15 yards from the castle keep they halted. In the dim interior of the guards' hut, they could just make out two corpulent soldiers sitting on stools, avoiding the afternoon heat. They were reclining against the back wall of the enclosure. Although their uniforms were similar to those Jotham had seen in the village, their carelessness marked these guards as decidedly inferior.

He motioned to his band with his hand. The three others crawled up alongside of him. Jotham pointed at Carisa and Bart, then at the hut. They fitted their weapons, drawing taut their bows. Jotham took a deep breath, nodded grimly and dropped his hand. At Jotham's signal, Carisa and Bart stood up and released their projectiles.

With a crash, the metal dart smashed into the stones while Bart's arrow exploded next to it; the wall disintegrated, exposing the stunned soldiers. The stone wall behind them bowed and gave way; as it did, the guards tipped backwards, sprawling heavily on the ground.

Jotham raced forward, swung his whip and smacked one of the scrambling soldiers on his back. There was a loud pop, a scream and a splash as he was catapulted into the moat. Before Jotham could swing again, the other guard waddled to his feet, and with a look of terror over his shoulder, followed suit.

A cauldron of bubbles boiled up from the green, murky water. There were two loud gurgling belches, and the moat grew still.

Bart looked at the blackened, crumbled stones. "That was easy," he said.

"Yeah . . . too easy," Jotham responded. "Let's keep moving."

Arranging themselves in two pairs, Jotham and Abe stood in front on the walkway with the twins five paces behind. Jotham raised his whip and aimed for the two-headed reptile's curling tail, while Bart and Carisa pointed their projectiles at each of the arrogant heads. When his whip struck, they released their arrows, striking the silver crowns simultaneously. Expecting a huge bang, the Paladins' hearts dropped when they only heard three pops, followed by little wisps of smoke; then silence.

Abe noticed Jotham's expression of confusion and fear. He secretly sneered.

Carisa opened her mouth to shout out a warning, but the words died on her lips as the rivets began to turn color. An inner flame was heating them into a fire of such intensity that the Paladins had to jump back. Soon, the rivets were beginning to liquefy into a white, smoking lava. Suddenly, the door erupted into furious flames. The waves of heat were so strong that the Paladins were forced to crouch behind the smoldering pile of rocks at the gateway. Waves of hot air and smoke billowed over them; and in less than a minute, the huge gate had been turned into a mass of smoking, gray ash.

The entrance to the castle now stood open and undefended. The Paladins leaped over the mound, their weapons ready. They ran down a long hall, then stopped at an arched doorway with large double doors. Overhead, in large gothic script was the motto: *Divide et Imperia.* Its meaning filtered into Jotham's consciousness from an old Latin lesson: "Divide and Conquer." The words made his skin crawl.

The clinking of metal, the thudding of plates and the loud snorting and growling of intoxicated creatures indicated that only a few inches of oiled wood separated them from a multitude of Ghnostar's troops. It sounded as if the room was packed with them. The Paladins looked at each other, a momentary uncertainty freezing them. Jotham met Carisa's gaze. There was a new wild defiance there which compelled him to act.

Jotham flung the doors open. They were in a great hall filled with several dozen long, wooden tables. Ten or more wolfish Ghargs sat at each one, squabbling drunkenly and tearing hunks of meat from platters in front of them. From the rafters hung rows of black banners on which Ghnostar's upside-down crown were ominously emblazoned.

Against the back wall, approximately 20 yards away, a raised platform was erected on which stood a single table, loaded down with the large body of a baked pig. Behind the table was a gilded throne covered with crushed velvet. The occupant was heaping slabs of pork onto his plate.

Carisa's jaw fell open.

It was Abner!

Chapter Twenty Three

Abe's face went dark. Imbedded in the hog's charred forehead was his battle-ax! His vision narrowed, closing out everything except his stolen weapon. A ferocious boldness was coursing through him.

Carisa moved quickly, preparing for action. This was her chance, and she was going to make the most of it. She began fitting a polished steel bolt into her crossbow.

The Ghargs closest to the door gaped at the Paladins. Chunks of bloody meat fell from their stiffened claws. Their glazed eyes sought to focus on the intruders. Those whose backs were turned ignored the screech of the hinges and greedily tore the meat from the table, stuffing it into their own snouts.

Abner's bloodshot eyes turned insolently toward them. They narrowed, and a cruel laugh burst from his lips.

Feverish growling erupted from scores of Ghargs who were startled into alertness at the harsh sound. Thirty or more of them stood up on their benches, swaying and snarling belligerently, their spiny plates fanning out in an evil halo, white foam beginning to drip from their bared fangs as they recognized the four trespassers.

Jotham, in the lead, was momentarily paralyzed by the menacing creatures. The Ghargs clawed closer, holding him with their eyes. Abner's white teeth flashed at his opponent who stood immobilized just ten yards away. "So Jotham," he laughed scornfully, "still alive, are we? Well, not for long!"

With a swift movement, Abner lunged for the ax and yanked it free. Jotham still stood locked in place. The moment his arm swung forward to hurl the ax, Carisa released the lever of her bow. Her dart flew high, striking Abner's forearm. Its force drove him backwards, pinning his arm to the stone wall behind him. He shrieked as the ax dropped from his hand, landing with a heavy clang at the foot of the dais.

Abner shrieked, "Kill them!"

Three Ghargs at the nearest table lurched into the air. Bart's arrow pierced the chest of one, who exploded into a reddish fog. Jotham's whip flattened another.

Abe, in a cold fury, was racing down the aisle, past rows of dazed Ghargs, toward Abner who was writhing and bellowing with pain.

Bart squinted his eyes. It seemed as though a halo surrounded Abe's body.

Seeing the enraged Paladin racing toward him, Abner pulled out his sword with his free hand and flung it at Abe's head. The broadsword spun toward him like a twirling saw blade. Abe dove feet first, and the sword flew past. He slid hard into the platform, his ankle twisting on the ax handle. He snatched it quickly, grabbing it with both hands. With a yell, he leaped up and threw it with all his strength.

There was a thud as it hit the wall behind Abner's head, then a huge crash which knocked Abe off his feet. Abner and the platform erupted, catapulting the pig's flaming body into the air in an eerie swan dive. The carcass landed with a fizzling crash on top of several Ghargs, lighting them up like Roman candles. Dense, greasy smoke along with the nauseating smell of scorched hair filled the room.

Shrill shrieks rebounded off the stone walls. The scratching of claws and the flapping of wings jolted the Paladins. The Ghargs were scrambling and flying about the room in confusion. The Paladins drew their swords and retreated so that their backs were against the wooden frame.

Abe stumbled to his feet, sword ready. As the thick smoke slowly dissipated, he could see streams of Ghargs pouring out the open windows, clawing at each other in a desperate battle to escape. Within minutes, their enemies had fled, leaving them alone with the smoking remains of the pig's carcass, and the stone sepulcher covering Abner's body.

Abe walked over to what was left of the dais. It lay in a charcoal ruin. The only evidence left of their enemy was Abner's forearm, which had fallen to the floor. The hand was open and on its palm was Ghnostar's tattoo.

Bart put his arm around Abe's shoulders and gently turned him away from the gruesome sight. "That was excellent Abe! You did great."

Carisa ran forward and hugged Abe tightly. "Oh Abe, that was incredible! When he threw the sword at you, I was sure you weren't . . ." she grinned shakily at him, "but you were amazing! Wasn't he, Jo?"

Jotham was hunting through the debris, distancing himself from the accolades being heaped on Abe. He was embarrassed by his indecision during the battle and hated being shown up his little brother.

"Yeah, he did all right," he responded halfheartedly. "But it was your arrow that really did it. If you hadn't stuck Abner against the wall, who knows *what* would have happened."

"I don't know, Jotham. I think Abe was the hero." Carisa smiled at Abe, ruffling his hair.

Jotham continued to dig through the pile. "Here it is!" he exclaimed, pushing aside a charred plank and holding aloft Abe's battle-ax. Though covered with soot, it was apparently intact.

He tossed it over to Abe, "Don't let anyone take it again."

Abe caught the handle, his ears turning beet red. "Thanks for the advice, Jo. I'll keep that in mind."

"Justar said there would be prisoners—let's go find them," Bart interjected, heading for the door.

Walking through the arched doorway, they turned left and made their way down another long passage. To their right was a courtyard with a stagnant pool and fountain filled with garbage.

Abe found the door first. It was small and had a narrow, barred window through which they could see stone steps winding down in a tight, dark spiral. It was unlocked. He ducked his head as he stepped in. The rest followed closely behind.

The air grew rapidly cooler as they moved down. There were no torches or natural lighting, so with each step they were descending further into complete darkness.

At the bottom of the stairs, they went through another archway and found themselves in a narrow passage at the end of which was a gate made of thick iron bars. On the walls were two smoking torches. From the darkness beyond the bars they could hear the clinking of chains, pitiful crying and the low moaning of voices hoarse with misery. The smell was foul: a mixture of excrement, unwashed bodies and fear.

Jotham shook the bars. The gate was locked.

He motioned the others back, swung his whip and split the lock with an explosive slap. Silence settled on those imprisoned inside the dark dungeon. Jotham stepped into the dim interior holding a torch in front of him. He was in a huge room with narrow slits cut high into the walls, which

170

grudgingly let in minimal air and light. On the floor in heaps, along the walls—everywhere he looked—he could make out ragged shapes of all sizes. They were all in chains. Most of the faces were deeply lined, and the thin, wasted bodies were bowed with age or despair.

As Jotham took another step, he heard a rustling and scraping as if large rats were scurrying for cover. Most of the prisoners had been so brutalized, their gaunt faces remained expressionless, their gazes blank and fixed. The dark circles around their eyes looked like ragged holes burnt into dry parchment. Their suffering had been so profound; they were little more than hollow shells.

The three other Paladins were standing quietly behind him. The harsh sounds of sobbing startled him. He turned and saw Abe on his knees, tears streaming from his eyes. "You will feel what I feel. . . ." Justar's promise to his younger brother echoed in Jotham's mind. Carisa placed her hands on Abe's shoulders as they shook with the force of his emotion.

As Jotham surveyed the tragic scene, a geyser of anger erupted inside him.

He didn't know from where it came, perhaps it was the memory of the silver knight, combined with words from Justar's commission; but before he had time to evaluate it, the declaration bubbled up and out of him—a command of unmistakable authority: "Be free!" he shouted. "Be free in Justar's name!"

The echo of his words was drowned out by the crashing din of hundreds of iron chains clattering and smashing onto the stone floor. Faintly at first, then louder, from scores of voices came a low wailing of such ecstatic relief and pent-up anguish that Jotham had to bite his lip to keep from sobbing out loud. He felt Carisa grab his hand and squeeze it with shaking fingers. Soon, hundreds of bodies had risen from the floor and were shuffling toward them, their hands raised high as tears of joy and gratitude soaked their faces. The Paladins were awestruck by this holy moment of deliverance.

Rapturous joy shone from the red-rimmed eyes of the prisoners. They were so utterly stunned by their sudden liberation that they had no words to express their thanks. Many ran gaunt, skeletal fingers lovingly over the Paladins' white tunics, their wet eyes eloquent in silent thanksgiving; although most seemed incapable of even this inarticulate communication. As the released captives moved through the shattered gate and up toward the stairs, a miracle occurred. Their bodies straightened, their muscles grew stronger, and the deep lines of sorrow etched on their faces were erased.

From the hallway behind them, the Paladins could hear the reverberations of slow, deliberate shuffling turn into the strong slapping of firm feet running toward daylight. It was exhilarating.

Jotham had never heard anything so wonderful.

* * * * * * * * *

That evening, a huge feast was given in the Paladins' honor. They were seated on a dais in the banquet hall, next to the baroness, Dame Fionna de Bracey, who had been released by one of the prisoners from her cell high in the tallest tower. Jotham was on her left, and Abe, the hero of the battle, was on her right—the position of honor, as they had all been informed.

During the lengthy, extravagant meal, a minstrel sang the sad tale of the castle's conquest and the murder of their gracious baron, Edgard de Bracey. Afterwards, the Paladins were pressed into relating every detail of the assault on the castle. When they were finished, they had to repeat it again. There was much whooping and shouting, but the loudest exultation was reserved for Abe's now famous slide, leading to Abner's explosive demise. At the conclusion of the sixth retelling, to honor his bravery, Abe was presented with a jeweled medallion, inscribed with the name of the castle, *Orion.*

The baroness gave them each a graceful curtsy, as the hall rang with loud applause. "Although our hospitality is somewhat constrained at present," she said, "as a reward, we wish to offer you your choice of anything in our realm. If it is in our power to give, it shall be yours."

Jotham lifted his hand, and gave her a surprisingly elegant bow in return. "Thank you so much, Dame de Bracey, but we can't accept your kind offer. Justar has already promised us sufficient reward when we complete our mission. It is—" He was interrupted by Carisa's hand on his arm. Jotham bent over as she whispered something in his ear.

He smiled sheepishly at the baroness, "Carisa, well . . . I guess we all would like to request one thing: Would it be possible to . . . to have some hot water to bathe in?"

The baroness laughed lightly, nodding understandingly at Carisa, who was trying to hide her blushing face behind her brother. "I understand, dear

172

friends; I enjoy an occasional hot bath myself. We have several wooden tubs which the Baron had the blacksmith and farrier construct for us. They will be waiting for you in the solar." Noting their quizzical expressions, she explained. "Those are the upper sleeping chambers, reserved for our honored guests. I trust they will meet with your satisfaction."

The four were led up a circular stairway to their own bedchambers. Each one was simply furnished with wooden chests at the end of the bed, a desk and a chair placed along the wall. Thick, beautifully woven tapestries decorated the floor and walls where large windows opened on verandahs overlooking the outer wall.

As promised, each Paladin had their own wooden tub, approximately five feet in diameter, filled with steaming water. The tubs were made from slats, banded around by steel strips, and looked like the bottom half of huge wine casks. One glance at her tub, and Carisa slammed her door shut. The others heard her splash into the water before they had finished removing their sandals.

"I guess girls can move quickly if they want to," Bart commented.

Abe lay down on his bed, stretching out luxuriously. "Hey don't forget your bath," Jotham said.

"I'll have it tomorrow," Abe muttered sleepily, rolling over on his side.

"What? You haven't been downwind of yourself lately, buddy. If anybody needs to clean up, it's you." Abe just shrugged his shoulders.

"Yeah," agreed Bart, joining in the fun. "There are two ways to do this," he said, planting himself next to Jotham, who was standing by Abe's bed, "the easy way or the hard way. . . . You choose."

"Come on," grumbled Abe, "Leave me alone."

Jotham jerked his thumb at Bart who winked back slyly.

Jotham held up one finger, then two, and then three.

They threw themselves on the bed, grabbed Abe's hands and feet and before he had time to protest, they tossed him unceremoniously into the tub.

"Aaahh!" he screamed, the hot water shocking him awake.

Bursting into laughter, Jotham put both hands on Abe's shoulders and dunked him under; when his brother's red face resurfaced, Jotham and Bart headed for the door. Anticipating a watery retaliation, Jotham yelled from behind the door, holding it open like a shield, "Make sure you clean yourself good; I don't want to be smelling your stale B.O. any longer."

Abe's lips were fixed in a fierce grimace. A cauldron of boiling resentment was ready to explode inside him. For a few moments, he fantasized about yelling for the guards and telling them to throw Jotham and Bart into the dungeon for assaulting the hero of the raid on Orion. He closed his eyes and imagined their horrified expressions. It was a delightful idea. Abe let the picture simmer. Whatever happened, he would think of some way to get even with his cocky brother.

After his bath, Jotham lay awake on his bed. Although exhausted, he was unable to calm his feverish thoughts. Like a movie screen, he kept seeing the events of the last few days being played over and over before his eyes. He tossed from side to side. The bed was too soft and creaked every time he moved. He stared down at the oblong patch of moonlight on his blanket and recalled the light which enfolded them the day Justar commissioned them as Paladins. He was plagued by accusations that kept battering him like a fist pounding a lump of dough.

You failure—you led the band into the lizard den and almost got Bart killed—what if he goes blind in that eye? You believed Abner—You didn't read the instructions before battle. . . . And you thought you were going to be such an awesome leader! You were so pathetic, even your little brother showed you up.

Face it: you're a loser . . .

. . . a loser!

He seemed incapable of defending himself against the incessant barrage. Throwing a blanket over his shoulder, he went over to the window and opened it. The moat 100 feet below him sparkled like an onyx as it reflected the torchlight from the guards patrolling the wall walk. There was a dangerous allure to its dark depths. He breathed in deeply, trying to exorcise the bitter despondency from his lungs. The cool night air smelled of orange blossoms and honeysuckle. It reminded him of the king's castle.

There was a metallic clink behind. His head jerked around.

Justar was standing next to his bed, staring intently at him.

Chapter Twenty Four

Jotham's legs felt as heavy as wet sandbags. An acrid weight of remorse dragged at him, pulling his shoulders down like anchors lashed to his wrists. His heart began thudding in his chest—a wild animal crashing against the bars of its cage. For a brief moment he wanted to fall prostrate on the stone floor, pouring out his shameful confession. Then he stopped himself; an iron gate came crashing down inside him, blocking out the sting of disgrace.

King Justar was standing motionless on the other side of the room, sparks of light flashing from him. An orb of fierce golden energy surrounded him. His sword was sheathed, and his strong hands were empty. There was a purposefulness about him that indicated he had come on a mission that would not be thwarted.

Jotham's jaw was clenched in anger. He steeled himself against the King's inevitable condemnation. Memories of his final encounter with his father flashed through his mind. He began preparing his defense. *It wasn't my fault—it was yours! I didn't ask to be captain. And your instructions . . . they were barely intelligible. If I was supposed to follow them, then you should have made them clearer. . . .*

The Great General took a deliberate step toward him, his eyes fixed on Jotham's. It was clear he knew what Jotham was thinking. Jotham's back stiffened; the back of his neck tingled.

Whoever heard of sending four teenagers to fight against hordes of monsters, anyway. . . . And the other Paladins aren't the most responsive group to try to lead. . . . They act more like brainless kids than real warriors! Jotham was whipping himself into a spitting fury.

Justar drew closer, his fiery green eyes steady as a marksman's.

Jotham blinked away tears of anger. "It wasn't my fault!" he yelled. "Why did you make me take charge? You must have wanted me to fail, just to humiliate me. . . ." Jotham's knees began to shake. He opened his mouth, croaking out, "It wasn't my . . ." He couldn't finish, his lips and jaw quivered; a sorrow as black and as empty as an eclipse threatened to consume him.

The King took a final step forward. Jotham's eyes were fixed on the floor. He was shaking from head to foot. King Justar lifted his arms and placed his hands squarely on Jotham's shoulders. Had those firm hands not held him up, he would have dropped to the floor.

"Look at me," the King commanded. His voice betrayed neither anger nor compassion.

Justar looked at him intently and in a quiet voice asked, "Jotham, why did you not follow my commands?" Though the words were spoken softly, without a trace of rancor, they cut through Jotham like a razor. He felt as if he'd been stripped to the core of his being; every argument dismantled and crushed before they could even be marshaled.

Jotham opened his mouth, but nothing came out. In an agony of guilt, he lifted his gaze to meet Justar's. The King's golden green eyes beamed with such fierce purity and tenderness that it shattered his pride and melted every trace of resentment.

There was nothing he could say. He felt uncontrollable sobs threatening to overwhelm him. Justar placed his hand firmly under Jotham's chin and lifted up his head. "I know what you've done. I also know your heart and that you love me. Listen, my child: you have not failed me." Heat was now flowing into Jotham's head and throughout his body. A wall of ice seemed to be melting in his chest. "I have chosen you for a purpose," Justar continued. "Your commission is not withdrawn but reaffirmed."

Jotham could not restrain himself any longer. Deep wrenching sobs rose from the chasm inside him, shaking him convulsively. Through the sobs, he was able to choke out the words, "Justar . . . I'm sorry. . . . I'm so sorry."

The King's response was immediate and direct. Jotham could feel the words resonating inside his chest: "Do not fear, Jotham, I will be with you. But, henceforth, follow my commands." Jotham didn't know how long Justar held him, nor could he remember how he got to his bed, but he somehow fell asleep with that promise throbbing in his ears.

A warm shaft of sun broke through his window, and the landed on Jotham's eyes, forcing them open. The memory of his encounter with

Justar was vivid in his mind. He could still actually feel the weight of Justar's warm hand on his head. He felt as free and as light as a little child.

Jotham stretched the muscles in his arms. He looked at his wrists and noticed that they were again poking out from his sleeves. The biking top was stretched even more tautly across his skin. Each encounter with Justar seemed to result in a major growth spurt.

A delightful expectation began bubbling up like an artesian well. He glanced over at the fireplace to see if there were any coals left to start a fire and warm some water. Then he noticed that the door connecting his brother's room with his was open. He strained to hear some sound from the next room. It was strangely silent. A hollow pang pricked him. The memory of the hurt in Abe's eyes as his head came out of the water suddenly reproached him. He jumped out of bed and peered through the archway.

His brother's bed was empty; Abe was gone.

* * * * * * * * *

Sometime after midnight, Abe was jolted awake by the sound of snickering and the feeling of sharp claws digging into his chest.

He threw off his covers, but there was nothing to see. Unable to fall back asleep, he lay back and began rehearsing the personal slights received from his older brother, nursing his wounded feelings. Every thoughtless act, magnified by years of competitive rivalry, swarmed through his mind. Each cruel affront was presented in vivid detail with the skill of a master prosecutor. Shortly before dawn, self-pity had festered into bitter resentment, spawning a reckless plan.

It had been a heady experience to be elevated to such an impressive height in the estimation of the populace. He had basked in their praise and admiration—a stark contrast to the disrespect he was usually accorded as the youngest member of the Paladins. It was great to be finally surrounded by those who truly appreciated him.

He had spoken with several of Orion's soldiers, who seemed to hold him in a position of almost godlike stature. In their conversations they had assured him that the second stronghold (Ursula's Fortress) was an unimpressive affair, which would certainly be no match for them. Because of its relative insignificance, it had always been lightly garrisoned and should prove an easy conquest for the Paladins.

177

Abe rehearsed a young soldier's words of praise. He had approached Abe with star-struck eyes saying, "To a mighty warrior such as yourself, sir, it would be but child's play to capture her." Those flattering words began to exert a fascinating appeal. As he savored them he became convinced that they had actually been an invocation of destiny. It was surely a declaration of his calling: a call to bold, aggressive action.

In a surge of elation, he decided to set off for Ursula's fortress by himself and launch a breathtaking, single-handed assault on the fortification. With one mighty feat of daring, he would disprove, once and forever, Jotham's vaunted superiority. The prospect of turning the tables on his arrogant older brother filled him with a rush of excitement.

By the time the sun's rays were beginning to lick the horizon, he was packed and on his way. It had not been difficult to convince the guards that Orion's hero had to leave surreptitiously, early and alone. They had been honored by the opportunity to assist in provisioning him for the secretive journey. Abe left the castle with enough food and drink for a weeklong journey.

An hour later, as the sun was evaporating the dew and warming the hard ground under his feet, Abe was startled to again hear the sounds of snickering in the trees along the path. He looked up, but the limbs were bare; there were no leaves to provide any protective covering, so he dismissed it with a shrug.

Although there was no wind, the branches shook. Abe was in too great a hurry to notice. Soon, there was a flapping overhead. Unable to see any cause for alarm, he continued trudging toward the range of hills in the distance.

Suddenly, what felt like a thick cord struck him flush in the face. Red sparks exploded; he stumbled and fell, his eyes streaming water. He jerked his head around wildly, but there was still nothing to see. Again the cord slapped him, knocking him to his knees. This time it scraped around his neck, tightened and yanked him up. He struggled to his feet. An invisible rope was choking him and lifting him off the ground. He wrenched his body and kicked his legs, but it kept lifting him higher.

He couldn't breathe. With both hands he clawed at the cord, pulling at it to decrease the pressure around his throat. His head felt like it would explode.

The last thing he remembered was the hazy outline of huge wings beating the air above him.

178

Chapter Twenty Five

The discovery of Abe's absence sent Jotham rushing to the other bed-rooms to awaken Bart and Carisa. They threw their clothes on and raced down the stairs to the main gate. The three anxious Paladins gathered the squad of guards, but none of them had seen anybody pass.

"If we see anything, we will alert you immediately, sir," the captain assured Jotham.

One of the guards bent down on one knee in front of the Paladins, his arms spread wide with palms open. "And, m-may I s-say kind s-sirs and lady," he stuttered awkwardly, "th-that w-we is ever s-so grateful for your l-l-leading us out of the d-dungeon. Th-thank you s-so m-much." His cheeks were flushed, and his eyes filled with tears.

Carisa leaned over and pulled him to his feet. "And you're ever so wel-come. It was our privilege to be able to be of service. If you really want to thank someone, thank Justar the King."

They quickly traversed the circular route along the wall to the rear of the castle. The soldiers at the back gate had been the ones to assist Abe's escape.

"But sirs, we was told not to let anyone in; we didna know that we wasn't s'posed to let anyone out, and in particular, the hero of Orion!"

"We're not accusing you of disobeying your instructions; we just need to know when he left," Jotham explained testily. His brother's title rankled him more than he cared to admit.

"Must've been perhaps two . . . three hours ago. . . ." The stout spokesman glanced at his quiet companion who was standing red-faced, holding his pike rigidly at this side, "Wouldn't you say, Elias?"

He nodded in agreement.

"How far away is the next stronghold from here?" Jotham asked.

The quiet one found his voice. "Bout a day'n a half, yore honors," he answered, flashing a gap-toothed smile hopefully at them. "That's whot we told Sir Abe."

"That'd be Lady Ursula's castle, sors," the portly one chimed in, nodding his head in jerky movements.

The three Paladins hastily packed food in their packs, obtained directions from the baroness, and after a hurried farewell, ran out of the castle in hopes of overtaking Abe.

The morning was cool, but the cloudless sky indicated that the day could prove to be a scorcher. They decided to try and make good time before the sun began to bake them in earnest. The flat, reddish terrain stretched out in front of them, interrupted by rocky formations which jutted high into the azure sky. Dry brush was scattered about in parched clumps, along with a few trees which had been so blasted by heat and lack of moisture that they could provide the travelers with little protection from the unremitting sun. Despite its barrenness, there was a harsh, arid beauty to the landscape that Jotham found compelling.

About half a mile down the well-worn dirt path, Bart abruptly held up his hand slowing their jog to a brisk walk. "Guys, haven't we forgotten something?"

Carisa and Jotham looked at him quizzically. They came to a standstill. "The scrolls!" they exclaimed in unison, grabbing for their pouches.

Jotham slapped Bart on the back. "Thanks, man. I can't believe I forgot again!"

Bart had his out first. "Yup, like I thought, the words are totally different. Pretty cool—they must change when we're asleep." He began to read his, "'As mighty Paladins of yore . . .'" He looked down at his scroll. "That's all that it says. . . . What is that supposed to mean?"

"I think I get it!" exclaimed Jotham, "It's supposed to be read in parts. Read yours, Carisa."

She shook her head, "No, you go first." Her voice was distant and weak.

"OK." He shrugged his shoulders. "It says, 'Again you go to war, to war.'"

Carisa continued the message: "'I send you off . . .'" her voice caught, ". . . a band of four."

Dismal silence settled on the three. They began to move along the path, their pace now slowed to a leaden walk.

Carisa cleared her voice. "Justar must have sent us those words before Abe left. We've got to catch up to him. His parchment must complete the message."

"You're right, Carisa, let's get moving," Jotham agreed. "He can't be too far ahead of us."

Jotham took off with quick strides. "I don't want to think about what might happen if Abe attacks Ursula's stronghold against Justar's directions." Bart followed close behind.

"Why would he head off alone, anyway?" Carisa asked, catching up to them. The two boys looked away. Suddenly suspicious, she said, "It's something you guys did to him, isn't it?"

"We were just playing around," Bart said.

As they ran, Jotham briefly described what had happened with Abe and the tub.

Carisa shook her head at them in disbelief. "I can't believe you guys; that poor kid . . ." her voice trailed away. She threw her hands up in the air and headed down the path in the lead.

The terrain was rugged and dry, and they had not passed any water since leaving Orion. The three settled for a steady jog and made good progress. After covering several dusty miles, they agreed to stop. Sweat was pouring down their faces, and the suits of mail in their packs felt like bowling balls strapped to their backs. They threw themselves down beneath a rugged outcropping, which resembled a huge inverted paintbrush.

Bart held his water bag at arm's length and poured a stream into his open mouth.

"Don't drink too much," Jotham warned. "We have no idea how long it will be before we can refill our bags."

Bart lowered the container as some water splashed into his nostrils. "Aye, aye cap'n," he coughed.

They ate their bread and smoked fish quickly along with some sweet nectarines. Hurriedly massaging their legs, they prepared for an uphill climb.

"Abe's also got to rest; he can't be too far ahead now," Carisa said.

"I just hope he doesn't get lost. . . . Jo, how's his sense of direction?" Bart asked.

Jotham stood and tossed his pack over his shoulder. "I'll put it this way, it's a lot better than yours." He waved for the twins to follow him. "We've got to get to him before sundown."

181

The climb was quite steep, and soon the Paladins were panting heavily. They had gone up and down an interminable series of rises, and the three were beginning to feel lightheaded. After reaching another peak, they were assaulted by a horde of small flies that divebombed the Paladins, buzzing into their eyes, ears and noses. The cloud of insects spurred the three into a burst of energy that drove them to the top of the next rise at a half-run.

Jotham's legs were now so rubbery he was afraid they would lock up and send him sprawling face first down the granite slope. When he reached the top, exhausted, he let out a huge sigh of relief. At his feet stretched the valley of Lady Ursula, and nestled at the foot of a craggy mountain, just as it had been described, was her castle. He dropped down on top of a large rock that dominated the summit. There was a wonderful breeze which blew the minute pests away as quickly as they had appeared.

Carisa and Bart sat down next to him overlooking the valley and tried to catch their breath. "The baroness was right; Ursula's castle does look pretty close from up here," Carisa said. "If she hadn't warned us, I would have sworn that we could reach it before dusk."

"I guess the altitude must do strange things with perspective," Jotham said.

Bart nodded. "I know it was doing weird things with my head."

Carisa stuck her elbow in his ribs, almost shoving him off the rock. "It wouldn't take much," she grinned.

"You'd better watch it. Unlike our noble friend Flaggon, I have no scruples about putting a girl in her place."

Jotham stood up on uncertain legs. "It doesn't look like we're going to catch Abe today," he said quietly. He took a few tentative steps forward. "He's definitely not anywhere in the valley. Hopefully, he's camping out in a cave somewhere. We'd better find a place ourselves to spend the night. I want to make sure we have plenty of daylight left to prepare for the night."

The sun was painting the sky with pale gold, pink and rose brush strokes by the time they found a cave entrance half hidden by low shrubs, bushes and fallen trees. The cave had several large fissures in the roof, which let in fresh air and would allow them to build a fire far enough back from the entrance to avoid detection. They gathered several mounds of sticks to keep their fire going through the night.

By the time the cold evening was settling upon the valley, the Paladins had a cheery blaze going inside their shelter. But despite the warmth of the fire, their hearts were heavy. After supper, the three wrapped themselves in their cloaks, lay down listening to the symphonic chirping of frogs and crickets and tried to avoid thinking about Abe.

Bart was the first to fall asleep. Carisa and Jotham were lying next to each other on their stomachs, staring quietly at the dancing flames. It was a comfortable silence. After a while, Carisa glanced over at Jotham to see if he was still awake. "Jotham?" she whispered.

He turned toward her. The flames were flicking golden sparkles in her dark eyes. He realized suddenly that, for the first time since meeting again, he and Carisa were virtually alone. He realized too that it was hard for him to look at her too long because it made his heart pound and his throat tighten.

"For some reason I was thinking about that day we were spin-cycled into Issatar." They both smiled at the memory. "I always meant to ask you about what happened at Trisha's house with my dad. It was pretty obvious that you and he didn't want to talk much about it, but I've been really curious. Besides the scratches on his face, there was something about him that seemed . . . really . . . different. I wanted to talk to you about it before, but it never seemed to be the right time."

Jotham groaned inwardly, wanting to stall, but realized there was no way out. He'd desperately wanted to erase the entire incident from his mind, but suddenly, he wanted to tell her all about it. He sat up, crossed his legs and gazed into the fire. "It seems like forever ago; it's like it never really happened or happened in another life. I guess in a way it did. The strange thing is, yesterday after we were attacked by the Ghargs something made me remember that day too."

He picked up some sticks and tossed them onto the embers. Frankly, it's been something I really wanted to forget."

She reached out and touched his arm. "It's all right, Jo, you don't—"

"Naah, I probably need to talk to somebody about that mess. It was very bizarre and confusing." He described the encounter in Trent's bedroom with as much detail as he could bear to give.

"Wow . . . my poor dad . . ." She let out a long breath. "No wonder he looked the way he did when he got back." She studied the flames for a few moments.

Her next question surprised him. "How did Trisha . . . look?"

He shrugged. "She was scared to death. It was like she was almost in shock."

She laughed nervously, "No, I mean how is she now? I haven't seen her for so long. . . . I was just wondering."

"Oh! . . . Well, she's—you know—the typical cheerleader."

"Yeah, I figured as much."

He hurried on, sensing thin ice but unsure how to navigate between the shoals of honesty and diplomacy. "She's . . . nice. She's got long, blond hair now. She's also quite a bit shorter than you."

"Most girls *are*. . . . I've always been a giant. . . ." she sighed.

Inwardly he kicked himself. "Come on, Car, I never thought you were too tall. . . . Well, in fifth and sixth grade maybe," he grinned, "but I think you're just fine now. Besides, I've always liked tall girls myself."

"Oh really?" She paused, "Umm, how many . . . tall girls have you liked?"

Brilliant, Einstein. "I didn't mean . . ."

She smiled crookedly at him, "Relax, I was just pulling your leg. So, how long have you and Trisha been dating?"

He hesitated. "We've never dated. She's been going out with a friend on the football team."

Apparently satisfied, she gave him a searching look and asked him, "What was it yesterday that reminded you of Trent's house?"

"It was really odd. When those Ghargs slimed us, the stench was the same as what I thought I smelled on the stairs outside his door."

Carisa was quiet for several moments. "Jo, do you think—I don't know how to say it—but I've been wondering for the past couple days if there is some kind of . . . connection between what's happening here and . . . over there?"

"It's strange you should ask that. I've been thinking a lot about that myself. I'm starting to suspect that there may be some sort of . . . link, but I don't know what it is. I have a sneaking suspicion about it but . . . it's too way out."

"Yeah, I know what you mean. . . ." She sat up and grabbed her knees as she stared into the flames. Jotham's chest tightened—she looked even prettier than she had the night in the cabin. He wished he dared touch the satiny smoothness of her long tawny hair. She stirred the fire with a long stick, the sparks illuminating her features with a golden halo. "Sometimes I get the feeling that there is more to this than meets the eye—kind of like those movie sets where it looks like you're in the Old West but its really just a Hollywood studio."

"Exactly . . . only backwards somehow." Since their arrival in Issatar, he'd been struggling to make sense out of it. "The setting makes you think you're in a movie except that you *really are* in the Old West. Or something like that. . . . I just can't explain it." After a pause, he decided to give it another try. "I guess what I'm trying to say is—although sometimes it seems that this is only pretend, the truth is that somehow this is more real than our 'real' lives in Rockville."

Carisa nodded vigorously. "That's it! I've been trying and trying to figure out how to put it into words, and you just did. That's exactly how I've been feeling." Her golden eyes were locked on his. There seemed to be the ghost of a question in them. He couldn't recall ever seeing that there before.

His breath caught in a lump in his throat. He sat up and threw another branch into the flames. "But even so," he went on with a slight smile, "I still find myself walking around thinking that at any moment someone's going to jump out from behind a rock or tree and yell: "Surprise, you're on Candid Camera!"

Carisa threw back her head and laughed. "You too?"

It felt good to hear her laugh. Her whole face seemed to shine.

What an incredible smile!

She sensed him staring at her. Their eyes met, locked and held. Carisa turned suddenly serious. "Jotham, you don't laugh very much, at least not as much as when we were kids."

Jotham shrugged, attempting a pretense of indifference, but conveying instead a sad vulnerability.

She rested her hand lightly on his arm. "I don't mean to pry, but I'd really like to know what happened between you and your father. Don't feel like you've got to tell me or anything. I only want to know because . . . well, I . . . I care about you . . . and Abe. You were our closest friends, and Bart and I—Mom and Dad too—wondered about it a lot." Jotham stared solemnly at the embers now glowing a deep orange.

"We felt so badly for all of you but didn't really know a whole lot." She stopped, letting her hand fall to her side. "I'm sorry Jotham; here I'm going on and on. Forget I asked; I don't want to force you . . ."

He reached out and gripped her fingers. "No . . . no. You're not forcing me. It's something I think I've really needed to talk about. There was just never anybody around who I knew . . . really cared." His cheeks flushed, he

185

became acutely aware of her hand in his. He let her fingers go, running his hand nervously through his hair.

"It's hard to talk about, and I guess it's tough to know where to start." He decided to simply plunge forward.

"You know my Dad began drinking heavily about the time when his business went bad. Well, as it headed into bankruptcy, his drinking got even worse. In less than a year, he was coming home drunk most of the time. He got really mean with Mom and me. For some reason, he left Abe pretty much alone. I was scared to death of him when he got that way. Pretty soon I guess I just started to hate him . . ." His voice trailed off. Carisa's golden brown eyes were soft as she waited patiently for him to continue.

She looked intently at him, encouraging him on.

"This went on for several years. Anyway, Mom told Dad that he couldn't keep coming home drunk, and that he'd have to find some other place to live. Plus, she had found out that he'd been seeing some other woman he met at the bar. Mom wouldn't hardly even use the word *divorce*, so you know things must have gotten really bad at that point." Jotham paused, "So, Dad . . . left," he finished awkwardly.

Jotham was surprised at how badly he felt. He'd thought sharing these painful memories with Carisa would somehow be cathartic; instead, he was feeling worse by the minute. But now that he was in the middle of it, there was no way to go back.

"Mom didn't want us to think he was a total scum, so she let us know that he was sending money pretty regularly to help out. Although he lived in an apartment somewhere, every once in a while he would come over, sometimes sober . . . sometimes not."

His voice caught. "Then . . . one night he came over . . . really drunk." Tension was etched along the corners of his mouth.

Carisa sat next to him, as still as a statue. Her face was drawn. It hurt to watch the pain twisting his eyes.

The details of that evening had been burned indelibly into Jotham's memory. He had held this memory inside himself for so long, but now that it was rising to the surface, he could no longer hold it back. It had a life and power of its own, and was pouring over like a pot of scalded milk.

"I didn't actually intend to hurt him. . . ." his voice quavered, but he went on. "I was alone in the house; he came in smelling like a stinking bar and asked me where Mom was. Something about the way he came in, like nothing had happened, and the smell of smoke and beer all over him, got to me. I asked him what he wanted from her. I could tell that made him mad, but I didn't care."

"He yelled back at me: 'I'm not here to ask her for anything. I came to give her something.'"

"I made some kind of sarcastic remark. It felt like something was coming unglued inside, and all I wanted to do was to get even with him for all the hurt he'd caused us. So I told him, 'the only thing you know how to give is pain.'"

Jotham's throat constricted, the memory of the look that had flashed through his father's eyes cut him to the quick. He'd wished a thousand times he could recall those words.

"He just stood there like I'd stuck him with a knife." Jotham let out a slow breath. "For a minute I thought he was going to cry. . . . Instead . . . he turned away without saying a word and walked into the dining room. After what seemed like forever, he turned toward me and said softly, like he was really hurt: 'You've never respected me—have you?'"

Carisa's eyes were wide. "What did you say?"

"I didn't know what to say. All of a sudden I was starting to feel really sorry for him, I wanted to go over to him and . . . and hug him or something, but I just stood there. Anyway, he began talking louder and louder and pretty soon he was yelling at me again about not knowing how good I had it, and stuff about how hard it was for him to be raised by his stepfather. He just kind of went crazy and screamed that I had no business judging him and that I had never given him the respect he deserved. By that point I was really ticked off again, and I lost it too. So I just yelled back, 'What is there to respect?'"

Carisa tensed, "So, what happened then?"

"It was . . . weird. All of a sudden, his face grew . . . dark and . . . kind of evil. He began walking towards me slowly, mumbling under his breath, 'You have no right to judge me!'"

"I couldn't move away; it felt as if some force had grabbed hold of me and stuck me to the floor. When he was right in my face, he yelled something like: 'You've always hated me . . . well then, go ahead and do something about it.' But before I even knew what to do, he slapped me . . . hard. It knocked me down onto the couch, and then he grabbed me and yanked me back to my feet."

Carisa sucked her breath in as if she had received the blow. She lowered her head, wiping a tear with the back of her hand.

Jotham's voice was growing faint, but he proceeded in a dull monotone. "He lifted his arm to hit me again. I screamed for him to stop and . . . I must have shoved him. He lost his balance and hit his forehead on the corner of the coffee table. He lay on the carpet a few moments groaning. Blood was everywhere. He pushed my hand away when I tried to help him up. But before walking out the door, he took an envelope from his pocket and threw it on the table. Inside was a check for my mom for $500 and a note telling her he was sorry. That was about a year and a half ago. . . ." She could now barely hear his voice. "I haven't seen Dad since."

"Oh Jotham," Carisa grabbed his hand, "I'm sorry . . . I'm so sorry; I didn't know. . . ."

He lay back down on the straw, exhausted. It was as if retelling the incident had drained him of his last reserves of energy. He fell into a troubled sleep, feeling Carisa's hand gently stroking his hair.

Chapter Twenty Six

Thin streams of light were cutting through the gloom from the cracks in the pitted ceiling. Jotham rubbed his eyes. As he recalled what he had finally been able to share with Carisa, inside him, a hollow melancholy vied with a strange exhilaration. He stared at the luminous shafts that seemed to be pouring particles of dancing light into the darkness. It was a morning filled with sorrow, yet sprinkled with a haunting promise of joy.

Suddenly, a picture of Abe's wet face set in an expression of anger and humiliation flashed into his memory. He jumped to his feet, an aching fear rising in his chest and walked over to their packs tossed along the side wall. More than anything, he wanted to find his younger brother and apologize to him. "Have you guys eaten already?" he called out to the two at the cave's entrance. "We'd better get going."

"I don't think we should eat today," Carisa answered, looking out over the valley.

"Why not?"

She held up her scroll. "Read this."

He walked out and stood next to them. Bart looked at him. "We haven't seen Abe anywhere, Jo. He's either lost or he's already at the castle. I dunno, maybe there's a shortcut or he walked through the night."

Fear began rising and tightened into a chokehold.

Jotham glanced quickly over her scroll. The poignant words from the previous day were still there, "I send you off a band of four," and, underneath, was a new phrase, in the center of the parchment, "Don't break your fast, and your strength will last."

"That's strange," he murmured, handing it back to her.

"Read yours, Jo. Car and I were thinking that Justar might make some changes in our battle strategy if we're still no longer four when we get to the castle."

Jotham unrolled his scroll, and to his surprise, found that there were no amendments to the message he'd read the day before.

"Mine hasn't changed either," Bart remarked.

"I guess the plans remain the same as they were yesterday—whatever they were," Jotham said, remembering the incomplete instructions due to Abe's absence. "With one exception," he grimaced, "we won't be eating today." He turned to look down at the valley, staring with troubled eyes at the tall turrets of Ursula's Fortress, the tops of which were still obscured by the morning mist. It had apparently been built on an island in the middle of a small lake. From their vantage point, it looked like a pearl seated on a swath of dark satin.

Carisa nudged her brother. "Go ahead and tell him."

"Naah . . . it was no big deal," Bart grumbled. "It was just a dumb dream."

"So? Tell him anyway."

He complied with reluctance. "Abe was in the sky, except that he wasn't really flying," he explained. "It only looked like it because he was in the air, but he was actually being carried."

"How?" Jotham asked, his fear contracting tighter in a painful knot.

Bart looked away. "Well . . . it was just . . ." Carisa stared at her brother with grim insistence. His shoulders slumped. "OK . . . There were two big Ghargs, and he was hanging by their tails. Each had a hold of one of his arms. He was kicking his legs trying to get loose, but he couldn't break their grip."

The icy knot was now threatening to strangle him. "Was that it?" Jotham was barely able to get the words out.

Carisa's eyes bore holes through Bart again. "Cut it out, Car," he protested. "It was only a dream anyway! All I could make out was that he was being taken into a dark place and was chained to a wall . . ." With a trapped look, he concluded. ". . . and it kind of looked like there were claw marks on his back."

Jotham slumped down against a craggy boulder.

Bart gazed morosely at the far-off castle, "Maybe I just dreamed that because I was feeling guilty over Abe."

"I hope so," murmured Jotham, following them inside.

"Whatever it means," Carisa said, "we'd better hurry." After covering the coals with dirt and strapping on their packs, they hurried out of the cool cave into the bright morning sun.

The Paladins jogged toward the stronghold in brooding silence. Of the band, Bart seemed to be the one carrying the greatest weight, as if he were laboring under a secret which he could not divulge.

The valley was covered with scrub brush, and in places large cracks testified to the soil's aching thirst. It was a bleak vista that spread out in front of them. The trees were gnarled and twisted, blasted by the intense heat into contorted claws, raking the dry air in parched frenzy.

After several miles traversing the hard-packed earth, Jotham signalled that it was time to stop and take a drink. They collapsed in the mottled shade of a splintered tree trunk and unplugged their water bottles. Bart and Jotham let the cool water stream over their faces and run down onto their tunics. Carisa took several deep swallows, then dampened a cloth and wiped her face.

Bart rubbed his stomach. "How long do you think we were supposed to go without food?"

"I know what you mean," Jotham lamented. "What I wouldn't give for deluxe burgers and a chocolate shake."

"Cut it out!" Carisa moaned. She tied the damp cloth around her neck.

A few minutes later, stepping back out into the baking sun, Bart told Jotham, "There was something else about that dream that may be important."

Jotham had been steeling himself for this further revelation. Something in Bart's face had told him everything had not been divulged at the cave.

"Somehow we got ahold of Abe's ax, and you began to play a dance tune on it. In the dream, I remember thinking that you were doing the strangest thing. I don't know why, but it just seemed really out of place." He paused. "I guess it was 'cause I think you were crying as you played."

Jotham felt a lump forming in his throat. He took off in a slow jog. Like a dead fish floating to the surface, an appalling fear was beginning to rise inside him.

They were about a mile from the castle when Jotham stopped dead in his tracks. His heart lurched madly, hoping against hope. Sitting against the thin trunk of a tall sparse tree that looked like an elongated mushroom, was a figure dressed in a Paladin's tunic. He was holding his head in his hands. With Bart and Carisa at his heels, Jotham raced forward, almost shouting with joy.

At the sound of their feet, the pensive figure lifted his head and gazed dully at the approaching runners. Jotham's heart sank like an anchor.

191

Although the Paladin's hair was dark and curly, he could see now that it was actually dark red. He also appeared to be considerably older than all of them. His face remained expressionless. He almost seemed to be expecting them.

The three Paladins surrounded the morose stranger who remained sitting as he squinted up at them through the sun's glare. Jotham was struggling to regain his breath, biting his lip in bitter disappointment. Something about the man reminded him of Abner. Jotham felt a sudden surge of rage and drew his sword.

The stranger stood to his feet, the white folds of his tunic unfolding and revealing a thin, angular frame draped in the attire of a Paladin. By his side hung a battered broadsword. It looked well used. He dropped his hands to his side, and with careless indifference, opened his pouch and withdrew a parchment. As if he were fencing, he thrust the scroll forward, sticking it on the point of Jotham's sword, declaring insolently, "I deflect your misguided thrust and parry with my own rapier."

Jotham arched his eyebrows at the tall Paladin who stood impassively, his long fingers open at his sides. Jotham drew back the scroll which dangled ludicrously from his sword tip.

"What's your name?" Carisa asked coolly. Memories of Abner's deceit restrained her natural friendliness.

The stranger drew himself even more erect, his chest puffing out as if he were standing in military review. His lean, serious face was balanced by large ears which stood out dramatically from the sides of his head. His red hair was shaved high on each side, which served to accentuate his ears, making them appear as if they were stranded on each side of his head. "I am a Paladin," he barked. "I am known as Trellawton the Third."

Jotham finished reading the parchment and handed it to Bart. "Looks like you're a Paladin all right," he said, "judging from the looks of the scroll. We're all Paladins here, so how about we call you by your name? Since it's a mouthful, we'll call you Law for short." He didn't bother asking for the stranger's permission.

Bart stared at Jotham, astonished at his credulity.

The stranger's mouth curved in a tight frown; he opened his mouth to argue, but checked himself with effort and finally nodded. After the three Paladins introduced themselves, Bart and Carisa looked over Law's parchment.

Bart whistled in surprise. The letters had the same internal light which marked their own scrolls. The statement, however, was striking: "A strand of one is soon undone, but when it's four it's fit for war." The three gazed silently at the stranger. Apparently Justar had sent him as Abe's replacement.

Jotham's throat again constricted painfully. He was beginning to feel sick with worry.

He wanted to scream, *What's happening to him inside that castle?*

Chapter Twenty Seven

Bart was staring at the emblem of the lion on Law's tunic. "So you're the real McCoy, eh?" Bart asked.

"I am not!" Law retorted, his freckled cheeks turning a fiery red. "I am a Paladin of the order of Prince Gabriel the Lionhearted . . ." gesturing at his black leggings and sleeves, "as is apparent by my uniform." He glanced with disdain at their biking attire. "And which order, may I ask, is yours?" Jotham felt rage building. They had no time for this arrogant clown.

Carisa answered quickly, "We're of no particular order. We simply serve Justar the King."

Law tossed his head and gazed patronizingly down at her. "We are the highest order of Paladins, and are, therefore, granted the most difficult assignments. Glancing pointedly at their sandalled feet, he went on, "Unlike others, we go barefoot as proof of our strength of will."

"It is our code not to intermingle with those of lesser rank or station." he said, flicking some burrs off his tunic. "I have never before violated the prohibition against the unequal yoke, and I cannot understand why the script would require me to do so now. It flies in the face of all reason and tradition."

"What's this unequal yoke deal?" Jotham asked coolly, his fury barely contained.

Law reverently opened his black, engraved leather pouch and withdrew a scroll tied with a gold satin ribbon. Touching the scroll to his lips, then unrolling it haughtily, he explained, "A fundamental doctrine of our order is that we are, and I quote . . ." he scanned the parchment, his lips moving soundlessly as he searched for the words, "never to put a horse and a mule in the same harness." Noting their confusion, he continued slowly as if speaking to idiots, "What that means is that we who belong to the Order of the Lionhearted are to remain separate from all others, lest we be contaminated—you *do* know what that means?—Good!—by their lack of discipline and by their tendency to compromise."

194

A tight smile played on the corners of Bart's lips. He was envisioning tossing Law against the tree trunk with a wicked judo toss. "I don't think we need to ask who the mules might be in this particular situation, do we?" Bart inquired, a hard edge to his voice.

Carisa elbowed him.

Law ignored it, continuing with his recitation of their catechism. "However, we are sworn to follow the instructions of the scripts of Gabriel to the letter, 'and verily, verily deviate never, neither by jot nor even by tittle.' The scripts supersede the Code's authority, and in the event of a conflict, are controlling in all matters of conduct and warfare." He looked down at their dusty leather pouches. "We use only the version authorized by Prince Gabriel, of course. May I ask, which version do you use?"

Again noticing the blank looks on their faces, he waved his hand dismissively. "Never mind, I can gather what the answer is. In any event, as you see, the words of the script (which are infallible and not subject to question) make it clear that you are to join me as your leader for the ensuing battle."

Jotham was on the verge of violence. "Law, let's get this straight from the beginning—*I* am the captain, appointed by Justar himself, and I'm not stepping down unless he tells me so, direct." Flinging out his hand, he grabbed the front of the red-headed stranger's tunic. "In fact . . ."

Instead of recoiling, strangely, Law only nodded, grimly.

Bart gripped Jotham's arm. "Excuse us, Law, give us a minute. . . ." He drew Jotham away, and the three gathered in a small huddle on the other side of the mound.

"Hold on, man. Don't go punching the guy's lights out," Bart urged. "I'd like to teach this dude a lesson myself, but we've got to decide if he's for real; and more important, we've got to get going toward that castle."

"Yeah," Carisa agreed. "Is he a real Paladin or an impersonator like Abner?"

Jotham had been glaring at Law, who was scowling back at him. Jotham again unrolled Law's scroll. "Look at the letters. . . . They are identical to ours. There are lots of things Ghnostar can imitate, but I don't think that's one of them."

Bart touched them with his fingertips. They shimmered over the surface of the parchment. "If he could copy them, it sure seems like he would have done so on Abner's scroll."

Carisa looked back at Law who was tapping the ground impatiently with his foot. "When you think about it," she said, "would an impostor act like such a jerk if he wanted to convince us to trust him?"

Bart gave a sidelong glance. "Good point." Then he turned to Jotham, "So what's the plan?"

"His scroll matches ours," Jotham conceded. "Abe is nowhere around and we need four for the battle. I don't think we have any choice but to let him join us . . . but there's no way . . ."

Carisa patted him on the arm and grinned. "We wouldn't let him take over either, Captain."

When they rejoined Law, Jotham silenced him with an upturned hand. Bart and Carisa flanked their leader with hands firmly on their hilts.

"The words of our scrolls match yours," Jotham began. "We have been ordered—before you received your orders, by the way—to fight as a band of four. Apparently, you are going to make up for . . . the other member of our band. You can link up with us, or you can go find some other strands or yokes, or whatever, to join." Jotham stormed off, waving at Carisa and Bart to follow him.

Law stared at the retreating figures, realizing that his argument was hopelessly lost. Replacing his scroll quickly in his pouch, with his long strides he caught up to them quickly. "Wait. There is no reason to lose our heads over this matter. I am willing to defer to you on the issue of leadership; however, I would strongly suggest that we remain here to coordinate an evening assault to rescue your brother."

The three stopped and turned slowly around.

"I am assuming, of course, that you have an established plan of attack." He looked pointedly at the Paladins. "I would like to know what it is."

The three glared at him with mounting suspicion.

"Jotham, you are the Captain; therefore, it falls to you to clarify tactics. Do you or do you not have a strategy for taking the fortress?"

Jotham sucked in a harsh breath, then let it out very slowly. His fingers were clenched on the hilt of his sword. "How did *you* know . . . about my brother?" he intoned with dangerous deliberation.

Bart readied his sword, and Carisa unslung her crossbow.

Red splotches appeared on Law's cheeks. Instead of fear, an embarrassed expression flitted across his narrow face.

"Ahhem, well, this is most unusual I can tell you. I must say, I generally put no stock in such things but I-I, well . . ."

Jotham's jaws were clenched, and the muscles along his jaw line were twitching. "Spit it out Law, or, I swear, I'll split you in half."

"Yes, yes. I see that." He ran a nervous hand through his red mop. "Before you arrived, I had a . . . well, what some would call . . . a . . . well, not to put too fine a point on it . . . a vision." He thrust his hands out as if personally dismayed. "There, you have it!"

"More!" commanded Jotham.

"Ahh, now mind you, as a matter of principle, I frown on such immaterial fancies—"

"Law!" Jotham's fury was evident. "Out with it. We're wasting time, and something tells me you're stalling."

The stranger's cheeks were flushed; his eyes were staring at his feet in embarrassment. "Of course, of course. Just before you arrived, as if I were dreaming—except I knew I was fully awake—I saw four Paladins." Law's eyes briefly touched theirs and quickly looked away. "Then, one of them was snatched and taken to a dark prison. I heard a voice—highly irregular, I must say—which sounded very much like that of the Great General King Justar declare: 'Don't trust your sight, attack at night. Wait for the light, then trust my might.'"

He hesitated, clearing a lump from his throat. "I-I believe he said that the captured Paladin's name was Abe." Law's vision combined with the vivid details of Bart's dream struck the Paladins to the heart. Jotham felt as though he'd been hit with a Warrior's fist. Bart's face was ashen. "Oh Abe," Carisa moaned.

Jotham's heart felt ready to explode. His brimming eyes stung. He swallowed but could make no sound. Finally, after several trembling breaths, he asked in a shaky voice, "H-how did you know he was *my* brother?"

Law nodded, "The voice said that Abe was the brother of the Paladin who would threaten to strike me." He gestured to the lengthening shadow, "Now, may we sit?"

The four warriors sat down. There was a long silence. No one wanted to be the first to speak. The late afternoon sun was still hot. They unstopped their water bags and drank deeply.

Law coughed loudly and gulped as if something was caught in his throat. He smiled apologetically at the three Paladins next to him, looking at them solemnly with watery eyes. "I ahh . . . believe I owe you an apology. When we met, I wasn't overly pleasant."

"Now that's an understatement!" Bart murmured.

"I have to admit I was very displeased with my instructions . . . Once you get used to fighting alone, it is difficult to have to join in with others, and I'm afraid, I took out my anger on you. It was conduct unbecoming of a Paladin of the Order of the Lionhearted."

The three nodded, accepting the apology.

Law stared down at his bony knees. "I have something else that I need to state. I was not commissioned initially to battle alone. I had a comrade-in-arms. His name was Ellwynn, and we became fast friends. We met with great initial success, but I grew overconfident and launched a hasty attack." He rubbed his sleeve across his wet forehead. "We were ambushed and I was able to escape . . . Ellwynn, however, was captured. I heard later that he had been terribly . . . tortured." Sorrow twisted his face. "I've never seen or heard about him again! He simply disappeared."

Carisa put her hand on Law's shoulder. He covered his face with his hands and tried to stifle the sobs. Jotham and Bart exchanged awkward glances.

After several moments, Law blinked his eyes, took a slow breath and looked toward the glistening castle. "If you don't mind, Jotham, I think it time to begin preparing for battle."

"Do you have any suggestions?" Jotham asked.

"First, I think we should eat. I have a goodly amount of provisions and, if I may say so, you have the look of hunger about you."

Jotham explained the instructions they had received that morning. Law nodded his head sympathetically.

"Well then, a fast it is," he said, closing his pack. "The first day is always the hardest."

Carisa asked, "So, you've had to do it before?"

"Yes, many times. Though it makes one feel weak, it tends to improve other more important faculties. I remember that Prince Gabriel once told us that sacrifice releases a hidden power; and that the greater the sacrifice, the greater the reservoir of power." He spread out his hands in front of him, his eyes widening. "It is a mystery."

"Let's hope we get a real boost tonight, because I'm starting to feel like a hollow tube about now," Bart groaned.

"If we can't eat," Jotham said, "we'd at least better try to get some rest and conserve whatever strength we have left. Something tells me that tonight we're going to need every bit of it."

Chapter Twenty Eight

Bart and Jotham made beds of their cloaks and lay down. Carisa sat down next to the new member of their band, who was sitting cross-legged staring at the castle. "Law, you mentioned something that I've been wanting to ask someone since we arrived here . . . What happened to Prince Gabriel?"

His eyes didn't leave the fortification. He sat quietly for several minutes, and Carisa was about to repeat the question when he began to speak, his voice soft and sad. "It is a sad tale, Carisa, and one that I do not fully comprehend. It is a dark, dark chapter that is difficult to talk about. But it is one that you need to know." He tugged thoughtfully on his ear, his face growing cloudy.

"Justar had commissioned our Prince to attack Ghnostar's Lair." He gestured to the mountains lying south of the castle. "It is hidden somewhere behind that range, protected by a spell." He lifted up his leather water bag. "Would you care for some refreshment?"

She took it from him. The water tasted faintly of lime. She looked at him in surprise. "Ummm, that's good."

Law smiled, "It's an old campaigner's trick. It's good for the digestion, it protects from illness and is more refreshing too." He took a deep drink. "The entire Order was mustered for this confrontation on a broad plateau on top of the mountain. We, of course, had superior leadership and discipline—Ghnostar's forces can never match us there; but, he has great craft on his side. Before the battle, we could hear the dragon regaling his troops with the boast that though King Justar had given great power to the Prince, age and treachery would inevitably triumph . . ." his jaws clenched, "and so it proved."

"How could that ever happen?"

"I don't think anyone who was there could answer that question. I know it was such a terrible affair that many who survived actually surrendered their commission and joined themselves to Ghnostar's army. They've been transformed into awful creatures and have become his most wicked warriors." He stopped, took a deep breath, then letting it out slowly, continued. "Let me go back to the beginning. Though we had marched for days, the battle did not last very long. It was actually over before many even knew it, but that didn't diminish the horror of it—especially for Prince Gabriel. If you'd known him, you would understand."

"If he was anything like his father, I can imagine pretty well what he must have been like," Carisa said.

Jotham turned over on his side. Carisa looked at him and saw that he was wide awake.

"The father and son had much in common, there's no denying that," Law agreed, "but there was an adventurous exuberance, a wonderful wildness about Prince Gabriel that made your heart race just to be near him. Not meaning any disrespect, the Prince laughed much more than the Great General. Actually, he seemed to smile all the time. That's why many called him Bonnie Prince Gabriel." Law smiled wanly with sorrowful eyes. "He loved a good joke. . . . Although, to tell you the truth, his puns were quite terrible. We all would laugh anyway, and not just to humor him, mind you, but because he enjoyed them so fiercely . . . You should have heard his laugh! It could make you weep with the sheer delight of it." His blue eyes clouded.

"I miss him terribly! In him there seemed to be no sadness. He could walk into a room and the glow of his face could make the worst darkness or heaviness seem light. He was like no other man I have ever known. All his men loved him," he paused, "except, of course, for Rinnard the Lanslot, who betrayed us."

Bart, who had been laying on his side, rolled toward them. "How did that happen?" he asked.

"It was after the initial sortie—several thousand had been killed or wounded, much more on their side than ours. The ground was littered with bodies. It seemed preposterous that there could be so many dead in such a short time. We had effectively decimated Ghnostar's elite troops—rather too easily as it later proved. It was the consensus of our generals that Ghnostar had been holding back the Kravens, and that while they were invisible, they had wheeled around our exposed flanks and were now awaiting his command."

Jotham drew close. "What are they?" he asked.

"They are the dragon's shock troops, his hand-picked guards. They are taller than I am and are a terrifying combination of vulture and leopard. They are singularly awful creatures."

Carisa shuddered and glanced around, sweeping the sky with her eyes.

"You have nothing to fear from them here," Law said. "Their exclusive function is to guard Ghnostar's Lair."

"Doesn't sound like a very pleasant bunch." Bart remarked.

Law went on. "The Ghargs had taken some of our men captive, the betrayer Rinnard being one of them. He was returned with a message that Ghnostar wanted a truce so they could go out and pick up their wounded. Rinnard got alone with the Prince and informed him that the Kravens had fled after seeing proof of our superiority—Ghnostar's forces are notoriously undisciplined so that was not out of the question. However, what Rinnard divulged next was 'the hook.' He told Prince Gabriel that after the enemy gathered up their wounded, Ghnostar intended to slaughter them as an example to his army."

Law clenched his fist and punched the knapsack on the ground. "It was clever . . . so clever. Ghnostar knew exactly what he was doing. Prince Gabriel could not allow the wounded to be killed. Whether they were theirs or ours was inconsequential, so he agreed to a truce. But he demanded that *we* be allowed to pick up *all* the wounded so they could be treated properly in a secure location behind our lines. With a great show of reluctance, the dragon agreed, and we did just that. A large group of us sheathed our weapons and carried the wounded off by the hundreds. However, before we were able to totally clear the ground, Ghnostar released the Kravens."

Law squeezed his eyes closed. He was holding the water bottle so tightly that it looked ready to burst. "I've never seen such a horrifying sight. The sky was black with huge hairy wings and spotted bodies. At the same moment, the 'wounded' we had placed behind us sprang to their feet, drew their weapons and surrounded us: most had only been feigning their injuries. They fell upon us from all sides. I received a severe wound on my leg and arm. I lay on the ground, blood pouring out of me." Law dropped his head into his hands.

"Our men were falling all over the field. However, out of love for our Prince, we still could have fended them off, though at the loss of more than half our men. But, Prince Gabriel would countenance no such slaughter. He released a terrible howl of anger; then, at the top of his voice, so that the ground shook with the awful sound of it, he screamed: 'Stop!' Everyone was frozen in their tracks. Prince Gabriel stepped forward through the immobilized warriors and offered himself as hostage for his men. The dragon, with slavering insolence, accepted the terms and led Prince Gabriel to a hill overlooking the evil pond in front of his castle. All Ghnostar's troops surrounded the lake, while behind them, we watched with breaking hearts as he gloated over and mocked our Prince. . . ."

Law let out a low moan.

The Paladins waited silently, in the grip of a dreadful expectancy.

"I-I can barely stand to recall this . . . Rinnard took a dagger and sliced the clothes off our Prince, cutting his body as he did so, then threw them at us. The Prince stood there naked, unafraid." Law's eyes widened with horror. His voice was almost too low to be heard. "Ghnostar lifted up his gruesome tail; and with a scornful snort, thrust it into the Prince's chest. The dragon, not content to simply kill him, picked him high into the air and began waving him about, shaming our Prince before our eyes." Law lifted his face, his eyes streaming unashamedly.

"Finally, tired of his sport, Ghnostar flung Prince Gabriel's body into that filthy pond. When his body smacked the water, the loathsome dragon raised his front claws and began prancing about arrogantly in an awful victory jig. It was more than some of us could stand. Some warriors even lost their minds."

Law stopped, swallowed painfully, then looked directly at them. "When Ghnostar drove his stinger into the Prince's chest, the strangest thing happened: all those on our side who had been wounded were immediately healed! That is why I am alive today. If it had not been for him, I would have bled to death." His eyes grew suddenly distant. "I'd never thought about it before . . . but I wonder whether that may have something to do with what Gabriel said about sacrifice and the release of power."

Carisa's face was ashen; she licked her dry lips. "Law," she whispered, "Were . . ." she hesitated uncertainly, "were the Prince's clothes made from white linen?"

Law was no longer able to speak. He had the haggard look of a man crushed and lost. Unable to look at her, he nodded his head numbly.

Her eyes grew wide, but she remained silent.

After Law's story, none of them felt like talking further. They each lay down with their own thoughts, and soon much-needed sleep overtook them. Dusk fell quickly in the mountain valley as the Paladins napped. The sun plunged behind the far-off range as if hurrying to depart the arena of conflict. The four were awakened by the cool evening breeze. After examining their weapons, slipping on their suits of mail and clarifying the details of the attack, they made their way toward Ursula's Fortress. Twinkling stars festooned the dark canopy overhead as they crept toward the castle. A shooting star blazed briefly above the ramparts.

"We proceed *'bonis avibus'*" whispered Law who was crouched next to Bart.

"Indeed," Bart responded, racking his brain for the translation; then it came to him. "Law says that we proceed to battle under good auspices," he muttered to Jotham and Carisa in the lead. "That star was apparently a good omen."

"I certainly hope so," Carisa said.

There were no lights in the fortress. It stood black against the clear, autumn sky. Its tall pointed spires reminded Carisa of an enchanted castle she'd seen in a fairy tale book. It was eerily quiet, as if it were holding its breath. The long, wooden walkway leading to the entrance gate was actually a high bridge over an empty lake bed. The drought had evaporated the water, leaving a deep crater around the circumference of the castle walls. From the mouth of the cave, what had looked like water surrounding the castle had actually been the cavity left by the dry moat.

It was so silent that the four found themselves barely daring to breathe. They crept slowly over the bridge until they were directly in front of the castle gate.

"What do we do now?" Bart asked as they stood in a huddle, dwarfed by the barred door.

"Watch and wait," murmured their captain.

"Great!" Bart grumbled. "I'm feeling a lot better already. . . . Do you know what we're watching for?"

"No . . . but we'll know when we see it."

"Makes sense to me, how about you?" Bart asked his sister, shaking his head.

She put her fingers to her lips and looked up at the walls looming in front of them. They were so tall, the sky was now blocked completely from view.

Growing tired of standing, they sat down on the bridge's wooden planks to maintain their vigil. A cold wind began to blow, whipping the ends of their cloaks. To keep them from flapping and snapping against the wood beneath them, they drew the thick material more tightly around them and waited.

Around midnight, Law grabbed Jotham's arm, jerking him to his feet. He pointed emphatically to an upper window. A lantern was swinging back and forth. It was immediately extinguished. Just as abruptly, it blazed and began to swing again. Bart and Carisa were now standing next to them. This was repeated four times.

"Was that it?" Carisa asked.

"The instruction said to wait for the light. I'm certain that was the sign we were to watch for," Law whispered. "Draw your weapons," he told them. "Our foe is treacherous, and we must take nothing for granted."

Taking several steps backwards, still facing the gate, they held their swords at the ready.

A breathless minute later, there was a scratching and a jingling of metal several feet to their right. A key was being placed in a small door they had not noticed, hidden next to the main gate. It swung open on well-oiled hinges, and the dim light of a slatted lantern shone on the form of a broad-shouldered man. He was dressed in filthy clothes resembling those of their new companion. When he held up the light to his face, they could see that his skin was a dark ebony. His hair was also black except for a patch of pure white on the crown of his head.

Law stiffened and lunged forward; Jotham grabbed him to keep him from falling to the ground.

"Ellwynn!" Law gasped.

Chapter Twenty Nine

Jotham steadied Law, and they soundlessly followed the ragged figure who was motioning for them to keep quiet and hurry into the castle. They entered a small landing with one set of stone steps leading up and another leading down.

"Are you all inside?" their guide whispered, his deep voice echoing hollowly off the stone walls. "Where are you, Trellawton?" Law was standing directly in front of him, tears streaming down his face. "I'm sorry, my friend," Ellwynn continued, "but I can no longer rely on my sight."

The Paladins were shocked to realize that what they had taken to be deep-set eyes were actually empty sockets left by a torturer's brand. Ellwynn's reassuring smile flashed at them in the light of the lantern. He held out his hand. "You and I both know they weren't the best, anyhow." Law threw himself weeping upon his friend's neck.

"Come, come," he murmured, his large hand patting Law on the shoulder, "there's a time for everything, and the time for sorrow is past. Now 'tis the time for war." He headed purposefully down the stairs. "Follow me."

Ellwynn opened a door at the first landing and entered. It was a kitchen, and a welcoming fire was burning in the open oven. Long-handled copper pots of all sizes, along with ladles and brass cooking utensils, hung from hooks on the walls. They sat down at a long table on which a pitcher and five glasses had been placed. "I would have offered you food to go with your drink, but I was warned of your fast, so that must wait. In any event, we don't have much time before the guards will waken to man their posts. All the prisoners have been blinded, so the soldiers have fallen into the habit of sleeping through the early watch and getting up just before their superiors come down for inspection."

"How did you know we were coming?" Law asked.

It almost looked as if their new friend were blushing. He cleared his throat, rubbed his mouth with the back of his hand and said, "It was most unusual. . . . I've never known anything quite like it." He handed the pitcher to Law who began filling the glasses. "You and I used to scoff at those gullible types who believed in such nonsense, but it happened to me and I can't deny it."

Law gazed at him intently. "What was it?"

The other Paladins were drinking deeply. The drink had a tangy taste of cider and mixed with it were pieces of orange, melon, and peach. It was delicious and helped ease the pain in their grumbling stomachs.

"I heard the voice of . . . well . . . How shall I say this? The voice was like that of . . . Blast! I might as well say it. I heard the voice of Prince Gabriel, himself." He raised his hand toward his comrade. "I know it sounds preposterous, but I would recognize that voice among a thousand. He spoke to me as clearly as you are—" He bit his lip which had begun to tremble. "I even felt his hand on my head. It was him, Trellawton. . . . I could smell him!"

"What did he say?" Law asked in an awestruck whisper.

"He . . . he laughed—but his words were sharp; there was fire in them. You know how he could get. Anyhow, he explained that we were going to pull a trick on Ghnostar's troops, so that the blood that had been spilt would be 'well and truly avenged.' He said you would be coming with a band of three others, and we were to show no mercy. He also gave me a special message for Jotham, the captain."

"Is it to be delivered in private?" Law asked.

"No." He turned his head toward the others around the table. "Where are you sitting, Jotham?"

"Here," Jotham reached out and touched Ellwynn's hand.

Ellwynn grasped his fingers, swallowing Jotham's hand in his. "The Prince says to tell you that he spoke on his father's behalf and that you were not to lose hope, but to trust completely in the Great King. Then he gave me a message from King Justar which I was entrusted to deliver, verbatim:

Do not despair, though sorrow tears;
My hand upon you, your burden bears.
All that's wrong will be made right,
For in your darkness I'll make it bright,
Then play it fiercely, with all your might,
To destroy the enemy, and win the fight.

Jotham again felt the icy prickling in his chest. He squeezed Ellwynn's fingers. "Do you know . . ." he paused ". . . where my brother is?"

"Yes. He is here. He was brought in late last night. The word among the prisoners is that he displayed tremendous bravery. The Ghargs were instructed to force him to betray you. But he refused to break."

"Is he . . . still alive?"

"Yes, he is. At least, I believe so. He is a brave young man."

Jotham leaped to his feet. "Let's go! Take me to him."

Ellwynn stood up. "I will show you where they are keeping him. The cook, who is the only captive with eyesight, will take the other three to find the rest of the prisoners."

Jotham was opening the door they had recently entered. "No," Ellwynn said, "not that way—you must stay behind me." Without hesitation, Ellwynn stepped toward a small door hidden in the shadows. "The rest of you are to follow Cook who is waiting on the other side of the door opposite the stove. You will recognize him by his girth, and by his eyes, of course."

Leading Jotham through the narrow doorway, Ellwynn added, "Trellawton, another thing—Prince Gabriel made it very clear that the girl is to use her gift on the blind."

Jotham's heart was hammering. He could barely restrain his desire to dash down the stairs shrieking Abe's name, letting him know he was coming to rescue him.

The circular stairway seemed to grow tighter as they progressed down into the lower level of the castle. The walls were covered with thick greenish-black moss, and there was a musty heaviness hung in the dank air. With each step, Jotham found it harder to breathe. Both the walls around him and the fear and tension within were squeezing in upon him. He felt as though he were moving progressively deeper into the belly of a monstrous carnivore. Despite the coolness of the passageway, a clammy sweat broke out on his face. His teeth began to clatter in nervous tension.

After the 16th turn, Ellwynn stopped and held up one finger. Jotham was overcome with a terrible dread that they were too late. Suddenly, he wanted to bolt back up the stairs. He was terrified of what he would find around the bend, but more horrible was the fear of what he would never find if he ran away now.

Ellwynn squeezed his arm, giving him the signal. Jotham filled his cramped lungs with the fetid air and yanked out his sword. As they inched around the last curve, they heard hissing and then a sound torn from the pages of Jotham's childhood—the rasping wails of his little brother in the throes of an awful nightmare. Jotham sunk to one knee, bile rising in his throat. He gritted his teeth, choking it down. A roaring filled his ears; he pressed his feverish forehead flat against the dank coolness of the stone wall. It felt like a vise was crushing his chest.

Ellwynn helped him back to his feet. The hilt of his sword was now burning in Jotham's palm. They were standing in a narrow, smoky hall. The gate in an arched doorway at the end was less than 20 feet away. Torches flickered, casting wicked shadows on the wall and inside the prison cell.

The horrible sounds were coming from that dim room.

Ellwynn grabbed his arm and placed his lips to Jotham's ear. "Be careful, Jotham. There are two guards in there. Better to draw one of them out first."

Jotham uncoiled his whip and held his sword in front of him as he stepped forward. When he was within six feet of the open door, he stopped.

The Ghargs had their backs to him and were grunting in rage. One held a torch and a whip, while the other was holding something that glowed.

He took another step. The vise around his chest tightened another notch.

His heart froze, pinning his lungs against his ribs. His dread had taken a ghastly form, materializing in a shape far worse than he could have imagined.

Abe was hanging from chains in the center of the barred cell. Livid welts crisscrossed his chest and thighs. He was shaking his head slowly from side to side, and when one of the Ghargs lifted its arm, with a sickening rush Jotham understood why. The guard was menacing his brother with a red-hot poker, its blistering tip only inches from Abe's eyes.

Explosive rage burst from Jotham's throat. He screamed in fury, swinging the whip. A torch exploded in a shower of sparks, plunging the hall into darkness. A snarling Gharg jerked its corpulent body around and clambered out of the murky cell; the barred gate clanged shut behind him.

Jotham was in a frenzy. He shrieked out his brother's name. The fleshy Gharg stared insolently at Jotham, a long studded whip in its clawed hand, and in the other he brandished a torch. He waved it, attempting to keep Jotham at bay.

Jotham flung himself at the creature, his own whip high overhead. It ripped through the guard's right arm, tearing it off at the shoulder. The wolfish snout opened in a howling scream. It retreated, hissing, until its back was pressed against the closed bars. Snarling and panting, it barred Jotham's entrance into the cell. Jotham threw his body at his enemy. The last thing the Gharg saw was the edge of Jotham's blade. The creature exploded. From inside the cell, there was the scuttling of claws desperately trying to get a grip on the smooth stones.

Behind him, Ellwynn yelled, "Well done, Jotham. Take care; the other one will be waiting."

"Stand back!" Jotham screamed, swinging his whip at the gate. The explosive bang in the small stone chamber was deafening. The gate and bars disintegrated. Before the smoke cleared, Jotham jumped into the room, swinging his sword wildly in front of him.

"Where are you?" he raged, thrusting his sword from side to side. Abe's pallid body directly in front of him remained motionless, suspended in the air, his arms stretched above his head. The poker glowed a dull red on the clammy stones beneath Abe's feet. The other guard was nowhere to be seen.

Jotham heard the snort above and behind him, but it was too late. Vicious claws dug deep furrows into his shoulders and back. The Gharg had been clinging to the ledge over the doorway waiting for Jotham's exposed back. Jotham fell to his knees. His attacker's claws were imbedded deeply in his flesh.

He did not feel a thing. In an incoherent rage, he lurched to his feet, almost toppling over with the weight high on his back and shoulders. Gripping his sword hilt with both hands, with one huge thrust backwards, he plunged its point into the Gharg's chest. Hissing out its pain and venomous hatred, it released its grip and fluttered to the floor, dragging itself backwards toward the far corner.

Jotham picked up the whip and aimed for the retreating yellow eyes. The Gharg reached the corner first and floundered into the air, reaching out to grab something. It was too weak and fell back on the wet stones. Its wings flopped uselessly against the cold wall. The tip of Jotham's whip twisted around the creature's throat and pulled its face to the floor with a thud. Then, in a rush of vengeful disgust, Jotham gave the whip a violent jerk, flinging it backwards then forward, smashing the Gharg from one side of the cell to the other. It exploded in a foul, yellow-green mist.

Panting out his rage, Jotham dashed over to Abe and threw himself against his brother's chest. He could still make out a faint beat.

"Ellwynn, come here . . . hurry!" he yelled.

Ellwynn was already at the door. Jotham pulled him forward, placing his hands on Abe's waist. "Just hold him. I'm gonna' break off the top chain. Don't let him fall."

Jotham aimed for the ceiling ring. There was a loud crack and the clanking of metal links. Before he could jump back, a length of heavy chain struck him on the head as it fell to the floor. He was on his hands and knees, stunned. He blinked and wiped the blood away with the sleeve of his tunic.

He stood up groggily and saw Ellwynn carrying his brother's body into the hallway. As Jotham stumbled out behind them, he noticed a leather bottle by an overturned stool. He smelled the spout. It was strong cider.

Ellwyn dropped to his knees, cradling Abe's limp body across his lap.

Jotham held Abe's head as he poured the cider into his bloody mouth. His lips were cracked, and his tongue was bruised and swollen. Abe coughed and grimaced as the cider burned its way down his mouth and throat. He moaned faintly. It sounded like he had called out Jotham's name.

Jotham's pulse began to race with hope. He used water from the bottle over his shoulder to rinse off Abe's misshapen face. His eyelids fluttered and opened. A wave of relief threatened to sweep him away. The Ghargs had not gotten to his brother's eyes.

They had rescued Abe just in time!

Jotham again placed his head against Abe's chest. The heartbeat was still terribly faint. It sounded irregular, like an engine coughing and sputtering. Cold sweat again broke out on Jotham's forehead. Abe's dark brown eyes were unfocused but widened in recognition as they settled on his older brother. A twisted smile formed on Abe's lips as he looked up at him.

"It's me, Abe; I'm here!" Jotham pressed his face against his brother's. "Hang on buddy, we're getting you out of here. . . . You're gonna make it. Trust me, you're going to be all right."

Abe coughed dryly, and Jotham placed the blackened leather container against his lips and gave him more to drink.

Abe nodded his appreciation, his lips forming indistinct words. Jotham placed his ear by his lips. "Better . . ." Abe whispered, ". . . than . . . Flaggon's brew." The corner of Abe's mouth was turned up in a lopsided grin. His cracked lips began to move. "I . . . didn't think . . . I'd see you . . . again," he whispered.

Jotham's throat and chest felt as if they were on fire. If he didn't make it right immediately, he would explode. "Abe . . . I-I'm . . . sorry . . . really sorry," his voice caught.

Abe's hand twitched. Jotham shook his head and placed his hand over his brother's weak fingers. Abe's skin was an awful grayish white. *He looks like a corpse,* Jotham thought, his throat constricting.

". . . I'm . . . sorry too," Abe choked out, "I . . . shouldn't have left." As he spoke, his eyes lost and then regained focus.

"No, no . . . *you* don't," Jotham moaned, "I need to ask you . . . to forgive *me*," Jotham felt Abe's fingers begin to close gently over his. Abe shut his eyes and nodded his head imperceptibly. The muscles in his face went slack, and Jotham jerked his brother until Abe's eyelids opened, halfway.

"You've got to stay with us. I'm going to find Carisa so she can give you her medicine." As Jotham tried to get up, Abe's hand tightened on his.

Jotham crouched over him. Abe's hold on his hand grew tighter, and he took a long, shallow breath. His eyes widened, and his pupils slowly dilated. They locked desperately onto those of his older brother.

". . . Jo . . . I . . . I . . ." he gasped. His eyes closed. His fingers went limp.

Jotham jumped to his feet, choking down the sobs that threatened to overwhelm him. As he raced toward the steps he yelled, "Hold onto him! I'm getting Carisa. Give Abe more drink and try to keep him awake!"

He raced up the stairs two at a time. By the time he rounded the last bend, he was getting dizzy. Faint light was now breaking through the archers' windows along the outer wall. A peculiar thought came into Jotham's mind as he flung himself into the kitchen: *today the drought will break.* He ran headlong into the cook who was standing with his back toward Jotham, chopping vegetables and meat on the long wooden table.

The cook spun around with the surprising grace of a large man and jerked his cleaver at Jotham. Startled, Jotham jumped back and tripped over a dog lying on the floor. Before he could fall, the cook reached out and grabbed his tunic. Recognizing Justar's emblem, the portly figure drove the tip of his razor-sharp knife into the table top and wrapped his beefy arms around Jotham, squeezing him to his ample chest, planting a kiss on both cheeks. He smiled a huge grin.

"You are de Captain Jotham, no? I see you are in great hurry; I will not detain you. Your comrades are in upper prison chambers working miracles weeth de captives. . . ." He was pointing to a portal opposite the fireplace.

Jotham raced toward the door. The cook continued talking, "I prepare feast to celebrate our veectory, but . . . if de steenkeen monsters come, I will tell dem it is for de celebration. Haaah! Dat is a good one, no?" Jotham ran through the doorway. He heard the cook drive the cleaver back into the table, snorting, "Prepare to die you steenkeen monsters!"

Jotham leapt up the stairs. This stairway went straight up, but at the top angled sharply to the left. As he raced upwards, Jotham began to hear the incongruous sounds of restrained laughter interspersed with an occasional distant shriek. Jotham burst through the archway on which a charred gate hung drunkenly from a bent hinge.

It was a long room with a row of double arches running down the center supporting a low ceiling. Along the entire course of the walls were large iron rings and chains now smashed and twisted. Law and Bart were handing weapons of all varieties to tattered men and women who were huddled in clusters around the bases of the supports. They were blinking and rubbing their eyes, their faces wreathed with incredulous smiles.

"Hey!" Bart shouted as Jotham sped past.

Jotham didn't hear him. He was looking around frantically. Sitting next to a window slit at the far end of the room, he saw her. Carisa was sitting on the floor, surrounded by a large group of blind captives. She was dabbing a damp cloth on the eyes of an emaciated boy. A small girl who looked like the waif's little sister stood next to Carisa staring adoringly up at her.

"What's your name?" he heard Carisa ask as she stroked the girl's head.

"Meeshah," she replied.

Carisa's smile was wiped away at the sight of the streaks of blood and the look of desperation on Jotham's face.

"Where's . . . ?" she began, jumping immediately to her feet.

"Follow me and bring your bottle," he rasped, breathing heavily. He began to run out of the room, pulling her behind him.

"Bart," she yelled, throwing the damp cloth at her brother, "finish helping the rest."

Carisa didn't say a word as they bolted down the stairs, through the

212

kitchen, and down the dungeon steps. The cook nodded silently as they passed him. Rounding the last turn of the spiral stairs, they heard a low voice.

Ellwynn was on the floor, holding Abe's head on his lap. Abe's body was still, and his arms hung limply at his sides, the backs of his fingers brushing the stone floor. The sickly whiteness of his skin against Ellwynn's rich blackness was an unbearable and shocking contrast. Abe looked like cold, white marble. Deep lines of sorrow were etched in Ellwynn's face as the Paladins raced toward him. He was cradling Abe's body moaning, "Why? . . . Why? He was so young. . . ."

Jotham fell down next to his brother and lifted him in his arms. Abe's skin was terribly cold. His head fell back, his mouth and his eyes remaining open. There was no longer any heartbeat.

"No! . . . No!" Jotham shrieked. "Not Abe! Not my brother!" A frigid, hollow hole seemed to be opening beneath him, threatening to swallow him in one cruel gulp. Jotham turned his streaming eyes to Carisa. She had sunk to her knees and was covering her mouth with shaking hands as she stared at Abe's open eyes.

"Give him your stuff!" Jotham screamed. "Pour it in his mouth. It's not too late . . . It can't be!" Jotham dragged his brother's body toward her, placing his head on her shaking knees.

He tore the bottle from her listless fingers, letting the contents pour into Abe's mouth, but his head fell sideways and the amber liquid ran down the side of his face. Her eyes darkened in horror. She gripped Abe tightly to her chest, her tears drenching his rigid face. Looking up at Jotham she sobbed, "Oh Jotham, he's dead. . . . Abe's dead."

Chapter Thirty

Jotham pulled out his sword and slammed the blade against the wooden stool. Chunks of wood splintered into the air. He slashed at the leather cider bottle, and with one furious sweep sent it spinning into the dark recesses of the cell, spraying frothy liquid over the stones. He followed it, stumbling and weeping into the dingy interior. Seeing the iron chains laying on the filthy floor, he began hacking and chopping, sparks flying as steel struck stone. Exhausted, he fell down on his knees, panting out his aching sobs. Grabbing the bits of twisted metal, he flung them against the wall. They tinkled in derision as they bounced off the blackened stones. Jotham began to wail his brother's name as the despairing darkness crashed down over him like a huge, black swell.

For several long minutes he was unaware of anything around him. When he came to, he found himself sprawled on the stone floor, his back against the wall, his right hand grasping the hilt of the sword beside him. He looked down at its bright sharpness and raised its tip. He pressed his palm down on it. The point was razor sharp; soon blood was running down the inside of his hand. He stared numbly at the red smear on the sword-tip.

It would be a quick death, he thought. Closing his eyes, he imagined falling on the sword. Immediately, a grinning skull's head came into focus; a burning red candle was pouring bloody tears down its sides. It had once flickered like a warning light outside the McCauley's house; now, it mocked him with its evil, empty sneer.

I can't, he moaned to himself. He grabbed the sharp steel with his left hand and tossed it away. The picture of the skull evaporated. A sharp, slicing pain now throbbed in both palms. Blood ran down his forearms and dripped from his elbows onto the floor. He cried out Abe's name, again and again until his voice was raw. Sorrow, loathing, fear and pain rose up within him, threatening to rupture his chest. He gagged, and then with a wrenching gasp, emptied his stomach against the damp wall. He heaved until there was nothing left.

The feel of gentle hands on his wrists brought Jotham back to consciousness. Carisa was bending over him, strands of hair partially obscuring her red-rimmed eyes; her cheeks were streaked. Crouched next to him, she wiped dried blood from his face, hands and arms. When he opened his eyes, she pulled him to her, wrapping her arms around him, sobbing quietly against his chest. The silky softness of her hair lay against his cheek, but it might as well have been strands of rope. He had fallen into an abyss of suffocating, empty blackness.

He had no more tears.

He was a hollow shell: empty of thought or feeling.

"I told Ellwynn to take Abe upstairs and clean him up," she said.

Jotham stared at her dully.

"Ellwynn can see now," she went on, as if her words would hold the pain at bay. "I put some of the ointment on his eyes; he's regained his sight!"

Jotham's eyes narrowed briefly; at least she could see a dark spark of anger rising out of the void. It melted immediately back into the icy depths.

"We'd better get out of here," she suggested.

Suddenly, running feet could be heard racing down the stone stairs. Law's voice bounced down into the hall way. "Jotham . . . come . . . the battle . . . !

He burst in upon the two Paladins huddled on the floor.

"Come, Jotham. . . ."

Law dropped to his knees next to him.

"Why should I?" Jotham asked in a flat voice.

"Because, you're our . . ." Law stopped himself; a greenish light was hovering about six feet up on the opposite wall.

"What is that?" Carisa asked.

Jotham stared blankly at the light.

Law walked over to the corner, sword ready. A glowing object was lying on a shelf in the corner where the Gharg had scurried for cover.

"What did you find?" Carisa asked.

"It's an ax," he said, pulling it off the dusty shelf. Holding the luminous weapon in his hands, he noticed the row of even holes on the handle. Law spun and ran toward Carisa and Jotham.

"Look . . . is this Abe's ax?" He held it out toward them.

"Yes it is," she said.

King Justar's message that Ellwynn had quoted flashed into Law's mind. He knelt next to Jotham, wiping the ax with his tunic. "This is for you, Jotham. You need to play it." He handed the shaft to him. It dropped from Jotham's fingers, and the steel head hit the floor heavily. Law put it back in his hands, wrapping his fingers around Jotham's. "Remember? That's what the King's message must have meant. He would make the darkness bright, and when you found Abe's ax you were to play it *with all your might.*"

Jotham's eyes grew hard.

Law shook Jotham's shoulders. "I know you're grieving over Abe, Jotham, but—"

"But what?" Jotham cried. "But in the vast scheme of things, it doesn't matter? That there are more important things to worry about? That the people in this castle are depending on me . . . their fearless leader?" He turned his face away. "Don't you get it? I'm a failure, Law—my brother's dead, and it's my fault!" He picked up the ax and tossed it against the opposite wall.

Law rose to retrieve the ax and the sword. "Jotham, the Ghargs outnumber the prisoners three to one, and most of them are still very weak. If we just give up, Abe won't be the only one who will die!" He kneeled beside Jotham. "We can't bring him back," he added gently, "but we can keep the Ghargs from slaughtering everyone who's left."

Jotham lurched to his feet and clutched Law's tunic. Their faces were only inches apart. "Guess what, *Trellawton the third . . .*" he said, flinging Law forcefully against the back wall. "I don't care! I don't give a—"

Carisa stepped between them, grasping Jotham's arm in her hands and pushing him back. "Jotham," she cried, "don't take it out on Law. . . . It's not his fault. . . . It just . . . happened, that's all."

Law slowly stepped toward Jotham, a resolute expression on his face. Jotham tensed, his fists clenched.

"I know how you feel," Law began.

Jotham shoved him away again. "No, you don't!" he cried furiously. Jotham stared at them, confusion and anger twisting his face into an awful mask. He turned away and struck his forehead against the wall. Carisa walked up behind him and quietly laid her hand on his back. Her throat ached, but she was unable to find words to comfort him.

216

"What are we doing here?" he moaned, a plaintive plea in his voice. She put her arm around him, her tears falling onto the dirty stones next to her sandals.

Jotham hit his head against the wall again. "I thought this was some sort of game . . . or dream. I was expecting that sooner or later I'd wake up in my room. . . ." He stared at her with wild desperation. "We don't belong here!" he screamed, pounding the wall with his fist. "We're supposed to be in Rockville. . . . This can't be happening . . . this isn't real!" Sobs shook him; then, his body slumped and he crumpled to the floor. Carisa kneeled by his side, her arm around his quivering shoulders.

Law stood over him for several seconds, his face grim. "Jotham, I do not make light of your pain. . . . I've never lost a brother. . . ." Law was fighting to keep his voice from breaking. ". . . But I have lost one I loved as dearly as anyone could love a brother, and I know the blackness and the pain of despair, my friend."

He pulled out his parchment. "Let me recite a passage from the scripts which speak of a great hope—one that I am only now beginning to understand."

"Sorrow comes in the night," he read, "but a great and immense joy will certainly come in the morning. Though the dark night of the soul may befall you, though the darkness may reach out and call forth your name, never forget that it is only a night, and that it too shall pass. And, indeed, I will call you by name."

Law placed a tentative hand on Jotham's bowed head. "There is a great mystery in this, but I am certain that you have yet to experience the fullness of the meaning of Justar's message. I believe it contains his promise to make your dark night bright . . . and Justar always keeps his word." He paused for a moment, squeezing his eyes as if uncertain how to continue; then carefully placed the ax in Jotham's hands, closing his fingers around the handle. "Don't give up hope; put your trust in Justar's word. Now play . . . Captain."

Jotham slowly lifted his head, two muddy trails streaking the dirt on his cheeks. "But why . . . ?"

"Because Justar said that's what you were to do. He commanded it for a reason. He put his confidence in you. Jotham, please don't let him down."

At that, a hoarse cry of betrayal erupted out of his shattered heart: "But he let me down! Why should I care . . . ?" He looked with haunted eyes at Trellawton, "Didn't Justar say he would make it right?"

217

Carisa put her finger gently on his lips. "He's right, Jo. Play, Jotham . . . play!"

Jotham had lost the ability to resist. He knew he could keep asking questions that would never be answered, or he could obey. He gritted his teeth, shut his red-rimmed eyes and gripped the instrument between both hands as if to snap it in half. Carisa was staring at him, willing him to pick it up and blow into the hollow tube.

He clenched his jaws, then lifted it to his trembling lips. At first, all that came out was a harsh, woody tone. But with it the entire castle tensed and grew still, as if in dread or anticipation. Jotham's face twisted in a spasm of pain, and he choked down a sob. He drew another shaky breath, then abandoned himself to the instrument, letting his fingers float over the carved shaft.

Like a festering splinter being drawn out by expert hands, the instrument pulled from Jotham a wrenching lament. The tune was so raw in its unrelenting grief that Carisa had to bit down on her lip to keep from crying out. Tears were dripping from Law's eyes. As the mournful sounds filtered upward from the depths of the castle, intermittent rumblings began shaking the foundations of the fortress, followed by muffled booms. It sounded as though huge cannons were being discharged overhead. Jotham was oblivious to the reverberations. Carisa turned to see Law race up the stairs.

She closed her eyes. The painful dirge washed over her in waves of piercing sorrow. Slowly, scattered incongruously among the mournful notes, Carisa began to detect an unusual undercurrent that reminded her somehow of Abe. Blended with the notes of aching sorrow were brief discordant clashings of delight. The instrument was pouring out a melody which embraced both the depth of lowest grief and the trembling heights of joy. Carisa was lost in it. The castle shook; then she could no longer feel it. It seemed as if another country in another time were wooing her—a lover was drawing her, calling out to her. Her heart yearned and resonated with its irresistible pull.

What sounded like the pounding of thousands of relentless fists caused her eyes to open in alarm. She let out a deep, aching breath. She put her hand on Jotham's arm. The music stopped.

"Come on, Jo, we've got to go up and find out what's happening!"

Without a word, he slung the ax over his shoulder and picked up his sword. Carisa took his hand and they ran for the stairway. The rumbling and crashing became louder and the hammering stronger as they climbed above the water level markings on the stone wall. From the slit windows they saw a ragged flash of lightning and immediately heard a resounding crack. The hammering was the pelting sound of a deluge of rain. The drought had indeed ended.

They followed the sounds of shrieking to a hallway that surrounded a large, square courtyard. Groups of a score or more newly-released prisoners were standing guard at each of the 12 doors. They were outfitted with a variety of weaponry, impatiently awaiting the order to attack. Several saluted, shouting questions as they ran by.

A large peasant with a surly face was thrusting at a door with a pitchfork, its tines jabbing like long metal claws at the scarred wood. When Jotham passed, he pointed a dirty thumb in his direction. "Now *there* be the Cap'n . . ." he muttered out of the corner of his mouth. "I takes me orders from such as him."

Many of the doors had jagged claw marks and in some places had begun to splinter; but from the screaming, hissing, and bellowing inside, it was evident that the Ghargs had not been able to coordinate any effective assault. There was also a strange tension in the hall that Carisa could not understand.

Law ran up to them, "Good, you're here! We didn't know how long some of these doors would hold, but we waited until you were ready. You have suffered greatly, Jotham. . . . Now it's time to cause the enemy to suffer." He rushed toward the East hall. "Follow me. Bartholomew is on the other side. The attack must begin there and you must lead."

Outside a pair of inlaid, rounded doors stood Ellwynn with Bart by his side. When Bart saw Jotham, he grabbed him by the arms then embraced him tightly. "Law told me about Abe. . . ." His voice caught.

Ellwynn put a strong hand on both their shoulders. "You must gather yourselves . . . the battle is at hand." Bart and Jotham stepped back, their swords ready. Ellwynn indicated that Jotham was to place his sword back in its sheath.

"I'm glad to report that the odds have improved dramatically, Captain. About a third of the enemy are now blind. As each of us recovered our sight, one of them lost theirs." Sounds of flapping and screeching near their door interrupted Ellwynn. "You are to blow on that ax, and we are prepared to charge in and pay back our enemies blow for blow." He planted his legs and saluted Jotham. "We intend on calling this battle the Charge of Jotham's Brigade."

Jotham stood in front of the doors and put the shaft to his lips. It felt ready. A high, piercing note flew out of the ax. It had an almost liquid power, as if a high-pressure valve had opened, shooting out a concentrated stream of energy. The wood began to vibrate. The hinges rattled as the wood throbbed and pulsated. Suddenly, both sides were ripped off their hinges, and the door collapsed inward. This was followed by the rhythmic crashing of 11 other doors as they were smashed flat against the stone floor of the courtyard.

At that signal, hundreds of vengeful, former prisoners—now fearless warriors—rushed into the huge square. It was infested with bat-like creatures scurrying and climbing in all directions like monstrous ants fleeing from a crushed anthill. Some were attempting to escape the downpour by crouching under the large, circular stone fountain which dominated the middle of the square. The heavy rain was drenching hundreds who were clawing their way up and over the slippery walls. Jotham's blast seemed to have stunned and disoriented them. Because their wings were soaked, many were only able to hop up to chest-level where they beat each other down with their sinewy wings, scraping and clawing in terror.

It was not a battle suited to arrows: there were too many of the enemy teeming about in disorganized packs. The Paladins discovered their swords to be as sharp as razors and were using them with great effect. With each slash, they could destroy a handful of the enemy. The prisoners' spears, pitchforks, pikes, staves and rakes were also being used successfully. Most of the forces who had once been swaggering conquerors were now retreating in abject defeat. Shouts of vengeance and victory mingled with shrieks, cries of anger and the dull popping of exploding bodies resounded off the tall walls of the square.

Bart felt claws raking his back as a Gharg attacked wildly from behind. An instant later he heard a pop, and his eyes were stung by an acrid mist. Spinning around, he saw Law grinning at him, his wet hair plastered over his forehead, holding a sword covered with an oily smear. Bart touched the tip of his own sword to his forehead, in a grateful salute.

Ellwynn was busily engaged swinging a broadsword almost as tall as his body. He had five Gharg's clawing backwards. Tiring of the pursuit, he lunged forward and with one mighty swing cut all of them in half. He threw back his strong head and into the rain bellowed out a roar of triumph into the rain. Shaking his mane of grizzled curly hair, a spray of sweat and water flew from him. As he turned to face more aggressors, a smile lit his face, but his eyes were cold as ice.

Jotham had chosen to forego the sword and use the battle-ax instead. There was something terribly satisfying about pouring out his rage through the savage strokes of Abe's weapon. He was exacting retribution with the instrument of war stolen from his brother. It was fitting.

The ax was light in his hand. There was a reservoir of strength in him that seemed limitless. His reflexes became as quick as a gymnast's. From a second-story balcony, two crazed Ghargs leaped down at him. Jotham threw the ax. It sliced cleanly through one of their wings; and pulling out his sword, he flicked it up just in time to skewer the other creature as it dropped on top of him. Catching the ax with his free hand, he dispatched the remaining Gharg with a wicked blow. Jotham smiled grimly; counting those two, there were 23 less of Ghnostar's forces.

On the other side of the courtyard, Carisa had cut though more than a dozen herself, but was tiring rapidly. The lack of food had drained her endurance. Her shoulders were beginning to lose strength, and her arms were growing numb. She sat down on the lower edge of the marble fountain, resting her back against the tail of a leaping dolphin, trying to catch her breath. Her tunic was drenched. She wiped the water and strands of wet hair from her eyes.

Out of the corner of his eye, Bart noticed that his sister was weakening. He began angling his way across the wet courtyard toward her. He spun just in time to avoid a leaping Gharg; it missed his face by inches. Bart struck its bony back with the flat of his blade, and a leaping soldier impaled it with a wooden pitchfork as it lay stunned on the stones. Bart turned back towards the fountain.

He froze.

Two large yellow eyes and a huge, wrinkled snout were peering down over the top edge at his sister. There was too much noise for him to yell a warning, and there was no time to fit an arrow. The Gharg's wet claws were scrambling for a grip on the stonework; it was preparing to pounce. With a huge heave, Bart threw his sword. It spun through the air, spraying rain-drops off its twirling tip. The hilt caught the Gharg full in the chest. The creature fell back into the stone bowl with a grunt.

Bart raced up to the fountain, past his startled sister, lunging for the sword which had clanged to the cobblestones and jumped up, grabbing the dolphin's tail for support. His foot slipped on the slick rounded stone. He grabbed the lip of the upper bowl just as the Gharg was lifting itself out of the water. Its hair was plastered to the sides of its gruesome snout; it stared up at him with malevolent eyes, gulping for air. It lifted its dripping claws, raising itself from the scummy water. Holding the smooth stone with one hand, Bart took a wide swing and tore the Gharg's head off its shoulders. He swirled the blade in the bloody pool and jumped down by his sister.

Her sword hung limply from her hand. She seemed to be near exhaustion.

"Thanks," she whispered in a hoarse voice.

He put his arm around her. "It was nothing," he said, puffing out his chest. "He made my day."

Shouts of triumph were now showering all around them as the courtyard was being swept clean of their enemy. The Ghargs were in a total rout. The rains stopped, and like theater curtains being pulled back from a stage, the late-morning sun broke through the thick clouds. Its rays exposed hundreds of Ghargs perched on the top of the outer wall flapping their wet wings madly, impatient to make good their escape.

Ellwynn strode up to Jotham, his chest heaving, the huge grin still on his swarthy face. He gestured at the ax. "May I request a more invigorating tune this time captain? And, remember . . . play it 'fiercely.'"

Jotham nodded, blowing forcefully into the shaft. Instantly, the sounds of Abe's Highland fling bounded triumphantly throughout the court. The Ghargs on the wall began screeching and hopping from foot to foot as if the stones were on fire, trying unsuccessfully to cover their ears. Soon, they were twitching spasmodically as the lilting refrain careened merrily off the stones. In a crazed torment, they threw themselves off the parapets, sinking down to the bottom of the moat, now flooded by the downpour.

The prisoners, unable to contain their glee, began dancing about in circles, grabbing each other's arms, skipping and shouting like little children in time with the music. Bart draped his arm around Carisa's shoulders and walked together toward the celebrating prisoners. "I guess that's two fortresses down, two more to go," he said, watching the laughing crowd. They continued walking silently toward Law who was deep in conversation with his old friend.

Since Ursula had died during her imprisonment, the four Paladins voted to put Ellwynn in charge. Reluctantly he agreed, after making clear that he would do so only as interim commander until the King appointed a more suitable ruler. Ellwynn then ordered the courtyard cleared and tables and benches brought out to seat the celebrants; the captives had been so long enclosed in darkness, they could not bear to hold this momentous celebration anywhere but under the gloriously blue sky.

The castle shone with a fresh radiance. The driving rain had washed it clean and new. There was a crispness to the air, and the skies smiled indulgently upon the hundreds of workers busily engaged in arranging the long rows of wooden tables. To provide decorative color, elegant vases and beautiful bowls were brought out, which according to Ellwynn, had made Ursula's Fortress known far and wide. These stood empty, since the Ghargs and the drought had long since removed all the flowers from the valley. The handcrafted earthenware glistened brightly, their lavish colors providing a pleasing replacement for the blossoms that would eventually return.

As each piece was brought out, a score of artisans would rush forward, staring hungrily at it, some covering their open mouths. Their newly-opened eyes seemed unable to take in enough color, contour and texture. They were starved for beauty. The older craftsmen gazed quietly, tears winding down furrowed cheeks onto their damp white beards.

Jotham picked up a distinctive piece. He ran his fingers over the glaze. A memory of his father removing pottery from his kiln came into his mind. He was surprised that a flash of anger and resentment did not come rushing in close on its heels. Instead, there was sorrow combined with something new, something which felt strangely like compassion. He carefully set the pot down again, letting his hand slide gently down its curved side.

After giving directions for the erection of the platform upon which the Paladins would be seated, Ellwynn drew Jotham into the hall and up a long flight of stairs. These led to the dizzying height of the northeast corner of the wallwalk. It was actually a well-protected patio with two embrasures at each end and a well with a bucket hanging from a winch in the center. From that vantage point, they could overlook the entire length of the valley. Small lakes and ponds were now scattered about like blue-green sapphires; and in place of infertile bleakness, a lush green carpet was spread out before them. The spell of barrenness had been shattered with the defeat of the Ghargs.

Ellwynn looked deeply at his companion, the corners of his dark eyes wrinkled sympathetically. "Jotham, first of all, let me tell you how grieved I am at your terrible loss."

Jotham looked at the beautiful valley and tried unsuccessfully to swallow the lump in his throat.

"I wanted to thank you personally for bringing deliverance . . . and much more . . . to us." Ellwynn's rough fingers gripped Jotham's forearm. "To tell the truth, I also needed to talk to you alone about something that I hope will provide some . . . perspective. It has also raised questions for me which are quite troubling, I must say; but I'm beginning to suspect that paradox may not be the bane of sluggish, undisciplined minds, as I once thought." He rubbed his bristly chin. "What I mean is, I now see that there are realities beyond our abilities to systematize and define."

A light flickered in Jotham's eyes. "Yeah, I think I understand what you're saying. I've felt that too ever since we arrived in Issatar, although I haven't been able to explain it very well."

Ellwynn smiled. "I'm glad you comprehend. . . . I'm not sure I fully do. You see, Jotham, Trellawton and myself are from the Prince's band of Warrior-Teachers. We are trained to be able to articulate and elucidate, to detect error and communicate truth. Reason is our stock in trade, you might say."

He stared off at the verdant growth spreading out along the length of the valley. "Our Code instructs us to trust in our intellect and not our emotions, much less our experience. It strongly and repeatedly enjoins us to preserve a calm mind: '*Aequam servare mentem.*' As my father and mentor, Ellwynn deGrier, would frequently say: 'We are to maintain objective distance, a calm detachment for the cool space of reason.' He was a master of debate and when he would inevitably best me, he loved to shout out (rather emotionally I always thought) *Cadit Quaestro!*—'the argument collapses!'" A wide smile lit his dark face. "All that to say that our class, steeped in Aristophelian logic as it is, is taught to be very dubious of the subjective." He turned to watch the preparations in the square below.

"Everything turned upside down when I heard Prince Gabriel's voice yesterday. I know myself and I know him, and I am unable to reach any other conclusion but that I heard him speak to me. That he is alive in some fashion is not my difficulty. The basis of my confusion is that he directly instructed me outside the confines of his scripts, which I've been taught were his exclusive means of communication and direction since his death."

Ellwynn waved his arm to signal Law, the foreman and the cook who were in a heated conversation below. The cook was waving his arms wildly, while Law and the foreman shook their heads vehemently. Ellwynn whistled shrilly, the sound easily carrying to the angry huddle. They looked up, and Law motioned for Ellwynn and Jotham to come down.

"It appears that the festivities are ready, so I will make this concise. While we were dancing in the courtyard after defeating the Ghargs—something I've never done before, I must admit," he laughed, "there was something else that happened." Ellwynn looked down at his feet, momentarily embarrassed. "I think . . . well, I *heard* the Prince speak again."

Jotham's head lifted, "What did he say?"

Ellwynn looked directly at Jotham. "Only this one thing: 'Tell him to await the Great Dance.'"

"Who was he talking about?"

"I took it to mean you, although I'm not sure why. Perhaps I made a wrong assumption, but I . . . felt . . . tsomehow, that he was referring to you."

"Are you sure it was me?"

"Yes . . . No . . . Well, I believe so. It may have been you only or maybe you and others like you. I can't be absolutely certain. I apologize for my lack of definitiveness—that's part of the paradox I was speaking about earlier. . . ." Ellwynn began walking to the stairs.

Jotham held his arm. "Wait, Ellwynn . . . tell me, what's the Great Dance?"

"It is an enigma. You see, not much is actually known about it. At least not much has been written clearly. The accepted majority position is that it is an allegory of the cycles of nature: death and life, you know. It comes from an ancient legend about the ultimate battle with the dragon. When he is defeated, so it runs, there will be a cataclysmic release of energy, and the dark spell over the cosmos will be broken."

"What spell?"

Ellwynn wrinkled his forehead and rubbed the bridge of his nose. "It was supposedly cast long before Ghnostar's time, so it is shrouded in deep mystery. But the legend does indicate that the spell has to do with death. In any event, at that time—if time is still in effect—the entire natural order will rejoice and supposedly erupt into a wild dance of celebration. Different metaphors are used, such as vegetation clapping its hands, animals singing, and waterfalls cavorting like music, to name only a few. I have always believed it was symbolic—a poetic allegory—but after what has happened

225

here, I'm no longer so certain. Frankly," he concluded, a shy smile filling his eyes, "I am beginning to hope I've been wrong."

He began walking pensively down the steps, then turned around. "Jotham, I am grateful to you most of all for giving me a great hope."

"How? What do you mean?"

"When you were playing that instrument in the dungeon, it was so sorrowful yet so full of . . . joy. It seemed to impregnate the stones of the castle with a hunger, a desire that was both wonderful and painful at the same time. As it filled the hallway around the courtyard something hard broke inside me . . . and I felt something I haven't felt since I was a child." Ellwynn's eyes brimmed. "I began to long for the Dance."

He squeezed Jotham's shoulders in strong ebony hands. "Thank you, my friend . . . . Thank you."

As Jotham looked down at the chiseled steps and nodded, an unexplained thrill of excitement caused his spine to tingle.

When they had joined the others and were all seated, the feasting and singing began. It lasted for hours into the late afternoon. It had been a full day since the Paladins had eaten; yet because of Abe's absence, they were unable to enter into the delights of the meal. They ate but barely tasted the food.

It had been a long time since the inhabitants of Ursula's castle had eaten like this. Course after course was brought up by the cook and his helpers. Finally, the beaming cook and three of his crew brought out the dessert on their shoulders: a frosted cake in the shape of a roaring lion, on its hind legs. The entire crowd stood to its feet and roared with approval.

Ellwynn then led the crowd in an emotional toast to Justar, the Prince, and their four rescuers. The thunderous applause almost shook the cake apart. After they had finished large wedges of the delectable lemon and raspberry cream confection, Ellwynn presented a final toast. He then handed each Paladin a silver chalice, inscribed with their names, as a token of their gratitude.

Although it was not yet evening, the three youths were exhausted. The fasting and battling, combined with their wrenching sorrow had drained them. Ellwynn caught Jotham's eye and with a nod to a tow-headed page had them led to their bedchambers, where iron tubs of steaming water had been prepared for them. Apparently word had traveled from Orion to Ursula's Fortress of the Paladins' strange obsession.

226

Soaking in the water helped to refresh their bodies, but it was impossible for Jotham to keep the recriminating thoughts at bay. He began to feel as though he were sinking under the weight of the reproach when a knock startled him.

"Sir, excuse me, with your permission sir, you have a visitor . . . He says he knows you," came the voice from outside his door.

Jotham groaned and mopped at his face with a thick cloth. "Tell him he'll have to wait till I'm finished."

"Very well, sir." The sounds of footsteps began to retreat.

"Who is it anyway?" he yelled weakly.

He could hear the sounds of feet hastening back to his door. "If I may say so, sir, perhaps, 'what' is more accurate. It is not—one of our kind, sir . . . . It is a dwarf, and a rather insolent one at that."

Chapter Thirty One

"Show him up right away!" Jotham shouted, jumping out of the tub, drying off and throwing on his tunic, which was hanging by the fire.

Within minutes, Jotham heard their friend coming up the hall: "Leaves me be, I tells you, or it will be the worse for you," Flaggon's voice was threatening.

"If you weren't on friendly terms with Captain Jotham, I'd teach you a thing or two, you dirty, insolent little creature," retorted the guard in a condescending snarl that galled Jotham.

He flung his door open before the startled guard could knock. Flaggon was standing next to a short, barrel-chested soldier with a scraggly mustache and small eyes. The red-faced dwarf's sword was half out of its sheath.

Jotham grabbed the front of the guard's shirt. "Watch your tongue," he ordered. The guard's narrow eyes flinched. "Flaggon is my friend and what you say to him you say to me. Unless you want to be reported to your superior, I expect an apology immediately."

The irate soldier looked incredulously at Jotham and then at Flaggon, who was staring straight ahead. His bald head shone an angry pink.

After several long moments in which his eyes seemed to grow smaller, the soldier cleared his throat: "I apologize for my remarks, Flaggon . . . *sir*." There were icicles clinging to each grudging word. They fell from his mouth and splintered frostily on the floor.

Flaggon, still staring a hole through the wall, puffed out his chest and muttered, "I accepts your apology. But I does warns you to mind your manners around your betters." The soldier's face flamed. "Next time, you may find you've bitten off more than you can chew."

Flaggon turned to face the soldier. "And one word of wisdom for you," he lifted a stubby forefinger into the air and shook it gravely, "the worth of a man is not measured by the size of his legs, but by the *heart* he fights with!"

The soldier spun on his heels and marched down the hall, muttering and huffing furiously to himself.

Seeing his friend again brought back a flood of emotion. Jotham fought the tears. Flaggon took Jotham's hands in his, also gulping hard. "I wants you to know, sor . . ." he blinked fiercely, "how sorry . . . We never . . ." He held up his hand, then pushed past Jotham who was still standing in the doorway. "I shan't continue. . . . 'Tis not my place."

"What are you doing here, Flaggon?" Jotham finally was able to ask.

"Justar commands and I obeys, says I." He rubbed his throat and smacked his lips. "It's been a long time since I had a swallow sor; mind if I take one before relayin' the particulars of me mission?"

Flaggon drank deeply from his leather bottle. He sighed contentedly, wiped his lips, then continued. "Justar bid me come and give you aid in light of your . . . loss. I am to go with you and take you to the next battle. We are to leave at first light to avoid the conflict which Justar says is brewin' here."

"What do you mean? We got rid of all the Ghargs, didn't we?"

"Yes you did, but these captives have been in Ghnostar's clutches so long their minds has been poisoned. That is why the Teacher Paladins must remain here to pull out those rotten weeds. Justar says if you stays, it will go all the harder for Ellwynn and make the Teachers' task all the more difficult." Flaggon held up his hand to ward off another question. "The prisoners, most of them at least, wants you to be their leader. They don't want to follow Ellwynn because they disrespects any as looks different as them."

"So *that's* why . . ." Jotham murmured, gritting his teeth.

Flaggon puffed his cheeks and snorted. "Yes sor. That's why they also be plannin' secret-like to make you their baron. I already spokes to Trellawton and he knows what to say to the people tomorrow, but Justar thinks it best that you be gone by that time."

"Very good, I'll go tell the others then."

Flaggon drew himself up. "No sor, that be my responsibility. Yores is to get some rest and prepare for the adventures of the morrow. It will come soon enough, mark me word." He reached up and opened the door. "Keep it unlocked, sor. I will come in later and find a place to sleep on the floor." He again waved Jotham's concern aside. "I prefers the stones, sor. As me grandfadder said, 'there's so much of them, better to make one's peace with it.'" Flaggon closed the door before he could argue.

* * * * * * * * *

A silvery blue glow radiated over the quiet glen. It was still as death. A terrible horror clutched at Jotham's throat as his feet moved of their own accord, pulled by invisible strings. He glided, rather than walked, toward the tree. An awful expectancy, a yawning dread engulfed him. He was under a terrible spell too great to resist. The huge oak seemed to be growing larger as he drew near. He was attracted and yet repulsed. Suddenly, he knew why: the tree's branches were flailing like a thousand serpents. One colorless branch undulated sinuously toward him. As it hovered inches away, its tip enlarged and took on the shape of Abe's battered face; its long white body, that of his dead brother's. Jotham slashed at it in fear and loathing, and the face disappeared.

The trunk began to moan, an awful sound of longing and pain. Slowly, the trunk twisted and turned. Its writhing was hypnotic. A flash of searing anger cracked the tree's hold over him. He yanked out his sword, and in an insane spasm thrust it deep through the oak's woody heart. There was a high wail of anguish. Jotham thought he heard his name, then it trailed off into a low, sobbing moan. Its groaning became a low, mournful whisper. It was shriveling in front of him, its branches crinkling, then falling off. Soon, all that was left was a thin, dry trunk which decomposed into a reproachful heap at his feet.

"Jotham . . . Jotham . . ." someone was calling his name.

He opened his eyes to see Flaggon standing over him with a lamp in his hand. Jotham's throat was raw and his eyes stung.

"You were dreamin', sor. . . . Are you all right?"

"Yes, thanks Flaggon. . . . Go back to sleep; I'm fine." He rolled over quickly to hide the wetness of his cheeks. He hoped he hadn't sobbed out loud.

He fell asleep with the angry questions whirling in his head: *Why, Justar? Why? Why did you let my brother die?*

230

Chapter Thirty Two

Flaggon was up as the sun made its first appearance over the blue peaks along the eastern rim of the valley. The sounds of scratching and clinking metal brought Jotham slowly into consciousness. He wrinkled his nose—there was a pungent aroma filling the room. Flaggon was sitting next to the open window, rubbing a cloth over Jotham's sword.

"What's that smell?" Jotham mumbled groggily.

"What's that ya' said, sor?. . . . I'm sorry. I was thinkin' . . . Oh, the smell! You was askin' about that were ya, Cap'n?

Jotham put his hand over his mouth to stifle his yawn.

"Same as I asked me fadder, when I wotched him cleanin' his weapons after battle. . . . 'Ya know, me boy,' he says, 'weapons don't clean their-selves. . . . A dirty weapon is a useless weapon . . . and don't ya forgets it now.'" Flaggon wiped a bead of sweat from his large nose. "I'se been doin' it now so long, I don't even notices the smell." He lifted a bowl of damp sand, showing it to Jotham.

"The smell's the vinegar, sor. I mixes it with the sand like me fadder and grandfadder before him done." He grimaced, "I prefers apple, but all the cook had was wine vinegar." He sighed deeply, "Must makes do with what one 'as." He picked up Abe's ax and began rubbing its head with the smelly abrasive.

At the sight of the ax, Jotham fell back heavily on the tasseled pillow and closed his eyes. Flaggon set the weapon down and walked quietly over to Jotham's side. Laying a hand on his arm, he said, "Sor, beggin' yore par-don, 'tis time to be goin'. Justar says we must be gone before breakfast is served to the inhabitants. We only has little more than an hour, and I must wake Master Bart and Lady Carisa."

Jotham rolled over on his stomach. "I can't. How can I leave my broth-er here?" he moaned.

231

"Where did they take him? Jotham asked. "I have to go see him." He looked intently at the dwarf. "I want to take him with us. I can't leave him here, Flaggon!"

"There, there now, young sor . . . perfectly understandable, that is." Flaggon's voice was gentle as he took Jotham's arm and led him to the door. "Abe will be all right here. His body is in good care. Follow me quiet-like and I will shows you. But first, let me wakes your comrades."

Jotham leaped out of bed, ran to the table and threw water on his face. Drying himself quickly, he matched strides with his bearded guide.

After alerting the other two, the dwarf led Jotham up several flights of stairs into an elegant octagonal library with mahogany bookshelves spanning the length of the walls. Large, leather bound volumes of every size and color filled the room. Jotham was amazed to recognize some of them; a number of them were even ones Glumpuddle had read to them years earlier.

Flaggon stood looking around the room for a moment. He pointed at a stained-glass window depicting a knight riding a black horse and began to count the bookshelves to the right. He walked over to the seventh one. "This is the quickest way to the resting chamber, sor." He pulled on the seventh book on the seventh shelf from the bottom.

The bookshelf shook, and ground its way backwards, the counterweight turning it slowly into the wall. As he walked through the stone entrance, Jotham glanced at the book Flaggon had pulled out from the rest. Embossed in exquisite detail on the dark red leather was its title: *Ivanhoe*. A memory flared briefly, but disappeared as quickly as it came. He followed Flaggon up broad stairs illumined by round windows which wound their way up the tower stairway.

Flaggon stopped in front of a wide, polished door which gleamed like raw honey. He turned the handle and stepped aside to let Jotham in. Flaggon closed the door quietly behind him, leaving Jotham alone in the dim room.

Candles glowed from ornate candelabras on the wall, gauze curtains covered three narrow leaded glass windows and in the center of the round room was a low table on which Abe's body lay. The early morning sun filtered through the thin curtains, casting a soft hue over everything in the room. The still form on the table was bathed in a warm glow. At the sight of his younger brother looking so restful and content, Jotham felt a new wave of sorrow overwhelm him. His feet, like lead weights, moved mechanically toward the body.

232

Abe had been washed and dressed in a spotless, shimmering white tunic. On his dark, curly head was a thin circlet of golden leaves with a large pearl in the center. In the middle was inscribed the same embellished letter M that was on Warrior's crown. Jotham fell down on his knees next to the table.

"Oh Abe . . ." he moaned, his forehead rested on his brother's chest. The tears left dark circles on the white tunic. "Justar, why . . . why?"

As he wept, a slight breeze lifted the opaque curtain over the window directly in front of him. Jotham lifted his head and saw that he was not alone as he had first thought. A servant girl was standing shyly near the farthest window, a shaft of light illuminating her golden hair. She wore a white apron, tied at the waist, and held a straw broom in her hands. Her hair was pulled back in long braids, which drew attention to her sparkling sapphire eyes fixed on him.

"I'm sorry if I startled you," she said in a surprisingly clear voice. She glanced at Abe. "I'm sure he was a wonderful boy." She walked gravely over to Jotham and put her small hand over his.

For some reason, Jotham knew the girl would have the answer. "What does that letter represent," he asked pointing at the fragile crown.

Her clear blue eyes gazed earnestly down into his. "That would be the symbol of martyrdom. It is a sign of highest honor, Sir Jotham."

Her voice was infinitely calming. "And, do not fear," she continued, with a penetrating look that laid his heart bare, "Justar is with you." Her eyes twinkled in the diffused sunlight as she stressed the final words, "And with him is *hope*." She laid her hand gently on top of his head. A comforting warmth flowed over him. She smiled again, turned and left the room.

Jotham stared after her for several moments. He turned back to look at his brother's still form and reached out carefully to adjust the coronet on his head. He rested his hand lightly on Abe's chest, then stood up quickly and walked to the door.

Flaggon nodded as Jotham came through the doorway. "You all right now, sor?"

"Yes, Flaggon, thanks for bringing me here." He looked past him and down the stairs. "Where did she go?"

"Who, sor?" Flaggon looked up questioningly.

"The servant girl . . . She came out just a few minutes before I did."

Flaggon's puzzled expression deepened. "No sor, you must be mistaken. No one's come out this door but you."

"Flaggon, she had blond hair and a broom in her hands. Are you sure you didn't leave for a few minutes?"

The dwarf puffed his chest out, and his cheeks began to grow dangerously red. *"Young sor,"* he huffed, "'twas my sworn duty to stand guard, and I done me duty and I tells you no girl or otherwise left that room." Not wanting to continue the argument further, Flaggon headed down the stairs. "We must hurry now; not much time is left."

Jotham stared at his reflection in the polished door. He placed his fingers on it then slowly turned, following Flaggon down the steps.

Chapter Thirty Three

Walking through the false door, Jotham reached out for the embossed volume that had opened it. It had obviously been read often. Beautiful, hand-painted illustrations were interspersed throughout the book. He wished he could take it with him. He turned to the first page.

"Come, come, sor," Flaggon was pulling at his arm.

Jotham ignored him.

Written on the flyleaf were the words, EX LIBRIS REX JUSTAR. A vague memory began to float into his consciousness, but it listed and sank away before coming into view. Underneath the bold phrase, in a meticulous, feminine hand was the sentence: *"Dulce et decorum est pro rex mori."*

Flaggon was now insistent. "We must be off, Cap'n; we barely has time now for our breakfast." Jotham replaced the volume and left the room.

While hastily consuming the dried fruit, milk and nut bread, Jotham caught Flaggon eyeing him rather strangely. It seemed to him that the dwarf looked slightly affronted or disappointed, somehow. The dwarf turned his head, and Jotham decided he'd misread him. Taking final hurried swallows of cold milk, the three Paladins followed Flaggon out of the castle.

Before they could leave the kitchen, the cook grabbed them and kissed each Paladin resoundingly on both cheeks. Flaggon glowered and puffed his cheeks out so fiercely that the cook stepped back, his arms dropping to his sides.

"Captain Jotham," the round-bellied cook smiled with moist eyes. "We will remember you and Lady Carisa and Bartolome fondly. You are always welcome to come and visit us. Now, please go or I will cry."

They walked quickly out the small door they had entered two days earlier. There they found the two Teacher Paladins on the walkway waiting to bid them farewell.

After shaking hands, Ellwynn and Law saluted the warriors, sword points to the sky. "It has been an honor," they declared in unison, staring straight ahead at the blue horizon.

Carisa walked up beside Law and gave him a kiss on his freckled cheek. "We'll miss you, Law." Her eyes twinkled, "All is forgiven and forgotten."

He gulped as his ears began to turn red.

Ellwynn sheathed his weapon. "I'm neither fond of nor good at farewells. But I will say that I consider it a rare privilege to call you my friends." With the open palm of his right hand, he struck his chest. His dark eyes glowed fiercely, "Paladins, I salute you."

The band struck theirs, "And we salute you."

Flaggon hesitated before making his way down the wooden bridge. He seemed ready to speak; instead, he puffed his cheeks out sternly, and grumbling under his breath, he led the band away from the castle with his quick, choppy strides.

The air was warm and still, and there were only a few white puffs of cottony clouds speckled across the azure sky as they trekked up the mountain. Flaggon had warned them that it would be a long, steep hike, and he was right. Following Bart's lead, Jotham and Carisa wrapped a damp cloth around their foreheads to provide protection from the sun's rays. Several hours later, they took their first rest. They had been climbing steadily over sharp rocks and boulders, and Ursula's Fortress now gleamed far below, an elegant pendant resting on shimmering black silk.

"The path ahead is dangerous, so be very careful," Flaggon warned, opening his pack and withdrawing a long rope. "Tie this round yore waists. It will keep you from slidin' off the mountain."

They climbed up the steep incline in single-file onto a narrow shelf that protruded from the mountain's rocky face. After awhile, Flaggon slowed down considerably in order to climb more carefully over the loose shale. Although the sun was hot in the deep blue sky, a mountain breeze cooled their sweaty skin. On distant peaks they could make out the stark whiteness of glistening snow. Frequently, loose stones would be kicked off their path, and the bouncing projectile would plummet hundreds of feet before smashing on the boulders below. The sound was a reminder for the Paladins to hug the cliff and inch forward with care.

The path began to widen, and Flaggon had them stop for lunch outside the mouth of a small cave. From this height, they also could just see make out a glinting turret of Castle Orion far in the distance. It reminded Carisa

236

of the globe she had in her bedroom at home. Inside the crystal globe was a miniature elfin castle which, whenever she shook it, would be covered with artificial snow.

As Jotham gazed down at the castle, the only thing he could see was Abe sliding toward Abner's dais and flinging the ax at their enemy. He bit his lip. Carisa looked over at him, her eyes growing soft and sympathetic. She rested her hand on his. He held it briefly, looked down at the grass, and let it go.

After putting their food away, Flaggon stood up, straightening his pack high on his back. "We are goin' to go through this cave. At the end is a gorge, and on the other side is the fortress. I has a small oil lamp with me, but it gives little light, so stay close."

The cave was actually a tunnel which had been excavated through the mountain centuries earlier. It was narrow and must have been dug by dwarfs. The Paladins followed their guide in an uncomfortable crouch.

Over the past miles, Jotham couldn't shake the impression that the bearded dwarf, whom he was now directly behind, was displeased with him. He decided to ask him about it the next time they were alone.

Flaggon was whistling as he strode ahead with nearly a foot of head room.

"There be times height be no advantage. Is that not true, sor?"

Jotham winced; even the joke seemed to have a barb to it.

After several minutes, the Paladins began noticing that drawings of animals and trees covered the walls. Although quite crude (they were little more than stick figures), they still spoke eloquently of the artists' loves and longings.

They told a story about a forest and a river, and about the men and animals who lived there. A large dragon with two heads eventually made his appearance, and it trampled down the forest and drank the river dry. A long section depicted pain, struggle and despair. This was followed by a vast panorama of battle in which hundreds of warriors were locked in conflict. The final scenes showed a small group of fighters confronting the dragon, several lying on the ground dead at its feet. The last drawings were blurry, as if someone had sought to erase them. Jotham peered closely at them. Something was clinging to the dragon's neck, then there was a fire, and finally, what looked like people and trees dancing by the banks of a broad river.

237

Flaggon stood in front of what Jotham decided was a depiction of the Great Dance. The dwarf looked disconcertingly at Jotham and kept walking toward the dim light at the end of the tunnel.

The rain was falling in a steady drizzle on this side of the mountain. Instead of deep blue sky, there was now a shifting mass of thick gray clouds overhead. The band gathered at the mouth of the tunnel and watched the water drip gloomily off the rocky outcroppings. The drops plip-plopped in a puddle at their feet. They put on their heavy cloaks. The air had suddenly become chilly.

Not more than 200 yards away was the gorge. It was about 50 feet wide, and from the muffled rumble of rushing water at its base, sounded very deep. The ground stretched out in front of them more or less smoothly with an occasional pile of boulders and debris: formations left by the erosion of wind and rain, and the inevitable mountain rock slides. Small scraggly brush and a few sparse trees broke the flat monotony. The ravine, which split the dismal plain, looked like a jagged tear, as if a mighty cleaver had dealt the land a brutal blow, cracking and ripping it apart in a painful gash. There was a sadness to the scene that silenced the already quiet band.

The twisted branches of a small tree perched at the brink of the chasm caught Jotham's attention. There was something arresting about its precarious position, teetering towards the yawning mouth which threatened to consume it. It seemed suddenly to be a stark parable. Most of his life he'd felt as if he were living on the razor's edge of disastrous failure. He was hounded by that secret, gnawing dread which ate at him. Abruptly, the living metaphor shifted and took on a resemblance to the writhing oak of which he'd so recently dreamed. He squeezed his eyes closed. When he opened them again, all he could distinguish was a wet, scrubby tree dripping water into an abyss.

"Flaggon, it doesn't look like the rain is going to break any time soon. I think we should keep going," Jotham said.

"I reckons you're right, sor, although one thing I've had my stomach full of is marching in the rain." Flaggon tossed the hood of his cloak over his bald head. "Can't say as I ever made my peace with that."

Bart was peering uncertainly at the drips. "Neither have I, Flaggon. I'd just as soon build a fire and wait it out."

Carisa moved over next to her brother. "Makes me think of those rainy days by the cozy fire in Glumpuddle's library." She stopped, noticing

Flaggon's quizzical expression, then explained, "That was the name we gave to an old friend of ours . . . in the other world."

He waved away her explanation. "Yes, I knows him, m'lady. . . . Lord Glump told us about that. Master Slimgilley and he used to laugh . . ." Flaggon wrinkled his face, the lines intersecting across his brown face. He put a hand to his mouth. "Ahh. I be not permitted to speak of other travelers." He squeezed his jaw shut in grim determination.

Carisa stared at him, her mouth open. "You met Glumpuddle?"

The dwarf pursed his lips guiltily, his cheeks as red as his beard. "I canna' speaks more about it. Master Slimgilley would have me tongue if he knew." Flaggon shut his mouth in a tight line, looked suspiciously out of the corners of his eyes, then whispered, "I will say this, he was a strange one . . . he was. Every time I called him Master Glumpuddle, he would allus says to me: 'Glump will suit just fine.' It was what his best friends called him, so he said."

Flaggon looked anxiously behind them; then, putting a conspiratorial finger to his thick lips, he continued, "He and me Master got on famously. An' I will say this, Lord Glump spoke very fondly of you . . ." His eyes narrowed, "but I shan't speaks no more about it." He turned on his heel and walked out through the dripping screen toward the gorge.

Jotham followed close behind.

Flaggon called back to the remaining two in the tunnel. "Don't be laggin' now. We need to reach Andromedous by mid-afternoon."

Jotham walked up beside him; he decided he would wait to question his guide about his misgivings. "I've been surprised we've not seen more Ghargs as we've traveled on our way. Is that unusual?"

Flaggon wiped the water from his bushy eyebrows. "We travels in the day because that's when most of them are asleep. They sleeps in the day so they can have plenty of energy to practice all manner of mischief at night. In Issatar it is never safe to be about when the sun sets—that's when Ghnostar's forces are at their meanest."

Bart was hunched over into his cloak, walking next to his sister. "If I lived here, I'd be sleeping too. . . . What a miserable place," he muttered to Carisa.

"I'd just like to be sitting in our kitchen drinking some of Mom's hot chocolate," she whispered from inside the red hood.

"Do you think we're ever going to return?" he asked, growing very sober.

"I'm sure of it, Bart; Justar promised."

He trudged over the dreary terrain, trying to keep the rain out of his good eye.

Jotham and Flaggon were now waiting for them by a bridge that spanned the ravine. It inclined sharply up toward the opposite ledge and was made of rope with narrow wooden slats along the walkway. These were joined tightly so that only a few inches of space separated the boards. Thick ropes were strung on both sides of the walkway and served as flexible handrails. It had clearly been constructed by expert craftsmen.

Jotham instructed Bart to proceed behind Carisa. He would follow Flaggon, who would be taking the lead over the canyon. Flaggon strode forward, holding tightly to the ropes attached to posts on either side of the divide. The end of the bridge angled up and was obscured by a fine mist that rose from the canyon.

Jotham stepped onto the bridge and took hold of the two support ropes. He began walking carefully, taking short steps over the wet slats. His stomach lurched as the bridge swayed gently under his feet. "Hold on tight," he yelled back at Bart and Carisa.

"No kidding . . ." Bart grumbled, eyeing the bottom far below.

Carisa's mouth was dry as parchment as she stepped on the bridge. Unlike Bart, she had never been afraid of heights: the taller the tree limb, the better, but this was something entirely different. Those were stable; this was not. She was not in control of this situation, and it terrified her. The bridge groaned as it trembled and swung in the slashing wind that tore through the gorge. With each step forward, it seemed to sway more and more emphatically—a bucking bronco intent on dismounting them. Far, far below, a mountain stream frothed and foamed, tumbling over rocks and fallen limbs. The walls of the narrow canyon trembled with the crashing of the roiling waters.

Carisa's chest began to feel painfully constricted. Her foot stumbled and slid on the wet boards. She felt dangerously lightheaded. Up ahead, Flaggon was walking gingerly, looking nervously back at her and Bart. He waved his arm for them to hurry toward him. Flaggon shouted something, but his words were blown like confetti into the canyon. The rain was now falling at a sharp angle, stinging her exposed cheeks and dripping into her eyes. The wind also seemed to be picking up intensity, as if conspiring to fling her and her brother into the chasm below.

Her stomach was in knots. She was becoming disoriented, and a clammy sweat broke out on her flushed face. She realized suddenly that she could not go on. She turned her head to tell Bart to go back and wait for the wind to die down. When she released her grip, it happened: the board under her foot broke, and the rope strands connecting the boardwalk together popped.

She screamed as her feet fell from under her.

The bridge began unraveling beneath her as rows of loose slats cascaded like a shattered keyboard into the canyon. With both hands Carisa grabbed one of the rope supports, her feet hanging loosely underneath her. She stared in unbelief as the rough cord she was grasping began to shred before her eyes. The smooth, sinister slice was all too obvious now. It gave way as she was making a desperate grab for the other support.

She fell, clutching the end of the frayed rope, her body swinging toward the canyon wall. When she struck the rocky cliff, she was jarred loose, her limp form plummeting into the heart of the rumbling gorge.

Chapter Thirty Four

The other three were hanging precariously from the remaining support rope. They had been struggling so desperately to maintain a hold on the swaying rope, they did not see Carisa's body drop down into the roaring mist.

The wet rope was biting into Bart's hands, and his grip was beginning to loosen. He strained to pull his feet up so that he could loop his legs over the rope. After several tries, he was able to hook his ankles around the support rope. His legs now bearing the weight of his body, he was able to inch his way back down the 15 feet to the foot of the bridge. Gasping, he dropped to the muddy ground, his fingers raw, his shoulders and arms trembling with the exertion. He crawled over to the edge of the canyon, hoping against hope to see his sister holding on to the end of the torn rope. His face blanched when he saw the loose end whipping back and forth in the biting wind.

"Carisa!" he screamed into the rumbling depths of the jagged crevice. Her name echoed mockingly back up to him.

"Stay where you are!" yelled Jotham from the upper end of the gorge where he and Flaggon had managed to crawl. "We're gonna slide down on the rope."

"Carisa's gone," Bart yelled back, his throat constricting. "Do you see her?"

Jotham had made a loop with his whip and was placing it over the rope. "No . . . not from here. Just hold on and we'll be right there," he hollered back. He let his body fall off the edge holding the ends of the loop and slid down toward Bart in short, swaying jerks.

"I can't see her," Bart's voice was quavering. His wet face twisted in agony as Jotham dropped down next to him. He was gazing with desperate eyes at the rocky face which fell away at an acute angle below him. Panic threatened to overwhelm Jotham, but he forced himself to speak with a calm he did not feel.

"Don't worry, Bart; we'll go down and find her. Flaggon will find a way."

Flaggon was sliding down on a loop made from the torn rope support. The friction of rope against rope caused him to slow almost to a stop; but by swinging his body he was able to maintain his momentum. When he reached the approximate place where the left support rope had broken, he let his weight drag him to a halt.

"What are you doing?" Jotham yelled.

"I sees something white on a ledge, sor," the dwarf panted, his beard blowing over his shoulder like a red pennant. "I thinks it may be Lady Carisa."

Bart stood up and put his hands around his mouth to form a bullhorn. "Can we reach her?" he bellowed.

"I thinks so." Flaggon pumped his stout body and began to slide toward the two Paladins again.

Taking the rope they had used on the way up the mountain and tying it to the rope that had torn, they were able to extend its length considerably. Flaggon expertly tied it around the stake that anchored the bridge supports. "Stand on the other side of this post, and belay the rope slowly as I goes down. If I finds somethin' I will give a tug and you pulls it up." Then, without another word, he slipped over the edge of the gorge.

The two fed the rope carefully and held their breath waiting for Flaggon's command. They had almost reached the last foot of rope when they finally heard his voice being tossed up to them on the swirling winds. "I've—found —bleeding bad—"

Bart thrust his head over the lip and yelled down into the void. "Use the liquid from the bottle—Hurry!"

After several moments, Flaggon's voice bounced up toward them. "—smashed, sors—liquid—gone!"

Feeling a tug, Jotham yelled, "We're gonna pull her up now." Steel was in his voice. Hand over hand they began drawing the wounded girl toward them. Her limp body was surprisingly heavy. It took all their strength to drag her up the cliff wall.

Bart's head drooped over the cliff's edge, oblivious to the yawning precipice. "Carisa, hang on!" he cried, his words falling into the pitiless, surging mist.

A few moments later he yelled, "I see her! Careful, we've got to get her over this lip." Within moments she was lying on the ground on top of her cloak. Her cheeks were gray and her pulse was very weak. Jotham threw the rope down and pulled Flaggon up the face of the canyon.

Bart tried to pour some of Flaggon's brew into her mouth, but her lips were slack, and her eyelids remained motionless. There was a dark spreading bruise on her forehead. Dark blood was seeping from the torn skin and running down her cheek. Bart wiped off her face, and with strips torn from his cloak, wrapped her head in a thick bandage. It was soon spotted with a dark stain.

Jotham wanted to throw himself down next to her and hold her cold body, forcing her to regain consciousness. Her limp white fingers lay on the muddy grass. His last memory of Abe flashed before his eyes. A hard, painful lump rose to his throat as he looked at her. He dropped to his knees by her prone body and began to scream, "No! No! Not Carisa too . . ." Disconsolately, he repeated Justar's name, moaning, "Justar! Justar, help us." His tears dropped onto her filthy tunic. He felt Flaggon's stubby palm resting heavily on his back.

Jotham's eyes flew open. He had heard Justar speak!

The words were clear and unmistakable: "I have authorized you to use my name." They were a gentle reminder but carried with them immense power. They throbbed within him as if a mallet had struck the taut skin of a kettle drum. He understood.

Jotham placed both hands on Carisa's bandaged head. The words: "In Justar's name be healed!" broke out of his lips as if on their own accord.

The corners of Carisa's mouth twitched and a restful contentment settled over her. She looked as if she were dreaming. She remained motionless for several minutes. The Paladins waited silently.

Her eyelids fluttered, then opened. Her gaze was locked on Jotham. She smiled into his eyes with a warmth that made his throat tighten.

Bart threw his arms up in the air. "Thank you, Justar!" he whooped. He slapped Jotham's back. Jotham was staring into Carisa's golden eyes; his throat felt too thick to trust himself to speak.

At Bart's exclamation of gratitude, the wind suddenly ceased, and with it, the rain. The clouds scattered across the sky like street urchins being chased away from a storefront. In their wake, the warm sunshine began to filter through the thinning clouds.

"Well done, Cap'n," chortled Flaggon. "I thinks I now knows why Justar formed the order of Warrior Priests. I always said Justar knew what he was doin'." He raised his stubby arms overhead, waving them back and forth, skipping in delight around the three on the ground. Bart stood, grabbing ahold of the dwarf's hands, joining him in his merry dance.

Impulsively, Jotham leaped to his feet, linked up with the others and formed a dancing circle whirling around Carisa, who was now sitting up, laughing happily at the comical trio.

The speed of her recuperation amazed them. Within the hour she appeared to be completely healed. She assured her solicitous brother that she was fully capable of traversing the gorge on the remaining rope.

"I've never felt better," she stated emphatically. "I mean it." Noticing his dubious expression, she asked him, "Want to arm wrestle?" The color had returned to her tan cheeks, and her dark eyes sparkled vivaciously. He had to concede that she did look better—better even than she had before her fall.

Flaggon climbed on the rope first, locking his ankles tightly around the cord. He was followed closely by Carisa and Bart immediately behind her. Jotham brought up the rear. Without the wind and the rain in their faces they made surprisingly fast progress, pulling themselves hand over hand to the other side. Soon they had all hoisted themselves over the upper edge of the canyon.

They stood in a line staring silently up the hill at the vast fortress which rose up before them. It was actually more a walled city than a castle. Along the exterior of the black stone wall, at intervals of ten yards, were large embrasures with loopholes from which guards could easily repel any assault. The stronghold sat on a craggy cliff, its back against a rocky drop-off and its front protected by a man-made lake. There was no way to get over the lake except by barge, and should anyone approach, its towering castle gate was enclosed by parapets from which guards could rain down arrows at will.

Jotham's heart dropped. Even Flaggon looked shocked; he had never seen a more formidable stronghold. The mammoth Castle Andromedous looked impregnable.

Its reflection in the lurid pool, with its multitude of dark towers and parapets lunging into the sky, gave it the appearance of a monstrous black spider lunging to snare its hapless victims. Jotham winced and turned his head away.

He suddenly felt that a terrible trap was awaiting them on the inside of that dreadful structure.

Chapter Thirty Five

Noticing his crestfallen expression, the dwarf gave Jotham a slap on the back. "It's not as bad as all that, sor. Appearances can be deceivin', ya know."

Jotham was not convinced. It sounded to him like Flaggon was trying to convince himself, as much as the Paladins. Reaching to adjust his sword, he felt the worn leather wallet hanging at his waist. A hot flush of embarrassment crossed his face. He now understood Flaggon's unspoken hostility.

Jotham waved the others toward him. "We had to leave in such a rush this morning, we—I mean, I," he added with uncharacteristic meekness, "forgot to read Justar's scrolls. We're going to read them now before we take another step."

"Hear, hear," bellowed the dwarf happily, taking a long pull from his bottle. He winked at Jotham, smacked his lips and grinned at the others. "Looks like your Cap'n has learnt himself another lesson."

The Paladins fumbled with their pouches, studiously avoiding each other's eyes.

Flaggon spread his short legs out, furrowing his large red eyebrows and puffed out his cheeks importantly. "Now, let us listen very careful to what our King says. Many be the battles as been lost for lack of attention to instructions." He squinted somberly at the three Paladins, a study in profound concentration.

Jotham looked at Flaggon sheepishly, "I'm afraid I'm going to need some help with mine; it's in Latin. I'm afraid I've forgotten most of the vocabulary I memorized." He handed his scroll to Bart. "I never thought I'd ever really be using it."

Flaggon's face now wore a disapproving frown. "As me fadder said on many occasions, 'learnin' is never wasted,' sor. One never knows when it will be useful." He snorted and clasped his hands behind his back. "It's best to take yore education very serious-like. . . . If I may repeat me fadder one more time, if he told me once, he told me a thousand times, 'bein' a leader is not for the slothful' . . . sor." As he spoke, he made a point to look over Jotham's shoulder.

Bart was having a difficult time with the translation. "'*Festina lente,*' he read. Flaggon's smile was goading him on. "We are to be slow . . . No, no. We . . . are to hurry, or make haste . . . slowly." Bart looked up in relief; the dwarf was glowing his approval.

"In other words—we are to take our time, but hurry up!" Jotham said. "That's a little confusing," he mused.

"I believe it means that we're supposed to travel quickly, but carefully," Bart explained.

Flaggon beamed his approval.

"Mine reads: '*Amor vincet omnia,*'" Carisa said, "which means, 'love rules or conquers everything.'" Flaggon's eyes were dancing happily.

Bart was disappointed that his scroll required no translation, yet he read the words aloud:

When the leader is bound, no strength can he wield;
Your joy will abound, for your victory is sealed.
When battle is over, three Paladins leave;
Haste to your last conflict; no longer to grieve.

"Geez, that was simple," he grumbled, stuffing the parchment back into his pouch.

Jotham glanced back at the looming fortress. "Who's the ruler of Andromedous, Flaggon?"

He stroked his beard for a moment, and answered, "He is known as Creost the Glute, Cap'n."

"Sounds to me like the plan is to find and destroy him. Once he's removed, Justar is promising us that the castle will be ours. What do you think, Carisa?"

She had been rubbing the letters on her parchment with a detached expression on her face. "W-what? Oh, the castle . . . yes, Jotham I think that is a good strategy."

Bart asked Flaggon, "What does your scroll say? I'm sure Justar must have something for you too."

Flaggon's face broke out in a wide grin as he read his instructions, then began chuckling loudly. "I never knows what's to expect from King Justar." He wiped his eyes. "Just when I thinks I knows him well, he does something like this. 'Unpredictable' is what Master Slimgilley calls him."

Carisa drew the scroll towards her. "So what did he say?" Flaggon pulled it away to deliver the punch line himself. "Well, the King wants me to be ever so careful when we gets into the fortress. He warns me: *'Cave cannum';* beware the dog." The dwarf burst out laughing again. "It's a sayin' we use in Issatar. Whenever we goes on a trip, we warns each other, very serious-like: 'now watch out for the dog.' We means it as a joke, of course." He threw his head back and guffawed.

His mirth was so infectious, the Paladins had to join in.

Flaggon grew serious. "The guards here are famous for their laziness. We call them Cretians, but even a Cretian's nap doesn't last forever. We must hurry," he raised a finger and winked, "slowly—of course—and cross the lake before they awaken. Once they're all awake it may be too late, there being too many enemies for us to fight all at once." Flaggon took off in a waddling trot toward the lake.

The Latin instructions had reminded Jotham of what he'd intended to ask Bart. He pulled him aside, letting Carisa run ahead alongside Flaggon.

Jotham explained what he'd read on the front cover of *Ivanhoe* in Ursula's library.

Bart's eyes clouded momentarily. "You sure that's what it said? *'Dulce et decorum est pro rex mori?'*"

Jotham nodded, "Those are the exact words."

Bart looked very uncomfortable. "What Ursula wrote was: 'It is a fitting thing to die for one's king.'"

Jotham's eyes did not waver. "That's what I thought," he said.

The black lake, which protected the front of the fortress, shimmered with a greasy slickness. The water was thick and placid. The only living creatures appeared to be the mosquitoes that had been lancing them unmercifully since they neared the stagnant water. The ferryman's cottage, a stone's throw away, seemed to be deserted. Across the lake, tied to a post about ten feet from the castle's outer wall, floated the wooden craft which served as the castle's only transport. Opposite was another post of the same height. Jotham surmised that they were the supports upon which the drawbridge rested when it was lowered to receive cargo.

Flaggon put his finger to his lips and pointed to the ferry. A large bundle had been left on top of it. When a puffy hand waved off a mosquito, the Paladins realized that it was the sleeping ferryman.

They huddled together to discuss the plan for crossing the lake. "We must find a log which has been deposited somewhere on this shore," Flaggon explained. "We will use it to float to the castle." He gestured with his forefinger, anticipating their questions. "There is a tunnel at the western wall that we will use to enter."

Bart and Carisa headed to the right, and Jotham followed Flaggon in the opposite direction.

"A tunnel?" Jotham asked the dwarf. "What's it for?" Flaggon didn't meet his eye when he answered, "Well, it is more like a tube. . . . It's for removin' refuse, sor." The dwarf walked away quickly and began looking into the weeds.

Jotham was glad Carisa hadn't heard.

Their legs and tunics were splattered with oily mud by the time Bart stumbled over the log. It had been draped with weeds and daubed with the dark mud and was almost impossible to see. They removed the heavy round shields and packs off their backs, slung them on the short branch stumps that stuck out from its sides and pushed the log away from shore. The water was warm and heavy on their bodies and smelled of oil. The four clung to the slippery log and kicked their legs, feeling their feet sliding through the ooze. Holding on with their arms, they used their legs to propel themselves and their craft toward Andromedous.

Something wrapped itself around Carisa's legs. She almost cried out, until she realized it was a submerged weed. With a few rapid kicks, it was dislodged. As they approached the sprawling fortification, the weeds again became an impediment. Carisa tried to raise her paddling feet high behind her to avoid getting tangled in them—they felt like long, slimy fingers clinging to her body. She shuddered as they traced their way over her legs.

They could now see that the enormous fortress was not black, as it appeared to be from the opposite shore, but was covered with dark ivy which completely obscured the stone. The twining growth gave the castle an ancient, foreboding appearance. The imposing structure seemed to be leaning back scornfully, tolerating their advance with haughty indifference.

As they paddled cautiously to the far end of the castle, the surface of the lake remained deathly still. However, on a few occasions, Carisa thought she saw large tail fins stirring the water near them. She pointed out one particularly strong ripple to Bart.

His eyes widened, and he whispered dramatically, "Catfish. Big ones! Be glad you're not a mouse."

Carisa rolled her eyes at him, but her legs began pumping faster. Their raft was now gliding into the shadow cast by the round tower looming ahead of them. They were within 15 feet of the fortress.

She felt another tug on her leg. She kicked again, but this time could not break loose. Electricity seemed to crackle in her hair. A buzzing sound filled her ears. She felt her muscles quivering. Her left leg and then the entire left side of her body began to tremble.

At the same moment, Flaggon hissed. "Somethin' has me leg. I thot it were weeds, but—" His words were cut off, his throat constricted. His larynx appeared to be paralyzed.

Jotham reached down to feel for the entanglement. A prickly vise clamped down on his arm. He shook it, but the pressure and stinging increased.

He stared at the water in horror.

Two dead eyes were staring up at him from the oily depths, and what looked like the finned tail of an enormous worm was wriggling next to his leg. An eerie blue light sheathed the length of its undulating body, which was as long as Jotham's. Its protruding jaw was clamped over his forearm, sending painful shocks of current coursing through his body.

He jerked his arm again, but the eel's underjaw had hooked him in a tenacious grip, that threatened to snap the bone. The phosphorescent light ran up over the obscene jaw and over Jotham's right side, sending shooting spasms up through his shoulder. Next to him he could hear Flaggon thrashing in the water and the terrified voices of the other Paladins.

The giant worm jerked its head sideways, nearly breaking Jotham's grip on the log. He could feel the needle-like teeth piercing the metal links covering his arm. The creature's strength and tenacity were horrifying. It yanked again, and his fingers began to slip.

"Bart—hel . . ." he gasped, as his head slid toward the water.

Bart thrust his sword down into the blackness near Jotham's arm.

"Again!" Jotham cried, his facial muscles growing numb. His ears were popping and his eyes bulged with the strain.

Bart thrust again and made contact with a dense, sinewy body. As Jotham's fingers gave way, he felt a convulsion and sharp teeth releasing their hold. Bart reached down and grabbed a fistful of Jotham's hair, pulling his face out of the water. The huge eel plunged downward, spewing blood into the rancid waters. Flaggon's attacker let go of his leg and greedily followed the descending trail to feast at the bottom.

Carisa screamed. Two huge shimmering bodies were insinuating themselves around her. Locking their jaws on her legs, they tried to pull her under. The water around her was percolating; thin tendrils of steam rose from the bubbling surface.

Flaggon pulled himself on top of the log and clambered quickly to her. "Hold on m'lady," he grunted hoarsely, drawing out his dagger and clenching it between his teeth. Carisa's eyes were wide and desperate, begging him to save her. He reached for her hand; but as he did, her fingers stiffened and slipped off the log.

Flaggon dove into the water. He stroked down and with one hand grabbed hold of her arm and pulled up, slowing her descent. With the other, he tore the dagger from his mouth and swung it in a vicious arc. The sharp tip sliced through greasy water and the roots of giant lily pads. He yanked at Carisa again and kicked down at the same time, thrusting his body down toward her legs. With reckless abandon, he released Carisa and kicked down even further. His hand was stung by the electricity along the eel's shimmering body. Ignoring it, he raked at it with the dagger and felt it connect. Rubbery skin peeled open; a thick warmth and then buffeting waves hit him in the face. The grotesque creature fell away, thrashing violently.

By its electrical glow, he could see where the remaining eel was attached to Carisa's body. He was running out of air. Aiming his thrust at its head, he jabbed down with the last of his strength. The dagger plunged through the monster's eye, immobilizing it instantly. The eel's jaws went slack, its sinewy body dropping like a stone.

Out of breath, he felt the strong hands of the two others pulling him and Carisa to the surface. Bart and Jotham yanked their companions' heads out of the water and dragged them back toward their raft. Flaggon and Carisa were barely able to drag themselves up over the log, where they lay taking in huge gulps of air.

They floated in silence, the four warriors waiting to recover their strength. After several minutes, they could see a metal grate which was now visible above the waterline at the base of the tower. It was rusty, and other than some moss growing on the upper bars, was surprisingly clean.

"Looks like it's been licked spotless," offered Bart who had overheard Flaggon's description of their doorway into the castle, "but how do we get in? It's locked shut, right?" he asked, pointing to the iron lock fixed to the top of the metal bars.

"Yeah, definitely looks like it," Jotham agreed. "We can't use my whip; if the guards haven't heard us already, the explosion would give us away for sure."

Flaggon's voice was still hoarse, but he was now sitting up. "If you gets us close to it, I thinks I can open it." They paddled the log till it came to a rest against the bars. Hoisting the dwarf up so that he stood on Jotham's shoulders, Flaggon stuck the tip of his dagger into the rusty key-hole. He jiggled it back and forth for several moments; then, with a clack, it sprung open. The four warriors wrestled with the grate. With a squeal, it swung down and splashed into the lake.

They peered through the entrance into a wide tube which slanted upward at a sharp angle. There were ridges along its length with rows of rivets connecting the sections of metal tubing. It was tall enough for them to fit through on hands and knees, and the grooves gave footholds upon which to climb.

Jotham went in first, followed by Flaggon, Carisa and Bart. The column moved quickly, unsure whether their fight with the eels or the sound of the grate hitting the water had alerted the guards. Though it was greasy and slippery, by keeping their hands and feet spread high along the sides, they could pull themselves up without too much difficulty. Despite the tube's solid construction, when the four were all inside, their movements caused it to shake. It was clearly not bolted tightly, either at the top or bottom. It swayed gently, at first, but the swinging became more pronounced the higher they climbed. Squeaking and grating sounds now filled their hollow chamber as if rusty gears were grinding out a protest.

Bart, who was in the rear, was almost enjoying the challenge of keeping up with his sister above him. His knees scraped across a thick ridge in the tunnel. Instantly, a sharp jerk was followed by a sound like a large chain rattling slowly through an iron keyhole. It began to pick up speed until the entire tube began shaking and slanting down at an increasing angle.

"Go back," Jotham yelled, struggling to slide backwards to stop the tube's downward momentum.

It was too late: their weight had swung the top of the tube down with such velocity that they could not stop themselves from being plunged head-first into the dark bowels of the fortress.

"Hold on, m'lady. . . ." Flaggon's voice reverberated distantly through the cylinder.

"Grab something!" Jotham yelled, his fingers gripping the head of a loose rivet. The tube slammed to a sudden stop, jerking the Paladins loose and plummeting them down the slick sides. The rivets, which had assisted their ascent, were now pounding and scraping their chest and legs without mercy. Jotham covered his head as he thudded his way down, the amplified grunts and cries of his companions slapping at him in the darkness.

Carisa's voice wailed. There was a deafening clang, and Jotham's body was flung out into the darkness.

His head struck something hard. He heard a jarring crack. Sparks of brilliant light exploded; then he felt nothing.

Chapter Thirty Six

Flaggon and Carisa flew out the cylinder's mouth together, landing heavily on a heap of hard, brittle objects. The wall of the stone chamber in which they found themselves, rang with loud cracking and snapping, as if porcelain plates were being smashed. Carisa fell on top of Flaggon, who groaned once, but did not move. Carisa's body remained still.

Bart had been the most successful in slowing his descent. When he slid out of the tunnel, he was able to tuck himself into a ball and roll down the crumbling mass, thudding to a stop on the dusty floor. Round objects like hollow coconuts and long, thick shafts cascaded down the side of the mound around him, sounding like die rattling about a huge roulette wheel. He found himself lying on his back, his head resting on one of the brittle, rounded surfaces.

They were somewhere in the inner core of Andromedous. He was unable to see where he was; it was completely dark. Judging by how the noises bounced off the hard walls, the room was not very large, though it was very dusty and dry. His eyes smarted. He pinched his nostrils to avoid a bellowing sneeze.

"Carisa, where are you? Are you all right?" Bart whispered. There was no answer.

He turned his head. "Flaggon? . . . Jotham?" He reached out his hand and picked up a hollow spherical object. His fingers traced over the smooth surface. It was clearly not a coconut. There were ridges that intersected over the rounded top; and as he ran his fingertips over its dusty contours, he felt it jut out slightly and then curve inward. His fingers slid into two circular holes and his thumb felt a sharp protrusion over another jagged cavity.

Then he felt a row of smooth teeth.

The hairs on the back of his neck bristled. He dropped the skull as if it had been on fire; the Paladins had landed on a mountain of skulls.

They were inside the castle's burial chambers! The waste tunnel they had been climbing apparently also doubled as a chute for cadavers. He broke out in a cold sweat and tried to shut out of his mind the stacks of ghoulish companions that no doubt littered the dungeon around him. A chilling wave of panic began rising inside him.

Raising himself slowly, so as to avoid dislodging any more skulls, he stood to his feet. His nose and eyes began stinging. He gritted his teeth but could no longer restrain himself. The layers of dust were more than he could withstand. The raucous sneeze careened off the stone walls. There was a loud crash as a skeleton propped next to him fell over, shattering into loose pieces. He sneezed two more times in rapid succession; then, as he caught his breath, he heard a groan.

It was Carisa; she was on the opposite side of the mound.

He was beginning to feel his way around the base of the heap when he remembered the instructions. It was more than a memory of words; he was actually hearing them. The voice of their King was reciting a stanza from the scrolls he had given them at their commission.

On your way, my words obey,
Read them faithfully day by day;
Then ev'n the darkness will be bright,
For, you will see, they give you light.

When they had first read these words alongside the stream, they'd interpreted the command figuratively, but now Bart realized there might also be another meaning. His dusty fingers fumbled with the clasp on his leather wallet. Unrolling the parchment, he discovered that the sentences he'd read that morning had expanded to cover its entire surface and were casting a soft amber light as they hovered over the paper. The light increased in intensity as he exposed it to the darkness around him. It cast a halo which illuminated a circle several feet around him.

Bart held the parchment out in front of him. He wiped his watery eyes with his sleeve and blinked his right eye repeatedly. Although he hadn't mentioned it to Carisa, that eye had not improved at all. There still seemed to be an opaque film over it that cast a milky pallor over everything.

The light revealed that they were in a room carved out of rock, with a low ceiling and a far wall comprised of bars running from top to bottom. As he suspected, there were hundreds of skeletons stacked in heaps along the walls, many covered in decaying rags. Along one of the walls, lying on narrow ledges, were more skeletons—judging by the quality of the tattered clothing, these were the remains of the castle's dignitaries—and over everything, a thick mantle of dust.

Shoving aside some long bones criss-crossed in his path, he heard King Justar's voice again. The words were simple: "Look and see, and he will be free." About 12 feet away, Jotham was standing and smiling. His body was transparent and had a bluish glow. Before Bart could call out his name, he evaporated and was replaced by the shape of a girl. She was stunningly beautiful. There was something about her that Justar wanted him to notice. *What was it?* He strained to see, but the ghostly form rose and vanished before he could make it out. In her place, Jotham again materialized, but this time he was wrestling a Gharg. Bart stepped forward to get a closer look, but the combatants were gone.

Something odd about the girl had struck him; he just couldn't put his finger on it. He kept walking, and the circle of light illumined Carisa's leg. Crouching next to his sister, he was able to make out Flaggon's red beard under her shoulder. She groaned and Flaggon's nose twitched. Bart jerked his head away as the dwarf roared out a mighty sneeze. Dust descended like a fog all around them.

Carisa shook her head and rubbed the dust from her face and eyes. She rolled over and sat up next to Flaggon, who was wiping his nose and shaking his head vigorously.

"How are you feeling?" Bart asked, holding the scroll alongside his sister's face. Although pale and disoriented, she appeared to be fine.

Bart could hear Jotham clambering and clattering down the side of the pile. Several skulls were dislodged and one rolled over toward them. Bart swung the parchment over and its light illuminated the bony sphere resting against Carisa's foot.

She stiffened but did not make a sound; her body was as taut as a guitar string ready to snap. Her eyes were fixed unblinkingly on the round object; it seemed to be leering up at her. Bart smacked it with his foot and lofted it over the burial pyre, smashing it against the bars along the far wall.

Jotham had now joined them; he was holding Carisa's shield in his hand. It had apparently flown off when she fell out of the tube. He rubbed a bump on the back of his head. "Man, I really got my bell rung. . . . Hey!" he touched the parchment in Bart's hand, "How did . . . ?" The memory of

Justar's rhythmic stanzas stopped him. He grinned, "Good thinking, man," he said, slapping Bart on the back. "I had no idea that's what the words meant."

"Where's me bottle?" Flaggon growled groggily, trying to clear his head. Bart shone the scroll and illuminated the leather bag draped over a detached thighbone. Jotham picked it up and brought it to the dwarf, who was attempting to stand on wobbly legs.

"Stay down until you've had a little of this," Jotham instructed.

Flaggon sat down uncomplainingly, uncapped the bottle and tipped back his head, letting the stream of cool liquid hit the back of his throat. He took several long swallows, then rose to his feet, seemingly fully recovered.

"We needs to be movin' now, sors and lady." He glanced solicitously at Carisa. Her face was ashen. Her eyes stared vacantly into the distance. She seemed intent on blocking out everything in the room.

"Come, follow me; we needs to gets out of this place."

The light revealed an iron gate which squealed as they pushed it open. On the other side, they found themselves in a narrow hallway with stairs leading up at one end and a low door directly to their right. It was about four feet tall. Bart moved the scroll over the wooden planks. There was no handle or keyhole visible.

"I don't see how it's supposed to open," he said, letting the light play on the stones that framed it.

"Let's see if I can force it open," Jotham said. He kicked it hard with the sole of his foot. Nothing happened. He kicked it again. It didn't move. Jotham took three steps and slammed his body against the door. It wobbled a bit but refused to budge.

Jotham rubbed the muscles in his neck and shoulder. "I don't know, guys; it's either locked from the inside, or there's something holding it closed."

Flaggon had been quietly studying the construction of the gate. He bent down and began sweeping aside the dirt at the bottom of the wooden planks. "Sor, could you bring the scroll a little closer?" Bart held it out over the dwarf's head. The top of his head gleamed dully in the diffused light.

"Just as I thot . . . there it is!" He grasped hold of a short rope and pulled up. The wooden door slid up, opening smoothly. It was held open by a counterweight hidden in the wall.

"Good show, Flaggon!" Bart said. The dwarf stepped back to allow the

257

scroll to shed light into the dark interior. Jotham was preparing to hand Carisa's shield back to her, when he stopped himself and turned to their bearded companion.

"I wonder if we should bother with our shields. They haven't been terribly helpful in the past."

The dwarf took it and gave it to Carisa. "Sor, they works just fine when you fights where and when Justar tells you."

Jotham felt a warm flush rise in his face. Ignoring the mild rebuke, he unrolled his scroll as he crouched through the low opening.

The amber light revealed a circular chamber nine feet in diameter with no windows. Jotham could not see the ceiling far above them. By the stray husks and piles of grain scattered over the floor, it was evident that they were inside a grain silo. An iron ladder was bolted into the wall and ran the entire height of the chamber.

Jotham gave the ladder a sharp pull. It held firm. "This is better than using stairs, and it will give us the element of surprise." He looked around at his small band for confirmation. "What do you think?"

Carisa finally spoke up. "I agree. We won't find anyone guarding the top."

Bart and Flaggon didn't object, so they began their ascent.

Though rusty and covered with grain dust, the sturdy ladder held up easily under their weight. It had been imbedded firmly into the stones. About 50 feet up, Jotham's scroll revealed another wooden door of similar construction. He found the short rope attached to the bottom and carefully pulled it up. It slid open easily.

He poked his head into the opening. He was looking into the interior of a very warm, darkened room. Most of the sunlight was blocked out by thick wooden slats covering the windows along the length of the room. It appeared to be empty. Although Jotham couldn't see anyone, there were strange whistling sounds coming from overhead. He moved the scroll slowly from side to side, but its circle of light revealed no danger.

He rolled up the parchment, clamped down lightly on it with his teeth and with both hands on the sides of the narrow doorway, pulled himself through. There was a musty dampness in the air. Standing inside the airless room, the whistling and huffing was much more distinct. It was clearly coming from above.

There was a heavy thud on the wooden floor.

He jerked his head to his right. In the dim light he could see the leathery wings first. A tall Gharg with large shoulders and a thickly muscled torso was walking toward him. His green eyes locked on Jotham. He was smiling wickedly, as saliva drooled from his mouth.

Chapter Thirty Seven

Jotham grabbed for his sword, but something about the Gharg's eyes gave him pause. There was a strange, vacuous dullness in them. The creature appeared not to be staring *at* him but *through* him. Jotham slid his feet sideways, holding his sword steady, aiming at its broad chest. The Gharg continued walking forward, his eyes still fixed on the spot where Jotham had been an instant before.

Jotham took two more slow, sliding steps away. His body was rigid as he readied to strike the first blow.

Flaggon's whisper drew his attention. From the corner of his eye, a few feet above the baseboard he could see the dwarf's face peering though the open gate directly in the path of the oncoming Gharg. Jotham tried to signal his companion, but the Gharg was upon him. Its outstretched wings hit the wall first; then its snout smacked into the boards, followed by its hairy chest. The dwarf ducked his head back into the silo, three talons missing his fingers by inches.

The Gharg snorted and snarled, blinked its reptilian eyes groggily, then turned and flapped its sinewy brown wings, flying up into the rafters. With practiced precision, it grabbed one with the claws on the end of its wings and spun, hanging headfirst and resumed its nap.

From the flapping of wings and snorting which ensued, with a sickening rush, Jotham understood the reason for the sounds that filled the room. They were inside a sleeping chamber, and the only way out was through a metal door at the opposite end of the room.

He knelt down by the wooden door and whispered for Flaggon to tell the others to follow him up into the room.

"I thought the Ghargakon had gotten you, sor," Flaggon murmured when he crawled through the opening. "But when it hit the wall, I suspected he were sleep walkin'. Thanks be to Justar."

260

Carisa and Bart had now joined the huddle. Jotham pointed to the dark mass in the rafters and then to the door.

"We've got to get through here; maybe it leads to Creost's bedroom."

The Paladins drew their swords with infinite care, stepping quietly over the wooden floorboards. The snoring and wheezing muffled any noises made by their sandalled feet on the floor.

A Gharg directly over Carisa's head coughed. She stopped, her body tense with fear. Bart's hand on her back gently pushed her forward. The room was as warm as a sauna. Soon sweat was running down the sides of their faces and the middle of their backs. They walked with slow caution, their eyes straining upward.

They were within ten feet of the door when Bart caught his toe on a half-empty wine bottle on the floor. Carisa heard Bart stumble and made a lunge for his arm, missed, and grabbed the edge of his tunic. The fabric held, and Bart was able to steady himself.

Carisa's heart was pounding so loudly she was certain it would rouse the sleeping monsters. But instead, it was the noise of the leather bottle thudding against the side wall that almost gave them away. At the sound, several Ghargs flapped their wings and readjusted their perch.

Flaggon and the three Paladins froze.

A thin Gharg directly above Flaggon unfolded his wings and stretched, yawning loudly. The claw at the tip of his wing swung within an inch of the dwarf's nose. After a loud belch, it retracted its wing and began to snore again.

The sweat was now soaking through their tunics and running uncomfortably underneath the mail. The polished door was only four feet away.

There was a cough, then a sneeze, followed by the sound of large wings and talons hitting the floor.

Carisa's heart stopped.

Bart, who was behind her, spun soundlessly on his heels.

A Gharg with its back toward them was walking toward the opposite wall. Bart could barely see the shape of its body as it made its way into the dim corner. The sound of water spraying the wall and splashing onto the floor let him know why the creature had awakened. They had only a few seconds before it would turn around and see them.

Bart jerked his thumb toward the metal door and motioned for Jotham to get to it quick. Bart kept his eye trained on the far corner. Jotham covered the last distance in one bound. He grabbed the handle and turned it as hard and as softly as he could.

It wouldn't move. The door was locked!

He knew he couldn't use the whip; the explosion would set the Ghargs upon them in a smothering wave of teeth and talons. And even if they could burst through, they might need to place the metal door between themselves and their awakened enemies.

Jotham grasped Flaggon's tunic and pointed at the lock.

Flaggon nodded, pulled out his dagger and slipped its point into the narrow keyhole. Pressing his ear against the metal, he twisted the blade from side to side. There was a metallic snap, and the handle turned.

The Gharg snorted in surprise, twisting its head around suspiciously. Its dull eyes suddenly focused on the four of them, and it began hissing violently. The skeletal monster opened its snout and let out a screeching bellow as the Paladins swung the door open. Startled Ghargs began raining down from the ceiling as the four warriors ran through the doorway, slamming it with a clang. Through the door they could hear the screams and cawing of scores of Ghargs, followed by the painful squealing of claws raking the metal behind them. Jotham slammed the outside bolt home.

Flaggon ran over to the east wall and flung back the velvet drapes that covered the tall windows. Light streamed in, illuminating the darkened room. Horror and surprise registered on all their faces.

The light revealed a dais about eye-level 20 feet away, draped with an ornate gold-tasseled rug. On top of it lay a huge cream-colored worm, its sticky sides wrinkled and pallid like moist skin covered too long by a tight bandage.

Creost's throne was a large pile of decaying food. It snuffed scornfully, and opened its ridged black lips, long hairy filaments hanging from the corners of his mouth like a foul mustache. It reminding Carisa of a corpulent, bleached catfish. With a forked tongue as long as Jotham's whip, Creost picked up a half-devoured chicken, along with the head of an eel, chewed, swallowed loudly and belched. The pouches around its red eyes narrowed lustfully as it fixed its eyes on Carisa. Its bloated tail, split like that of the huge lizards in the cavern, thumped once, sending foul garbage raining down onto the floor.

Jotham read the look and stepped forward, his sword gripped firmly in both hands. *For that I'll kill you myself, Creost,* he promised himself.

Flaggon put his hand on Jotham's arm. "Jotham, wait! Somethin's amiss, sor. I can smell it!"

Jotham stopped. Then, suddenly, he smelled it also: above the smell of decaying garbage, he could again detect the telltale stench of bile and rancid meat.

Flaggon looked down at Jotham's sword hand and noticed that the wrist strap attached to the hilt was hanging loose. He gestured angrily at the strap, "Sor, never fight without that around your hand. It may save your life—it has mine."

Jotham quickly slipped his hand through and Bart did the same. Jotham turned to look at Carisa. She raised her hand showing him the strap tied carefully around her wrist.

The worm belched again, raised its glistening row of stubby, milky white arms; and instantly, at the foot of the dais, ten fierce creatures materialized. Their upper bodies were that of vultures and below were the glossy black legs of leopards. Out of their beaks long, red pointed tongues flicked angrily. They spread out their powerful wings in silence, staring coldly at the Paladins, and formed a black shield around their leader.

Flaggon sucked in a breath and gasped hoarsely, "Kravens!" They were face to face with Ghnostar's elite troops.

Horrified, Jotham looked at Flaggon, "Law told us they only guarded Ghnostar!" he hissed.

Flaggon's bushy eyebrows rose in bewilderment. "That's wot I were told as well, sor. . . . They must be changin' their tactics for some reason."

The Kravens' hairy, muscular legs were bent, ready to spring. The claws on their large, padded paws were fully extended, ready for the kill. Although their reptilian tongues darted in and out of cruel beaks, they made no sound. Their only other movement was the confident twitching of their sinuous tails. Jotham looked into the dead pools of their eyes and saw no emotion—no anger or hatred—only an impersonal, coldly calculating, killing instinct.

He felt his insides freeze. Their soulless eyes were dismembering him with ruthless detachment.

The scraping and clawing against the metal door at their backs was becoming louder. Jotham tested the bolt. It would hold.

Bart and Carisa hurriedly armed their bows. Bart's arrow slipped from his fingers. He picked it up quickly and fit it back into his bowstring.

Seeing the polished arrows, the Kravens' eyes hooded dangerously.

Immediately, they began to vanish. Only a dim gray outline was discernible as the Paladins lifted their bows.

"Aim high," yelled Jotham.

Carisa dropped the lever on her crossbow, and Bart's arrow flew an instant later, both at head level. Two black, smoky flashes erupted seven feet in the air. Jotham could smell burning feathers. Even in death the Kravens were utterly silent.

Creost threw its fleshy head back, opened its thin black lips and emitted a blast like the braying of an enraged elephant. It was as loud and deafening as the screeching blare of a tornado warning alarm. The Paladins felt as if their insides were being shaken loose. The Ghargs on the other side of the door grew suddenly quiet.

The room again looked deserted, except for the worm-like Glute on the dais.

"Backs to the wall!" Flaggon ordered, his sword flicking warily from side to side. "Try and hit the Glute," he yelled at Bart and Carisa. "Remember the King's instruction."

The obscene creature stared at them with its beady red eyes. They released their arrows, but they fell harmlessly to the stone floor in front of Creost's platform. He slathered his scorn over them with a barking laugh. Apparently, the ruler of the castle had the power to control the trajectory of any missiles aimed at him. Their arrows would be useless against him.

Bart and Carisa unsheathed their swords.

"Show yourselves, you filthy cowards," the dwarf yelled, his dark eyes flashing, his bald head growing red with anger. "Whatever you do, don't expose your backs," he warned, "They loves to latch onto the spine!"

Suddenly, a corner of the drapes was gripped by invisible claws and yanked closed with a thud. Darkness surrounded them. The four began swinging their swords with greater speed and waited for their eyes to adjust to the dim light.

Jotham remembered Slimgilley's explanation about defeating Ghnostar's forces: "If we can keep them away, they'll have to show themselves eventually." The four thrust and parried into the air, swinging and jabbing erratically to keep the Kravens off balance. Their unpredictable razor points were thus far proving effective, but the Paladins could feel their arms tiring. It was becoming more difficult to keep the points of their sword up.

Sensing their exhaustion, Flaggon yelled at Bart. "We need more light, sor—take your bow and aims it right next to me."

The bearded dwarf began sliding to his left along the back wall, waving his sword in front of him. He turned the corner, his back flat against the stones. Each gliding step brought him closer to the thick velvet covering the window. His blade darted like the flicking tongue of a cobra, his wild eyes shifting back and forth expecting an invisible slash at any moment. He reached out to grab the material, but just as quickly jerked it back, three bloody furrows showing on the back of his hand.

He bit back a scream.

At the same moment, Bart released his arrow and it struck the wall to the right of Flaggon's head. It missed the Kraven but exploded next to the velvet. Red-hot sparks showered the drape. Within seconds it erupted in flames.

Jotham heard a whistling of talons sweep past his face. His sword grazed a body lunging away.

"They're coming closer!" he yelled.

The velvet was beginning to burn with intensity. With a roar, the drapes burst into huge flames. The claws were again hammering and grating against the metal door behind them.

Flaggon was inching back toward the three Paladins, whipping his sword blindly as the blood from his left hand dripped onto the floor. He snapped his head sideways, and livid claw marks appeared on his cheek.

"It be flyin'," he screamed to Bart. "Aim higher!"

Bart's next arrow flew several feet above Flaggon's head. It penetrated the Kraven with a soft thump. There was a flash, a scorched plume of smoke, then silence. The instant the arrow made contact, Flaggon dashed back toward the Paladins.

The metal door was now shaking with the persistent scratching and scraping. The frame jerked violently as one Gharg after another launched themselves madly against the door. It bulged as angry fists struck fierce blows against the metal. Several rivets popped loose. A crack was appearing along the wooden outer frame.

The Paladins were exhausted. Their arms and shoulders were numb with fatigue.

"Don't let them points sink down," urged Flaggon, ignoring the gouges on his face. His blade was slicing the air with abandon, its tip dancing

265

proudly. The drapes fell off the large window in a charred lump, and light again streamed into the room.

Their attention was caught by the burning velvet. None of them saw the first Kraven's silhouette begin to appear; it was the shortest one. He was sliding along the wall against which the Paladins were standing. Approaching from Bart's blind side, he crouched only a wingspan away. Turning his head, Flaggon caught a glimpse of its outline as it prepared to pounce.

"Look out!" he screamed, but the warning came too late. The Kraven uncoiled and was upon Bart before he could turn to face the ambush. He fell on his back, the Kraven on top of him. The hooked beak slashed at his face and stripped his sword from his hand.

When Bart fell, two other Kravens became visible. They were bounding toward Carisa and Jotham, the talons on the tips of their wings fully extended. Jotham had no time to reach for his whip.

Flaggon drove his dagger into the back of the creature who was on Bart's chest. A deep, oily furrow appeared on the black feathers. Undaunted, it continued to scratch and bite at Bart, trying to force him over.

The dwarf, almost hysterical, leaped on top of the Kraven's head, clutching a handful of feathers in one hand. With a vicious chopping motion he sliced its head from its shoulders. "This is for me fadder!" he screamed, kicking the twitching body off Bart.

Flinging the head aside, Flaggon dropped into a crouch. Another Kraven had leaped at Bart, who was wiping the blood away from his good eye. Flaggon lunged, thrusting his short body forward, the sword point angling sharply into the creature's stomach. As it fell, they both landed on Bart, sending him reeling backwards against the wall. With a whooshing expulsion of air, the creature evaporated, leaving a black smear on the floor and wall.

The remaining Kravens were now completely visible. Carisa and Jotham had blood on their arms and shoulders from talons and beaks that had nearly found their mark.

Carisa was aiming her crossbow at the Kraven nearest her. It flapped its huge wings but couldn't lift off the ground in time. The dart hit directly in the center of its forehead, hurling it backwards. Its head exploded with the thump of a crushed watermelon. The projectile drove through the vulture's skull, embedding itself in the wall behind it. The explosion blew a hole as large as Flaggon's body in the stonework. The Kraven's headless form slipped slowly to the floor, then burst apart in a spray of bone, feathers and fur.

Jotham helped Bart to his feet and handed him his sword.

"You okay?" he asked, seeing the blood covering his friend's face.

"I'm fine," Bart grunted, blinking furiously. "Let's get 'em." Jotham and Bart swung their swords at two Kravens who were rising into the air in front of the window. They sliced through the leathery wings, and as the Kravens fell, with two fierce jabs, the Paladins stabbed them in the chest.

Flaggon was being harried by several Kravens. Another was crouched low, six feet away, undecided, staring at Carisa with hungry eyes. Bart threw his sword, knocking the Kraven back. At that moment, Jotham freed his whip and snapped it, missing the snarling beak by inches. The creature flapped its wings furiously and flew into the rafters.

Flaggon was gasping loudly, both his hands clenched around the hilt of his sword. Carisa spun toward him. He was penned in.

Her dart slammed into the feathery back of a Kraven who was striking with his clawed wing. The dwarf, taking advantage of the explosion, lunged upward, slicing off the foreleg of the hovering Kraven. It shrieked, then flung itself on top of him. Dropping to his knees, he drove the sword tip upward, tearing a hole in the vulture's neck. It dropped to the floor at Flaggon's feet. It first sizzled and smoked; then it disintegrated.

Looking up at the Kraven in the rafters, Bart yelled, "Leave him to me." Wiping his eyes clear, he fitted a long arrow into the bowstring. The Kraven flew higher and perched on a ledge 30 feet above them.

Bart aimed high. "I'm gonna' take your ugly head off," he promised. The arrow missed, but the explosion dislodged the Kraven from its perch, sending it swooping down, its forked tongue flicking wickedly. It banked and flung itself against a shuttered window opposite the dais and began tearing large hunks of wood from it. Bart aimed again and blew off one of its legs.

Carisa anxiously looked over at Bart. She bit back a cry—blood was streaming from his forehead and his right eye.

The Kraven spun around, enraged, snapping at them with its wet beak. Delirious with hatred and pain, it launched itself at Bart, but the explosive crack of Jotham's whip caught it flush in the chest, catapulting the creature through the window and down into the lake.

267

Jotham failed to see Bart slump to the floor.

Creost, seeing his guards dismantled, raised his corpulent head and trumpeted another blaring cry. This time it was mixed with a strain of desperate fear.

"This one is mine," Jotham declared, unwrapping the ax he had strapped on his back.

Creost roared out a blubbering cry again.

Jotham ran his finger over the sharp edge of the ax and raised it high above his head. The polished iron seemed to flame in the orange glow of the late afternoon rays which poured through the broken window. Creost the Glute had grown still and was puffing up his fleshy body in a grotesque display of bravado. His red eyes glowed with an insane, evil intent.

As Jotham swung the ax, he yelled, "And this is for my brother!"

The monster's fear had robbed it of its power, for the ax flew straight and true. It struck the detestable maggot and disappeared into its fatty tissue. Then, an instant later, the dais and its occupant erupted in a foaming geyser, tearing a gaping cavity in the back wall.

The clawing on the metal door immediately ceased, but now through the ragged opening in front of them, the Paladins could hear shouting and the clattering of chains.

Jotham ran over to where the dais had been and retrieved Abe's ax. He poured water over it and wiped it hurriedly before strapping it onto his back. He was about to step through the hole when he realized the others were not behind him. He turned and saw Carisa kneeling beside her brother. She was dabbing a cloth on Bart's face. It looked like a gray mask. She glanced at Jotham only briefly.

"I don't feel so great," Bart muttered.

"You'll feel a lot better once we get you out of here and get you some air," Jotham said hopefully, walking up next to him. "You ready?" he asked.

"Yep, never readier," Bart replied in a weak voice, trying to smile. Jotham lifted him to his feet and draped Bart's arm around his shoulders. Carisa put her arm around his waist as they walked through the yawning hole.

Chapter Thirty Eight

After getting into the next room, Bart, drained from his wounds, sank down and let his back rest against the rear wall. Carisa stood by him, her hand on his head.

Flaggon noticed the cages first. They were suspended from the ceiling and were littered with motionless shapes. He removed a torch from a wall bracket and struck flint to steel, lighting it at the first attempt.

A piercing wail of anguish and terror froze them into place. A woman was standing inside a nearby cage, her matted white hair streaming over her shoulders. She was shaking the metal bars with both hands, pounding her head against them as the light approached. Flaggon took another step forward, and a shrill clamoring erupted from the other hanging cells. Chains clanged and cages shook.

The torchlight revealed hundreds of filthy prisoners, their faces white and emaciated, bony fingers clawing at their eyes like rabid animals. The suspended cages rocked back and forth as the prisoners threw themselves against the bars trying to flee from the light. The huge cells creaked and groaned as they swung and spun above them.

"Flaggon, lower your torch!" yelled Jotham. He stepped in front of the dwarf, his back shielding the terrorized prisoners from its beams. "We have come to free you!" he yelled. Bedlam erupted in the cages and along the walls where others were chained. The prisoners on the floor began swinging their long wrist chains over their heads, while others hunched over and growled threateningly.

"Tell them Justar sent us," suggested Carisa. Her voice was taut with pity and apprehension. She was torn by a longing to comfort them and terror of the demented captives.

Jotham called out, "King Justar has commissioned us to give you back your freedom." At that, some of the prisoners grew silent. Waves of fear seemed to crackle throughout the room; then, with one voice, the captives shrieked out their response: "Noooo!" It was drawn out in a long, crazed wail suffused with infinite horror.

The figures in the cages began rocking disconsolately, their heads thrown back; that one word continuing to pour out of their throats. The piercing, repetitive chant was slowly wrapping a noose of despair around the Paladins, which was threatening to strangle them all.

"Stop!" yelled Jotham, taking a resolute step forward, fire flashing from his eyes.

Jotham's voice stirred the prisoners into a renewed frenzy. The room erupted, as if a wasp's nest had been thrown into their midst. Fearful bellows and spine-tingling screams shook the walls. The floor-chained prisoners began whipping their chains, threatening Jotham. Several were making lunges at him, but were restrained by thick neck bracelets.

A muscular giant of a man with a waist-length beard picked up a rock the size of a watermelon. Holding it overhead, he roared at Jotham, "I Arbakon, and I not 'fraid of you or your weakling King!" He menaced Jotham, who had his whip ready.

"No, Jotham . . . don't do it!" yelled Carisa, running forward and grabbing his arm. "Justar sent us to release the prisoners, not fight them." She placed her body in front of him, staring directly into the hulking giant's face. "We are not your enemy!" she declared. Something in her clear, strong voice silenced the screaming prisoners.

The large rock was lowered to chest level.

Arbakon stared back at Carisa, his wild eyes narrowed in rage and suspicion. He looked from her to Jotham and then back. His eyes blazed with a sudden, yellow hate as he once again lifted the rock. Perspiration ran down the sides of his bearded cheeks as he took aim. Something in his manic expression stirred a memory in the back of Jotham's mind.

Carisa threw her head back, a surprising calmness overtaking her. Her fear had fled. She gazed deeply into the eyes of the giant, and with power stirring in her voice declared, "I command you to stop, in Justar's name!" She stood motionless facing the towering prisoner, her fists clenched; only the corners of her mouth quivered. "By the authority of King Justar, drop the rock." Her firm tone permeated the cold room with a commanding quiet.

The fire dimmed in Arbakon's eyes. The rock dropped from his enormous hands like a bird from a dog's mouth.

"You will not harm us," she told the other prisoners whose chains were now hanging limply from their hands. They lowered their eyes, shame covering their faces.

Arbakon continued to stare at Carisa, his eyes glazed, teeth clenched. The quiet was electric as the room grew still.

Suddenly, Jotham understood what was familiar about this titan. Though a stranger loomed before him, the gravely voice and crazed eyes were identical to those of Trent McCauley! That was exactly how he had looked when he'd flung himself on Pastor Mark. The sensation of icy fingers ran up Jotham's back.

Carisa continued to stare at Arbakon. There was now something unexpected in his face: a desperate plea for help. Her heart ached with pity. She was about to open her mouth to speak again when she looked up and saw a huge Gharg with the wingspan of a condor wheeling above Jotham, its tail poised for attack. "I am Arbakon," it growled in a harsh voice identical to that of the giant. Its grotesque swollen features were twisted in disdain.

Jotham stepped backwards toward the wall.

"I am not afraid of you or your weakling King," the winged-creature repeated the scornful boast. As it was speaking it swooped down, and veered quickly, spinning away just out of the reach of Jotham's whip. Arbakon was quick and crafty.

Jotham let the leather lash hang limply from his hand. He kept his eyes trained on his enemy.

"Justar is a fool to send children against the likes of me," the boastful Gharg continued, flying in quick, powerful bursts above him. "Leave now, and I won't hurt you; but if you stay, I will tear your heart out."

The Gharg twisted suddenly and dropped. Just as quickly, Jotham fell to his knees and swung, but the tip of his whip flicked past his assailant. Long talons tore through Jotham's tunic along both shoulders, sliding off the smooth mail underneath. The winged creature flew up cackling in delight, leaving a foul, vaporous trail in its wake.

Obscured in the thick smog, Jotham dropped his whip and pulled out his sword. He groveled on the stones, pretending to be seriously wounded. Out of the corner of his eye, he saw Bart still sitting, his bow in his hands aiming upwards.

"I warned you, fool!" the Gharg gloated, releasing another cloud of rancid smoke. Jotham coughed and choked, exaggerating the effect of the fumes. Seeing his opportunity, his attacker flung himself at Jotham's exposed back.

Bart's arrow sang. It thudded into the Gharg's throat.

The moment Arbakon disintegrated, the bearded giant, who had been hiding in the darkness, threw his hands into the air shouting, "I free, I free!" He covered his face weeping.

Jotham scrambled to his feet, his eyes streaming in the caustic smog.

Scores of prisoners began rattling their chains and cells pleading for the Paladins to release them.

Jotham ran into the middle of the room and with a loud voice yelled, "In Justar's name, be free!" Instantly, the chains on the necks and wrists of the prisoners fell off, and the barred walls of the cells swung open. The caged prisoners leaped about in joyful frenzy as prisoners on the ground began to lower the cells to the floor.

The released captives were leaping and grabbing at each other, hugging and kissing each other's cheeks with delight. A group in a corner, too weak to run about, thrust their arms into the air yelling, "Thank you, Justar, thank you."

Others linked hands, forming a large human chain. Jotham was unable to resist as they pulled him into their joyful dance.

Arbakon broke through the line and pulled Jotham loose, gripping Jotham's shoulders in his huge hands. "Sir, thank you . . . I sorry for . . . ." Tears were running down into his beard.

Jotham's eyes were level with his chest. He grinned up at the large, bearded face which now glowed with a childlike innocence, "No . . . don't. It's all right, I understand." The bearded giant, overcome, wrapped his meaty arms around Jotham and kissed him gratefully on the top of his head. He pulled back and pointed toward a doorway in the west wall that was now open. "I took friends outside, sir. I carried one on shoulder. I think he hurt bad."

Jotham's heart sank. "Please take me to them."

He followed Arbakon through a chamber where many windows had been smashed. "Bad guards ran away here," his guide said, pointing at the tufts of brown hair clinging to the glass in the broken panes. They walked down several flights of stairs and out into a lush garden.

"There, sir," the giant gestured toward an elegant pool. Bart was propped against a low wall embellished with a colorful mosaic. The bright

272

colors made his face appear even more pallid. Flaggon was sitting next to Bart, rubbing his wrists as Carisa dabbed a wet cloth against his forehead. The muscular prisoner squeezed Jotham's arm and turned back.

Jotham didn't feel a thing. His heart had turned to lead.

He walked slowly over to his friends, assailed by claws of cold fear. He could see that there were long scratches on Bart's cheeks and over his right eye.

Carisa's voice was barely controlled. "He couldn't see it coming. . . . The Gharg hit him from his right side." The old hardness in her words stung him.

He felt as though Carisa had plunged a dagger into him.

Bart moaned and wiped the fresh trickle of blood from his cheek. She did not have to look at Jotham for him to feel the unpardoning accusation in her steely eyes. The blistering silence seared him like a fiery brand.

The excitement and relief following their hard-fought victory drained from him, leaking out onto the ground. Waves of guilt smashed against currents of anger at Carisa's humiliating indictment. He knew she was blaming him not only for Bart's injuries but Abe's death as well.

Rage burning hot in his chest, he spun away, heading back to the prison room. He told himself he needed to find Abe's ax; in reality, he wanted to get as far away from her as he could. He stalked back through the doorway into the prison chamber. The prisoners were gone. All that remained were broken chains and empty cages littering the room.

The ax was lying in the center of the room. He picked it up and turned to leave.

He was arrested by the soft scuffling of hands and knees in a far corner of the room. Lifting Abe's ax to chest level, he spun on his heels, poised to repel the ambush.

Chapter Thirty Nine

A dark shape moved in the corner of the dungeon. Jotham tensed, his hand gripping the shaft of the ax. The movement stopped. He yanked a torch from the wall, lit it and stepped forward. Although drained by the battle, he was primed for any adversary. It would feel good to take out his fury on another Gharg.

He held the torch out in front of his body and walked toward the sound, his ax angled expectantly.

"Who goes there?" he yelled, waving the light toward the far wall. "Show yourself, whoever you are." He took another step toward the sound, ready to fling his weapon. He was disappointed when the flickering light revealed a tattered captive, his head covered by a dark green hood. He'd been huddling alone in the furthest corner from the open doorway. He was of slight build and was crawling on the floor, attempting to gather up his pitiful collection of belongings. When the torchlight illuminated him he jumped up, his back pressed against the stones, crouched and breathing heavily like a trapped animal.

Jotham strode forward, pushed back the green hood and gaped. The light exposed not the face of a boy but that of a young woman. Though her face was vandalized by sorrow, her beauty was dazzling. The golden light caused her whole face to glow, illuminating every detail for him. She was unlike any girl he'd ever seen.

Despite the mud on her clothes and face, when her hood was thrown back, it released a perfumed scent of such delicacy that it caused Jotham's head to reel. Her long hair, which hung over her chest, shone a burnished gold in the torchlight. Her deep violet eyes were wide set and fringed by thick eyelashes, reminding Jotham of a frightened fawn. Smudges of dirt covered her cheeks, which she was attempting to rub away with the sleeve of her dress. It served only to accentuate her stunning beauty.

She looked up at him fearfully, then her features softened as if she recognized him. Widening her eyes questioningly, she pleaded in a low, hoarse voice, "Brave sir . . . I apologize for being so forward, but . . . I am . . . so thirsty . . . might you be so kind as to give me a drink?"

Taking a deep breath, he unslung the leather flask from his shoulder and uncorked it. As he bent forward to give it to her, she put both her hands around his and drew the flask to her lips. Her hands were surprisingly soft. There were livid scratches on them which looked recent.

As she drank, she slowly lifted her face and looked deeply at him. Her lovely eyes held him. She seemed to be looking into the depths of his being. Overwhelming sensations careened through his mind and body; he hoped she would drink forever. His desires and emotions seemed to be running riot. There was a mysterious profundity in her gaze that drew at something deep inside him. He was intoxicated and confused: wanting to be with her, yet fighting a conflicting desire to break away and run for his life.

When she was finished drinking, still holding his hands gently in hers, she softly said, "Thank you so much, Sir Jotham." Then, smiling sweetly, she dropped her delicate hands and said, "I should introduce myself. My name is Deidrah."

Jotham smiled back, "You apparently already know mine."

"Oh yes," her cheeks flushed, "I heard your friend use your name during the battle." She shuddered. "You were so brave, Sir Jotham." She rested her fingers lightly on his forearm. "It is obvious that you are a mighty warrior." Her eyes shone up at him with an almost worshipful glow.

The bitter weight of recriminations had now vanished completely. Jotham wondered smugly what Carisa would think if she saw how Deidrah was looking at him. His head seemed to be in a whirl. Deidrah's scent was affecting both his concentration and his equilibrium. Her frank admiration was also intoxicating.

She took a step back openly appraising him. An intriguing, bold curiosity had crept into her face. "The warrior who spoke your name, she is very pretty. . . . Are you lovers?" she asked, looking directly at him.

He tried to keep his gaze level as color rose in his cheeks. "No . . . not at all," he stammered. "We are . . . just friends," he said, smiling what he hoped was a tolerant, sophisticated smile, ". . . merely comrades in arms, you might say." Deidrah cocked an eyebrow at him. Trying to remain nonchalant, Jotham continued, "We've known each other since we were small children.

Our relationship ends there." His cheeks were still warm. He switched the subject abruptly. "How long have you been a prisoner?"

Her violet eyes clouded. "It feels like I've been a slave in this dreadful place forever, although it must be about three years. The truth is," her throaty voice had become very soft, "I stopped keeping track after my mother and father were . . ." Trembling, her voice broke; her head dropped, her hair covered her face behind a veil of pain and sorrow.

"It's all right; you don't have to go on," Jotham said, patting her arm. "I understand." Her arm was firm and smooth under the thin material of her dress. His fingertips tingled.

"No, no, I must tell you, Sir Jotham. You are entitled to know the truth—after all, you saved my life."

"You don't have to . . . really." He looked around at the filthy surroundings. "Wouldn't you rather go outside into the sunlight?"

She looked up, fear flashing briefly behind her eyes. She dropped her gaze in embarrassment. "I'm afraid I am in an awful state. I've been hiding in this dirty corner for days, and my dress is frightful."

"Don't worry about that," Jotham assured her. "You are the most . . ." his voice thickened, ". . . beautiful girl I've ever met."

Her eyes held him captive. Her even white teeth glowed in a radiant smile. This time she rewarded him with an elaborate curtsy. "Sir Jotham, you are not only a brave warrior but a true knight. I thank you for your compliment." She straightened herself and came over to him, taking his right hand in both of hers, holding them up to her chest. "I-I'm not looked on very. . . . What I'm trying to say is . . . the townspeople hate me, and the truth is, I don't blame them myself." Her cheeks flamed as she went on in a rush, "And, Sir Jotham, I wouldn't blame you if you hated me too." Her eyes were now brimming with tears.

"Deidrah, nothing you say could make me hate you," he said as he placed the torch in a bracket, and still holding her hand, led her to a ledge near the doorway. "Let's sit down here. Please tell me all about it . . . and just call me Jotham. Okay?" He drank in deeply the wine in her eyes, his breath tight in his chest. "You don't need to worry about my response."

"I would expect such gallantry from you, but I fear you may soon wish to retract your words."

She removed the cloth satchel that had been hanging over her shoulder and set it down on the stone, using it as a small cushion. Her fingers began nervously folding the pleats of her dress. "My parents and I were captured by the Ghargs several years ago. My father was a builder in a nearby town. He drafted the plans for the tunnels under this castle. When he heard that the Ghargs were close by, he hid the plans in a secret compartment. That night they broke into our house and dragged my father and mother into the street. The beasts forced me to watch as they hung them to a tree." Her hands were clenched into small, white fists.

"The Ghargs lashed them and threatened to . . . to gouge out their eyes if I refused to tell them where the parchments were hidden." She clutched at his arm silently begging him to understand. "Jotham, I couldn't stand to see my father and mother suffer like that. I wanted to kill those Ghargs, but I was helpless. There was nothing I could do. . . . I couldn't let them kill my parents, so . . . I told them."

Wiping the tears from her cheeks, she pressed on. "The Ghargs used the plans to infiltrate and conquer Andromedous and brought us here to serve them as slaves. When my father refused to build their prisons, they spread the lie that he was a collaborator who'd helped them evade the town's defenses. The townspeople turned on us and one morning . . . I found him dead. My mother died of shock a few days later. He was so brave . . . he never told anyone the truth about me." She dropped her head down onto her knees to stifle her sobs. "I killed my father," she moaned.

Jotham lifted her chin. "Stop, Deidrah. Don't say that ever again. You didn't kill him, and you don't deserve to be hated. It's those filthy, wretched . . ." He was barely able to restrain himself from screaming out his fury. He continued, his voice quavering with rage, "It was not your fault—I would have done the same thing." He reached around her, drawing her head against his shoulder. "You aren't the one to blame. If I could get my hands on those Ghargs right now, I'd make them suffer."

She gazed up at him gratefully, tears trembling on the ends of her lashes. "You've been so kind to me. I don't deserve your sympathy." She looked down at her lap shyly. "You don't know how safe I feel being with you. I don't want you to ever leave." She squeezed his hand. "Oh, Jotham, I don't have anywhere to go. . . . I don't mean to presume on your kindness, but do you think I could come with you?"

Jotham felt his pulse begin to race. Her candor and the wistful longing in her voice threw him off balance. He ached with all his being to be able to shout, "Yes!" but King Justar's scroll had been very clear. It had stated unambiguously: 'When battle is over, three Paladins leave.' Surely they could make some arrangement. "Deidrah, I would love for you to come with me . . . I mean us . . . But I-I don't know, I'd need to talk with the others first."

Deidrah stood up, and despite her fragile appearance, grasped his wrists with surprising strength, raising him to his feet. "You are a brave warrior and an honorable knight. You are so strong and so kind; I know I can trust you. You're the *only* one I can trust. Please, please let me come with you."

She stood trembling in front of him, almost touching him. Although her clothes were in tatters, Jotham could not help but notice the lovely contours of her body. He felt his heart hammering inside his chest, and the blood rising high in his cheeks. He knew that, somehow, he would find a way for her to come, and that he would fight anyone who tried to keep her away.

At the same time, Jotham felt a growing certainty inside him: *Justar would understand. He would want me to protect her.* Stilling the avalanche of reckless emotion, Jotham was finally able to whisper the words: "Of course, Deidrah . . . you can come."

Her dazzling smile melted him.

"Thank you, Jotham. I knew you were good." Deidrah stood abruptly on her tiptoes and pressed a soft kiss on his cheek. His head was spinning madly; he felt drunk. Her perfume caused his senses to reel.

Ignoring his embarrassment, she laughed deep in her throat, "I would so love to meet your brave friends; could you take me to meet them?"

He hesitated, not wishing to share her with anyone. What he wanted was to be alone with her forever, but he answered, "Ahh . . . certainly, I'd be glad to introduce you to them." She picked up her small parcel, removed some slightly soiled gloves, and with an apologetic smile, slipped them on. Grasping his hand, she followed him out of the dim prison chamber.

Although late afternoon, the sunlight stung their eyes. After adjusting to the brightness, they walked hand in hand to find the rest of the band. The Paladins were no longer in the small garden, but the sounds of delightful revelry led them to a nearby park where crowds of prisoners were celebrating beside the banks of a lovely lake, whose emerald waters sparkled happily.

The couple walked past clusters of frolicking people. Many shouted out their thanks, some of the more bold ran up to shake his hand. Their overwhelming joy, which had recently moved Jotham, was now only a source of irritation. All he could think about was Deidrah. He was overcome with the nearness of her body and the warmth of her fingers. The melodious singing was drowned out by the roaring inside his head.

Flaggon broke away from the noisy crowd and bounded toward them, his face glistening. "Sor, Bart has completely recovered," he shouted gleefully. Suddenly self-conscious, Jotham released Deidrah's hand. The dwarf pulled up short when he saw her. His nose twitched and he rubbed it vigorously.

"What do you mean?" Jotham asked.

"You wouldna' believe it, sor! After you left, Bart whispered to Lady Carisa that he'd seen a picture-like of a pilgrim's scrip with a bottle inside." The dwarf rubbed his bald head excitedly. "It were the most astonishing thing! Lady Carisa opened her scrip and found her little green bottle . . . and it were full. When she rubbed the oil over his injuries he could see perfect out of both eyes." Flaggon's eyes narrowed as he looked at Deidrah. "We were looking all over for you, sor—especially the Lady Carisa—very impatient, if you catch me meanin'."

Flaggon lead them toward a large circle of dancers. Bart was wedged between two men with full gray beards; they were all laughing as he tried to keep up with their intricate steps.

Bart whirled past, hopping and tripping over his feet. "Where've you been?" he yelled. "You're missing all the fun." At the far end of the loop, Bart got a clear look at Deidrah. His eyes widened in surprise. He broke away immediately and trotted over to them; his attention riveted on the girl.

"Aren't you going to tell me who your friend is?" Bart asked, his expression leaving no question about the impression Deidrah had made on him.

Jotham introduced them; then, in a flat voice, summarized her story. "I found her alone in the dungeon," he explained, as if he held Bart personally responsible. Flaggon, who was standing behind Deidrah, sneezed loudly. Her perfume seemed to be bothering his sensitive nose.

Deidrah stepped forward, holding out her hands to the tall Paladin.

"I so wanted to thank you, Sir Bart, for helping to free us. I know you suffered much. You were all so brave." She took Bart's hand, placing a light kiss on the back of his fingers. A pang of jealousy burned through Jotham. He decided he needed to get her away from this competitor as quickly as possible.

"My eyes are perfectly fine now; and let me tell you, this is a wonderful way to celebrate the recovery of my sight." Bart's gaze had not left her face. "As we say, you are a sight for sore eyes," he said chuckling at his own joke.

Jotham pulled her away, explaining in an officious tone, "I must go find Carisa, she needs to report on what's been transpiring. I'll take Deidrah with me." With a thin smile and glaring eyes, he tossed back over his shoulder. "You can go back to your fun, Bart, and you can dance a jig for me."

Bart's face was sheathed in innocence. "Oh, I don't know, Jotham, I don't think that would be a very good idea. We haven't scouted out the entire town yet, and for all we know, there could still be Ghargs lurking about. I'd hate to have you and Deidrah face them alone." Bart beamed at them with exaggerated sincerity, "Besides, I know where Carisa is, and I'd feel terrible if you got lost."

Deidrah couldn't restrain her laughter. She took Bart's arm in one hand and Jotham's in the other. "What lady has ever had such handsome and gallant protectors," she said, reassuring Jotham with a meaningful glance. "Sir Bart, lead us to your friend." Still seething, Jotham let her pull him forward.

They walked through narrow cobblestone alleys, past people who were talking excitedly. Some were already beginning to clear away the dirt that cluttered the streets and storefronts. Joyful crowds were filling carts with refuse and hauling them away to remove from the castle all memory of its evil oppressors. Andromedous was being cleansed and reborn before their eyes.

Bart led them to an open gate in a high wall surrounding a large plaza. In the center by a splashing fountain, Carisa was kneeling among a throng of people—many of whom looked dangerously ill—and others who were crippled and blind.

While the celebration had been going on in the town's main park, Carisa had found a quiet place to treat the neediest of the captives. Her hair was disheveled and her face was flushed. As she heard the Paladins approach, she stood up and greeted them with a tired smile that evaporated at the sight of the girl on Jotham's arm.

Slight color rose to her cheeks when Jotham introduced Deidrah. The golden-haired girl thanked Carisa with more restraint than she had shown the two other Paladins.

"I'm very pleased, Deidrah, to meet you too," Carisa said rubbing her forehead with the back of her hand, leaving a dark smudge behind. "We are very grateful that Justar used us to help free Andromedous, but without his instructions and weapons we wouldn't have stood a chance." As she spoke, Carisa was appraising Deidrah carefully. After a moment Carisa added, "You look different than the others I've met here. Are you from this town?"

Deidrah looked down, her face flushing slightly, "No, I . . ."

Jotham put his arm around Deidrah's shoulders. Carisa's eyes sparked momentarily.

"She has nowhere else to go, Carisa. Ghnostar destroyed her family . . . so I've asked her to come with us."

Carisa was stunned. "But Jotham, the King's words were clear! We can't disobey them!" she cried out in disbelief. "Bart's scroll said that—"

Jotham waved aside her objection and began speaking with increasing speed and conviction. "I'm certain that Justar would allow for this exception. You and I know that he is loving and good. It's not his desire that any defenseless creature should suffer. Justar could not have intended us to leave Deidrah all alone. You can see how weak she is, and you heard how these people don't trust her. I've thought it over, and she's coming!" He concluded fiercely.

"But Justar's words were clear: 'Paladins three!'" Carisa interjected, her mouth set in a taut line. Over her shoulder, she saw Flaggon leaving the square. Deidrah's eyes also appeared to be following his departure.

Jotham's eyes bore holes through the opposition. "We're taking her with us, Carisa—and that's final."

Despite Jotham's barely suppressed rage, Bart waded into the fray. "We all agreed to obey Justar's word. It would be wrong not to do what he told us."

"He's right, Jotham; disobedience could be very dangerous," Carisa said grabbing his arm and pulling him aside. "I think we'd better talk this over alone," she murmured, eyeing Deidrah warily.

Deidrah was staring nervously at the twirling sprays of water in the ornate fountain.

"No!" Jotham shouted yanking his arm free. "I gave her my word. There is nothing more to discuss. Justar put me in charge, and I've made the decision. We're not leaving her behind . . . she needs us."

Bart came up behind them. "Maybe it's you who needs her," he interjected.

"Shut up, Bart!" Jotham spat out. "You always think you're so comical.

You're just jealous, that's all." His face was livid. "If you don't want Deidrah to come with us, you'll have to go without me," he barked. Without waiting for their response, he went back and gripped Deidrah's wrist and stormed away with Deidrah stumbling behind him, her cloth satchel flying at her side.

After tripping over her skirt and nearly falling several times, Deidrah gasped, "Jotham, stop. Please . . . you're hurting me." He halted, whirling around, his eyes still blazing. His gaze softened as her saw the hair matted against her red cheeks.

"I'm sorry, Deidrah. I didn't mean to . . ." He dropped her wrist in embarrassment, then gently pushed her blond hair away from her face.

Struggling to catch her breath, she said, ". . . Jotham . . . I didn't intend to come between you and your friends. . . . You risked your lives to save ours . . . I couldn't bear to be the cause of your separation. Please leave me; go back to your friends. I'm so sorry. . . ." Her eyes filled with tears, and she fell against him, burying her head in his chest. He held her tightly against him.

"It isn't your fault," he responded bitterly. "They're so selfish. They don't care what will happen to you. All they're thinking about is themselves. Justar would want us to take care of you. I know he wants you to come with me."

Her violet eyes were shining up at him. "Oh, Jotham, are you sure?"

"Absolutely! I won't let anything happen to you . . . ever. You are more important than . . ." he faltered, the words were choked by the thickness in his throat. He was trembling, both with anger and with longing for this beautiful girl who had captivated him. But he could only stand there, mute, trying to swallow the lump lodged in his throat.

Deidrah sighed, "Jotham, I am the most fortunate girl in all the world. Justar has been so good to send you to me. You know, I was hoping just when you rushed into my prison that Justar would deliver me from that horrible place." Her face grew pale at the memory of her captivity.

"I don't want you to ever think of that dungeon again. I'm so glad I was able to save you." Deidrah gazed at him with an allure that sent waves of fire through him. Slowly, he lowered his face to hers and closed his eyes. He could feel her breath against his lips; then, abruptly, she disentangled herself, her eyes sparkling mischievously. She drew back from him, objecting in mock dismay, "My, my, sir: you are a bold one!"

He stared at her in dumb adoration, struggling to collect what remained of his faculties. All coherent thought seemed to have been struck from his mind.

When he finally spoke, his voice was low and thick. "Deidrah, I think you were the reason why I was sent to do battle in that wicked place. . . . I'm sure Justar meant for us to be together. . . ." She stopped him with a finger against his lips.

Her eyes bright with promise, she grabbed his hand, lifting her skirt above her ankles so she could run. Then, pulling Jotham meekly behind, she urged him with a coquettish glance, "Let me show you a secret place where no one can find us."

Shoulder to shoulder, they ran into a small grove that was nestled near the base of the western wall. She led him to a small cove next to a stream meandering serenely among the quiet trees. Underneath a large willow, they sat down on the cool grass, staring at the sparkling brook. They sat in silent reverie until Jotham said, "I don't want to have to fight any more battles. Deidrah, I want to stay with you forever."

"Maybe you can," she responded with an inscrutable smile. "As we say in my town, sweet knight, 'let's be merry for who knows what the morrow will bring.'" She skipped over to where she had dropped her satchel, took off her gloves, and removed a purple cruse. Jotham gazed intensely at her appealing figure, then lay down with a luxurious sigh and closed his eyes.

Deidrah sat down by him, lifting his head onto her lap. She ran her fingers lazily through his hair. With a flourish, she opened the bottle and placed it carefully against his lips. He took a long draught of the cool, delicious liquid and felt a comforting heat flowing into him.

"Umm, I've never had anything that tasted like *that* before. . . ." Jotham murmured.

She leaned over and gazed at him intently. "It is good, isn't it? Have some more." She held him with her eyes. They seemed to him like dark, mysterious pools slowly expanding and drowning him in their depths. Jotham caught the soft hand that was caressing his head and pressed it to his lips, briefly noticing a delicate mark in the center of her palm. As he kissed it, his chest suddenly felt heavy, and his head began to reel. Deidrah's face was becoming blurry; it was fading quickly. Blinking his eyes didn't help; everything was out of focus. Somewhere above him, he heard a slight hissing sound.

His stomach tightened. It sounded like a Gharg was close by and was coming after his Deidrah.

A fire was now pouring into his belly. He struggled to get to his knees, still blinking furiously. His eyes momentarily cleared, and a terrifying chill froze in icicles up and down his spine. He stared with horrified eyes at Deidrah's hand lying open on the grass. The mark he had kissed was a tattoo—an upside down three-pronged crown—Ghnostar's secret insignia!

Jotham gagged. The hissing over him grew louder.

He looked up into eyes that were no longer violet, but were now hooded and green: the reptilian eyes of a leering Gharg, its split tongue flickering in and out of its snout. It hissed at him malevolently as it raised its body over him. In sensuous delight it allowed the claws on the tips of its wings to slowly extend and trace a line down Jotham's cheek, savoring the certain victory at hand.

The burning in his stomach was now an inferno. The poison was doing its deadly work and had put him at the mercy of this loathsome creature.

The Gharg's crouched legs stiffened, its only movement a slight twitching at the end of its thick tail; then, it pounced, its talons bared. Jotham twisted away, knowing even as he did so he couldn't evade the attack. Instinctively, he threw out his hand to block the blow. Claws pierced through his open hand, their razor points protruding through the other side. The pain compressed his lungs in a crushing vise; and a sound he'd never heard before burst from his open mouth: a wail of pure agony.

It sounded terribly far away.

With a triumphant snarl, the Gharg leaped upon Jotham, chugging greedily deep in its throat. With a violent, slashing fury, its claws raked furrows through the mail and into the Paladin's chest. Jotham felt his skin tear and the warm blood seeping down over his chest.

Blackness crashed in upon him.

Chapter Forty

As Jotham had run out of the park dragging Deidrah behind, Bart made a move to follow. Carisa held him back.

"No!" she bit off the word sharply, her eyes dark and hard as flint. "He's got to learn that he can't just boss everybody around. Let him learn his lesson the hard way."

"But, Carisa . . ." She waved him quiet with her hand.

"You did that just like our beloved captain," Bart said, imitating the dismissive toss of her hand.

Carisa glared bullets at him.

"Hey, relax; Jotham will be back. Just wait: he'll come dragging his tail between his legs when he realizes what an idiot he's been."

Carisa shook her head. "I doubt it," she said, looking down the path that Jotham had taken. Flaggon trotted back into the plaza. "Did either of you think there was something strange about that girl?" she asked, as Flaggon drew near, panting.

Bart laughed, "Yeah. The most beautiful woman I've ever seen acts like she actually finds Jotham more attractive than me."

Carisa rolled her eyes in dismay.

Flaggon interjected, "Yes, m'lady . . . I noticed it."

"What was it? All the time she was here it kept bothering me, but I couldn't put my finger on it."

"A slight trace of jealousy, maybe?" Bart needled her.

Flaggon and Carisa ignored him. "Me fadder—may he rest in peace—passed on to me a big nose and a big smeller. Anyways, I can usually tells if an enemy is around by the smell. Like you, sor Bart, I thought that Deidrah was very beautiful—too beautiful if you understands what I mean—and she smelled very ladylike and all, but I wondered if it might be coverin' up somethin'. The perfume was too strong so I couldna' be certain, mind you, but the longer I smelled her the more I thought I was smellin' a Gharg."

"Come on, Flaggon. You've got to be joking," Bart chortled. "I've seen my share of Ghargs, and that was not one. If she is, we're all in big trouble."

"Speak for yourself," snapped his sister. "And if Flaggon is right . . . Jotham is the one in big trouble."

"But . . . I don't—" Bart protested.

Flaggon raised his finger, impatience edging his voice. "If you will recollect, sor, Master Slimgilley explained to you in our cottage that one of the Ghargs abilities is to take any shape they desire. Abner was a spy for Ghnostar, but he didna' look like a Gharg." He pulled at his beard. "I hates to say it, but I believes that Deidrah could be one too."

Bart stared at Flaggon, weighing the dwarf's words. He was still unconvinced. "I don't know, Flaggon. There was nothing about her that seemed like a Gharg. She was just the most incredible woman. . . ."

Carisa rubbed her eyes with the palms of her hands, alarm beginning to show in them. "Yeah, maybe too incredible. I've never seen anyone so beautiful."

"You sure you're not reading into this because you're mad at Jotham?" her brother asked.

She shook her head. "All I know is that there was something not quite right with her. For some reason, I kept looking at her gloves, but couldn't put it together. I should have warned Jotham . . . or challenged Deidrah. I was tired and mad," she admitted. "I just wasn't thinking very straight."

"Oh no." Bart's face suddenly stiffened, his eyes distant. "Justar *warned* me about this . . ."

Carisa's face blanched. "What do you mean?"

". . . When we were in the burial chamber in the castle. I saw . . . this picture of Jotham and a girl. . . . It was her! The King told me that I was to see and that '*he*' would go free." Bart slapped his palm against his head. "Justar was warning me about a trap being set for Jotham, and I blew it! There was something odd about the girl in that vision. . . . Now I know what it was: it was her hands! She was beautifully dressed, but she was wearing *filthy gloves*." He clenched his teeth. "I saw, but didn't see . . ." He shook his head miserably.

Flaggon nodded. "They were probably coverin' the mark on her palm. We must go find them."

Carisa spun around with a look of wild desperation. "But how will we find them? They could be anywhere."

"I took the liberty of finding out, m'lady," Flaggon said, as he ran over to a bench, jumped on top, and began waving his arms. He caught the attention of a sentry in a tower above the western wall. The guard lowered his bow and pointed it directly at them.

"Don't move," the dwarf yelled over his shoulder. "That's Arbakon—he's been keeping watch for me, and I believes he has a message for us."

A few seconds later, the whistling sound of an arrow bore down at them. It passed six feet over their heads, ripping through foliage and sticking fast to the elm nearest them. A parchment was tied around the shaft.

Bart tore it off and handed it to Flaggon. They dropped to their knees as he smoothed it out on the ground. It was a rough map, with a line leading to a small park along the west wall. There were two "x" marks at that point.

Flaggon jabbed his stubby forefinger at the map. "That's where they be," he exclaimed.

The Paladins jumped to their feet. "Have your bottle ready, m'lady," Flaggon yelled, taking the lead.

The dwarf was like a bloodhound on a hot scent. His short legs moved faster than they had ever seen. He had an unerring sense of direction, and they only had to double back once.

As they ran over the winding cobblestone paths which honeycombed the fortress, the phrase Carisa had read many hours earlier: "*Amor Vincet Omnia*," kept resonating in her head. "Love covers all." She felt her cheeks burn as she recalled her harsh words and conduct.

"Please Justar, let us get there in time—please . . . please!" she pled quietly, brushing tears from her face.

Carisa slowed to fit a dart into her crossbow, her lips in a taut line. Her weapon would be ready.

The three ran past a long row of whitewashed houses. Approaching an intersection where the path took a sharp turn toward the fortress wall, Flaggon raised his hand. "They're behind that building," he panted, pointing to a gray structure with pillars along the front. Noticing the crossbow in Carisa's hands, he nodded. "Very good, m'lady, but aim a little high. According to the map it may be an uphill shot." He took a deep breath. "When we turns the corner, spread out so that you do not get in each other's way."

Bart readied his bow quickly.

On Flaggon's signal, they dodged around the wide building, racing toward the trees 30 yards away. They ran up to the hillock in the center of the grove. It was bare.

They raced over its crest, and below them, near a stream, was the Gharg, sitting on Jotham's chest, its snout open and dripping.

Carisa skidded to a standstill, her crossbow fixed on its cruel jaws.

The Gharg jerked its head sideways, nostrils flaring. It had caught their scent.

Carisa and Bart were unwilling to release their arrows. The dimness of the grove plus the proximity of the Gharg to Jotham's prone body made it a chancy shot.

Flaggon didn't stop. He was screaming something unintelligible at the snarling creature who had plastered its reptilian body over Jotham's. It glared at the onrushing dwarf, its long green torso rigid except for the blunt tip of its tail, which flicked dangerously. As the dwarf ran forward his sword raised above his head, the powerful muscles in the Gharg's hind legs began to twitch. Flaggon flung himself at the Gharg.

The reptile sprang sideways rolling onto its back and kicked at the dwarf's belly flying over him. One foot caught Flaggon's thigh. The dwarf made no sound. He landed on the grass, rolling over on his shoulder and leaped up with a grimace, waving his sword at the Gharg who was scuttling toward a gnarled elm tree.

The two Paladins finally had a clear shot. They released their arrows as the Gharg clambered into the undergrowth. Carisa's dart plunged into the tree, blowing the trunk apart in a shower of scorched splinters. Bart's arrow was high and flew past its outspread wings.

The Gharg leaped into the air, clawing for a low-hanging willow branch. Flaggon hobbled forward and swung at the snarling, scrambling creature. The monster's tail whipped around and knocked him off his feet. As Flaggon toppled over, his slashing blade caught the tail, slicing it off onto the grass. Carisa released another dart and caught its leg, ripping it in half. Crawling and jumping through the thick branches, the Gharg spat out its agonized fury as it leaped over to another tree whose branches almost touched the thick castle wall. Bart's arrow blew a hole in the bulwark as it dove over the wall and flew off into the darkness.

Flaggon limped over to the tail, still jerking spasmodically on the ground, his face crimson. His wound was pouring blood; the pain had etched deep lines along his eyes and mouth. He struck at the tail until it looked like links of sausage littered on the grass.

He found Bart and Carisa kneeling down by Jotham's head. She had uncorked her small vial, which was full once again. She handed Bart a dampened cloth to wrap around the dwarf's leg. The bleeding stopped immediately.

Carisa poured the liquid out directly on Jotham's torn and bleeding chest.

Bart looked down at his friend's face. "We're too late," he said, his voice like stone. "Flaggon, I think he's dead." The dwarf bent over to take a closer look. Jotham's mouth was bluish and frozen in a terrible grimace. His eyes were jaundiced, and his face was a sickly green. Flaggon knelt down over Jotham and sniffed his mouth.

"Lady Carisa, hurry! Pour Justar's brew into his mouth—he's been poisoned."

As she obeyed, Carisa clamped her teeth over her lip to keep from crying out. Jotham's body was stiff and cold.

And there was no pulse.

Chapter Forty One

As he lay on the cool grass surrounded by his frantic friends, Jotham sensed himself floating away. He felt like he was in a dream, yet was fully aware of himself and his surroundings. *Perhaps I'm having a vision . . . or maybe I'm . . . dead.* He didn't know what was happening other than he was gradually disengaging, leaving his body behind. *I look pretty awful,* he observed with detachment as he floated higher and higher above the branches of the tallest tree.

He could still see the small circle clustered around him in the darkening grove. He was somewhere above them looking down at the heartbroken band, yet strangely untouched by the pathos of the scene. It seemed that his emotions had been cut away when he'd separated from his body. Like a feather dancing in the evening breeze, he hovered, then blown by a sudden gust of wind, spun crazily away.

He was twisting lightly in the darkness, disconnected images flashing around him. A bright light in the distance began to pull at him. It was King Justar.

Justar didn't say a word. He was standing in front of Jotham, in a quiet garden, his white tunic blazing brilliantly. The sky was a deep blue, and a few puffy clouds were trailing overhead. The King was waiting for him, quiet and still. His massive broadsword was in his right hand. The first move clearly was to be Jotham's.

The image of Abe's torn body hanging inside the dank cell exploded in Jotham's mind like lightning. The power of that picture was so intense it caused him to gasp; his hands and legs shook with the force of it. His emotions had returned with a vengeance. A black, agonizing rage burned its way up from his stomach and out of his mouth.

He found himself screaming, "It was your fault! Why did you . . . ?"

In his hand he felt the smooth contours of his sword hilt as he rushed at Justar. His lunge was blocked by Justar's flashing blade.

"You could have stopped it. . . . Why didn't you?" he sobbed, his sword slamming down again on the King's inflexible steel.

Jotham swung again; the King side-stepped deftly and struck Jotham's blade sharply with the flat of his own sword. Jotham spun around panting, harsh sobs clutching at his throat, letting the impetus of his twisting blade carry him in a full circle. He thrust again. Blocked and parried on each occasion, Jotham was unable to penetrate the King's defenses. Back and forth they fought on the soft carpet of green grass, steel against steel, the clanging and ringing of blades a strange counterpoint to the gentle quiet of the peaceful glen.

Justar's eyes were locked on Jotham. His mouth was set in a firm, hard line, his golden eyes seemed to be flashing crystalline fire. Jotham was gasping and weeping, his arms barely able to raise his weapon, yet he refused to give. He was choking on his anger and grief. With each slashing stroke, he raged out the bitter question. "Why? . . . Why?"

Justar's blade dipped, and Jotham seized the opening, staggering forward. King Justar stepped back calmly, his sword curving up, catching Jotham unprepared. Turning his wrist, Justar abruptly flicked the blade out of his opponent's hand. It plunged into the ground where it wobbled crookedly, then fell over, its hilt embedded in the soft soil. The King stepped forwards, and with a twitch of his wrist, a fine red line appeared across Jotham's cheek and jaw.

The King's eyes were showering Jotham with sparks of hot light. He lowered his sword tip and pointed it directly at Jotham's heart. It touched Jotham's tunic, pushed through the mail and pricked his flesh. Jotham was being drenched in sparks that were raining over him like flecks of white lava. The heat was so intense Jotham didn't feel the blade. His eyes were caught by Justar's golden gaze. A fierce burning caused him to look down. The King's blade was being slowly drawn out of his chest. There was no blood—just a blazing heat, and a great emptiness.

Something had been cut away.

The Great General sheathed his sword. Then he lifted his powerful arms and encircled him, drawing him close. The General King was not answering any questions; he was just holding him until the raging waves subsided.

Jotham moaned, huge angry sobs bursting from his mouth. Gradually, the swells quieted. Somehow, Jotham understood that he would receive no explanation, nothing to relieve the pain. There would be no answer—only the presence of his King. But something was different. He blinked his eyes and put his hand to his chest. The fury . . . the raging fury—it was *gone*, and along with it, the barrier in his heart. In its place was a clean, vulnerable space. Justar's voice was cascading fragrantly over him in a quiet whisper, "My child, I love you. . . . Do not fear."

Then, the King held him at arms length and looked deeply into the Paladin's eyes.

"Jotham, have you led well?" The very gentleness of the question almost undid him. There was no rebuke or accusation in the tone. It was a pure, piercing question by his King . . . by one who loved him without reservation.

His throat felt so thick he couldn't swallow, but he heard himself respond hoarsely, "No, my King . . . I have not."

"What you say is true. Child, you forgot the words Warrior gave to you. Don't you know why I wrote the names of your band on your chest?"

Jotham looked down. It was as if he were seeing the embroidered names of his three companions on his tunic for the first time. He had not thought about them since discovering his new attire at Slimgilley's house.

"I told you they were to be on your heart, not under your heel."

Jotham nodded his head numbly.

"And you were to lead them by service and example, with humility."

Jotham's shoulders slumped. He wanted to drop to the ground and sink under the grass. He had failed his King and had failed his band. And one of them was dead as a result.

"I am sorry, my King. I'm sorry . . ." his voice broke. "I was wrong." The words were wrung out of the depths of Jotham's being.

The heat from Justar's fiery presence grew more intense—he was burning with fire; then, just as suddenly, it cooled. Instead of the steel of the King's blade, he felt the comforting heaviness of his hand. "You are forgiven. Now go and lead well in my name."

The relief which flooded over him made his knees buckle. Jotham's head swam, and the constriction around his throat tightened. He longed to shout out his allegiance, his undying loyalty, but his throat was strangled in a painful grip.

Twinkling, glowing embers of golden light shot into the sky and arced gracefully back to the earth like a massive Roman candle exploding on the

Fourth of July. Justar, the sky, the glen were gone, and in their place was a vast twirling, shimmering mist. He was floating through a galaxy of golden stars.

He knew immediately that he was no longer in Issatar. He was somewhere back in his world. Headlights were whizzing past him. He was inside his grandfather's dilapidated station wagon. Jotham had seen faded photographs of it in his father's photo journal, and he knew it must be his grandfather who was driving. One hand was on the wheel, while the other held a bottle. His lips were curled into a vicious snarl; his face streaked with sweat. There was a little child sitting in the back seat. His head was bobbing and jerking as he fought to stay awake. Jotham realized suddenly: *I'm seeing my father as a boy riding in his dad's car.* The man tipped the bottle up and drank greedily, beads of condensation dripping like blood onto his pants.

He watched as the boy succumbed to sleep, the chin of his curly head falling on his red and white striped T-shirt. Sensing danger, Jotham wanted desperately to awaken the child, but was unable to intervene. His eyes were drawn to the rearview mirror, where he could see his grandfather's cold, blood-shot eyes narrowing, his face contorting wickedly. Everything slowed; each movement freeze-framed in a horrible, gliding, unstoppable drama. Jotham saw him toss the brown bottle aside. It floated through the air, twisting, foam sliding out of its mouth in a perfect arc. It hit the plastic door panel, spattering globules of amber liquid across the window, then dropped lazily to the mat on the passenger's side, where it lay. A large bubble formed on the blue rubber pad and popped. As if awaiting that signal, the speed of the action increased.

The drunken man twisted his head sideways, shifting his body toward the sleeping boy. He threw his right arm over the back of the driver's seat. Jotham's stomach was in a hard knot. Glancing quickly back to the road, then through the mirror at the child, the angry man whipped his open hand around. He slapped the sleeping boy across the face. The speed of the blow was like the strike of a cobra. The harsh sound of skin against skin snapped inside the car like a rifle shot.

The small child's eyes sprung open in shock. The naked look of bewilderment made Jotham's heart shiver, stealing the breath from him. It was if he had received the blow, not his father. The small face was twisted in pain and confusion. Deep down in the recesses of his eyes, rage was smoldering.

Jotham knew he'd seen that wounded look before; and that he'd been its cause.

The car twirled in a small cyclone of blurred images, then evaporated. Jotham was now on a farm. It was a place he'd never visited, although he recognized it immediately. It was the farm where his father had been raised after his mother remarried. Jotham was inside a dusty barn looking again at the same little boy now grown several years older. A farmer, the young boy's stepfather, was yanking a leather strap off a post. Jotham could see his father's small fists clenching and unclenching; otherwise he was motionless and silent. His slender back was ram-rod stiff, quietly awaiting the punishment. The farmer picked up a dirty shovel and threw it furiously against the barn door. A hen exploded into the air cackling its indignation.

Suddenly, Jotham was the one looking up at the farmer holding the strap. The raging man was bent over swearing down at him, his face contorted into a mask of brutal rage. His eyes seemed to blaze with insane ferocity. Jotham was paralyzed with fear as the strap whipped toward him, striking him across his back and shoulders. The strap whipped him again and again, the stinging and slapping of the thick leather frightening the ponies in the nearby stalls. They began to whinny in alarm. Though tears spurted out of his eyes, no sound escaped Jotham's lips. His back bent under the blows, his thin legs shook, but he didn't fall.

The farm and the barn spun out of sight, and Jotham was now inside a clapboard chapel. He was sitting on a pew, filthy toes sticking out the ends of torn boots. He felt indescribably tired. There was a hard, bulky mass in the pocket of his oversized coat. Pressing his hand against it, he felt the contours of a bottle; behind him the chapel door banged shut. The sound was unnaturally loud in the empty, sparsely furnished whitewashed building. Without turning his head, he knew that his father was shuffling in, steps slow yet purposeful. Unshaven, hair dirty and unkempt, he walked down the narrow aisle. He looked as though he'd been on the streets for a long time. Instead of judgment tearing a hole into him, Jotham felt an unusual, unexpected solidarity with the broken and tattered figure.

Something hard and cold had melted inside him. His father fell to his knees, moaning in front of a makeshift altar on which stood a simple crucifix. It was tilting and looked ready to fall. Another figure materialized. He was slightly built, had on a dark robe and held a large leather book in his hands. Tears were running down his cheeks as he looked down on Jotham's

294

father. He put his arm around the penitent figure on the floor, bent over and began to speak softly to him. Slowly his father grew quiet.

The priest opened the large book, setting it down on the altar. His father's eyes were glued to the words on the worn pages lying open before him. He whispered hoarsely to the priest, who nodded emphatically, pointing at the page, then at the crucifix. His shoulders and hands gradually stopped shaking; then, with an explosive, mournful groan his head dropped heavily onto the open book. The priest took a small bowl of water, dipped his fingers in it and lifting the penitent face up, traced a cross on his father's forehead. As if tossed by strong hands, his father fell prone before the crucifix, his arms spread out. He lay motionless.

The priest looked up at Jotham, his beautiful gold and green-flecked eyes smiling. The stoop-shouldered cleric's lips were moving. He heard no sound, though he felt the force of the words enter into him like a spear thrust: "My son, as you have been forgiven, you must forgive." The heat of the wordless communication was as piercing as Justar's flaming sword. Jotham fell backwards, blown over by an irresistible gust of cool wind. He lay on his back unable to move, but he was not afraid.

Jotham coughed uncontrollably, wheezing and sucking in huge mouthfuls of air. He heard Carisa gasp, then the gravely voice of Flaggon: "He's coming to, m'lady."

"Praise be to Justar!"

Chapter Forty Two

Although Jotham regained consciousness, the poison he had swallowed had affected him severely. For days he suffered with a brutal fever and was delirious for long hours. Carisa sat by his bed, wiping away the perspiration and feeding him as often as she could whenever the fever would decrease. Despite her tender and compassionate care, the poison was nearly too strong for the liquid from her bottle. Several times, Jotham appeared to be succumbing to its terrible power. However, on the seventh day, his fever broke and color began to return to his pallid face.

They decided to remain in Andromedous for another week while Jotham recuperated. In three days, he was able to get out of bed and begin getting exercise by wandering through the winding streets and small parks scattered throughout the expansive castle grounds. Despite its forbidding exterior, on the inside it was actually a very beautiful fortification. Whoever had designed the castle had clearly loved flowers, for they were scattered lavishly about—a gardener's paradise. Climbing rose bushes festooned the inner walls, intertwined with purple ivy, hyacinths and honeysuckle. Beds of purple begonias, lavender posies, and orange, red and yellow tulips ran along the borders of the serpentine paths.

It would have been an idyllic place were it not for the painful void left by Abe's absence. Jotham would catch himself waiting for his brother to appear at mealtimes or run up to him from around a corner while making a circuit of the labyrinthine streets. Despite the ache in his heart, and the plague of unanswered questions, Andromedous was perfectly suited to help him recoup his strength. What surprised him was that even though the pain did not leave, there was now an inexplicable peace that comforted him.

After a few days, Jotham was able to begin jogging around the wall with Bart. The guards in the parapets and embrasures followed them curiously with their eyes, occasionally gesturing incredulously at the sweaty runners. The quiet walks through the gardens and courtyards decorated with arabesque designs on porcelain and marble, Jotham reserved for Carisa.

One of the first things Jotham had noticed when he came to, was that Carisa and her brother were the same size they had been when they were first called into Issatar. Carisa had regained her attractive figure and was once again a lovely young woman. Pretending to be asleep, he would gaze at her sitting by his bed. She looked to him like an angel.

When he first asked her to accompany him on his exploration of the inner bailey, she agreed reluctantly, convinced only by his weakened condition that he needed her. They would walk for long periods in silence, and their conversation tended toward small talk. Neither wanted to be the one to concede fault or make an admission regarding Deidrah's treacherous scheme. Whenever the subject would threaten to arise, they would both run for cover; it was an incident too painful or shameful to discuss.

On the last day of their stay, Jotham decided to tell Carisa about his confrontation with Justar. It proved more difficult than he imagined. They'd become so accustomed to veering away from sensitive issues, he was finding it very hard to leap over the unspoken barrier this had created.

Jotham and Carisa headed in an easterly direction, both wanting to stay as far away from the western grove as they could. This evening, the silent omissions weighed heavily, serving only to strengthen the barricade between them. The sun was low on the horizon when Jotham decided to have out with it.

They sat down on a low pillared wall surrounding a wading pool, their feet kicking in the cool waters. The rays of the setting sun were casting a gold-lavender sheen on the unperturbed waters at their feet. He cleared his throat and said, "Carisa . . . I don't think I've ever really thanked you for . . . coming back to get me." He stared uncomfortably at the purplish streaks in the pool.

Carisa said nothing; her eyes were also fixed on the glorious palette in front of them.

His temple was throbbing, but he felt that if he chose to pull back into safety he would regret it forever. "You guys saved my life. . . ." He hesitated, then decided to plunge ahead with reckless abandon. "I was a fool to fall for Deidrah!"

Carisa glanced at him out of the corner of her eye, but said nothing.

A locked door seemed to be springing open inside him. He looked at her with a steadiness that surprised her. "I had a confrontation with Justar while I was unconscious. He showed me something about myself that I need to tell you about."

She picked up a rounded pebble and skipped it across the still waters. It bounced several times, hit the curved wall and left a scrape on the moss-covered stone. Carisa was intrigued, but she still remained silent.

He told her about the contest with the King and his own defeat. "When the King pointed out why your names were sewn on my tunic, I felt awful. I wanted to rip them off my chest and scream out what a lousy captain I'd been. I knew I had failed all of you." He stopped to settle the trembling in his voice. "You were right. . . . Justar shouldn't have picked me." His hazel eyes met hers squarely. "You would have made a much better leader."

Their eyes held briefly, then she looked away.

"I asked you to come out with me to tell you that and ask you to forgive me for letting you down and being such a stubborn idiot." His voice, though soft, had an undercurrent of strength, which added an even greater poignancy to his confession.

Carisa was drawn so strongly to him that it startled her. She felt the color rising in her cheeks. Her eyes stung with the realization of her own failures which were made even more pointed by Jotham's candid admission. Her heart was thudding against her chest. She tried to speak, but her mouth was as dry as parchment.

"Uhm, Jotham . . . You're wrong. . . . I don't think I would have made such a hot leader at all. I've been really stupid and cruel to you since the beginning, especially about Bart's eye."

"Yeah, but you were only—"

She ignored him. "I kept blaming you, and because of me, Deidrah was able to take advantage. . . . So I'm the one who needs to apologize to *you*. I've just been too proud to admit it." She bit her lip.

He reached out his hand and put it over hers. Her skin was cool and soft. "It's okay, Carisa; I don't blame you at all. . . . But, yes," he smiled, "I forgive you . . . if you forgive me."

She nodded, letting her hand rest comfortably under his.

". . . and about Deidrah," Jotham continued, ". . . I was a total moron. I was so mad at myself about Bart—you weren't the only one blaming me— I felt like an absolute failure. Anyway, I figured because of me he'd be blinded . . . and that, plus—Abe." Jotham's voice weakened. "She really set me up. . . . I believed everything she told me. He shook his head ruefully. "I just can't figure out what came over me."

Carisa's dark eyes smiled with a knowing twinkle. "You don't need to explain, Jotham; she was the most beautiful girl I've ever seen. Plus, she did have an advantage. . . ."

"What was that?"

Carisa grinned, "She, or it, as the case may be, had at least a couple hundred years of experience on you."

He gave her a sideways smile, "Are you accusing me of being inexperienced and naive?"

"Me? Never. No way!" Carisa laughed but grew serious again. "I understand perfectly, Jo; I really do. Remember, I was taken in myself, not so long ago." Her face hardened at the thought of Abner's gorgeous smile. "Ghnostar's forces are very, very clever. And, who knows what kind of hypnotic power they're able to exert."

Jotham winced. "Yeah, you're right. . . . In spite of how she looked, there was something about her that made me feel really weird. It was like someone else had control of my emotions."

She nodded in agreement, drawing his hand over onto her lap.

"As I think back on it," he continued, "she was just laughing at me. At first I thought she was mischievous, kind of like you," he blushed. "But really Deidrah was . . . toying with me—like a cat playing with a mouse." A little smile played at the corners of Carisa's mouth. "But I can see now she was really just laughing at me." His throat tightened; he was embarrassed and overcome at being close to Carisa again.

She slid her other hand shyly over his. "I know how you feel, Jo," she said, "like you were used . . . made a fool of. It feels terrible. . . ."

Jotham felt shivers run up his arm. Returning the pressure of her fingers, he was overwhelmed with the awareness of how unworthy he was of her. With difficulty he swallowed, and with his right hand reached over and brushed back the strands of hair which had fallen over her eyes. She looked directly at him, a question in her glance.

"Carisa, I was so wrong. Deidrah was nothing at all like you. She doesn't even come close. . . . You're the most wonderful person I've ever known in my life."

The sun had almost set. The water rippled with miniature orange crests.

A flock of geese honked overhead, while around them the tree frogs were beginning their nightly serenade. Her dark, lovely eyes, which had touched him the moment he had seen her outside his home, had never looked so beautiful. She glanced up at him and smiled. The bronze sky made her face glow and cast a halo around her hair. *You are a saint*, he thought to himself, *and I don't deserve you, but if I don't kiss you now I will never, ever forgive myself.*

He lowered his face, placing both hands on either side of her head, drawing her face up to his. He could feel the ridge of her ears through the glossy silkiness of her hair; then he felt the sweetness of her mouth, soft against his lips, returning the warmth of his kiss. Jotham's heart throbbed. Not knowing how long he could stand the overwhelming, dizzying delight of her lips, he lifted his head and brushed her hair with his mouth.

"Carisa, I love you," he whispered into her ear. "I think I've known it ever since I saw you jump out of your van."

Her eyes glistened as they held him. She turned her face to look at the horizon; then she jumped off the wall, pulling him up to his feet. She slipped her arms around his waist, locking her fingers lightly behind his back. "Captain, it's late. . . . I believe our comrades must be wondering about us—you know what a mother hen Flaggon is." She stood on her tiptoes and kissed him lightly on both cheeks. "We don't want them getting nervous about us, do we?"

Hand in hand they made their way back up the cobblestone path toward the castle keep. They waved at the guards walking along the tops of the walls above them, carrying lanterns. The soldiers responded with a respectful salute, standing at attention until they were out of sight.

"Are you worried about tomorrow and our last battle?" Carisa asked.

"Are you kidding? Remember who you're talking to—Jotham, your fearless leader. . . ." She glanced at him and he laughed. "You want the truth? . . . Yes I am . . . *very.*"

She squeezed his fingers. "That's nice to hear. For a second there I thought you were reverting back to your old ways." Carisa grinned up at him, her eyes twinkling by the flicker of the torch hung on the wall.

Jotham saluted another soldier who, upon seeing Carisa, removed his helmet and gave a low bow. She continued. "I felt pretty good yesterday after Flaggon told us that he thought we were finally ready for our last battle—until he reminded us of the words on Bart's script before we crossed the lake to attack this castle."

Jotham nodded his head, repeating the instructions: "When the battle is over, three Paladins leave." He shook his head as he stared at the setting sun. "I wonder why Justar wanted him to stay behind?"

"I can't imagine," Carisa responded. "At least Flaggon thinks we're ready; *I* sure don't feel like I am. I just wish he were coming with us."

"Yeah, tell me about it. Picturing the three of us battling alone has really scared me. I've gotten so used to relying on that crazy dwarf, I can't imagine fighting without him."

Carisa smiled. "For a short little guy, he's an incredible fighter." She hesitated with an unusual sparkle in her eyes. "Jotham, I think something is finally starting to sink in: as long as we follow Justar's instructions, the odds—no matter what they are—don't really matter. Know what I mean?"

"Yeah, I've been thinking about that too. It's made the thought of going to battle without Flaggon almost tolerable.

She stared soberly at him. "You and Flaggon have been keeping the details a secret for a while, Jotham. Can't you tell me where the final battle is going to be? I'll find out tomorrow anyway."

He stopped and put his hands around her neck so that his fingers met at the nape. His eyebrows were deeply furrowed. "I didn't want you to be worrying about it, so I decided to hold off until the final day. The main reason why we've been taking our time is to make sure we're all as well prepared as we can be for what's ahead."

"Come on, already, out with it. Where are we headed?"

Drawing her to him, he rested his cheek against her tawny hair. He held her close. "We're going to attack Ghnostar's Lair."

"I knew it, Jotham . . . but thanks for telling me, anyway," she whispered, gripping him tightly. "So, tomorrow we fight the dragon."

Chapter Forty Three

The day of their last battle dawned clear and bright. It was an unusual day, full of hope and tingling expectation, yet undercut with a sweet slice of suspense.

There was nothing about the morning which gave any hint that they were about to face their greatest test and their most dangerous enemy. Banks of cottony clouds were floating across the pale sky, and a chorus of birds outside his window chirped extravagantly. It was as if they were singing out their own thanks for liberating them from Ghnostar's grasp.

Jotham walked over to the desk and sat down to his solitary breakfast. He could feel the familiar tightness in his chest. *But this is no game,* he told himself grimly, allowing himself briefly to think about Abe. The muscles in his stomach knotted with the memory.

Before retiring the previous evening, Flaggon had waggled his red eyebrows at them and said, in a voice that was more sober than usual, "In the mornin', you will each find food in your room. It is for you to breakfast alone. On the eve of a great battle, it is 'the better part of wisdom,' as me master says, to begin in quietness; 'to compose and clear the mind'—you understand." He rubbed his nose and coughed, "Tho' I admits I doesna practice what I preaches, in that regard, meself. But I needs to, and so does you. . . ."

Their red-bearded friend had made as if to leave; but instead, turning around in the doorway, he faced them solemnly, raised his hand and said, "There is a famous saying in Issatar, which we repeats before a great battle; it is a great comfort." There was a timbre of emotion in his voice which moved the Paladins. "It goes like this: 'though the war horse is made ready for battle, victory rests in the hands of the King.'" He blinked several times, rubbed his nose vigorously, and as he walked out, murmured, "May the peace of Justar be with you." Then he shut the door.

After finishing the meal of oatmeal cooked with raisins and brown sugar, cold milk and mugs of fruit juice, he had met the other Paladins on the causeway in front of the castle.

"I felt so good last night, I thought I was sleeping in my bed back home," Bart said, sitting cross-legged on the end of the wooden dock.

"Hopefully we'll be back there soon, if all goes well today," Jotham added.

Carisa noticed the flap of his wallet was undone. "Jo, what did your scroll say today?"

His hand rubbed the worn leather.

"You did read it, didn't you?" she asked in a motherly tone.

"Of course." He bristled, then seeing the laughter in her eyes, smiled. "I may be dense, but I'm not stupid."

"Well now, that's a matter of opinion," Bart interjected.

Jotham reached around Carisa and slapped him on the back of the head. "Watch it—I'm still the Captain of this rabble."

Carisa slid next to him, her head resting against his shoulder.

"The words weren't in Latin," Jotham continued, "and it was really short. It said: 'Fear not; a sacrifice that's great overcomes all hate.'"

"Mine were pretty similar," Bart said, trying not to stare at Jotham and his sister. "'Fear not; where I have overcome, the war's already won.'"

Carisa took her parchment out and read: "No need to fear my child, for I am near—my hands below—my face above; though small you be, I pledge to you these you shall see." She smiled, "I guess the message is pretty clear: we shouldn't be scared about the two-headed dragon."

"Who's afraid?" Jotham asked, grinning at her.

Carisa reached down to tie his wallet shut. Her fingers brushed his, sending a current through his arm.

"Your pouch will barely close," she said, struggling to tie the double-knot, "What do you have in there?"

Bart stared in amazement at the couple. Carisa looked back at him, her expression alternating between innocence and amusement. Casting a suspicious glance at Jotham, he stood up and turned toward the water.

Jotham looked pensively at his wallet, then quickly undid the knot and pulled out his scroll, handing it hurriedly to Carisa. From the bottom of the pouch he brought out another one, this one flattened and torn.

Carisa and Bart recognized it immediately as Abe's. They drew in their breath as Jotham began to uncurl it.

He took several shaky breaths as he read it, then, swallowing with difficulty, began to read out loud:

You are no longer four,
So heed, my children, timeless lore:
The brilliant splendor of the sun,
Redresses fully a loss of one.
The majestic pow'r of the King's son,
Ensures this boon; the warfare's won.

Bart's shout jerked Jotham's head around, causing him to almost drop the scrolls. He replaced them quickly in his pouch. "Hey, look guys, our transportation is here," Bart yelled, pointing at the sky.

Jotham and Carisa jumped when they heard the beating of mighty wings approaching at high speed. Three horses were flying towards them with a thundering of powerful wings. Their muscular, white bodies glimmered in the morning sun. Flaggon was riding the lead horse, which despite its size, alighted on the wooden dock with stunning elegance. The other two landed with equal grace, their gleaming white hooves barely making a sound on the planks. Flaggon's horse tossed its head proudly and whinnied a respectful greeting.

Carisa stepped forward eagerly, her hand outstretched to pat the silky strands between the black eyes of the horse nearest her. The mare reared back on her legs, pawing the air over her head and neighed angrily. The mare's eyes glowered dangerously. Flaggon's horse jerked his head toward Carisa baring its teeth. It struck the causeway a threatening blow.

"M'lady," Flaggon shouted, struggling to keep his mount from butting Carisa, "these war horses are not used to being taken lightly. . . ." the stallion whinnied loudly. "They expects to be treated with the same respect as you would expect."

Carisa stepped back quickly. The horses began to calm down, their wild eyes staring angrily at the Paladins, their massive flanks and long, satiny tails twitching nervously.

Flaggon waited for his horse to lower its head before jumping off. He turned and gave a bow of gratitude. The three horses nickered and shook their flowing manes, both accepting and waving off the dwarf's gesture at the same time. He turned to the Paladins. "You may touch them, but only if they gives you their permission. These be valiant warriors—not beasts of burden. They carry others rarely and only on express orders of the King."

The three Paladins noticed for the first time the horses' hooves that gleamed along viciously sharp edges. Their feet were clearly used for something more than galloping.

"This is Lexus," Flaggon said, gesturing to the stallion. "Spinx you have already met, Lady Carisa, and the other is Excall."

The Paladins, taking their cue from the dwarf, bowed deeply, their right arms sweeping the ground before them.

The three horses nickered with restrained acceptance.

"So, where are we headed?" Jotham asked.

"Ghnostar's Lair is over there," the dwarf growled, pointing north to a single far-off peak which jutted up into a dark gray cloud. It had not been visible when they had first come across the lake, but it now stood out like a jagged tooth in a warlock's mouth. "The war horses are under orders to take you there, but I don't expects them to stay. This is yore battle, and they won't interfere."

"What are you going to do here?" Carisa asked.

Flaggon shrugged, conveying both total ignorance and infinite understanding. "Me king has asked me to stays here and help appoints a worthy successor to the baron who ruled here but was killed by the Ghargs." He puffed out his cheek, "'Tis an important task, mind you," he lowered his voice, "though I'd rather be goin' with you, if you knows what I mean. I prefers battles to meetin's."

The thudding blow of a hoof striking wood interrupted him. Flaggon raised his finger toward Lexus, nodding affirmatively. "They are anxious to be off, sors and lady. They believes very strongly in not postponing unpleasantness. Where there is a battle to be met, they hates to waste a moment. Justar has inscribed the words: '*Carpe diem*' in a rock which overhangs the canyon where they live. They believes they are called to 'Seize the day,' and they expects others to do likewise. You must needs go."

He stopped, his Adam's apple bobbing like a cork in a hurricane, and gave his red nose a rub. Blinking his watery eyes, he withdrew his sword and held it out in front of him. "Ahem . . . it is time to bid each of you: *Ave atque vale*."

Bart leaned over, whispering to Jotham, "Hail and farewell."

Jotham bowed his head and touched his sword to the dwarf's. "*Ave atque vale* to you too, Flaggon."

Carisa and Bart stepped forward, their sword points touching the others, their blades forming four steel spokes connecting the brave circle of warriors. The light glinted brightly off the tips, the sparkle of flashing light the sun's contribution to their final salute.

Flaggon cleared his throat and in a quavering voice said, "May Justar go with you . . . my friends."

Replacing her sword, Carisa ran over to him, bent over and wrapped her arms around his neck. Flaggon puffed out his cheeks and squeezed his eyes shut, grimacing fiercely. A tear ran down his weathered cheek and onto his beard.

"We'll miss you," she said finally.

He nodded his head, his eyes still closed.

The three horses at that moment bent their forelegs and lowered their long, graceful necks.

"I think we've got our permission to mount," Bart said, climbing on to Excall's broad back, his legs behind the joints of the large, retracted wings.

Jotham lifted his leg and slid onto the stallion, its massive shoulder muscles quivering beneath the glistening white hair. Jotham could feel the restrained power impatient to be released. Carisa gingerly mounted Spinx, making sure she did so with the greatest respect. The horses' legs remained bent until Flaggon had said his individual good byes, giving each of the Paladins' forearms an emphatic and final shake.

Lexus spread his wings and with two powerful beats lifted himself and Jotham into the air. Excall and Spinx followed quickly, their wings thumping the air like huge canvas sails slapping the wind. With each thunderous stroke they rose higher; then in one coordinated movement, they spun and in a tight military formation hovered 50 feet above the placid lake, allowing the Paladins one last look at their friend below.

He was standing on the edge of the causeway—his feet spread, his back stiff and his sword held high. The three saluted him with their blades, and with one twisting glide they sped away toward the lone mountain.

Chapter Forty Four

The speed at which the war horses traveled was exhilarating. The rushing wind whipped their hair back and almost stole their breath away. Even Bart, "the king of vertigo," was thrilled by the velocity produced by the mighty wings. The horse's bunched muscles under the satiny, white skin were propelling them forward, tearing through the air with dizzying speed. Andromedous could no longer be seen.

Carisa had her fingers locked in Spinx's mane and was sitting upright, her head back, her long auburn hair flowing behind her like the beautiful mane of a chestnut at full gallop. Her face glowed with excitement. She looked over at Jotham next to her, his mouth open in a huge smile. He was laughing, although she couldn't hear it above the beat of the horse's wings. Looking over his shoulder at her, he let out a wild whooping battle cry. Lexus apparently interpreted the sound as a request for greater speed, and incredibly, lunged forward, his wings beating an even faster rhythm.

They were soon within the dense cloud surrounding the tip of the jagged brown mountainous tooth. As they flew into the yellowish gray mist, they were immediately buffeted by a sense of utter desolation and nameless terror. It dropped down upon them with the suddenness of a metal grate.

The three horses landed on the peak where a terrifying bleakness insinuated itself over them like a humid blanket. Cloying tentacles of fear wrapped around them with surprising force and rapidity. As exhilarating as had been their flight up to the mountain, the plummeting of their spirits into dark dread was even more intense.

The white chargers bent their necks low, allowing the three Paladins to dismount onto the dreadful plain. With a chorus of neighs and loud whinnies of encouragement, interspersed with a great tossing of manes and stamping of hooves, the horses leaped into the mist and flew away.

The Paladins felt as if all hope had gone. A numbing terror wrapped itself tightly about them. Their eyes darted over the ghastly peak; there was no place to hide. Despite themselves, they began to move forward. With each step, they were enveloped more deeply in fearful apprehension that had a life of its own. It battered them with hammer-like blows. Unable to escape, the Paladins were nonetheless being compelled to go forward.

The sandals on their feet clung to the marshy ground as they trudged toward the evil lake and the solitary edifice that dominated the landscape on the far shore. The sticky mud made sucking sounds, as if urging them to retreat.

Ghastly tree stems, blasted by decay, ringed the sullen waters of the black and lurid lake that lay between them and the derelict building. It lay like the eye of a monster frozen open in death; its still waters glazed in unruffled luster. Over the surface of the dank pond reeked a pestilent yellow vapor—dull, sluggish and thick—stinging the nostrils of the Paladins with its sulfuric stench. Their stomachs churning and their hearts as leaden as the reeking mist, they trudged up to the miry shore and stopped.

Across the water lay Ghnostar's Lair. The castle stood out against the unremitting flatness of the marshy summit, flanked on one side by rank swamp grass, and on the other by scattered, decayed trunks. The deteriorated building gave off an aura of excessive antiquity and decay. It had once been an impressive fortress; though now, its large gray stones were fissured and cracked. The tops of its three major towers were crumbled and diseased, its ramparts moldy and fallen in on themselves in rubbled heaps. The discoloration of the walls was great. Black fungi overspread the exterior and hung in a tangled webwork. Rotting cobwebs of dark mold climbed through the vacant eye-like windows. Although the stronghold appeared deserted, they knew that Ghnostar could appear at any moment. A foreboding horror, an awareness of impending disaster, draped itself over them. This sinister expectancy tightened like a noose. Coal black clouds skudded hurriedly, plastering inky layers across the sky, as if rushing to blot out the light. Within minutes, the blackness of the water matched the churning blackness of the sky. Light and sound had now been sucked up in the voracious horror of Ghnostar's domain.

The three warriors were in the grip of such intense fear that they could barely breathe. Carisa's body was trembling. Bart was taking in air in short, quick gasps, his hands shaking. Their gaze was fixed on the black lake in awful anticipation. Jotham couldn't stop his knees from quivering. If he didn't do something, he knew they would be overcome before the battle even began. His mind reeled in near panic; he was immobilized by the dreadful watery eye that lay open at his feet staring into his soul.

Jotham broke free of its fixed empty gaze and looked again at the castle. The derelict castle glared evilly at him. It seemed to be floating on the surface of the mist, its broken windows transformed into the empty eye sockets of a fleshless skull. That image shook a memory loose and freed Jotham momentarily from an hypnotic stranglehold. He suddenly understood that the battle had already been joined. The assault had begun the moment they set foot on the ghastly mountain top. While remaining hidden, Ghnostar had been mercilessly pummeling them with fear—his most formidable weapon.

The stillness grew even more unnerving. It was as if all sound had been swallowed up by the dense fog. The hairs on their necks bristled with an ominous expectation of a pervasive evil as old as time itself.

Something was coming.

Suddenly, an extended series of ragged lightning bolts tore open the vault of the dark cloudy sky, casting a lurid radiance on the crumbling edifice. The sullen waters began to glow with a phosphorescent light, revealing its depths. At the bottom of the lagoon, a grotesque shape became visible. As it swam, it released hot currents of evil that bubbled and popped on the water's torpid surface.

Jotham's racing hopelessness threatened to drown him. But the barrage of questions and doubts that assailed him was now interrupted by a firm, yet infinitely still, voice. The simple phrase they had recited on the causeway was now throbbing inside him like a two-note bass refrain: "Fear not . . . fear not . . . fear not."

Calming words began to quietly resist Ghnostar's onslaught: ". . . a sacrifice that's great overcomes all hate." His thoughts seemed to be regaining some order. Abruptly, as if a puzzle piece were falling into place, the lake triggered the memory of Prince Gabriel's sacrifice. *So this was the place.* Law had told them about this evil lagoon—it was where Ghnostar had treacherously killed the Prince and flung his body away.

Jotham suddenly recalled the odd question Carisa had asked at the end of Trellawton's story. He turned to her, his throat finally free. "Carisa! Remember what Law told you about the Prince's clothes?"

309

She did not look up from the water. It was becoming brighter. Silvery ripples, which had been racing from one edge to the other, were now swirling at a rapidly escalating pace. The light from beneath began to turn a burnt orange and pulsate from the center of the pond, radiating outward in concentric circles. Along the shoreline, the decayed trunks caught the lurid radiance and shone like ghostly specters.

He grabbed her shoulders. "Carisa, listen! . . . He confirmed your guess that Prince Gabriel's clothes were made of white linen."

Bart tore his eyes away from the threatening eddy to look at Jotham.

Carisa continued staring at the whirling waters in a stupor.

Jotham shook her, trying to break the spell. "The strips in our pouches are from his tunic!" he yelled. "They're spotted with his blood . . . his sacrifice—"

Bart's expression changed suddenly. "I get it! . . . and Justar's scroll promised that his sacrifice would overcome Ghnostar's hate."

The dull vacancy in Carisa's eyes broke. "Y-Yes," she nodded. "Yes, I remember! You're right," she affirmed hoarsely. "Take them out . . . quick!" With trembling fingers they opened their wallets.

Bart and Jotham wrapped their strips round their upper arms. Carisa tied hers around her head, pulling the loose strands of hair away from her face. A fierceness rose in her eyes which startled them. Unsheathing their swords and raising their shields to chest level, they prepared themselves for the worst.

The unnatural luminescence from the lake was now reflecting fiercely off the dark canopy of heavy black clouds overhead. The surface of the water began to discolor as if saturated with bright red blood. A palpitating gory light spread like an open wound around them. The burbling waves were spinning faster and faster. The creature was rising from the bottom of the pool. Violet beams from two pair of eyes glowered malevolently up at them.

From behind they heard a chorus of hissing and snorting and throaty cackling. The Paladins spun around to see 12 Kravens, each about seven feet tall. They were drenched in the crimson light emanating from the center of the lake.

Bart and Jotham drew close to Carisa, their swords ready for the charge, but something was wrong. Though the entire squad was slavering at them in fury, they appeared to be incapable of coming closer. It was as if an invisible barrier were keeping them at bay. Their yellow eyes were fixed with insane hatred at the cloth strips tied to the Paladins' bodies. Their leathery wings flapped in frustration.

"What's the matter with them?" she asked. "They can't seem to get any closer . . . Is it the strips?"

"Yeah, I bet it is!" Bart said.

Jotham nodded. "Look at them. They're terrified of the cloth!" As he spoke, the Kravens began to growl and shield their faces. Bart and Jotham turned to Carisa, whose strip had begun to glow ruby-red. The Kravens couldn't bear the sight of it.

An explosive hissing of water jerked their attention back to the lake. Ghnostar was rising up from the glistening, oily pool. Black droplets of water dripped from its two lizard-like heads covered with marbled skin. Their scales were a sinister patchwork of red and black. The snouts were identical: long and tapered, almost elegant, except for the steel ring at each tip. As if to compensate for the dullness of the iron bands, gaudy crowns adorned its heads, pressed between two pairs of thick, curving horns that were bent forward. On the frontpiece of one crown was a large milky-white stone with the word *Mentire* inscribed on it, and the other crown had the inscription, *Acusare*.

As its body rose majestically out of the water, they could see that Ghnostar was covered with bands of living color which flowed from one end to the other: waves of brilliant crimson merged with indigo, to bright green, then to golden yellow and back to red; the cycle repeating itself in steady rhythm. It was mesmerizing. The one constant was Ghnostar's heads, which retained their marbled coloration. The colors streamed down its large body, even altering the hue of the double row of spiked horns, which ran over the crest of its back and down its powerful tail. Its smooth, glistening body would have been a showpiece of sinewy perfection were it not for the two protruding nubs on its back and the dull iron rings in its nostrils, testimonies to Justar's mysterious discipline.

The three Paladins stood transfixed. The light from the dragon's body turned their white faces a lurid palate of fluorescent color, "This is not good!" Bart's voice quavered. "Just l-look at it. . . . It's—"

"Get your bows ready," Jotham snapped. Carisa and Bart obeyed, sheathing their swords and preparing to launch their arrows against this monstrous and beguiling enemy.

Ghnostar fixed the trembling warriors with its two pairs of eyes and held them. The Paladins were unprepared for such raw, sensual power. The monstrous lizard glided gracefully onto the shore only 20 yards away, its eyes locked on them. It stood upright on its muscular back legs, over 15 feet tall, the claws on its front arms retracted, its body aglow with fiery light: a living spectrum of shimmering color. Its elegant necks were arced in proud arrogant beauty. Once certain of the Paladins full attention, Ghnostar closed its eyes, and began waving its necks as if they were stroking themselves. It reveled in its own sensuous brilliance, utterly consumed with its own breathtaking beauty. The 12 Kravens dropped to their faces and lay prone on the marshy ground.

Mentire opened its reptilian eyes while Acusare continued to luxuriate, basking in its splendor. "You've been abandoned by your gutless king," Mentire declared, in a resonating rich bass voice. "He's afraid of me. . . . I took his son's life, you know. . . . Ever since, he's been terrified of me. All he does is keep sending poor, pathetic miserable children such as yourselves who wind up as meals for my troops." Its body shook with deep convulsions of laughter. "Do you know what my soldiers call you? 'Ghnostar fodder,'" the lizard snickered malevolently. "I must say, however, you do provide my army with practice." Their enemy roared out in derision.

"I will not dignify you by coming any closer," Ghnostar sneered. "My royal guards will be only too glad to tear you to shreds. They have heard of you and have been anticipating their revenge." The dragon looked down at his warriors.

"Arise," it bellowed, rancid spittle raining over them.

The Kravens leaped to their padded feet, their black tails flicking in anticipation.

"Attack!"

The Kravens shuddered, their eyes fixed on the glowing strips and on the three shields which had begun to burn with the same ruby glow.

"Keep your shields up!" Jotham yelled, "I don't think they can break through that power either—look at how they're glowing."

Ghnostar shrieked, "Attack, damn you. . . . I said attack!"

"Don't move!" Jotham thundered.

Driven beyond their fear of the Paladins by terror of their merciless commander, the Kravens lunged forward. When they were within a wingspan of the three, they were suspended in the air and then were catapulted backwards. It was as if they had hurled themselves against an invisible trampoline and had been flung off. They were tossed into a snarling, tangled heap, the talons on their wings raking each other in frustration.

Ghnostar roared in fury: an incredible, bellowing, air-shaking, mind-chilling sound. "You miserable, impotent fools . . . I will kill them myself," it bellowed.

It threw its twin heads back, slicing the sky with its horns. When its eyes were averted, Carisa fitted a dart into her bow. As the heads came down, she stepped forward, aimed and released.

There was a dull, thudding sound. The steel shaft entered Ghnostar's chest.

The twin jaws opened wide, one snout emitted a snarling laugh and the other closed down on the dart, pulling it out easily. Acusare snapped it like a twig between its front teeth.

"That was a mistake," Mentire growled. "You've made me angry, little girl. Now I'll have to hurt you."

The beast lowered its heads, with jaws open, preparing to attack. The earth shook, the huge lizard's back legs churning the marshy ground, showering gobs of mud as it began to race toward them.

Carisa aimed her crossbow and released another dart. Bart did the same. Ghnostar moved with unexpected fluidity. With a sweep of one neck, it knocked Carisa's dart aside; and shifting its body sideways, side-stepped Bart's arrow, which slid past merely scratching the dragon's scales. It lowered its head further, the four razor horns aimed for their chests. An ear-splitting hiss of rage poured out of the slavering jaws as it charged forward.

Bart and Carisa threw their bows down and yanked out their swords. Jotham had Abe's ax in his hands.

As the horns reached out for them, the Paladins shifted sideways and twisted their bodies, like bullfighters sidestepping a charging bull. Carisa lost her footing in the mud and slid onto her back. The pounding feet thundered past, splashing brown drops over her. The horns grazed Jotham's tunic. As they slid by, Jotham lunged, swinging his ax, slicing a thick spike off Mentire's head. On the opposite side, Bart's sword forced Acusare's head to jerk away, but not before he'd cut off the tips of both horns.

With relief at the surprising ease of this initial victory, Bart yelled at their enemy, "Take that, you filthy lizard." The sword in his hand was as shaky as his voice. Although his legs felt wobbly, his confidence was rushing back.

Ghnostar shrieked in anger, its body lifted high in the air, its front claws fully extended, gleaming a sinister ebony above them. Ghnostar trained its burning violet eyes on the exhilarated warriors and gazed at them with a disconcerting and scornful stare, then bent over and began to turn away.

This is going to be easier than I imagined, Bart thought to himself. *Ghnostar is all bluff, he just wants to try and scare us to death. . . .*

Bart reached to pick up his bow.

Jotham opened his mouth to scream a warning, but Ghnostar was too quick.

As it turned its body, the dragon spun its long, powerful tail around and with amazing agility struck the Paladins a crushing blow. They were sent flying toward the crouched Kravens who had been anticipating their commander's ploy. The shields were knocked out of the Paladins' hands; their wrist straps were all that prevented them from also losing their weapons.

With the Paladins' protective shields gone and their strips covered with mud, the Kravens seized the advantage. Immediately, three Kravens leaped on Jotham, and the rest slashed and tore at each other in a mad frenzy to reach the twins who were lying on their backs. The competition among the pack was vicious; they snarled and fought, biting savagely, drawing blood. Several Kravens were disabled by severe gouges and limped away angrily, nursing their wounds.

From the sounds to his left, Jotham could tell that his comrades had retained their blades and were using them on their attackers. Jotham had clung to Abe's ax and with one swipe had taken off the arm of one Kraven and with a back swing had almost decapitated another. Apparently, the strips were still releasing sufficient energy to allow him to fight with tremendous agility and power. His tunic was shredded, and he'd suffered a long gash along his thigh where savage talons had managed to slice through the mail, but now only one of his attackers remained. Jotham slung his shield over his back, unsheathed his sword and rushed at the Kraven, swinging both sword and ax at the vulture's head.

It leaped into the air as Jotham charged, the claws at the tips of its wide wings nearly blinding him, but ducking at the last moment, only cut into his cheek. Jotham flung the ax and buried it in the creature's chest. It exploded. To his left, he saw three Kravens sitting on the marsh, snarling and licking at flank and head wounds. One Kraven was on his back motionless. On the run, Jotham uncoiled his whip and ran screaming at the creatures who were swarming over his comrades.

He pulled free a shield that was sticking out of the mud and flung it in Carisa's direction. She was on her knees facing two attackers, her back exposed to a pouncing predator. The shield struck the Kraven and sent it sprawling. It lay still. Carisa grabbed the shield and held it in front of her.

Jotham's whip snapped, and the huge vulture who had been clawing at Bart's arm disintegrated. Another Kraven was on his friend's chest, his beak closing over Bart's face. The leather lash again coiled back and popped, shredding the vulture's wings. The Kraven shrieked and spun around. Jotham aimed low. His whip blew off the leopard legs. It fell to the ground writhing in agony, then exploded.

The Kravens who were stalking Carisa halted and turned toward the blast. Seizing the opening, Carisa dropped her shield and with both hands thrust her blade through one, pulled it out quickly and stabbed the other through the neck. The black creatures dropped down at her feet moaning. A moment later, they had erupted in acrid smoke.

The Kraven that had been stunned by Jotham's shield had dragged itself quietly behind Bart who was getting to his feet. It pounced forward, but the slurping sound of the marsh gave it away. Bart jerked his head and saw the ambush. All he could do was drop back down on his back. The vulture's talons ripped a chunk of hair from his head as it flew over him, and its claws tore a hole through the mail on his shoulder. Bart screamed in pain, rolled quickly, and jumped on the Kraven's back. He drove his sword into its back until it dropped back down in the muck.

The Paladins flung themselves at the wounded Kravens and slashed them to pieces. Behind them, a loud, grating laugh shook the ground. The huge dragon swaggered forward, its every movement an insolent dismissal. "That was only to soften you up," Mentire jeered.

With a start, the Paladins realized that the horns they had struck off had grown back. The monstrous lizard noticed their surprise. "You didn't think it would really be that easy, did you?" It advanced toward them with menacing grace. Ghnostar stopped and angled its body to look at its castle; the Paladins followed its gaze. From the decrepit stronghold across the lake, four long columns were marching: a full squadron of reinforcements.

Ghnostar's purple tongues flicked hatefully above them. From Acusare's mouth came a flowing stream of invectives, which hit the

Paladins with the stunning rapidity of a bantamweight's jab. As the one horned head spoke, Mentire stared at it with a mixture of worship and envy.

"How can you hope to defeat *me*, Ghnostar the Great, when you were such miserable failures with much lesser foes. You can't stand against me, you pathetic weaklings. You fell for every trick. None of the warriors chosen by Justar were as gullible, puny and ineffective as you've been." The dragon chortled; its split tongue now a formidable weapon.

Bart wiped the blood and muddy water off his face. He had a deep gouge along both cheeks. Acusare bent down, and the Paladins were assaulted with its putrid breath as the chiseled snout drew close to Bart. "Cut yourself shaving?" the lizard questioned maliciously. "Don't you know that it's only for big boys . . . not children?"

Bart's face flushed and his eyes sparked. He didn't have time to fit an arrow into his bow. The hilt of his sword felt hot and slick. It would just have to do.

As if reading his mind, Mentire snarled at him. "Don't think that your little play toys will have the same effect on me as on my inept soldiers. My skin is much too strong and—" Ghnostar stopped, turned its twin necks to gaze lustfully at its shimmering splendor, "—much too beautiful to make the slightest impression." Ghnostar snorted and threw its horned heads up in disgust. "As I said, you have no hope. . . . You should never have entered my domain." Angry ripples of luminous color flowed in currents across its sleek side. Contempt seeped like rancid oil from each preening movement.

A wave of futility crashed over the Paladins. In comparison to their dazzling opponent, they were nothing. They felt brutally exposed: inept, foolish and pathetic. Carisa bit down on her trembling lip to keep from crying out her humiliation. Bart's eyes were glazed over with tears, and he was swallowing great gulps in his effort to keep them from running down his face. Mentire's red eyes took in their distress and slowly bared its fangs, curling its upper lip back in disdain. He let out a contented, purring hiss.

Acusare lowered its head to look straight at Jotham and changed its tack. ". . . And you," its eyes narrowed wickedly, "you had such high opinions of yourself, didn't you?" Ghnostar sniggered malevolently. "But, a miserable failure is what you turned out to be. . . . You're . . . a zero, less than zero." Acusare sneered at him, its pronged tongue extended in derision. "Let me put your suspicions to rest—you—are—a—loser."

Jotham's heart turned to lead. Ghnostar was verbalizing the message he'd battled all his life. It was as if the dragon itself had scripted it. Jotham's head spun in a whirlwind of shame. Ghnostar had stripped him to the core. A roaring filled his ears.

A firm hand grasped his arm. He heard Carisa's gentle voice whisper: "It's not true, Jotham! Don't listen to it; listen to the King!"

He turned a wooden glance toward her.

"Listen to the King's voice," she repeated.

The rushing, spinning void slowly evaporated. Strength returned to his body.

Ghnostar's cruel voice was continuing as it turned his body to prepare for a final charge. ". . . and now I'm going to crush you like the miserable little worm you are."

He could barely hear the dragon's poisonous, intimidating barrage, for Jotham was now listening to another voice. His being was resonating with the rich, reassuring words of his King. "My child, I love you. . . . Do not fear. . . . Do not fear." A warm tingling prickled from the tips of his toes and fingers to the top of his head. His hands were trembling, they felt massive and strangely muscular. Power was entering into him.

He felt invincible.

Chapter Forty Five

Sheet lightning ripped through the dark expanse, coating the combatants with a ghastly bluish pallor. The Paladins resembled corpses frozen in battle.

The lightning flashed again, hitting a splintered trunk near the oncoming Kravens. It exploded in a mighty shower of orange, white and blue sparks. The columns marching toward them from the derelict castle fell apart as the reinforcements scattered for safety.

Ghnostar's snouts were dripping saliva, which fell to the earth like thick raindrops. The lizard flung itself high in an ecstasy of triumph, then lowered its twin heads, its horns thrust out menacingly. With its back trunk-like legs, it savaged the ground, the earth beneath quaking as if in terror. The tremors caused the water to ripple and splatter against the far shore. Ghnostar's jaws snapped as it prepared to launch itself against the three warriors, who were pressed against the brink of the lagoon.

Once more the dragon lifted its glorious body to its full terrifying height. A lightning bolt splintered the ebony sky, catching Ghnostar in horrific splendor. Jotham was dazzled by their enemy's raw magnificence. Instantly, a picture leaped to Jotham's mind: the story painting in the cave. In the last scene, the stick figure drawing of a dragon had something clinging to its neck.

He suddenly knew what he was supposed to do.

The horns were now level with them. Jotham yelled, "Raise your shields but stand your ground. Don't take a step back."

The ground was shaking as Ghnostar raced at them.

They lifted their shields high. As the dragon lunged toward them, Jotham's eyes were trained on their enemy. Every brilliant scale along its glistening body stood out in individual stark relief. Drops of saliva fell from its jaws like brilliant jewels. The dragon's eyes were blood-red; yet despite its palpable hatred, its appearance was stunning.

318

From deep inside Jotham, there rose an unshakable confidence and a wild fearlessness. Justar the Great General was pouring his courage into him, and every cell in his body was being saturated with it. A formidable shout poured out of his throat with shattering power, "Stop! We resist you in Justar's name."

Ghnostar slammed against their shields and was flung back as if it had hit a granite wall, his twin heads flopping fitfully. The monster lay on its side, its chest heaving.

The strip around Jotham's arm was throbbing and had turned a deep red. A hotness was bubbling inside him, as if his blood had become charged with fire. From his toes to the top of his feet, he was awash in a tingling, ecstatic strength which would have been frightening had it not been so sweet. He felt his bones and muscles expand as if he were gaining an incredible mass and density. He stared at his hands; they were vibrating. His fingers were thicker and had a tensile strength they'd never had before.

Carisa's eyes were fixed on Jotham. When he had shouted at the dragon, she thought she'd glimpsed another face superimposing itself over his—a brighter, more intense face, one made for glory. As she watched, Jotham tore his red strip loose and raced forward. He jumped, placing one foot on the ring in Acusare's snout, and swung around to grab ahold of its neck. Ghnostar staggered to its feet and tried to shake Jotham loose. The dragon made several listless attempts, but Jotham had grabbed a horn in each hand and refused to be dislodged. His legs were wrapped around the smooth scales of its sinewy neck, and with each swing Jotham seemed to attach himself more tenaciously to their foe.

Bart squinted his eyes. Jotham's entire body appeared to be glowing with the same golden light he had seen around Abe when he had rushed Abner's dais in Castle Orion. His hair fairly bristled with an electric energy. Carisa looked over at Bart, her eyes wide in amazement. There was a nobility and ferocity in Jotham's face that was frightening. The shape of his body was actually altering. His arms and legs were growing larger and his back was definitely broader. Everything about him appeared to have been enlarged and made more solid. The air around his head crackled with the currents of golden energy which encased him.

Jotham gripped Acusare's neck with his knees. Power was flowing through him. As Ghnostar bucked and shook, swinging and jerking its neck with increasing savagery, Jotham knew he could not be dislodged. He sensed that his King was not only with him, but somehow in him, and that victory was certain. With unhurried deliberation, he yanked the strip tightly around Acusare's twisting neck. Tossing his head back in triumph, Jotham screamed out a wild, undulating battle cry. The harsh ferocity of their captain's exultation sent shivers through his comrades beneath him.

With desperate brutality, the dragon spun, throwing its head high. Using his opponent's thrust to his advantage, Jotham flung himself away, twisted gracefully in the air, landing with both feet solidly on the ground.

A trumpeting shriek split the air. It was so loud the Paladins had to clap their hands over their ears. Acusare whipped its head back and forth in a terrible agony while Mentire snapped and raked at the red noose, which was now puckering the marbled skin as it continued to tighten on its own. Acusare's eyes were bulging, and foam was pouring from its lips. In a frenzy of fury and pain, Mentire bared its long fangs and tore madly at the linen. There was a horrible, snapping crunch as Acusare's proud head was ripped off along with the cloth.

Blood coursed down the stump of its neck as Ghnostar stood weaving back and forth before them. Mentire sucked in loud gasps of air, and its sides moved in and out with pain and exertion. The flow of colors along its body slowed. They soon came to a complete stop. Ghnostar's beautiful scales were quickly turning the color of rust. Its eyes were pools of yellow hate. Mentire's sinuous tongue licked at the blood covering its snout.

"You . . . miserable . . . little vermin . . ." it panted. "How dare you . . . think you can stand . . . against the great Ghnostar. You are cowards . . . hiding behind your shields. I spit on you and . . . your king." It coughed, spraying bloody spittle over them.

Carisa felt her strip throbbing against her temples. Slinging her shield around her neck, she pulled the linen loose. It was glowing again as she held it up in front of her. She motioned for Bart to do the same. He held his in front of him with both hands held high. Sparks of golden light shot out from the linen.

"We stand against you in the name of Justar the Great General and King!" they yelled. Their flashing eyes were as hard as polished steel.

A jagged bolt of lighting sprayed light, striking the dragon with such force that it made him stumble and fall to his knees. The two Paladins raised their linen again. Another flash of light erupted, then another, but it wasn't lightning. They were dazzling rays of concentrated phosphorescent light shooting out from their spotted cloths. They struck Acusare's head repeatedly, searing it with hot rays. Black smoke was pouring out of the dragon's ears and nose as the light beams burned through its rust-brown scales. The air stank like fish and rubber being put to the torch. The earth shook beneath them as their enemy's massive feet scraped the ground. Its tail flailed, thrashing up and down in agony.

Ghnostar gave one final earth-shattering bellow as its remaining skull erupted in flames. It stumbled, tottered, then fell headlong into the dark, waiting waters of the still pond. A rocket of incandescent sparks exploded into the sky as the dragon's body smacked the black pool. With a loud intake of air, the foul mist was sucked into the plume of fire, rushing into the vortex of shooting embers, turning the flames a vivid violet-orange.

The squadron of Kravens behind the Paladins were transfixed, their curved beaks frozen in open dismay. They stood rooted to their places, an agonized expectation of doom holding their paws in an iron grip.

Waves were dashing about the lake, reveling with delight over the removal of the oppressive, stagnating cloud. The water was becoming increasingly clear, and within moments the Paladins could see to the very bottom. A white, glowing shape was spinning in the depths of the crystalline waters. Slowly, the currents on the surface restrained their celebrations and began whirling in concert with the light which was rising majestically to the surface.

The Kravens' bodies were jerking spasmodically. Their lower limbs were trembling with exertion. Ghnostar's elite troops were wrestling with invisible forces pressing them to the ground.

The clouds began to roll backwards in all directions, uncovering a circle of clear blue sky directly over the lake. At the center of the pool, the whirling water was rising. Suddenly, a geyser of brilliant white burst into the air straight up into the circle of blue sky. It spun with the power of a tornado. The Kravens began shrieking in rage as up through the twirling tower of water a glowing figure rose in regal splendor. He wore a crown over his thick mane of red-gold hair which tumbled to his shoulders. He had no beard, but the resemblance was unmistakable.

It was the Prince—King Justar's son.

He was standing on the crest of a mighty fountain, his eyes a blazing fire. The geyser bent toward the Paladins in a graceful arc. It deposited the Prince next to a large tree, which only moments before had been a withered trunk. The entire mountaintop was now covered with great trees whose tops seemed to touch the puffy white clouds.

The Prince stood with his back to the three bowing warriors, whose swords points were embedded in the ground before them. He stared fiercely at the squadron of Kravens who were weakening in their struggle. At least 100 had fallen to the ground on knees bent in reluctant homage. The Prince lifted his great sword and pointed it at the front row. Their legs buckled, and they fell forward on all fours. The remaining columns dropped instantly to their knees, their wings spread out before them, as if huge boulders had flattened them. Although their backs were bent, the Kravens in the first row continued to resist. Every muscle in their bodies quivered with humiliation as they gave unwilling honor to the Prince. Finally, a host of them gave in and fell prostrate, their beaks thrust into the mud.

Gabriel stood before them, his broad chest heaving, and drove his sword point into the ground inches from a gigantic Kraven—the captain of the squad. Its bulbous vulture's head was down, but its eyes were turned up in arrogant challenge. The Prince pulled his sword out, carefully placed its muddy point in the center of the Kraven's long, black neck and waited.

In a voice quivering with rage, the Kraven growled hoarsely: "Justar . . . is . . . King."

"Again. All of you," commanded the Prince, his voice ringing with authority, "and louder!"

This time, the entire squadron snarled out their sullen declaration. The Paladins kept their heads low but heard Prince Gabriel whisper something to the Kravens' leader. This was followed by the sound of their enemies trudging back toward the dismal fortress.

Jotham felt the hands of the Prince on his head. He looked up. The young Prince's gray-green eyes glowed with approval. He was smiling broadly with a playful expression as if he'd just heard a humorous story. "Paladins, you have acquitted yourselves splendidly. My father's plan worked well. As I told Ellwynn, it turned out to be a quite a trick indeed." His voice was like Justar's, except with a delightful, winsome undercurrent of laughter. "You are to be congratulated, Paladins. Your reward awaits you, but before it is yours, there is one more task . . ." he turned toward Jotham, "and you must each do it alone."

Above him, Jotham could hear the faint throb of mighty wings approaching. Lexus spun in a graceful circle and landed on his back legs, followed by Spinx and Excall. When their forelegs touched ground, they immediately bowed their strong necks giving honor to the King's son. Their left wings were retracted covering their flanks, and their right wings were fully extended and covered their heads and legs. They remained in that position until Prince Gabriel greeted them, laying a hand on their muscular white shoulders.

Lexus raised his head and rested his muzzle on the Prince's hand before standing erect. "He will take you in goodspeed, Jotham. And do not worry about your friends," he said gesturing to Bart and Carisa. "You will see them in due time, after their mission is complete."

Spinx and Excall, who were standing expectantly behind the two Paladins, neighed excitedly.

The Prince continued, "I extend to you my thanks and that of all true Issatarians. You have defeated a mighty foe. . . . You are heroes, each one. You have fought bravely and gained great glory and immortal fame. . . . I salute you!"

Jotham climbed onto the broad back of the stallion. With a triple beat of its wings, they were in the air. As they flew over the lagoon, there was a loud splintering crack. Lexus looked down, and Jotham's body pitched forward dangerously. He gripped the horse's mane with both hands, causing Lexus to pull up quickly. Spreading his wings, the war horse angled his body to glide in a half-circle.

The sight below was shocking. Prince Gabriel was standing alone on the shore opposite the decayed castle, his sword extended. Great streams of bluish flame were shooting out from the blade, scorching both the castle and the Kravens that had returned to it. Large gaping fissures were opening up along the walls and ran crookedly out into the ground at their base. From above, it looked as if a claw were shredding the edifice, beginning at the tops of its walls and continuing down, scraping deep gouges in the earth. These cracks widened rapidly; then with the force of a fiery whirlwind and with the rushing sound of thundering waterfalls, the stone walls were torn apart and tumbled burning into the yawning cavity that had opened to receive them.

As the ground drew itself together, extinguishing all evidence of the stronghold's existence, the sound of a tolling bell shattered the quiet. It tolled

323

seven times and stopped. Directly beneath him, Jotham saw a huge, shimmering bubble floating up from the bottom of the lake. It rose quickly to the surface, swayed pendulously for several moments, then popped, spraying water in all directions. The towering ramparts of an exquisite castle emerged, resplendent in gleaming white marble. It was shaped in a perfect circle with seven round towers around the outer wall. Colorful banners and flags waved from each point.

Lexus dipped down suddenly, sending Jotham's stomach into his throat as he flew past the purple pennant that flapped at the tip of the highest tower. It declared the title of the castle's master. Jotham stared in amazement; a tingle ran over him.

On it was inscribed his name, "Lord Jotham."

With a low whinny, Lexus twisted and sped down to the plains below.

* * * * * * * *

In less time than it took to fly up to the gnarled mountain, they were speeding over a deep, lush valley. The thick, luxurious grass over which they flew appeared to be waist-high. They sped over rounded green-gold hills and broad meadows. Jotham's vantage point revealed vistas of higher hills overgrown with chaparral, valleys within the main valley where groves of tall, leafy trees flourished. Lexus slowed, then dove into a grove dominated by an especially large tree in the middle.

Jotham leaped off the horse's back and found himself in a silent glen staring up at a formidable tree. From the huge gnarled trunk came a deep, resonating groan. A current of cold electricity shivered up his spine.

He was staring at the mammoth oak from his nightmares.

Chapter Forty Six

Although the huge oak was much larger than it had appeared in his dreams, there was no question that it was the one he'd seen countless times before. Its mournful cry exerted a terrible yet familiar attraction over him, as though the tree were willing him to draw near. Irresistibly Jotham was drawn to the massive tree. Placing one foot slowly in front of the other, he approached with apprehension and a thrill of expectancy.

Would his questions finally be answered?

Standing a body length away from the huge tree, he detected a faint shudder coursing through the ancient knobby trunk and into the labyrinth of branches overhead. Pressure began gathering painfully in his chest, threatening to burst forth in a torrent of emotion.

The mournful sound shifted subtly, and Jotham recognized its tone immediately. He'd heard it in the vision of his father. It was the same sorrowful groan his father had uttered on his knees in front of the crucifix. It shook him. The oak groaned more insistently. Tears of compassion formed in his eyes. He was now trembling in front of the towering trunk, the weight of his blade heavy against his left thigh. His hands shook, but he knew there would be no need for either sword or knife—the hatred and anger had disappeared.

He lurched forward, his last steps blinded by tears, and thrust out his empty hand. Palm open, he laid it on the gnarled trunk. To his surprise, he was no longer wracked with sobs, and his tears were gone. In a voice resonating with authority, he declared: "You are free, in Justar's name!"

Immediately, Jotham heard what sounded like an intake of breath, a deep, profound gasp. The entire tree began shaking convulsively, its shuddering roots making the ground tremble underneath him. The mournful groan collapsed suddenly into a roaring bellow which sliced through Jotham like a cleaver. The sound swelled around him, crescendoing in swirling currents until it drove him to the ground.

Abruptly, everything became ominously still. Cautiously, he looked up and pulled himself erect. With a mighty, triumphant shake, as though it were casting off a crushing restraint, a rich, earthy cascade of relief broke out from the tree's core. Deep peals of laughter erupted with such unrestrained delight that Jotham was swept up into its joyful, infectious torrents. Riotous laughter erupted out of him, convulsing him and causing him to lose his balance. He fell backwards, holding his stomach, laughing until tears streamed down his face.

From all around the glen the other trees responded with equally uncontrollable glee. The sweet melody with its richly layered harmonies washed over Jotham, drenching him in waves of delight. He rested his weight on the trunk and attempted to stand. His entire being resonated to the music's pulsating rhythm and bold syncopation. The majestic symphony encased in sheets of breathtaking color was almost more than he could bear. It captivated and thrilled him, causing his heart to ache with the sheer weight of its beauty.

The fountain of resplendent color and sound began pouring into him like a crystalline waterfall changing his very essence. As it coursed through him he could feel himself becoming somehow more solid, more real. Unable any longer to remain upright he dropped, trembling, on his face. He remained motionless until something brushed his feet. Jotham turned his head and saw that the lower branches of the oak were bent toward him, shyly covering his feet. And next to him was a shimmering stream flowing from the heart of the glen.

The music and shouting quieted. A tingling anticipation swept through the grove. Suddenly a thunderous voice bellowed out the words they had all been waiting to hear: "Let the Dance begin!"

A thrill of expectant joy surged through Jotham as the oak slowly drew itself erect and began to sway gracefully.

Peals of praise began to erupt around him. The shouts: "Freedom! . . . The lords of the kingdom have been revealed! . . . Free at last!" catapulted over and collided with the roaring declarations: "Liberation Day has come—the curse is broken. . . . All glory to Justar . . . Justar is King!" This ecstatic cacophony coalesced into one triumphant symphony, and was joined by shimmering currents of light and music, which were pouring down from the sky. They swept over him welcoming him in a warm embrace.

326

Jotham realized instantly that a door had been opened to him that all his life, except for brief, tantalizing moments, had been closed shut. He knew that he was no longer outside and alone; he was home. Joy was no longer apart from him, it was now within—and in a way he could not explain—he was within it. Strangely, this joy seemed to be not so much an emotion but a powerful living thing. He felt it flowing with vitality through his veins as if it had become his lifeblood.

Gradually, the music began again, growing louder with each movement. The tree's branches kept time with the glorious music, which had now been joined by a vast chorus of voices. And weaving independently through the iridescent stream was a solitary antiphonal line which transfixed him. The limbs of the trees in the grove were swaying in an ecstasy of delight. As the leafy branches swung in a dance of deliverance, some began clapping together in exuberant off-tempo, adding a delightful counterpoint to the music.

A song erupted from Jotham's mouth. He didn't recognize the unusual words, but he knew instantly that it was an affirmation of allegiance to the Great King. He leaped impulsively into motion, his joyful song of praise compelling him to move. His legs carried him bounding over the soft grass in long, effortless strides along the bank of the wide stream that was fast becoming a mighty river. Mischievous, happy ripples followed him as he raced by. The tips of the tiny waves caught the sun's rays and refracted them into millions of glorious prisms. Soon he was running inside a canopy of a thousand dancing rainbows. The faster he ran, the more strength he seemed to possess. He sensed energy flowing into his legs, propelling him forward, giddy with delight. The exhilarating liberty of sheer speed overcame him, and he leaped delightedly into the air.

Infused with an impulse of irrepressible joy, he leapt higher, spinning in a graceful turn. What amazed him even more than accomplishing the move was his ability to continue to spin effortlessly with perfect control.

Caught up in his exultant dance, Jotham leapt, spun, then landed softly, continuing to run with tireless exuberance, only to bound back into the air in an ecstasy of joy. He was a participant in the Great Dance, for he was one whose heart had been set free.

Beginning another arcing vault, he was frozen in mid-air by the sight of a majestic figure standing by the river. It was King Justar!

He was glowing in a brilliant radiance, both arms in the air with his face upturned. Jotham was stunned. The Great King was singing and from his throat were pouring out that rich, entrancing antiphonal music. The notes pierced him, stealing his breath away. He dropped to the ground like a stone.

King Justar tossed back his splendid, silvery-white locks and let out a thunderous laugh that shook every bone in Jotham's body. It reverberated through the ground and into the sky. Terror gripped Jotham as his body resonated, threatening to explode. It was only the King's hand on his back which kept him from shattering into a million particles.

A fearful hush fell like the dense shadow of an eclipse. Jotham lifted his head and raised himself to his knees. The King stood in front of him, dressed in a glistening white tunic with purple border, the attire of a Warrior Paladin. On his chest was the royal insignia, and his head was graced by the elegant three-pronged crown. The sparkling jewels in each prong refracted bolts of light in thousands of glowing colors. In his hand was a huge double-edged broadsword which was pointing straight at his heart. The sword drew nearer and came to rest when its razor point touched Jotham's chest.

"Paladin! Stand and give an account!" rang out the Great King's voice in a tone of uncompromising authority.

Jotham felt himself being lifted off the ground and planted firmly on numbed feet. He was riveted in place by Justar's gaze. The King's eyes no longer glowed with warm delight; instead, the golden flecks were as sharp as diamonds. They gripped him in a ferocious fire of unyielding justice. There was no hint of compassion, only a flashing, a glowing of fierce, regal intensity.

"You have been given much," King Justar declared. "We shall see how much you have given away." The sword's tip held steady over Jotham's heart. "What you have kept for yourself you will lose, what you have given up, you can keep forever."

As the King uttered these portentous words, a shimmering light began dancing around his head and crown, until fire erupted out of him in all directions. From within the raging flames, Justar's burning eyes remained locked upon the young Paladin.

Jotham felt the point of the fiery broadsword penetrate. The pain was brief but scalding. The blade was withdrawn and placed on his head. A searing inferno poured through the core of Jotham's being, burning and purifying as it surged through him.

As the heat slowly diminished, Jotham was startled to see images racing before his eyes. They resembled parchments, and on them were scenes that had taken place since entering Issatar. Vivid pictures, freezing every painful incident, every shabby act and amazingly, every thought, sped past his vision. As they coursed by they burst into flames, the ashes disintegrating in the breeze. Occasionally, a parchment would resist the fire, curl in upon itself and fall heavily at his feet. The poignant train of images seemed to flow by in an endless panorama. Mercifully, the stream finally came to an end.

Jotham dropped his head, unable to bear the Great General's gaze.

His eyes grew wide.

At his feet, scattered before him on the grass, lay piles of jewels. There were a handful of small diamonds, and a few the size of walnuts. A large red ruby and an even larger emerald lay on its side touching his foot. He bent over in amazement and hesitantly picked up the green stone. It glowed with an alluring flame as he held it up to the sky.

"That is for the pain you suffered in my name."

Taking up the diamonds and letting them run through his fingers, he heard Justar say, ". . . and those are for the tears you shed for others."

Raising the ruby, Jotham drunk in its vermilion hues. Justar's hand was on his head, and his gentle voice said, "My son, that is yours for the blood you shed for me."

Jotham's legs gave way, and he fell heavily to his knees, choking sobs wrenching his body. He felt so ashamed, so utterly unworthy. He could have done so much more, could have been so much better for his King.

With his hand still resting softly on Jotham's head, Justar declared in that melodious voice that had filled the skies with shimmering joy: "Jotham, I am well pleased with you."

Jotham winced as if he'd been struck in the stomach; all his breath was driven from him. The unexpected accolade caused his head to spin. He fell flat on his face, all strength drained from his body. He was as limp and powerless as a little child. Unbearable gratitude threatened to burst his heart. Disbelief had been eradicated by the exquisite power of those words. He felt as if the jagged shards of his being were being welded into a completeness he'd never known.

This peaceful serenity was abruptly shattered by a brutal collage of bitter memories. Through his mind again raced the painful scenes of failures and defeat, welling up before him like moldering phantasms rising from the grave. Waves of humiliation swept over him until he felt he would drown.

"Look at me," Justar commanded, his hand lifting Jotham's chin.

On his knees, Jotham looked straight into the face of his King who beamed down at him, love and pleasure pulsating from him. "The past is forgiven and forever forgotten. It is not ever to be brought to mind. The old is gone and all is new; to signify this newness, I give you a new name," he declared.

A thrill of gratitude overwhelmed Jotham. He scooped up the jewels and poured out the beautiful gems in a cascade of lavish color over Justar's feet.

"Here . . . these . . ." Jotham fumbled for words, ". . . these . . . are for you. Thank you, thank you my King," Jotham almost sang out the words.

The King bent down, picked up the gems and held them tightly to his chest. When he unclasped his hands, Justar was holding a shining crown resplendent with the precious stones.

Jotham bent down on one knee.

The Great General King, pressed the crown firmly upon the Paladin's brow. He held out his sword, touching it lightly to Jotham's shoulder.

Gazing deeply at him, Justar proclaimed: "My child, your new name shall be Lord Justian the Righteous. I have met with your friends. They each have also received a new name; they, like you, are not to reveal it to anyone."

He sheathed his broadsword and stepped back, looking down approvingly upon the crowned Paladin. "Justian, the enemy you have defeated will not be your last. You will fight other foes, some visible and others not, though no less formidable because unseen. . . . Go now dear son, your band awaits you."

With those words, the King was gone.

He was surprised to hear a gentle, apologetic whinny behind him. Turning he saw Lexus standing in the knee-high grass, tossing his white mane. Jotham strode over and placed his hand on the horse's head, and instead of rearing back, a shiver of delight twitched through its muscular body. Lexus bent his proud neck acknowledging Jotham's regal status. With one easy leap, Jotham was on top of the war horse who sped upward with lightning speed.

Moments later they were circling downward, approaching the glen and the huge oak. Underneath its branches, Jotham could make out other mounted war horses. The riders were looking up at him waving their arms; a golden light surrounding them.

Jotham's heart swelled. There were three horses and riders, and one of the riders looked wonderfully familiar. As he drew nearer, he was certain. The dark curly hair and lopsided grin were unmistakable.

His brother Abe was standing in his stirrups, waving his sword and shouting out Jotham's name.

Chapter Forty Seven

Before Lexus planted all four feet on the ground, Jotham had leaped off and thrown his arms around his brother. He hugged Abe fiercely. The heaving in his chest choked off everything he wanted to say. The pressure became intolerable. Two rattling breaths tore loose, then he could restrain himself no longer. Hard, racking sobs broke from his lips as the tears poured down his cheeks.

Finally, Jotham was able to catch his breath and whisper, "Abe, I didn't think I'd . . ." his throat closed up again. Swallowing the painful lump, he managed to ask hoarsely, "What happened to you? How did . . . ?"

Abe tried to speak but couldn't.

"It was incredible," Bart exulted. Jotham looked over at his friend and noticed that he was also wearing a crown. His was studded with scores of rubies and emeralds.

Bart continued, "Prince Gabriel told us to go back to Ursula's Fortress to see Abe. When we entered the room where they were keeping him . . ." Bart stopped and looked up at his sister, "Carisa you tell it, after all you were the one . . ."

Carisa shook her head and motioned for him to continue. He shrugged, "Okay, anyway, there was this bluish light shining all around the table. Carisa walked over to Abe and placed her hands on his chest, like it was a perfectly normal thing to do. All of a sudden, Abe just sat up. He scared the daylights out of me, I can tell you!"

Carisa was smiling. Her brown eyes were so warm and alive. They were sparkling with joy and a wonderful serenity Jotham had not seen before. His heart ached at the sight of her. She wore an elegant coronet; it was clustered with sapphires and the diamond in the center was twice as big as any gem on Jotham's crown. He smiled happily at her, knowing it was her reward for selfless service.

"The first thing Abe said to me was that he wanted to get some hamburgers and French fries," Carisa laughed. "We had to remind him where he was—"

"Yeah, I had to settle for roast mutton, or something," Abe said, his throat finally free. "It was a sacrifice, but I managed to survive the ordeal. . . ." Abe looked up at his older brother and smiled, sensing an acceptance that surprised him. "By the way, Jo, I like your crown . . ." he stopped and grimaced, his eyes twinkling, "You're not a king by any chance, are you?"

"No, I'm not . . . and yours isn't bad either," Jotham said motioning toward Abe's simple gold circlet with the embossed M made of large pearls as its centerpiece. "It's just like Warrior's." He gripped his brother firmly around the shoulders, needing the reassurance that it was truly Abe standing next to him. "I'm so glad to see you again, man." Jotham's eyes glistened. "I can't believe how much I missed you."

Abe stared down at the grass, "Me too . . ." he murmured. "After I left Orion and was captured by the Ghargs, I thought I'd never see you guys again. . . . Boy, was I an idiot for going off like that."

Carisa leaned over and kissed his cheek. "Don't worry Abe, sometime we'll have to tell you about how brilliant *we've* been."

Jotham's face had grown somber. He dropped his arm from Abe's shoulder, took a step back and motioned for Abe to climb back on his horse. When they were all astride their horses, Jotham unsheathed his sword. "You know guys, one thing I've come to realize—I wish I'd figured it out sooner—was that being named your Captain was an incredible privilege. It was an honor I took for granted." He looked at each of them, his eyes bright with emotion. "I didn't deserve the position and I didn't deserve you guys. . . . I was a rotten leader and failed you in a lot of ways."

Bart was about to interject, but Carisa's hand on his arm stopped him. Jotham continued, "But, despite my failures, Justar has been with us just as he promised, and he helped us defeat Ghnostar." He raised his sword which shone brightly in the gentle afternoon rays. "I wanted to tell you that I think that you are one phenomenal band of warriors. You are awesome soldiers," his voice caught slightly, ". . . and I feel honored to have been able to fight with you."

To their surprise, he grinned. "This *has* been a great adventure." Stretching out his sword to meet the tips of their flashing blades, he shouted, "Paladins, I salute you!"

At those words there was flashing of light, a whoosh of air, and they were flung into the sky in a whirl of rushing wind. Beneath them a great door began to open in the oak's trunk. The wind whipped them around and around, then thrust them headlong into the opening in the tree.

They found themselves inside what looked like an endless tunnel, still mounted on their horses. The passage was very broad—wide enough to ride four abreast. Lamps were glowing down the extent of the passageway. In the air was the sweet smell of cinnamon and the freshness of mint. It was coming from the flickering wicks in the pots hanging from the walls. Ahead, flanking both sides of the tunnel, were the mighty men and women of valor they had seen in Justar's throne room.

Jotham was surprised to notice that their faces seemed less stern than when they had first seen them. Though the fierceness remained, it was now softened by what appeared to be expressions of deep respect. The warriors held their long lances at their sides, but as the four paraded past the first row of champions, there was a rush of plumes and feathers as the lance points shifted and were extended forward to form a beautiful canopy over-head. This continued as they rode deliberately down the hall. As the four Paladins rode past, the knights inclined their heads respectfully. Slowly a cadence could be heard behind them, mixing with the stately rhythm of the hoofbeats on the clay floor: it was the sound of clenched fists thudding against the breastplates of the soldiers they had passed. Soon the entire tunnel was reverberating with the throbbing beat of the warriors' salute.

At last the Paladins stood in front of a simple, wooden gateway. Unlike the tunnel, it was barely tall enough for them to walk through. Their horses bent their knees and lowered their heads, whinnying softly. The four Paladins dismounted; and as they did, Warrior stepped out from the line.

He seemed to be glowing more brightly than they had ever seen. His face shone its pleasure and approval as he strode in front of the door. Warrior struck his chest with a fist clothed in golden mail, then his voice thundered, "Paladins, your King bids you farewell. You have gained honor and glory and immortality."

He extended his muscular arm in tribute. "Paladins, we salute you."

At that the powerful voices of the valiant soldiers rang out, flooding the passageway with accolades and shouts of praise. Warrior turned, struck the door with his fist and stepped to the side. It sprang open, and as the Paladins ducked their heads and entered, they were swallowed up in darkness. The door closed behind them. The only sound they could hear was the tolling of a mighty bell growing stronger until they were suddenly flung into a familiar, spinning void.

When it stopped, they found themselves inside a dank earthen pit, standing on the rungs of a wooden ladder. Bart was at the top, Abe was somewhere below and Carisa and Jotham were in the middle.

"You can let go now," Carisa whispered, "I'm not going anywhere."

With a start, Jotham realized that he'd been gripping her ankle with his right hand.

"Sorry," he muttered, releasing his hold.

"I think we all know where we are," Bart said. "I can feel the trapdoor above me."

"Yeah," Abe whispered from underneath. "But I can't feel any door back here—it's just disappeared."

Jotham asked the question that was on all their minds. "But how long have we actually been gone?"

"And is that awful guy still prowling around?" Carisa added.

"The only way to find out is to go outside," Jotham said. "Bart, give the door another push. But keep quiet."

A shower of dirt and dry grass pelted the three underneath as Bart shoved his shoulder against the trapdoor. This time, it sprang open with ease, thrusting Bart's upper body out and on top of the door with a loud thud. He grunted as the wind was knocked out of him.

"Hey, I said, quiet!" Jotham hissed.

"So much for surprise," Abe muttered, his hollow voice rising up from the bottom of the cavity.

When the four had crept out, they heard an unusual sound. It was a roar, then loud scraping and skidding followed by the sounds of stones being sprayed against a wall.

It took a few moments for the four to realize what they were hearing. Their attacker's van was apparently spinning its tires, showering gravel behind it as it raced away from the Glampoole mansion. The driver was flooring the accelerator, desperate to make his escape. They ran through the woods and saw its taillights as it fishtailed around the curved driveway and out the gate.

Carisa shuddered. "I don't remember it being this cold."

Bart rubbed his arms vigorously in agreement.

335

It was late afternoon. Their bikes were where they had lain them next to the red-bordered "No Trespassing" sign on the front lawn. They appeared to be intact.

"Looks like the coast is clear," Abe said.

"Yep, the enemy has fled in disarray, Cap'n," Bart affirmed.

Jotham wasn't listening—the sight of Glumpuddle's house had stirred a memory. He was thinking back to what their old friend had said to the nurse in the hospital before he died. The odd name, "Ivan Eklibrius," had stuck in his mind throughout their adventures in Issatar. But it had leaped out at him in Ursula's Library when he'd opened the copy of *Ivanhoe*. The phrase *Ex Libris* in the fly leaf had caused a flashing, momentary connection that at the time had escaped him. Now he suspected he knew exactly what it was.

"Bart, Abe, I have an idea. Go into the library and look for Glump's copy of *Ivanhoe*. Bring it back home with you. Carisa and I are going to take a detour on our way. We'll meet you there."

Carisa looked at him quizzically.

Abe and Bart started walking up the splintered stairs. "Why are we doing this?" Bart yelled as they pushed open the impressive front door.

"Trust me," Jotham grinned, "have I ever steered you wrong before?"

"I think we'll plead the fifth on that one, your honor," Bart responded.

Before Abe's back disappeared into the dim interior, Jotham yelled, "By the way, let's not let our folks know where we've been just yet. I don't really want to give them grounds to question our sanity at this point, if you knows what I mean," he said, wagging his eyebrows, imitating their friend Flaggon.

Carisa slipped her hand into his. "Where are we going, Jo?"

"In the cave I told you that I kept having this strange feeling that there was more to what was happening in Issatar than met the eye. Like there was another level or meaning, somehow. Remember?"

Carisa nodded.

"There were weird parallels and most of them related to what happened at Trent's house." He handed Carisa her bike and climbed onto his. "I promised myself the first thing I would do when I got back was to go see him again. It finally came together for me during our battle with Ghnostar. . . and I realized what I needed to do."

That wild fearlessness in her face returned as understanding dawned on her. She nodded again and said, "Let's go do it."

About 30 minutes later they were riding their bikes up the McCauley's driveway. They laid them down next to a dark blue van with government plates parked where Jotham's Mustang had been hours earlier.

Trisha flung open the door the same moment Jotham placed his finger on the doorbell. Before he could introduce Carisa, Trisha had thrown her arms around her neck. "I just knew it was you. Thanks for coming!" she cried.

Trisha stepped back, brushed tears from her face and looked at Carisa. "You look great!" she gushed. "Looks like you've been in the sun. . . . I know I look terrible; it's been such an awful day. Jotham's probably told you all about Trent." She grabbed his arm, "Thanks for coming back. I was going to call you, but I've been busy with Mr. O'Tulley from the FBI. He's with Trent right now. I was looking out the front window when you rode up." She stopped and looked him over quizzically. "You look different, Jo . . . like you're . . ." she shook her head. "No, that's too weird."

He quickly changed the subject. "I felt like I'd really blown it with your brother this morn—I mean, this aft—" he stopped, "when was it? Oh yeah, this afternoon." He glanced at Carisa; they both grinned. "It's been kind of a long day for us too. Anyway, if you think it's okay, I'd like to see if I could talk to him again."

As he was speaking, a square-faced man with a dark baseball cap in his hand and a camera bag around his shoulder came down the stairs from Trent's room. He was placing a miniature recorder into the front pouch of the bag.

Trisha introduced him as Agent Jack O'Tulley.

"Just call me Jack," he said, in a gruff voice, as he shook their hands. "He refuses to talk," he told Trisha. He cleared his throat. "You'll have to excuse me, kids, I think I caught cold. . . . I told him about the conversation with Red and Pieters that I recorded at the old Glampoole place last night, but he won't say a word. He just stares at me like he wants to tear my head off."

"What happened there?" Carisa asked.

The agent described the circle of young people in the Glampoole living room, the skull and the cards they were holding. He told them he'd seen a black card with a skull on it in Trent's bedroom. "I'm pretty sure I know what it means; I just need him to confirm it," he said.

Jotham spoke first, "We had an unusual experience there ourselves," he said. He described the Suicide Club video they'd discovered inside the mansion and Red's subsequent attack.

The corners of O'Tulley's mouth grew taut as Jotham talked. "You were very lucky," he said. "Red Jaglowski is a killer. I've been tracking him for a couple of years. We've known that he was part of a drug ring that brought drugs from Georgia and Louisiana to the Midwest." He took a handkerchief, wiped his nose, and went on.

"I'd heard rumors that he was also branching out into slasher and suicide videos; that's why I followed him here. You're the first witnesses tying him to it. If we could only get Trent to talk, we could also get Red for supplying drugs, conspiracy, transportation of pornography over state lines, attempted murder, kidnapping—the works. We'd be able to put him away for a good long time."

Jotham looked up the stairs, "I know Trent; I saw him a few day . . . a while ago and I wanted to talk with him again. I think Carisa and I may be able to get through to him. Would that be all right?"

Jack O'Tulley hesitated, then shrugged, "Sure thing kids, it can't hurt. But give a holler if he starts acting in a threatening manner."

Trisha glanced fearfully up at her brother's room. "I'll stay here with Mr. O'Tulley. Would you like some coffee?" she asked, walking toward the kitchen.

"Sounds terrific," he answered and followed her through the doorway.

As Jotham and Carisa started up the stairs Jack yelled up at them, "Be careful. I'll be right down here if you need anything."

Standing outside Trent's bedroom, waiting to be allowed in, Jotham warned Carisa about Trent's ghoulish appearance. It was his advice to act naturally and not make a big deal out of his bizarre hairstyle.

She nodded somberly.

Jotham knocked twice; Trent ignored them each time. After jiggling the handle and finding it unlocked, he opened the door and they stepped into the room.

It was exactly as he remembered it. The incense was glowing on the shelf, although much lower than before, dimming the interior with dense smoke.

"I've come back to see you," Jotham said, sitting down in the beanbag next to Trent's bed. "I hope that's okay." Carisa pulled a chair over and sat next to him.

"I can't believe you came back for round two," Trent muttered. "I'm impressed—very." Trent's blood-shot eyes glared at him. "I thought you would have been scared away for good."

338

"I brought Carisa Crayford with me. You remember her, don't you?" The sullen eyes softened briefly in recognition.

"Yeah, I do. Hello, Ms. Crayford. Welcome to my humble abode."

Carisa smiled warmly, "Nice hair! I've tried to do my hair that color, but I can never quite get it."

Jotham stared at her reprovingly, but she kept smiling at Trent.

Trent looked a bit embarrassed, but smiled back at her.

Jotham sighed and went on,"We didn't come to yell at you or tell you what you need to do, Trent." There was a snort of disbelief from the bed. "We just wanted to find out if you would let us pray for you."

Instantly, a thick, foreboding silence settled over the room. Trent drew back and grew still, as if retreating into himself. His eyes slowly hooded; there was a reptilian quality about Trent's unblinking stare. It sent shivers up their spines; they'd seen that same expression too many times before. As Jotham was about to qualify his request, a sly smile skewered Trent's face.

"You wanna' pray?" the voice rasped. "Knock yourselves out. Go right ahead and do your little religious mumbo-jumbo." He hunched over, crouching on his knees and snarled, "I'm not scared of you or your God." Trent held up his hands in front of him, his fingers in the shape of a steeple. "All I need now is a little halo, huh?"

Carisa squeezed Jotham's hand. Both their palms were cold and clammy. "Trent, there is nothing to be afraid of," she said, taking a step forward. Trent snorted his disgust again. "Would you mind if we sat next to you?" she asked.

Trent stared balefully at her for several seconds. To Jotham it looked like he was sizing her up for a meal. His muscles tensed. *If he jumps I'll rip his head off,* he promised himself; *or die trying,* he added, remembering Trent's inhuman strength. Carisa was still smiling bravely. Finally, Trent answered. "That's fine."

Trent closed his eyes and lowered his head in sudden resignation, but when they placed their hands on his shoulders, Trent shuddered, hissed, then leaped into the air. He sprung over their heads with cat-like fluidity, landing behind them in a low crouch. His hands were extended in front of him like claws. The fingers of his hands reminded them of white talons.

He moved so quickly, Jotham was unable to fend him off. With a guttural snort, he grabbed Carisa. In one smooth movement, he flung her across the room, grabbed Jotham around the neck and threw him to the floor. Carisa's head hit the closet doors with a bang. Before Jotham could scramble to his feet, Trent was on top of him snarling and spitting in his face. A monstrous strength had taken over his body, and Jotham knew immediately that he had no chance of muscling Trent into submission.

Help me, God. Help me, he pleaded. Trent had his hand around his throat and was squeezing the air out of him. A roaring sound filled his ears.

Trent's face contorted into a hideous mask. He began to hiss. Hatred was pouring out of his body like poisonous gas. His eyes were filled with yellow fury. Clawed fingers began ripping at Jotham's sweatshirt, seeking to tear his chest open. Jotham twisted his body from side to side but couldn't dislodge his assailant. Trent's hold on top of him was as tenacious and as irresistible as that of a boa constrictor. Jotham felt as if his head were about to explode. Red stars began popping behind his eyes.

Carisa's voice rang out, "Stop, in Jesus' name!" She had crawled behind Trent and had one hand raised over his head.

A gurgling cry of despair broke from Trent's twisted mouth as his body went rigid. He fell on his back, his arms bent, his fingers still locked into stiff claws. Next to him, Jotham was sucking in huge mouthfuls of air. Carisa dropped to her knees, her hand on Trent's chest, praying silently.

Jotham took another deep breath; his throat was on fire. He knew that he should pray, but what he wanted to do was smack Trent in the face. Anger was boiling inside him. Carisa raised her head and was looking up at the ceiling, silent words moving her lips, tears running down her cheeks.

It was as if the priest with Justar's eyes was again standing before him, repeating the words he'd uttered in the vision: "My son, as you have been forgiven, you must forgive." The rage dissipated immediately, as if a bucket of water had been poured over hot embers.

He knelt next to Carisa and began praying. He'd never prayed with such passion in his life. Currents of heat raced over his body; sweat began running off his cheeks. His breathing became labored. Jotham understood that they were engaged in a struggle against an ancient power which was tenacious and supremely wicked.

The familiar, oily stench of decay descended around them.

He opened his eyes and again the outline of the skull, with its dripping candle, materialized over Trent's head.

A cold chill sped up his spine. His skin prickled. He prayed more insistently for God's power to bring deliverance. Instead of being paralyzed by

340

the heavy, fearful cloud, a deep confidence settled over him. It was as if a protective mantle were being wrapped around both their shoulders. He stopped, put his hand on Trent's dyed hair and declared: "We resist you in the name of the Lord Jesus Christ!"

His fingers tingled. A pulsating current ran through his body and down into his hand. Trent shook underneath him. His eyes rolled back in his head, and his body became limp.

Carisa placed both her hands on Trent's chest. "Let him go . . . let him go, I command you, let him go in Jesus' name," she repeated. His body began to shiver as if electricity were coursing through him.

Suddenly, Trent released a low groan. His eyes sprung open, and Jotham could see that they were utterly clear. The rage had dissolved, and with it, the image of the dripping skull.

It was almost an hour later when Carisa and Jotham came downstairs. Trent followed a few steps behind. His face was haggard but clean; it had been his decision to wash off the mascara before leaving his room. The peaceful calm that eddied from him was unmistakable. There was a kind of radiance on him: the quiet exultation of a released captive. As they walked into the living room, the McCauley's parakeet, which up to that moment had remained completely silent, began to chirp delightedly.

Jotham placed his hand on Trent's back. "I think Trent's willing to talk to you now Mr. O'Tulley."

The agent's mouth was open in amazement.

"Well, I never . . ." was all he could say.

While Trent was answering questions in the den, Jotham called to tell his mother when she could expect them back for supper. He smiled when she told him that Abe and Bart had a big surprise for them. By the time the questioning was over, the sun had gone down. Mr. O'Tulley offered to drive Jotham and Carisa back home. "We'll come back tomorrow to pick up the bikes," Carisa said. "We can talk then," she assured Trisha.

"Thanks, kids," Jack O'Tulley said, as they drove away. "You have no idea what a help you've been. I really thought that kid was a goner. . . . I've seen that type before. They usually wind up on a slab in a morgue somewhere." He wiped his nose with a red bandanna. "Trent's got a lot to be grateful for. You probably saved his life. He confirmed that he'd drawn the victim card at their last gathering and might have wound up on video tape as a sacrifice."

Carisa just stared at him in disbelief.

"Believe it or not, that's what Red and his boss were up to. There's a market for anything these days. It's a sick, sick world," he said in a tired voice. "I can't tell you much more about the case at this point, but for what it's worth . . . you helped me settle an old score; and as a freebie, we've also been able to trace the van to where Red's boss is holed up."

They drove silently for a while. Jack looked at them out of the corner of his eyes. He coughed. "I don't know what you kids did upstairs, but whatever it was, it was darn impressive. Trent mentioned something about the name of Jesus or some such thing. Is that right?"

They nodded.

"You won't believe this, but when he said that it reminded me of the craziest thing that happened when I was a little kid. I'd almost forgotten it, to tell you the truth. I was born and raised down South and my grandma actually stopped a lynchin' outside our house once. She stood in front of a crowd of crazy Clanners and told them to stop. When she yelled out the name of Jesus, they dropped that rope like it had burned 'em." He smiled at the memory. "I asked her 'bout it later and all she said was 'Jacko there's powah in the blood.'" He whistled in wonderment. "It was the dam—darndest thing I'd ever seen—I haven't thought about it for years."

Jotham looked at the square-faced man. "Maybe you ought to start thinking about it again."

Jack looked briefly at him, a question on his face.

There was a chill in the air, and the horizon shone a light pink as the FBI agent dropped Jotham and Carisa off at their front door.

"Thanks again, kids. Y'all look me up now if ever you're down Georgia-way."

"Your grandma was right, Mr. O'Tulley," Carisa said, closing the door. "You oughta check it out."

They waved at him as he drove off.

Carisa slipped her hand in Jotham's as they walked up to the front porch. "Seems weird to be back, doesn't it?" she murmured.

They stopped on the step, and Jotham smiled at her, "Feels like we've been gone a lifetime." He put his arms around her and held her tight. "I never want to let you go," he whispered.

"You'd better," she giggled. "I think I hear someone coming to the door, and I don't think Dad would quite understand . . . yet."

Bart threw the door open but thrust his body into the opening to block the view of those inside the house. "Everything cool?" he asked, glancing quickly at the couple. "We've been going crazy waiting for you guys." He ushered them into the house. "Wait till we show you what we found in the library."

Abe rushed at them, waving a piece of paper. For a second both Jotham and Carisa thought it was one of Justar's scrolls. "It's Glump's will . . . and you won't believe what it says—"

"Now, now Abe, there will be plenty of time for that later," Mrs. Lewis, interrupted him. "Their food's gotten cold. I'm sure the poor kids are starving by now." Her eyes caught the flush on Jotham's face and the brightness in Carisa's eyes. She smiled to herself.

At the table Abe showed them the will. It was very simple but gave "the four Paladins," naming them individually, ownership of the Glampoole mansion. The estate was set up in a trust fund, which according to their friend's wishes, was to be distributed in certain increments "to charities and institutions selected by the aforementioned Paladins." However, the library was theirs to do with as they wished.

Abe took out the copy of *Ivanhoe*. "When I opened it, I figured it out too, Jotham. In the hospital, he wasn't yelling out the name of some relative, he was trying to tell them the location of his will: *Ivanhoe, Ex Libris*." He grinned at his brother, "Pretty clever, Jo-man. Glump would be proud of you."

The microwave buzzer sounded at the same time as the telephone.

Mrs. Lewis picked up the phone, and by the frost in her voice Jotham knew immediately who was on the other end.

His mother's back had grown stiff. "Your timing is always—David, I don't—" A long silence followed. Her shoulders slumped as she listened, "—are you sure?—We have visitors—" she sighed heavily. "Okay, I'll ask him—" Mrs. Lewis covered the mouthpiece and looked at Jotham, her green eyes tired and hard. "It's your father, Jotham. Something . . ." she clenched her jaw, then let out a shaky breath, ". . . unusual, has happened to him. He wants to know whether you'd be willing to talk to him."

Carisa reached under the table and gave his hand a quick squeeze. Jotham looked up at his mother, his throat tight, his eyes moist.

"Tell him I'd love to."

EPILOGUE

Jotham's bed felt wonderful. Bart was snoring softly on a roll-out underneath his bedroom window, and Carisa was downstairs on the sleeper-sofa. The adults were still talking in the kitchen. To their parents' amazement, on their first evening together, the teenagers had voluntarily gone to bed early.

Though he felt exhausted, the memories of their recent experiences were still so vivid that Jotham could not fall asleep. But there was something blurred and indistinct at the edges of his consciousness that refused to come into focus. It remained at the periphery of his mental vision, just outside his reach. He felt certain there was some overall pattern he was missing.

Jotham looked over at his nightstand and saw that the Bible he'd left open that morning was back in its familiar place. He wondered if his mom had noticed his envelope-bookmark. *I'm sure she did; she must have seen Dad's fingerprint too. She doesn't miss a whole lot,* he told himself. *She was looking at Carisa and me pretty carefully tonight . . . I'll have to tell Mom about her tomorrow, and about what happened to Dad. She won't believe it.*

He flicked on the reading light and opened the pages to Romans 8, where he had left off another lifetime ago. He began reading, and his mouth dropped open. His throat tightened, and his breath caught in his throat at the words in front of him.

I consider that our present sufferings are not worth comparing with the glory that will be revealed in us. The creation waits in eager expectation for the sons of God to be revealed. For the creation was subjected to frustration, not by its own choice, but by the will of the one who subjected it, in hope that the creation itself will be liberated from its bondage to decay and brought into the glorious freedom of the children of God.

344

We know that the whole creation has been groaning as in the pains of childbirth right up to the present time. Not only so, but we ourselves, who have the firstfruits of the Spirit, groan inwardly as we wait eagerly for our adoption as sons, the redemption of our bodies. For in this hope we were saved.

His chest throbbed with a familiar pang, and the words on the page blurred. He was once again a part of the riotous celebration in the glen. The shouts of liberation, the glorious profusion of music and color, and the exhilaration of unbounded delight washed over him. When he closed his eyes to quiet the emotion, the image of the huge oak appeared. But it was no longer writhing. Instead, it was swaying in a graceful dance to the rhythm of a distant song.

Jotham slowly picked up the envelope lying next to him. He fingered its torn edges and looked intently at the stains, as if seeing them for the first time. The anger and the fear were gone, and in its place was an aching longing that burned like a white-hot flame. He placed his bookmark between the pages, closing the book with a wistful smile. Rising up like the foamy swell of an ocean wave was a great hope, and it was full of joy, for he now understood something he never had known or actually believed before: he, Jotham Lewis, was destined for honor and glory. And it felt good.

It felt *very good.*